Bruises

Is love enough to heal their bruises?

Louise Lindley

FriesenPress

Suite 300 – 852 Fort Street
Victoria, BC, Canada V8W 1H8
www.friesenpress.com

Copyright © 2014 by Louise Lindley
First Edition — 2014

All rights reserved.

No part of this publication may be reproduced in any form, or by any means, electronic or mechanical, including photocopying, recording, or any information browsing, storage, or retrieval system, without permission in writing from the publisher.

ISBN
978-1-4602-4611-5 (Hardcover)
978-1-4602-4612-2 (Paperback)
978-1-4602-4613-9 (eBook)

1. *Fiction, Erotica*

Distributed to the trade by The Ingram Book Company

For Stephanie… a true friend.

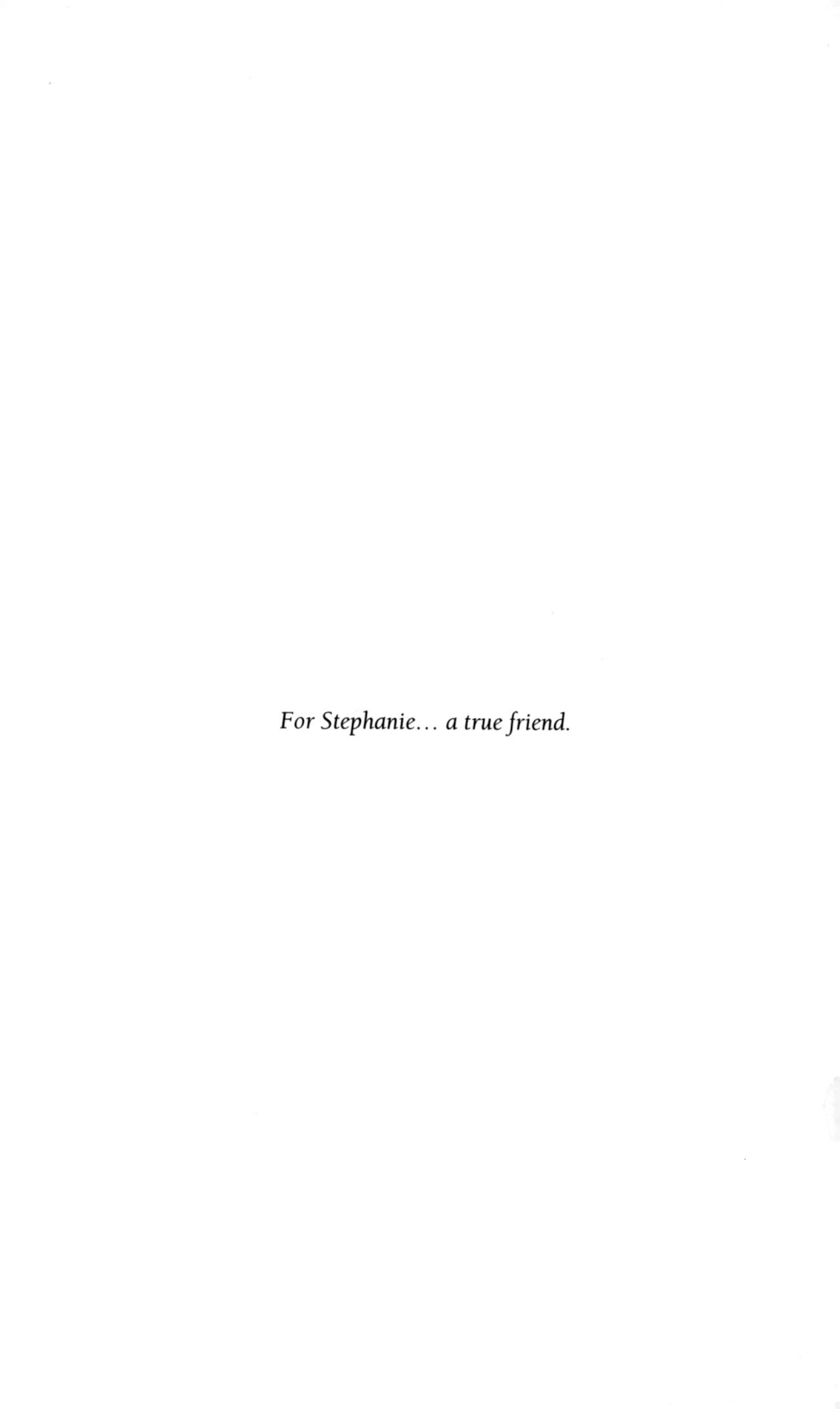

Chapter 1

As the plane approached the dark, wet runway of Newcastle International Airport, Frankie stared out of the window. This wasn't home anymore, just the place where she'd grown up. She thought about her apartment, her best friend and roommate, and the perfect life she'd temporarily put on hold. It was going to be a long six months.

As she stood watching the same three bags ride the carousel, she felt weary and sad. It had been five years since she had last stood in that very spot, wondering if she would ever get over the immense grief a daughter feels when she loses her mother. The reality was that you never got over it - as time passed, you just learned to live with it. Suddenly, a loud thump brought her back to reality, as the first bag from her flight dropped unceremoniously onto the belt. After twenty minutes of moaning to herself about the inefficiency of British airports, and hearing several announcements over the tannoy that were presumably meant to be in English, she finally spotted her familiar red and black plaid suitcase heading towards her. She breathed a sigh of relief and reached out to grab it before it tried to escape for another ride out into the miserable February weather.

As she approached the automatic doors that opened into Arrivals, she ran her fingers through her bad, long-haul-flight hair, in an attempt to make it look presentable. Once through the doors she scanned the crowd. There he was, waving furiously from behind some turbans, trying to get her attention. Her cousin Thomas was a tall, slender man with short dark hair and black-rimmed glasses. He always reminded her of Clark Kent, but without the super powers. Thomas pushed his way through the crowd to meet Frankie.

"Hi!" they both said simultaneously, and flung their arms around each other.

"Long time no see, here let me take that," Thomas said in his soft Geordie accent, reaching out for the handle of Frankie's one and only suitcase. "Is this all you have?" he asked, surprised. "You do know you're here for six months?"

"Yes, there are such things as washing machines you know, and I'm not exactly here to enjoy myself, am I?" she replied.

"I know, and I forget that yoga wear doesn't take up that much space," he teased.

"Ha-ha," she replied with a little smirk, "that isn't all us Vancouverites wear, thank you very much... sometimes we wear jeans!"

He laughed as they headed towards the pay station.

The journey into Newcastle was mostly filled with catch up chatter between the two cousins.

"Mam said she's stocked the fridge and cupboards for you with a few essentials to see you through the next couple of days. She's planning on calling you tomorrow to just touch base, make sure you're okay, you know," he said, as he slowed down at a red light.

"Ahh bless her, already looking after me," Frankie replied with a weak smile.

Frankie's Aunty Carol was her mum's younger sister by just over a year. The sisters had been very close all their lives, until Frankie's mum, Emily, had lost her battle with breast cancer five years ago. Frankie had always been close to Carol; her aunt had always been there for her and her brother Andrew. Now, during what was potentially another difficult time for Frankie, Carol was already trying to make things easier for her niece.

Finally, Thomas pulled up outside the small, old building in Jesmond that was his sister's home. Lucy, a Registered Nurse, was taking a year off to travel and work in Australia, following a messy break-up with her boyfriend of four years. A good friend of hers had been living in the two-bedroomed flat for the past six months, while her new place was being built. Luckily for Frankie, Lucy's place had become vacant just at the right time, and Lucy was thrilled to have her cousin live in it for the remaining time she was away.

"Well here we are, let me help you in with everything," Thomas said as he climbed out of his Toyota Rav4.

He pointed to the car parked in front of them, a black Smart car.

"Lucy's," he said, "Use it as much as you want, but don't expect to be able to do any serious shopping in it!"

Frankie gave a little laugh while raising her eyebrows.

Frankie had only been to Lucy's flat once before, when she had been in Newcastle for her mother's funeral. The 1910 building on Eskdale Terrace contained twelve flats, all very well preserved and cared for by the residents. A large, blue, wooden double door opened from the street into a simple, clean entrance hall. You stepped onto a beautifully tiled black and white Victorian style floor, with a sweeping staircase ahead of you, and doors to the flats on either side. This period style of building was common in Tyneside, but very different from Frankie's modern Vancouver apartment. Lucy's flat was on the first floor, towards the front of the building. Walking through the door, Frankie instantly felt welcome. The room had large cast iron radiators that reminded her of being at school, so the place was warm and cosy.

"There you go, my dear," said Thomas, as he dropped her bags just inside the doorway to the bedroom, "I think there's a file under the coffee table with everything in you need to know about the place. Here's your keys," he said, handing her a 'Keep Calm and Have A Pyjama Day' key ring. "I'm going to take off and let you get some sleep. As I said, Mam will call you tomorrow, but she's dying to see you so don't be surprised if she wants to pop in. You know where we are if you need anything. Jen and I will have you over in the next couple of weeks for dinner; we can catch up properly then." He gave Frankie a quick hug. "I'll see myself out, bath and bed for you, Doctor's orders!"

"Very funny," said Frankie. "Safe drive home and we'll speak soon."

The door closed and she was left standing alone in the quiet flat.

As she lifted her heavy head off the pillow, it took her a moment to register that she wasn't dreaming the phone ringing next to her.

"Hello," she said in a very sleepy, groggy voice.

"Frankie, pet, I'm sorry, did I wake you?"

"Aunty Carol!" Frankie sat up, thrilled to hear her dear aunt's voice.

"I feel terrible, I thought you would be up by now, it's nearly eleven!" Carol exclaimed.

"Really! I can't believe I slept so long, it's a good job you did wake me." Frankie climbed out of bed and headed into the open plan kitchen/living room, to make a cup of tea.

"Listen pet, you sort yourself out, wake up properly and call me back later," said Carol.

"Well, a little bird told me you were dying to see me, so why don't you come over in a hour or so?" said Frankie, talking into her left shoulder, where she had wedged the phone with her cheek in order to free up her hands to fill the kettle.

"Oh, go on then, if you insist!" Frankie could hear the excitement in Carol's voice. "I won't stay long, I know you'll want to get unpacked. Do you have everything you need, can I bring anything?"

"To be honest, I have no idea!" After the long journey from Vancouver the day before, she had been so tired once Thomas dropped her off, she had decided to skip the bath and go straight to bed. She therefore had no idea what supplies Carol had left her.

"Just bring your lovely self!" she said.

"Ahh, all right pet, well if you think of anything, let me know."

After a long, hot shower, Frankie slipped into her favourite black yoga pants and a sloppy, wide-necked sweatshirt. After two cups of tea and a pile of toast and marmalade, she started to feel human again, ready to unpack and explore what was to be her new home for the next six months.

The front door to the flat opened almost straight into the kitchen, with the end of a long breakfast bar just a couple of feet from the door. Across to the right, the main living area featured an original tiled fireplace with wooden surround that she couldn't help but admire. It 'popped' out of the wall, with a recessed bay either side. In the wall opposite the front door, one in the kitchen, one in the living room, two tall windows towered over the room and looked out onto the front street, giving the relatively compact space a feeling of openness.

Located to the left of the front door was the main bedroom, featuring two more large windows dominating the room on either side of a queen-sized bed. At the foot of the bed, leaning against the wall, stood the biggest, most ornate mirror Frankie had ever seen. She admired its position and imagined watching the reflection of a pert backside, the owner extremely hot and thrusting towards her, between her very spread legs...

"Oh yeah!" she whispered to herself, raising her eyebrows and smirking.

The wall containing the front door ran along to the right and housed three further doors. The first, opposite the breakfast bar, led into the bathroom, which housed the most enormous cast iron claw foot bath; the second opened into a large closet; and the third into a small second bedroom/office that contained a desk, a sofa bed, and a few shelves scattered with all kinds of books. Another large window dominated the room, but as it was on the side of the building, the room was quite dark. All the rooms, along with the kitchen cabinets, were painted the same shade of cream, but splashes of colour in the soft furnishings, wall pictures, and area rugs on the polished floorboards made each room individual. It was not really to Frankie's taste, but it seemed to work.

"Right!" she exclaimed, one hand on her hip while running the other through her untidy hair, "I need Train!"

She searched her bag for her iPhone, then her roll-on. Starting to panic slightly, quietly cursing to herself, she remembered texting her roommate and best friend Kayla to let her know she had arrived safely. She finally found it under her jacket, which was slung over the back of the sofa.

"It's all right everyone, panic over," she said, looking around the room while holding her arms up, as if someone were going to shoot her. It wasn't unusual for her to talk to herself like this.

She picked up her glasses from the coffee table in front of the sofa; putting them on as she walked towards the small table in the bay where the docking station was located, she selected all the Train songs. After sliding the iPhone into place she switched on the dock, pressed shuffle, and picked up the remote control. Within a few seconds a song entitled 'Homesick' started playing as she walked back towards the bedroom. She stopped at the breakfast bar and laid her hand on the counter top, sighing, "Oh come on Pat, really, that's a little unfair after less than twenty-four hours in the country!"

She turned and hit the forward button on the remote and waited for the next track to start playing. 'Drive By'. "That's more like it," she said, as she nodded her head to the beat and turned up the volume.

She had just put the last of her things away, as the song 'Respect' was finishing, when she heard a knock at the door. As she made her way to it, it started to open.

"Hello," a familiar voice called, in a broad Geordie accent.

Frankie hit the pause button on the remote before she flung her arms around her visitor.

"Aunty Carol!!"

"Oh Frankie, pet, it's so good to see you too."

The two women embraced for what seemed like an eternity before Carol pulled away and cupped her hands around Frankie's face.

"Let me look at you... God I wish I'd looked as good as you when I was 38, with jet lag! Still no man yet?"

Frankie laughed. Her love life was always of great interest to her aunt.

Why, Frankie had no idea. Maybe it was the fact she always seemed to pick the wrong guys. Like the barista she had briefly dated, who worked for a local Starbucks by day, but turned out to be a male escort by night. How did she find out? His 'employer' for the evening had booked a table at the same restaurant she and Kayla happened to be dining at.

"Oh you know me Aunty Carol, too busy, too old, too fussy!" She headed into the kitchen to put the kettle on.

"Give over, too busy and too fussy I'll agree with, but not too old! You're never too old; there was a couple on the telly the other night, 85 and 87; just got married, both for the first time, she wore white and everything!" Carol chuckled as she followed Frankie into the kitchen.

"Well I definitely won't be wearing white, especially if I don't get married until I'm nearly a hundred!" she said, reaching for two mugs and holding them up. "Cuppa?" she asked.

They both sat down on the comfy, red sofa in the living room. Carol placed her tea on the small wooden coffee table in front of them. "How was the flight?" she asked.

"Long, uncomfortable, hot... it was fine." Frankie took a drink of tea and continued, "A long haul flight is never going to be good when you're doing it because you have to, and not because you want to!"

"I know, pet," Carol replied, "Hands up to you, I couldn't do what you're doing. You know I'm here for you?"

"Yes Aunty, thank you." She managed a sad smile as Carol patted her knee with affection.

"Now then," Carol said, in a more jolly tone, "I'm going to continue to look after the place for you like I did for Rachel. Lucy insists and I agree; you're going to have enough to do, working and sorting out that house. So I'll pop in and clean on a Friday morning if that's okay, and I'll do Hercules' litter box while I'm here. Now, when shall I bring him over?"

"I guess whenever, it's his home so he doesn't need to settle in or anything. I start work on Tuesday so that gives him a couple of days to get used to me," she replied, shrugging her shoulders.

Hercules was Lucy's cat. A very large, very white fluffy thing that had flatly refused ever to go outside and was very spoilt as a result. Living in the comfort of Lucy's flat suited him fine. Despite the fact that he thought that all around him were his servants, he was, in fact, the most friendly and loveable creature, and as long as he was fed, brushed out regularly and had his radiator bed, he was happy. When Lucy went away, her friend Rachel had taken care of him. He had briefly been living with Carol and Frankie's Uncle Eric until Frankie arrived, but he was unimpressed with their twelve-year-old golden retriever, which the cat looked upon as some sort of alien life form.

"Well, how about tomorrow morning?" Carol asked.

"Sure!" said Frankie, "I'm actually quite looking forward to having the company."

The two women chatted and drank tea for an hour or so before Carol had to leave. They made arrangements for the following day and embraced each other again. Carol pushed Frankie away with her hands placed on her upper arms.

"Remember, pet, I'm always here, okay. Promise me you'll remember that," and she kissed her niece's forehead.

Frankie's eyes were starting to fill as she nodded.

Carol closed the door behind her and Frankie wiped the tears from her eyes.

Frankie spent the rest of her first full day back in England enjoying some of the delicious Marks & Spencer's goodies that Carol had left for her, before heading out for a stroll to re-acquaint herself with that area of Newcastle. It was early February, and she was pretty sure it was going to rain again. No problem; she was used to lots of rain, living on the west coast of Canada. She zipped her waterproof jacket up to her chin and carried on looking around, realising that, really, very little had changed in the last five years.

Jesmond, an affluent area of Newcastle she had once called home, and would briefly do so again, was made up of Victorian terraces, large detached houses from the same period, and a few modern dwellings. She noticed the streets appeared more congested than she remembered; parked cars seemed to be bumper to bumper everywhere she looked, but then it was a Saturday afternoon. Although she loved her more modern way of living on the west coast, she missed the history that a city like Newcastle-upon-Tyne provided. Many houses dated back to the turn of the century, and had their own stories and secrets to tell. Most of them had now had makeovers, and therefore lacked the character that the original features provided. Although the old dark red brick still stood, they now housed plastic windows and doors, with a lot of inconsistency in the look. Some were pretending to be dark wood, some plain white, and some leaded. As Frankie looked around at this mish mash of 'old timer meets new, young, and fresh', she already began to feel out of place. Although she loved Britain's history, she still thought her surroundings felt tired and strained, unclean and poorly maintained, dowdy and drab.

After two hours of fresh air, the jet lag started to get the better of her. She arrived back at the flat, pretty exhausted, just as it was getting dark. "A cup of tea and then a nice hot bath, I think," she said to herself.

While waiting for the kettle to boil, she texted Kayla. It was 4pm; so only 8am back in Vancouver.

Hey! How's it going? Fx

A few minutes later, while she was sat at the breakfast bar drinking her tea, she received a text back.

Lonely without you but I'm coping. Heading up to Cypress for a few runs with the girls this morning... sorry :-(How about you? Kx

Being able to ski on the local mountains was one of the great things about Vancouver. It had rained all week in the city, so Frankie knew the conditions on the mountain would be amazing. She replied:

Not even the slightest bit bothered... really! I'm fine, jet-lagged & lonely too. Once I start work on Tuesday it will be fine, I hope. Enjoy the snow, miss you! Fx

Almost instantly her phone buzzed again.

Will Do, Miss You Too. Kx

She had been looking forward to soaking in the bath all day. As she sank down into the steaming water, she got a feel for just how big the tub was. When she sat down on the bottom the water came to just below her armpits, and then, lying back, she discovered that being only five foot two inches tall meant touching the other end to stay above the water was not an option! However, she lay back all the same, held onto the sides, and relaxed for the first time in about two months; a very long and stressful two months that had now, temporarily, led her back to Newcastle.

It had all started about a year after her mum died, when her brother, Andrew, called her from his home in New York. It turned out that their father's sister, a miserable old spinster, whom they had never liked, had called Andrew, quite concerned about their father's behaviour.

Mr. Nicholas Robertson was an excellent and well-respected cardiac surgeon, in spite of his bad temper and arrogant behaviour. However, he appeared to be becoming forgetful and acting very strangely. His sister, Patricia, had visited him at home one day to find the house a complete pigsty and her brother, fully clothed with his pyjamas still on underneath, trying to light a gas fire by rubbing two wooden spoons together! Obviously very concerned for her brother's welfare, she contacted his doctor, who promptly admitted him to hospital. At some point the Chief of Surgery at the hospital in which he worked got involved. It turned out colleagues had been noticing odd behaviour, but with no spouse or other immediate family around, they were having great difficultly getting him help. Remarkably, he was still performing surgery without any problems.

Andrew's relationship with his father had been difficult all his life, even more so than his sister's; he really didn't feel anything for him. His father had disowned him after Andrew had told him that he was gay. From then, until their mother died, Andrew had had nothing to do with his father; hadn't so much as spoken to him. Emily's love for her son had been unconditional; his sexual orientation had never been an issue for her. Despite the rift however, Andrew, being two years older than Frankie, still always seemed to be the first to be informed of any news about their parents. The day Patricia found him in this mess at home, she felt it only right that his children know what was happening to their father, and called Andrew. Frankie and Andrew, who were very close siblings, discussed the situation at great length and decided that if one of them were required to return to England to deal with matters pertaining to their father, it would be Frankie. Shortly afterwards, their father was diagnosed with Alzheimer's, and eventually returned home, with help from his sister and services provided by the local Community Health Authority. He also took retirement due to ill health.

That was how it had been for the last four years. Neither Frankie nor her brother saw their father after his diagnosis, but periodically they had heard from Patricia about how he was deteriorating. Over the last year it had become increasingly apparent that living in his own home was unsafe. The home services had increased a little but not enough to care for him 24/7, which was now what he needed. To be fair to Patricia, she had done as much as she could for her brother. But at the end of November, she had made a very desperate call to Frankie, not knowing whom else to turn to for help.

After a long, sometimes heated discussion, Frankie had agreed to go to England. However, she wanted nothing to do with her father, despite his plight. Patricia, therefore, had agreed to find her brother a home and move him as soon as possible. It would be Frankie's job to sell the family home and clear it of its contents, something she knew would not be a quick or easy thing to do. Frankie had made sure that Andrew was fully aware and in agreement with this arrangement, which, of course, he had been.

So, after working as an anaesthetist for seven years at a large general hospital in Vancouver, Frankie negotiated a six-month sabbatical. It would be financially impossible for her to not earn for six months, so she then contacted an old mentor and friend in England. Dr. Kathy Barnes was now the Head of Anaesthesia at one of the biggest and busiest infirmaries in the North East of England. Frankie had known Kathy since her training days in Liverpool, when she had been a Senior House Officer in General Surgery; Kathy had been a Specialist Registrar in Anaesthesia. It was Kathy who had persuaded Frankie to go into anaesthesia; the two had been friends ever since.

Kathy was delighted to hear from Frankie. The call couldn't have come at a better time for her. She was looking for a locum to fill the position of a consultant colleague who had just suffered a large stroke. Dr. Liam Spencer had worked in the same job for the last thirty years. He was the oldest and longest serving member of the department, and close to retiring. The department was in shock, as was Frankie when she learned the news; she had worked with Liam during her Specialist Registrar training.

So, Kathy offered her the temporary position, with a number of theatre sessions that would equate to three working days. As Frankie was still registered to practice in England, the paperwork would be straightforward. She finished work in Vancouver in mid January, ready to start her new position at the beginning of February.

And so, there she was, soaking in the most amazing bathtub ever, about to start working in the very healthcare system and in the very country she had sworn she would never work or live in again. As she let go of the sides, so she could submerge herself completely in the hot, sweet-smelling water, she began to realise that you should never say never.

The following morning, Carol let herself into the flat, carrying a large pet carrier.

"Yoo-hoo!" she called, "it's only me!"

Frankie came out of the bedroom, having just finished drying her hair.

"Give us a hand pet, he weighs a ton!" Carol was struggling to fit through the door.

"Here, put him through first and I'll take him," said Frankie reaching for the pet carrier. "Bloody hell, cat! What does she feed you, steroids?" She almost put her back out when she took the full weight of Hercules.

"He's a boy that likes his food," replied Carol, "I'll just pop back down to the car to get the litter box and the rest of his things." The door shut behind her. Frankie placed the carrier on the floor and kneeled down beside it.

"Right big guy, let's have a look at you then," she said as she unhooked the door.

Hercules didn't hesitate; he strolled straight out and started rubbing himself against Frankie's knees. She stroked him in response to his affection. He was beautiful: pure white, fluffy, very affectionate, and very large!

"I think we're going to get along just fine," she said, as he started to purr deeply.

The front door opened again as Carol made her way inside carrying his litter box and a large bag that looked heavy.

"Ahh! I see you two are getting acquainted," she said, "and he's purring, always a good sign.... now!" she continued as she placed everything on the kitchen floor, "I will need to bring you more food and litter but there should be enough for a couple of weeks." She started to unpack the big bag, removing a large sheepskin from it. "This is his bed, he likes to sleep on that radiator by the window. His litter box goes in the cupboard..."

"Oh I wondered why there's a cat door into there," Frankie interrupted.

"Yes, well, your Uncle Eric installed it, but he didn't think to measure the height of the cat, so the poor thing has to almost slide in and out on his belly!" Carol replied, rolling her eyes.

"Oh dear," Frankie said, trying not to laugh. Her Uncle Eric, Carol's husband of nearly 35 years, was a lovely man who had recently retired from family dentistry and, despite what he would have you believe, he wasn't a handyman.

"Well at least it does the job," Frankie said.

"For now," Carol replied, "but if he gets much bigger, Eric will have to take the whole door off!"

Now Frankie was laughing. She had missed her aunt's sense of humour.

Carol helped Frankie get Hercules settled back into his home and it wasn't long before he was curled up on his radiator bed while the two women chatted over a cup of tea.

"When are you thinking of calling Aunt Spiker?" Carol asked. She was referring to Patricia; she had always called her Aunt Spiker since reading Roald Dahl's *James and the Giant Peach* with Lucy and Frankie when they were children.

"I probably should just get in touch out of courtesy," Frankie replied.

"And dare I ask if you're going to the Home?" Carol paused, knowing she was opening up an old wound, "at any point, maybe? You know, just to see him, just once?"

With a large sigh, Frankie replied, "Aunty, you know there is not one teeny, tiny bit of me that even wonders if he's okay. Besides, he barely recognised me before he became ill, I'm pretty sure there is even less chance of that now." Frankie's voice had a sad, slightly bitter tone to it.

Carol put her hand on Frankie's shoulder and started to rub it affectionately. "Well it's early days pet, you might feel differently when you've been back to the house."

Frankie pressed her lips together and looked at Carol.

Shortly after that, Carol left. She wished Frankie good luck in her job, insisted she call if there was anything she needed, and told her to pop round anytime.

"Keep smiling pet!" were her last words.

The rest of Sunday was spent doing exactly what Sundays were meant for: rest and relaxation. She wanted to make sure that Hercules settled back into his home, at least that was her excuse and she was sticking to it. It was a good opportunity to catch up on her cyber life, as she hadn't checked anything since arriving on Friday. She ensconced herself on the comfy red sofa with her iPad and a cup of tea. After making three trips back to the kitchen to refill her so-called 'mug', she finally made a mental note to purchase the biggest tea bucket she could possibly find when she was next shopping.

After emailing her brother, she discovered that according to her social networks, not much had happened in the New World since she had left it on Thursday, though there were some amazing photos that Kayla had posted on Facebook of the girls' ski trip to the local mountains. She felt a little envious that everyone else's lives were currently carrying on as normal, while she was now 5000 miles away, in a strange flat, in miserable Newcastle, with a big, fat, white cat who was currently using her iPad cover as a scratching post.

"Where did I go wrong?" she asked Hercules, as she rescued the cover from the cat so she could replace it over the screen. "I mean," she continued, as she lay back on the sofa and began to stroke his head, "I work hard and I'm a pretty good person, but here I am taking time off from my life to help a man I am embarrassed to call my father." Hercules was now rubbing himself along the side of her leg and purring deeply. "You have no idea how good you have it, not a care in the world because you're 'The Cat'. What I would give to be you for the next six months... let me know if you're interested in trading." As Hercules settled onto the sofa next to her, she suddenly caught herself. "Look at me, this is how pathetic I've become, talking to a cat I only met two hours ago. You must be thinking, 'Who is this basket case they've shacked me up with now!'"

As she laid her head back against the sofa, a wave of tiredness washed over her. The cat was clearly happy and settled, a large heap of warm, vibrating fur next to her. She couldn't help it, her eyes were heavy and closing. *Just a little power nap,* she thought as she drifted off.

When she opened them again, it was dark. She had no idea what time it was, but she was cold and stiff from falling deeply asleep on the sofa. At some point she must have moved from sitting to lying, because she remembered Hercules next to her, but now he was lying on top of her. Not surprisingly, that was the only bit of her that was warm; he was pretty mad about being moved from her very full bladder.

"How do you know?" she asked him as he gave out a disapproving meow. "You know, the full bladder thing!"

She flicked the main light on as she danced to the bathroom, and noticed the large clock on the wall.

"Bloody hell!" she exclaimed, "I'm sure I wasn't asleep that long." She looked back at Hercules, who was stretching on the back of the sofa, with his bum in the air, in that very elegant way that only cats can do. It was five to midnight.

She was now wide-awake and starving so, after two bowls of Crunchy Nut Cornflakes, a cereal she dearly missed in Canada, she decided to run a bath. She rarely did so at home, in the oversized shower tray that North Americans seemed to get away with advertising as a 'bath'. '*No, this is a bath*' she thought, with its sexy, curvy little feet, telephone tap, and great length, depth, and width...

"Oh, the things you could get up to in here!" she said to Hercules, who was perched on the wide ledge that surrounded the tub and was pawing at the bubbles. Andrea Bocelli was playing quietly in the distance of the living room.

"Oh, I love this one," she said as she shut her eyes and sank as far as she dared without going under. "I have no clue what the songs are called, or even what he's singing about, you know." Hercules walked along the bath as she spoke, shaking his soggy paw. "I mean," she continued, "he could be singing from a car manual, or the instructions from a box of tampons for all we know, right, but he just makes it sound so beautiful and romantic."

Classical music wasn't really her thing but she loved Bocelli's voice, so she had most of his music on her iPhone and her Nano. She tended to play it when she wanted to relax, and especially when she was reading; since she didn't understand the words, she couldn't sing along. She had always thought that it would be good music to make love to. Her mind started to wander... lying against a firm, smooth, six-pack of rippling muscle, his hands wrapped around her, spreading silky bubbles over her throbbing breasts while he gently and skillfully caressed her ear and neck with his tongue...

The song finished and she was brought back to reality by the change in tempo.

"Oh big guy," she sighed, "where is he? Mrs. Clit-tor-rus has been neglected for far too long," Her new companion made his way back along the edge towards her, meowing as if in sympathy. "Not here, that's for sure."

She put a wet hand up to the cat, which he affectionately rubbed his ear against, and started to purr. She gave him a sad smile, before getting out of the still-steaming water.

After not the best night's sleep, following her unplanned power nap on the sofa the night before, Frankie was showered, make up on, hair done and dressed in jeans and a simple black scoop neck sweater by 8.30 the following morning. She had arranged to meet Kathy for coffee at the hospital before she started work the following day. Despite the Anaesthesia Department secretary's efficiency in organising everything by email and a couple of phone calls, Frankie knew there would still be some form or other that needed completing. This was also an opportunity for her to test out the Metro; Newcastle's underground transport system. There was a station at the end of the road that would take her to the one stop right in the city centre. She could then walk the short distance to the hospital. She was used to cycling to work at home, so she needed some way of getting a little bit of exercise every day; besides which she knew that parking would be an expensive nightmare, even with only half a car! So, it was on with the waterproof jacket and boots, to brave the early February monsoon that appeared to be happening outside. Feeling a little apprehensive about the whole thing, she headed out.

The journey into the city was very straightforward, but the walk to the hospital took a few minutes longer than she had remembered. She arrived at the busy coffee shop, which was situated in the main entrance to the hospital, just before 10 am. There was no sign of Kathy, so Frankie secured the last two seats on the end of the wall-mounted bar. Just as she finished draping her jacket over the back of the tall bar seat she heard a familiar voice behind her.

"Well, well Dr. Robertson, you haven't changed a bit!" Kathy said, as she approached Frankie from behind, beaming at her.

Frankie swung around to open arms and hugged Kathy tightly.

"Hey! It's good to see you again," she said.

Kathy pulled away from Frankie, saying, "Look at you, the West Coast must agree with you, you look fantastic! Mind, you would look good in a clinical waste bag!" she exclaimed, smiling.

"Thanks Kathy, I do have a pretty nice life, thank you very much."

"Oh, and that's an interesting accent you have there now, my friend. What with that and your amazing figure, I'm surprised to find you're still single," Kathy said with raised eyebrows and a probing little smile.

"Yes, still looking for him... I think I still sound pretty British, but I guess not when I'm here."

She had never really had a strong Geordie accent, but after seven years in Canada it was now non-existent. She could still understand it, of course, and turn it on whenever she wanted. She now spoke with a slight Canadian twang.

"Well, with any luck you'll find him here and I'll get to keep you!" Kathy said with a little smirk.

"In your dreams, Dr. Barnes, I'm here to get rid of a man in my life, not gain one!"

"I know, sorry, I'm sure this isn't going to be easy for you. I'll do my best to help you out in any way... well, we should get down to business." Kathy handed Frankie a large brown envelope. "Here's the last of the paperwork that needs signing so we can pay you; and there's also a signed form in there from me so you can get hospital ID. I suggest you do that today. Have a look through everything while I grab us some drinks. Let me guess... a large latté with an extra shot?" She looked at Frankie, hopeful she'd remembered correctly.

"Well remembered!" she replied with a smile. She sighed, dug around in her bag to find her glasses, then opened the envelope and pulled out the papers.

After finishing the administration, which was the main purpose of their meeting, the two old friends chatted over coffee until Kathy was paged back to Theatres. Frankie then took the opportunity to take a little tour of the hospital; it had been nearly eight years since she had last worked there. The general layout remained the same, but a number of areas had been updated over the years. The most interesting change was the main entrance, which seemed to have turned into a shopping mall. After collecting her hospital ID, Frankie decided that enough was enough; she needed some air so she headed back out via the main entrance, towards the city centre.

If there was one thing Frankie missed about England it was Marks and Spencer's food. She decided that the only way she was going to get through the next six months was to eat as much of it as possible. Luckily for her, she would pass the large Newcastle store every day after work, and taking the Metro instead of driving would mean she wouldn't be able to carry too much. Therefore, she would need to buy little and often. *'There's a shame'*, she thought as she entered the store via the back entrance, straight into the wine section. This caused her to smile to herself as she grabbed a basket. She was like a child in a candy store, desperately trying not to show her obvious excitement to the general public as she picked up one of her all-time favourite dishes that only M&S did: Cumberland Pie. A variation of a cottage pie but much, much yummier and three times as many calories!

By the time she'd done her shopping, treated herself to lunch in the M&S café, waited twenty minutes for the Metro and lugged the four heavy bags of groceries and wine up the street in the freezing, pouring rain, it was mid-afternoon. As she climbed the stairs to the first floor flat, the door to her next-door-neighbour's was just opening, revealing an adorable little old lady, wearing small, round spectacles and with white hair swept back in a bun at the nape of her neck. Despite looking like a drowned rat, Frankie felt it would be rude not to introduce herself.

"Hi there," she said, "I'm Frankie, Lucy's cousin. I'm using her flat for a few months while she's away."

"Am sorry pet," the lady replied, "you'll have to speak up, I haven't got me hearing aids in!"

Just as the old lady was finishing speaking, a much younger version of her, with darker hair but without the bun or spectacles, came up behind her.

"Who on earth are you talking to, Mother?" The younger lady saw Frankie, and paused for a second before speaking again. "Oh!

Hello, I'm sorry, I didn't realise there was someone at the door, my apologies."

"No worries," Frankie replied putting down her bags before pushing her dripping hood off her head to reveal herself.

"I just wanted to introduce myself. I'm Frankie, Lucy's cousin."

The lady interrupted Frankie, saying, "Ah yes, Carol mentioned you a couple of weeks ago; from Canada, is that right?"

"Yes, I'll be here for the next six months, I leave just before Lucy gets back," Frankie informed her.

"You're a doctor, I believe, working at the Infirmary?" The lady continued.

"Yes, that's right, I'm an Anaesthetist."

"Really," the lady said, admiringly, "well, I'm Penny and this is my very deaf mother, Annie, or Mrs. Whitfield as most people call her. Delighted to meet you, I'm sure we'll bump into each other from time to time, if there's anything you need please don't hesitate... now Mother, come along let's find your hearing aids." Penny turned her mother around and back into her flat, her voice fading, "There's no point in going to bingo if you can't hear the caller..."

Frankie smiled at her retreating neighbours, bent down to pick up her bags and headed towards her flat.

"Hey big guy, sorry I was so long. I bought you a little treat from Mr. Marks and Mr. Spencer." Hercules greeted her by rubbing himself against her legs and arching his back, purring loudly. After changing into dry, comfy clothes, she clicked the kettle on and put her groceries away. There was a message on the answer phone from Thomas, hoping she had settled in, and inviting her over on Saturday evening for dinner. She made a cup of tea in the ridiculously enormous, pint-sized mug she had stumbled across in M&S, on a Valentines display. It came with chocolate-covered, heart-shaped biscuits inside, wrapped in red foil; the mug was white with red, pink and purple hearts all over it. It wouldn't normally have been her choice, but this was an emergency, before she ended up with too much blood in her tea stream!

Frankie lit the gas fire, which actually looked very realistic, before flopping onto the sofa to complete the forms Kathy had given her earlier. A very satisfied puss was washing himself systematically on the arm next to her, after having enjoyed half a tin of gourmet salmon. She returned Thomas's call, accepting the dinner invitation. The two cousins kept it short, as Thomas was in a meeting; they would talk again towards the end of the week to make arrangements. He wished her well in her new job, but he knew that she would be fine and that work was going to be the least of her worries for the next few months. By 9.30 Frankie was beat. She'd enjoyed her Cumberland Pie curled up on the sofa, while watching old British comedy on UK Gold. A very content Hercules lay, stretched out, on a hideous rug covered in poppies, in front of the fire. She hit the remote to switch off the small flat TV screen in the bay, to the right of the fireplace, and stood with her hands on her hips, looking down at the cat.

"Well big guy, time to hit the sack I'm afraid, it's going to be a long day tomorrow."

She switched the fire off and bent down to gently stroke the side of his face.

"Night, night... sleep well," she said to him, walking towards the bathroom.

Chapter 2

WHEN FRANKIE BUZZED the front door to the Anaesthesia department, a vaguely familiar voice came over the intercom.

"Anaesthesia, may I help you?" said Helen, the department secretary Frankie had corresponded with over the previous couple of months.

"Morning Helen, it's Frances Robertson."

"Dr. Robertson, welcome, push the door when you hear it click."

Sure enough, within a second or two, the door clicked and Frankie entered the office.

Helen was sat behind a desk on the right of the door Frankie had just come through. The layout of the office had changed, but Frankie was sure the furniture and decor were all the same. Helen was a tall, slim woman in her mid forties, with bouncy, thick, dark blonde, shoulder-length hair. She stood up to greet Frankie, wearing a black fitted shift dress and high heels. She was immaculately presented, even down to the perfectly manicured nails she held out to shake Frankie's hand.

"Lovely to finally meet you, Doctor, and to put a face to the name." She spoke in a soft Geordie accent.

"Nice to finally meet you too, and please, call me Frankie."

Frankie felt quite under-dressed in jeans and a sweater. She knew her casual West Coast style might be frowned upon here, but she wasn't very good at conforming just to fit in; they would have to like it or lump it!

"Okay.... Frankie," Helen said, looking slightly uncomfortable with the informal request, "can I get you a tea or coffee? Dr. Barnes will be with you shortly. I believe you have completed the last of the paperwork for me?"

"Sure, I have it right here, and a tea just with milk would be great, thanks." Frankie handed Helen the large brown envelope.

"Great, if there is anything else I need, I'll drop you an email or just pop a note in your post box." Helen pointed to the wall behind Frankie, which featured several shelves of black magazine boxes with names on the front.

"I try to keep them in alphabetical order, but I'm afraid they get moved around. I have already allocated one for you, but to be honest we try to keep everything paper-free if possible."

"Okay, thank you. I already sorted a hospital email with the I.T. Department, though they would only let me have it in my full, official name, which is a bit irritating."

"That's good to know. Well, it looks like Dr. Barnes is off the phone now. I'll bring you that tea and, please, if there is anything I can do to help you in any way, let me know." With a kind smile, Helen glided off.

Kathy's office was behind Helen's desk, with a small window in the door. Through this, Frankie could see that Kathy was sat at her desk. She gently tapped on the door, while looking through the window; Kathy was about to take a mouthful of coffee, but paused and waved Frankie in instead.

"Good morning, is this a good time?" Frankie asked as she entered the small, slightly disorganised space.

"Of course, good morning, I hope Helen has sorted you out with a drink?" Kathy replied.

"Yes, good to finally meet her, she seems really nice." Frankie slipped her backpack and jacket off and slid into the chair in front of Kathy's desk.

"Yes, she's only been with us a year now, but fingers crossed she'll stay. After Rosie left, it took us a long time, and a lot of useless secretaries, before we found her, and she's great!"

After a brief chat while the women finished their drinks, Kathy took Frankie over to the Theatres, where she changed into scrubs that were so big she could have pitched them to camp under. She'd brought her own work shoes, a bright red pair of Crocs, covered in Jibbitz. Kathy had arranged for her to spend the morning orientating herself, which would also give her some time to see her patients for the afternoon. She was scheduled to do an orthopaedic list with Mr. Patel, a surgeon she didn't know, but would be working with every Tuesday. It was normally a full day list, but by pure luck Mr. Patel was interviewing that morning, so his morning list had been cancelled. Kathy had described him as very pleasant to work with, but a bit on the slow side, and he liked to listen to Mozart while operating, which she thought made him even slower.

There were a few familiar faces from her training days a few years back, the most familiar being Gloria, the larger-than-life, broad Geordie receptionist, who manned the front desk. If you wanted to know anything about anything, you asked Gloria.

"Hey, Gloria how's it going?" Frankie said to her back as she approached the desk.

"Dr. Robertson! Hello pet, ah heard you was comin' back to us. Great to see you pet, you look smashin'!"

"Thanks," Frankie replied, "but I'm afraid it's only for six months."

"Aye, family stuff ah believe, sorry to hear about your dad. It always happens to the good'ens."

"Mmmm, well I'm just playing the dutiful daughter, then I am out of here... for good," she said with a sad smile.

She knew she was going to get this a lot; the world saw her father as a brilliant cardiac surgeon who had tragically lost his wife and was then diagnosed with a cruel disease himself. Only Frankie and Andrew knew differently. To them, he was just the man who happened to be their father; an aggressive, uncaring, unloving, selfish and self-centered creature that they had never really loved or even liked.

"Well pet, however short it is, it's lovely to see you again. Now pet, what can ah help you with, ah believe you're with Mr. Patel later, nice man, you'll like him, a bit slow mind you."

Frankie smiled to herself at the preconceived idea that she was being given of this poor man before she had even met him.

"I just need a copy of the list and where the patients are, so I can go and see them. Which OR will I be in?" Frankie asked.

"No problem pet, here you go, and am ah to presume by 'OR' you mean which theatre?"

Frankie let out a little laugh and a sigh both at the same time before replying, "Yes, sorry, you may have to keep me right... which theatre?"

"No problem pet," Gloria said, "that's a very canny accent you have there, ah like all those American dramas me, so ah knew what you meant... you're in Theatre 4."

'*Canny...*' now there was a word she hadn't heard in a long time. A very common word in a Geordie's vocabulary; the Scots also used it, but she wasn't sure if its meaning was the same. '*Its meaning... what was its meaning exactly?*' she thought as she thanked Gloria for her help and strolled off to find Theatre 4.

As she entered the anaesthetic room of Theatre 4, she interrupted two nurses in deep conversation over several bits of paper that were spread out across the bench.

"Oh, pardon me, I'm sorry I'll come..." Her apology was cut short by the older nurse.

"No, no problem, we can move... staffing problems, it will take a while. Please come in." The nurse started to gather up the papers.

"You must be Dr. Robertson? Welcome, I'm Denise, the Nurse Manager and this," she gestured towards the other nurse, who appeared much younger, "is Claire, one of my Senior Sisters."

"Hi, nice to meet you," said Claire who seemed far too young to be a Senior Sister.

'Sister'... there was a title she would have to get used to again. She was more familiar with Charge Nurse.

"Nice to meet you both too... please, please call me Frankie. I hate the formal titles," she said, almost pleading with them.

"Okay, Frankie it is, now we...."

Denise looked up as she was interrupted by a male voice whose owner was opening the door behind Frankie.

"Excuse me Dee, Ward 33 on the phone at the front desk, something about the emergency that's been added on to the end of Mr. Clark's list?" Frankie turned her head slightly to glance at the well-spoken man who wasn't quite visible through the window of the door.

"I'll take this, Dee," said Claire, "I know exactly what this is about. Excuse me," she said firmly, nodding to Frankie as she headed out the door.

The man was about to follow her when Denise called to stop him.

"Oh Jack, hold on a second, I should probably introduce you to our new doctor." Denise grabbed the door and opened it for the man called Jack to come into the room. As he did so, Frankie turned properly to look at him.

"Jack, this is Dr. Robertson. She'll be taking over Liam's lists for the next six months and I believe you'll be in here with her this afternoon." Denise then looked at Frankie and continued, "Jack is an Operating Department Practitioner, and a very good one at that. He's worked with Dr. Spencer quite a lot over the years, so he'll keep you right..."

Denise was talking and talking and talking, while Frankie stood staring up at steel blue eyes, a curl of dark hair poking out from the side of his hat, and stubble peeking up from a mask that was hanging from his ears, but half pushed under his chin. She was experiencing the most bizarre feeling, like stars twinkling inside her. She had no idea she'd been holding her breath, until Jack then spoke, which caused Frankie to suddenly pay attention.

"Pleased to meet you, Doctor," he said, nodding his head in Frankie's direction.

Frankie wasn't sure what was going to happen when she opened her mouth; she was on leave from all her faculties.

"Please... call me Frankie," was all she could manage.

"Frankie?" Jack asked. Her accent was unusual, he thought. "Okay," he said, as if she was asking him to call her Miss. Piggy or Rapunzel or something.

There was an awkward silence for a second, while Jack gazed down at two sparkling emeralds and the cutest little nose he'd ever seen on a woman. He caught himself having these thoughts and quickly spoke again, so he could just get out of there.

"Well, I'll be in soon to start setting up. I just have to finish next door and grab a bite of lunch." He kept his face expressionless, as he nodded slightly at both women, before leaving.

"He seems a bundle of laughs!" Frankie exclaimed, trying to play down the strange feeling this man had just given her.

"Go easy on him," Denise said, "he was very close to Liam Spencer and he's having a bad week... " Denise looked like she was about to say something else but instead smiled and nodded, then left the room too.

Jack walked into the anaesthetic room of Theatre 7. Two of his nurse colleagues were in there, huddled around an iPhone, giggling at something on the screen.

"Hey Jack, you should take a look at this," said Megan as she looked up, "You okay?" she asked him.

Jack stood for a moment trying to make sense of what had just happened. He realised his heart was thumping.

"It would appear that Dr. *Frankie* Robertson," he emphasised her name, "is a woman!"

"Yes, we knew that, did you not?" said Marie.

"Er, no, what sort of woman is called *Frankie*?" Again he emphasised her name.

"I think she's from America or somewhere, you know what they're like over there, anything goes!" said Megan.

"Some people were really excited about her coming back. She worked here a few years ago I think. Isn't her dad some high flying surgeon over at the Freeman?" said Marie, "Anyway Jacko, what's the big deal, are you scared of her?" Marie batted her eyelashes and slid up to Jack, reaching to touch his arm, which he pulled away.

Marie had been overtly throwing herself at Jack for as long as he could remember, even when he was married, but like most of the theatre staff, he couldn't stand her.

Jack retreated into Theatre 7; it was now empty, the morning list had just finished. He needed to clear away the unused drugs and equipment from the anaesthetic machine before he could have lunch. If the truth be known, he really wasn't in the mood to be around people right now and most of his colleagues understood this. However, he now had to spend the afternoon making small talk with some American woman called 'Frankie'. She made him feel strange. He decided that he had to be civil; he wasn't angry with her personally, he would have been angry at whoever filled Liam's shoes. He was especially angry at this time of year, this week in fact, Saturday to be precise.

'*She doesn't have to know,*' he thought to himself, '*I don't need to tell her. We'll just make small talk, it's only for the afternoon. It will be fine.*' He nodded his head slightly to himself and finished his work.

The theatre staff room was a large sitting area, with low, soft chairs arranged around the perimeter of the room and two rows of chairs placed back to back down the centre. A number of small coffee tables were dotted around, littered with gossip glossies, used cups, and coffee stains. A wall-mounted TV hung in the corner, showing awful daytime shows, and an open-plan kitchen at the far end provided a holiday destination for germs. '*It's a typical hospital staff room,*' Frankie thought as she looked around when she entered; they were obviously the same the world over. There were a number of people in the room; unfortunately the thing about theatres was that everyone looked the same. Unless you saw people out of work you had no idea what their hair colour or style was, because they wore a hat all day. You had no idea what shape they were because scrubs were the most unflattering, unfashionable and shapeless sacks a person could ever wear; especially if you had the misfortune of being the last person to get changed, as Frankie had been that day. It was a good job she was wearing one of her Power Y yoga tanks, because the neckline of her scrub top was close to being indecent. She could have fitted down one leg of the pants, and they were rolled up at least four times so that she didn't trip over the hems... Gorgeous, but nobody ever said medicine was a glamorous job!

She decided just to slide into a seat to the right of the door. As she was taking out her M&S pasta salad, a man sat in the centre row facing away from her, got up - a rather tall man who, she also noticed, was rather wide and clearly very fit. She half watched the man as he walked, still with his back to her, towards the sink in the kitchen. He rinsed his dishes and dried them before putting them in his backpack. As he turned, he looked straight at Frankie who, of course, was looking at him. She took a short, sharp intake of breath as she realised she was looking right at Jack. She couldn't just look away as he walked towards her, because she was sat right next to the door, so she gave a little smile of acknowledgement as her stomach tied itself in a knot.
"I'll be right with you, just give me five," she said to him as he reached out for the door handle.
"Take your time, Doctor, list doesn't start for another half an hour. I'll go and set up." He replied without taking his eyes off her, his hand missing the doorknob altogether.
She didn't quite manage to say anything - she couldn't even manage a 'thanks' - he was quick to get out of the door. She then had to try and eat something.

Fifteen minutes later Frankie entered the anaesthetic room of Theatre 4. Jack was standing with his very wide back to her, checking the monitor.
'*I bet he doesn't have problems finding scrubs that fit*' she thought to herself. Just as she, yet again, pulled the shoulder of her scrub top back into place, he turned around, his eyes going straight for the exposed shoulder she was rearranging.
"Having problems, Doctor?" he said, with very little expression.

"Just an XXL one. I've come to the conclusion in the last hour that the reason some nurses put on so much weight over the years is because they have to grow into the scrubs!" she replied. "Oops! Sorry that was my inside voice - she speaks without my knowledge."

Jack looked away from her. He couldn't help smiling at what she'd just said, but he wasn't going to let her see that.

"Interesting that you've made that observation now, after however many years in Theatre? Surely American nurses are just the same?" he questioned.

"I wouldn't know... I've never worked in the States!" This got her back up; why did everyone assume that her slight North American twang meant she was from America?

She slapped her backpack down on a long bench that ran along the entire length of the room and began digging for her glasses. Jack had finished checking the monitor and was now moving over to the bench where Frankie was standing.

"I just assumed..."

Frankie stopped him.

"Yes, everyone just assumes! Well, North America consists of more than just..." She put her right hand over her heart and said in a mock, high pitched, exaggerated American accent, "the United States of America."

Jack found it hard not to smile at her performance. Her glasses made her striking green eyes look even bigger and they were... sexy! He caught himself again and realised he was staring.

"Okay, my apologies," he finally said, looking away, "May I ask where you are from?"

"Sure," she looked up at him over the top of her glasses and replied in her best broad Geordie accent, "Newcastle!"

He did a sort of 'ha ha' smile back. *'Now she's just trying to be clever,'* he thought, as she continued speaking.

"But I've lived in Vancouver for the past seven years." She picked up the records of the first patient and leaned slightly towards him, pushing her glasses back onto her nose, quietly saying, "that's in Canada... West Coast."

Their eyes met, the temperature of the room shot up and Jack opened his mouth slightly, as if to say something, but really he was trying not to gasp. They must have been like that for only a second, but they both felt like minutes had passed. Frankie started to feel all twinkly inside and Jack suddenly realised he wasn't breathing. It was Frankie that broke their stare and the silence.

"Yes...well...that concludes today's geography lesson. Perhaps you could find your way to our first patient, or do you need a map?"

She offered him the patient records; he suddenly took a big breath in and practically snatched them from her. Re-arranging her scrub top again, she managed to smile at him.

"Good!" she said, trying to stand a little taller, feeling rather pleased with herself as she moved towards the anaesthetic machine to get ready for the patient. The door behind her creaked slightly and when she turned to look, a swift draught blew across her face and Jack was gone. She turned back to face the monitor, looked up slightly and took a few slow, deep breaths to calm herself.

"What the hell?" she said, quietly.

Despite the interesting start to the afternoon, Frankie and Jack were both very professional as they worked. The list was busy and Frankie couldn't deny that Jack was very good at his job. She wasn't always used to having an anaesthetic assistant in her regular job, but in the UK it was the norm; every anaesthetist was required to work with an Operating Department Practitioner. An ODP was more than just an assistant; they were trained in other areas and had knowledge and skills in scrubbing in for a case, or recovering a patient from their anaesthetic. She realised very quickly that he seemed to be one step ahead of her, knowing exactly what she would need. Her only complaint was the strange twinkly feeling he gave her. Every time he was near her, and especially when she had intubated her patient, not only did their bare arms touch, but also their fingers when he was securing the tube for her. It was the strangest thing, something she had never felt before with any man. It was ridiculous, she wasn't even sure she even liked the guy! She'd only known him three hours, but he was rather attractive and looked like he had the kind of body she only imagined in her naughtiest fantasies. She told herself to get a grip and focus.

At 5.45 they took the last patient to the recovery area. Jack went back to the room to tidy up, while Frankie handed over to the recovery nurse and made sure her records were complete. She entered the anaesthetic room to find Jack at the bench, disposing of the sharps into the container. She took a deep breath and let go of the door. Finding herself stood next to him, she noticed him glance sideways at her; their eyes met, but they both quickly looked away. Frankie took her glasses off and started to pack up her things.

"Thanks, Jack. Denise was right, you're very good at your job."

"Just doing what I'm paid to do," he replied, matter-of-factly, without looking at her.

They were side by side, their arms almost touching. Frankie couldn't help but notice how strong and muscular his arms were - his biceps almost filled the sleeve of his scrubs. She felt very tiny next to him. Despite being at the end of a full day's work, he smelt so good. Little did she know that he was stood there having similar thoughts.

Jack was suddenly aware that he was towering above her... he was tall, so he towered above most people... He thought, *'Why is she any different?'* The shoulder of her scrubs had slipped off again, but on this occasion she made no attempt to correct it.

"Well, I guess I'll see you around tomorrow," Frankie said as she clicked together the fastenings of her backpack, "I think I'm in OR 2 doing urology." She slung the backpack over her shoulder and looked up at him.

"In that case you will... I'm also in **Theatre** 2," he replied, correcting her, but looking at what he was doing and not at her.

"Oh!" The moment he said this she felt a shooting star take off from somewhere deep inside. "Well, in that case I'll see you in the morning in OR...sorry," she squeezed her eyes together then corrected herself, "*Theatre* 2."

"Yep I guess you will." He sounded like he was making fun of her, still making no eye contact.

"Well... have a good evening." She shrugged her shoulders; he said nothing in reply, and so she just pushed the door open and left.

The moment she was gone, Jack looked around; the door was still swinging. He turned to face the wall cupboards and rested his forehead against them with a slight thump, closing his eyes and breathing out slowly. He just wanted this week to be over, but then what? Another year would pass by and the same countdown would torture him until February 9th passed by again, then it would be three years, then four, five... Jack suddenly stood up straight, rubbed his face, and put his hands on his hips, looking around the room to see what else he needed to do. He was just about done when Marie walked into the room.

"Well?" she said, leaning against the bench with her arms folded, pushing her chest up so it looked even bigger than it already was.

"Well what?" said Jack, looking puzzled.

"How was the Yank?"

"She's actually not American." Jack didn't hesitate to correct Marie, "She's a local who now lives in Vancouver."

Jack remembered the way Frankie had sarcastically informed him where Vancouver was earlier in the day and decided to give Marie the same treatment. He said quietly, in the same tone Frankie had used, "That means she's Canadian." It worked. Marie's expression changed instantly.

"Ha-ha, very funny," she said, annoyed. "I came in to see if you needed a hand, but next time I won't bother!" She stormed out.

Jack walked to the sink to wash his hands before leaving, feeling slightly satisfied.

It was nearly 7pm before Frankie got home. She received a very warm welcome from Hercules as she walked through the flat door. She took off her hat, coat, and boots, as the cat weaved himself in and out of her legs, rubbing himself against her, purring.

"Hey big guy, how's it going?" She bent down to stroke him.

"You hungry?" she said, and he let out a loud meow. "Let me see, salmon or chicken?" There was another loud meow and she took that to mean salmon.

"Excellent choice, my friend!"

After slaving over the microwave to prepare an M&S ready-meal for herself, she ran a bath. Hercules joined her on the side of the tub, so he could paw at the bubbles. Bocelli sang in the background, possibly declaring war on a toaster for taking his bagel hostage and burning it to a crisp.

"So. How was your day?" she asked him as she sank further into the hot, velvety water. "Slept for most of it, I should imagine? I'm totally coming back as a cat, you know. What I would give to sleep all day and have a plate of salmon served to me without lifting a finger!"

Hercules was waving a paw furiously, trying to remove a large blob of bubbles from it.

"My day was a bit strange... it was okay until I met my ODP for the afternoon. He was good at his job, but a little rude, and I have to put up with him again tomorrow. But you know what was really weird? He gave me the strangest feeling whenever I was really close to him, or looked straight at him. What's that all about? I mean, how can you not know or like someone, yet they do that to you? He did smell really good, and dare I say it... he was pretty hot!"

She shut her eyes, breathing in the wonderful aroma of satsuma.

Her immediate thought was of Jack, his broad back, his thick muscular arms, that dark curl of hair peeking out of his hat, his stubble, and those steel blue eyes staring at her with a slight look of anger when she had the last word... all this flashed through her mind.

"See... for God's sake... I try to relax and there he is," she said to Hercules, angrily.

After her soak, she sent emails to her brother and to Kayla, letting them know how her first day had gone, omitting the obvious, most interesting bit of course. By about 10.30 she was beat and crawled into bed so she could recharge with a good night's sleep ready to face it all again tomorrow.

Chapter 3

FRANKIE WAS STILL fast asleep when the alarm went off at 6.30. She decided that, despite it only being her second day back in the NHS, she would resume her normal Vancouver work morning routine and dress code. She started with a shower to wake herself up. She washed her hair but never dried or styled it, because why would you when it was going to be hidden under a hat all day? She applied tinted moisturizer and mascara. There would be none of this dressing up for work nonsense, when she only had to change into a pair of unglamorous scrubs. No, not even jeans, because jeans meant underwear, and if there was one thing that Frankie hated more than anything in the world it was underwear! Panty lines and yoga pants are just plain unattractive. So yes, she was a commando girl. Sure, she owned underwear, but only wore it when appropriate or under jeans, because jeans can chafe something shocking. So she dressed in black yoga pants, a purple Scuba Hoodie with a lilac Power Y yoga tank underneath. No bra, because the tank top had built-in support.

Breakfast was a bucket of tea and granola, banana, and Greek yoghurt. She packed her backpack with her iPad, a healthy M&S lunch, a large bottle of water, and the one item she couldn't do without at work... her glasses. She only really needed them for reading, but found that at work she ended up wearing them most of the day, because it was a pain to take them on and off. She also thought they made her look quite intelligent. After feeding Hercules and tidying up his litter tray, she was out the door by 7.30.

Her short commute and walk to the hospital took her just under half an hour, so she walked through the anaesthetic office door just before 8am. To her surprise, the office was empty. She had forgotten that most people started a bit later in England. She checked her mailbox, finding a note from Helen inviting her to the 6th Annual Theatre Charity Event next Friday, February 15th. The ceilidh was to be held at the Gosforth Park Hotel, and would include raffles and a silent auction. All the proceeds would be donated to the Heart and Stroke Foundation this year, out of respect for Dr. Spencer. Tickets would be £35, with a buffet included in the price. *'Cool'*, she thought to herself as she scribbled a note to Helen, letting her know that she would love to attend, and that she would swing by at some point in the day to give her the money. She left the note on her desk before she left.

Despite being a little early, there still weren't any small scrubs. She huffed and puffed about the unsatisfactory size of the ones she would have to suffer again that day, then heard a voice from the other side of the lockers.
 "I think there should be a delivery from the laundry tomorrow...you're not alone, I have the same problem." The smiling, friendly face of a woman not much older than Frankie popped around the lockers, making Frankie jump.
 "Sorry, didn't mean to scare you. Hi, I'm Heather, Dr. Robertson or, wait, sorry... Frankie isn't it?"
 Frankie let out a slow sigh and smiled before replying.

"Yes, nice to meet you."

"I'm a scrub nurse, in fact I think I'm in with Mr. Anderson today in Theatre 2 - you're gassing in there too, I think?"

"Yes I am." Frankie was glad to know that a friendly face (or rather a pair of eyes, because that's all you see when people are scrubbed) would be around to break up the weirdness with Jack.

"Well, it should be a good day. Mr. Anderson is young, enthusiastic, very efficient, quite amusing and rather easy on the eyes, if you know what I mean!" Heather gave a little smile and a wink. "All helps to get you through a day of shoving things up men's willies! See you in a mo'." And she was off.

Frankie stood, looking slightly stunned for a minute, then burst out laughing; she instantly knew she would get on very well with Heather.

As Frankie approached the anaesthetic room of Theatre 2, she could see movement; there was someone already in there, and she knew who it would be. She started to feel all twinkly inside. After taking a couple of deep breaths, she looked through the small window in the door for a second, before entering. Jack had his back to her, as he checked the monitor. She confidently pushed the door open.

"Good morning, Jack," she said as she walked in.

"Good morning, Doctor," he replied, without even turning around.

Frankie stood for a second and stared at his back. She couldn't believe how rude he could be. She walked over to the bench to put her backpack down, saying rather cheerfully, "It's going to be one of those days is it?"

"One of what days?" He actually turned around this time when he replied, looking confused at Frankie's question.

"Jack," she said, placing one hand on her hip and turning towards him. "I have a pretty laid back approach to my job, but

I don't do rudeness well, even if it comes with good looks and professionalism. I'm filling the shoes of someone everyone was very fond of... I get it. But the show must go on. It would be nice if you could be a little friendlier."

She was quite proud of her little speech, but had she really just said that, the good looks part? *'Bloody inside voice again!'* she thought.

Jack was standing with his arms folded, looking down at the floor, when she finished speaking. There was a silent pause, for what felt like hours, before he looked up and spoke.

"Point taken, Doctor."

He couldn't help noticing her scrub top hanging off her left shoulder; it looked even bigger than one she'd fought with yesterday. What she wore underneath intrigued him; it was obviously not a bra, but some sort of fitness vest. The colour really suited her. He looked at her across the room, expecting her to say something, but she just seemed to be concentrating really hard, her lips parted slightly.

"May I make a suggestion?" he asked.

She shrugged her shoulders. "Sure." She assumed it was going to be about getting on better with each other, but he took her completely by surprise by walking towards her. He stopped for a second, right in front of her, and reached out for her name badge, which was pinned to the right side of her scrub top.

"May I?" he asked, as he started to unpin it.

"Looks like you already are!" She looked at him, very puzzled, her internal organs all swapping places, excited at the fact he was actually touching her. She was sure that if she opened her mouth again, thousands of butterflies were going to fly out.

Jack unpinned the badge, then carefully lifted her scrub top back onto her shoulder, before re-pinning the badge across the

V-neck at the front of the top, to make it smaller and stop it from exposing her again.

Jack was wondering what on earth he was doing. He had barely looked at another woman since his wife, let alone touched one, so what had possessed him to do this now, at this time; why not after this weekend at least? 'Why her?' he questioned himself. He was shaking slightly as he touched her; he had to think of something to say quickly before she noticed how she was affecting him.

"There you go. Now that you're decent, you'll look good and professional too," he said standing back, admiring his handiwork, thinking he'd won this round with what was a fairly harsh statement.

Frankie was completely frozen to the spot. He smelled so good, being so close, and she was looking head on into the 'V' of his scrubs, where tufts of chest hair were escaping for air... She knew how they would feel; she had to remind herself to breathe.

She let out a little laugh, completely taken aback by his words.

"Well," she said looking down, shaking her head, putting her hands on her hips again before looking up and straight at him.

"Okay! I appreciate the fashion advice, we can't have all those little old men getting stiffies before we ram a camera up it, can we?"

He bit his lip to stop himself from bursting out laughing. He kept his eyes fixed on hers for a couple of seconds before breaking free, becoming aware that she had made him blush.

"Another fair point, Doctor... I'll get the first patient." He reached his arm around her to pick up the patient records.

"Sure, I'll draw up my drugs," she said, as he started to push open the door. He stopped and looked back, "I've already done them." Their eyes met again.

"Oh," she replied, impressed. "Okay, great!"

"...but you might want to check them. I took an educated guess at what you might use."

"Sure... I'll do that... thanks."

The door was left swinging, causing a draught to blow across her face. She stood watching it, wondering what in the name of sedation that was all about!

"Good morning Dr. Robertson, pleased to meet you. Mike... Mike Anderson. I trust Mr. Davidson is suitably anaesthetised for me to explore his bladder?" Mr. Mike Anderson breezed into Theatre 2, fully gowned, masked, scrubbed, and ready for surgery.

The patient, a 72-year old man who was having a cystoscopy to explore his bladder to determine whether or not he had cancer, lay on the operating table, sleeping peacefully and breathing steadily. Frankie and Jack had worked well together again, despite their differences.

"Now then," Mike announced, "I think it's only fair that our new visitor introduce us to some tunes from the West Coast of Canada."

Frankie looked up, surprised.

"I trust you have an iPod, Doctor?" Mike said to her.

All eyes were on Frankie, waiting for her response.

"Sure, have you guys heard of Train?" she asked.

"Ahh, 'Drops of Jupiter' I do believe, I approve of your good taste. Now then, let's get this show on the road."

Mike and Heather, who was also scrubbed, proceeded to lay sterile drapes over the patient. Frankie reached for her iPhone.

"I have all their albums, do you have a preference?" Frankie asked.

"Oh, I think just shuffle the lot and surprise us!" Mike replied.

"Sure." Frankie smiled to herself; she already liked this guy and had a good feeling about the day.

A few minutes later the first song, 'She's On Fire', burst out of the speakers; this was one of Frankie's favourites. One of the good things about theatre masks was that no one could see her miming the words. It all made for a much more relaxed day that ran smoothly and efficiently. Even Jack seemed to be letting down his guard; Frankie noticed him nodding to the beat of the music occasionally.

At the end of the list Mike declared that, for the duration of Frankie's time at the Infirmary, every Wednesday would be a 'Train' day. This suited Frankie very well; she strongly believed she was their biggest fan and had no problem listening to them all day.

"Excellent!" she exclaimed, after Mike had made his announcement, "My work here is done!"

Even Jack joined in the laughter within Theatre 2. As he did so, his eyes met Frankie's as they wheeled the last patient out of the theatre to recovery. He actually smiled at her a little; neither of them was wearing a mask now that surgery was over. For the first time he noticed she had very fair eyebrows, which led him to believe she must be blonde.

"You're quite the comedian for an American!" he said.

"Why thank you," she replied in a mock, high-pitched American accent, trying not to let the excitement show that he was complimenting her.

They were chatting freely as they pushed their way through the recovery room doors. That was all about to change. Marie, who had been moved to recovery due to staffing problems, met them.

"Well good afternoon, Doctor... Mr. Lee."

Frankie instantly noticed that this not unattractive nurse was obviously flirting with Jack.

"Marie, I see you've been sent to the dark side, been a bad girl have we?" The way Jack spoke to her suggested that he was not in the slightest bit interested in this woman.

The three of them wheeled the patient into a vacant bed space.

"I just so happened to be working 11/7 today, and they were short in here, so I drew the short straw. Meet me after work though and I'll show you just how bad I can be!" Marie was giving Jack the full come on - eyelashes, cleavage, and smile that she must have thought looked seductive - but Frankie thought looked like she was about to burp! She interrupted her and said quietly, "Excuse me, Nurse, you obviously haven't noticed we're in a hospital here and not in a Bigg Market pub. So if you don't mind, can you save your trashy mouth for a more appropriate establishment and someone who might be vaguely interested in using you."

Frankie then continued to hand over the patient to Marie as if nothing had happened. Jack gathered the transfer equipment from the bed and immediately headed back to the theatre they had come from. He didn't once look at Marie, but he knew she was extremely pissed off. He also couldn't look at Frankie; after she had made her discreet little speech to Marie all he could think was how much he wanted to kiss her. He had been trying to put Marie in her place for years without success; this woman had done it after two days!

'Kiss her,' he thought as he put the equipment away, '*what the hell is happening here?*'

As he turned it over in his mind, Frankie walked back into Theatre 2. Jack was crouched down behind the anaesthetic machine trying to disconnect the ventilator tubing. He immediately stood up as she walked towards him.

"I'm sorry, Jack, inside voice again...she just doesn't know when to control herself. Not that I think she was out of order to say something." Frankie was cringing slightly as she thought back to her words.

"Don't apologise, please, she's had it coming to her for a long time. She's not a very popular member of staff, but her mum is the bed manager so she gets away with quite a lot."

"So was I right in sensing she's not going to get her way with you then? Oops there she goes again, none of my business, you don't have to answer that." Frankie was sure she knew the answer anyway.

"No it's fine, and you're right. I dread to think where that girl's been...huh, I guess that's my inside voice!"

They both looked at each other and burst out laughing. It was one of those looks when two people exchange something invisible but they're scared by what it might mean. They quickly looked away, each finding some tidying up to do. If the twinkling Frankie was feeling at that moment wasn't enough, the next thing Jack said nearly caused her to shoot into orbit!

Jack had no idea why he asked the next question; like the inside voice Frankie had introduced him to, it was out of his mouth before he could stop it.

"So, you're here with your... husband? Boyfriend? Significant other?"

She had her back to him so he couldn't see her face. She screwed it up in a kind of excited smile, took a short, sharp breath and composed herself before replying,

"Nope, alone, I have none of the above. Not for the want of trying mind you... I think my inside voice scared them all away... yourself?"

Frankie had to ask, he was a very good-looking guy; she was sure he had to be with someone. She braced herself, convinced he was going to say he was gay.

It never occurred to Jack that she would return the question. Now what? Should he tell her he had been married; should he tell her why he wasn't anymore? He couldn't. Any other time of the year, maybe, but not now.

"No, none of the above either." He didn't find it easy to get the words out; he tried to avoid the subject whenever possible. He couldn't look at her, he knew his face would give away more. In fact, he needed to leave the room; he needed space; he needed to have not put himself in this position!

"Excuse me, I just have to..."

Jack just left what he was doing and escaped out of the door.

Frankie spun around in surprise; where the hell had he gone? One minute they were actually having a normal, adult conversation and the next he'd gone. She poked her head out into the corridor... gone!

She shrugged her shoulders and sighed heavily.

About fifteen minutes later, Frankie had already finished clearing up her equipment and was just packing her backpack, when Heather walked in.

"Hey Frankie, just going to finish up here for Jack."

"Is everything okay? One minute we were chatting and the next minute he was gone!"

"I know, not a good week for him I'm afraid. Hopefully he won't blow so hot and cold once he gets Saturday out of the way," Heather said this as if Frankie was supposed to know what she was talking about.

"Saturday?" Frankie asked curiously, "Why Saturday?"

"Oh, you don't know. Well I suppose there's no reason why you should. I'm sure he won't mind me telling you; I know for a fact he won't say anything himself." Heather stopped what she was doing and turned to Frankie.

"Saturday will be the second anniversary of his wife's death," Heather said, with the saddest of looks.

"Oh my God!" Frankie hadn't seen that coming at all.

"I know, I was here the day it happened. I've never seen anyone look so shocked by a piece of news as he did that day; I thought he was going to collapse, honestly. Poor thing, he's never really gotten over it. Anyway, cut him some slack, he's a little fragile."

Frankie had no idea what to say to this. She thanked Heather for sharing the information with her; it was important she knew, in case she saw Jack on Friday. Then she left for home.

Chapter 4

THURSDAY WAS A day off for Frankie. She had hoped to sleep in, but her body clock had other ideas. Not only could she not get Jack out of her head, she knew she had to start dealing with the primary reason for her being there. Kayla was up late, having been at work until midnight, so she Face Timed with her, filling her in on life so far. Kayla, a recovery nurse, was not only her roommate; she was also her best friend. She and Frankie had met on their first day in the OR and hit it off right away. Kayla was from Melbourne, Australia, and a couple of years younger than Frankie. She, too, was making a fresh start in life, after having finally rid herself of her violent husband. Frankie couldn't fool Kayla; they had known each other for seven years. As soon as she mentioned Jack, Kayla saw that there were things Frankie wasn't telling her.

"I'm only gonna ask you this once hun, and I'll know if you're fibbing... you've got the hots for this guy haven't you?" she asked in her thick Aussie accent.

"I can't hide anything from you, can I!" Frankie was smirking slightly. She was actually quite glad to have someone other than Hercules to talk to about her crazy feelings.

"So let me get this straight... he's younger than you, he's hot, he's available and he's possibly into you too... and your problem with this is? Listen hun, with the amount of crap you're going to be dealing with while you're there, you'll deserve a bit of fun and if that fun is meaningless sex with this guy then Hell Yeah!!" Kayla was a typical Aussie, her inside voice was also her outside voice.

"Kay, the poor guy is still mourning the death of his wife."

"So he needs some distraction therapy, you know, help him move on."

Kayla was as a blunt as a butter knife, but it was one of the reasons Frankie loved her. However, she was temporarily forgetting the one rule they had made very early in their friendship... you don't date your colleagues. It ends up messy and awkward. Frankie was quick to point this out.

"But he's not really a work colleague is he, it's not your proper job... so you can kind of justify it."

"Kay, it's not going to happen, okay, I don't even know why we're thrashing this out."

"Okay hun, but I want all the details if it does... promise?"

"Yeah, whatever!" Frankie rolled her eyes a little, smirking.

After Frankie hung up with Kayla, she sent a quick update to her brother. She was going to their parents' house that afternoon, before she contacted the estate agent to enquire about putting it on the market. It was important that she kept Andrew informed. At some point he was going to come over from New York and collect whatever keepsakes, belongings, etc., he wanted from the house. Also, at the end of the day, it was the house they had both grown up in and, despite much unhappiness, Andrew wanted to visit it one last time.

Frankie then contacted Patricia, out of courtesy, to let her know her plans. Much to Frankie's relief, there was no answer, so she just left a message. She was nervous at just the thought of visiting.

She had no idea what to expect. It had been five years since she was last there. Although she had agreed with Andrew that she would do this, she now wished she wasn't doing it alone. This was only the beginning; where would she start even to begin clearing the house? After two large buckets of tea and a Cadbury's flake, she informed Hercules of her plan.

"You're probably wondering why I'm doing this? I sometimes wonder myself, but, at the end of the day he was... is my father. Just because I didn't get on with him doesn't mean I have to cut him off completely. I think I just have to take it a week at a time. Maybe set aside one or two days to go to the house. We can discuss my approach to the clearing side of things later over gin. What do you think?"

Hercules was lying on the back of the sofa, eyes open, purring into Frankie's right ear.

"I know for a fact that old prune face won't have done anything with the place, so I bet you I have to hire a skip to clear the ten tons of shit my father will have hoarded over the years."

At this point Hercules closed his eyes.

"I can see I've now lost you at the mere mention of him. Well, I guess on that note I should go, or I'll never do it, will I?"

Hercules then lay his head on a paw.

She got up and stroked his head gently. He purred a little louder, causing her to smile.

Frankie had never driven a Smart car before. She had always thought that they looked as if the company had run out of money to produce the front and back of the car that was originally designed, so they just made it without those bits and thought it looked cool! The only thing Frankie had ever thought was cool about them was the ability to park them in between two parked cars with the Smart's nose pointing into the road. She'd seen that in San Francisco once, while at a conference. At least Lucy's was just plain black and not some crazy colour, with advertising that made it stand out. The bottom line was, she was going to have to drive the thing to get to the house. As it happened it wasn't as bad as she thought it would be, despite driving on the opposite side of the road to that which she was now used to.

As she pulled into the driveway of the large, semi-detached, 1930s home, she felt slightly nauseous. At first she could only sit, staring at the bricks and mortar that she'd once called home. It took her ten minutes to finally get out of the car. It was then she noticed how overgrown and unkempt the garden had become. Her mum had been a very keen gardener; she would turn in her grave if she knew what it looked liked now. Frankie made a mental note to hire a landscaper to tidy it up as soon as possible. She slowly approached the solid oak front door, and searched around in her jacket pocket for the keys. She pulled them out, with the same Mickey Mouse key ring she'd been given for her thirteenth birthday, now faded and worn, dangling from the door key. The same door key she'd also been given on that same birthday, marking a milestone in independence and responsibility. It was now twenty-five years old. She clumsily pushed the key into the lock and noticed she was shaking slightly. She dropped her arms to her side, leaving the key in the door.
"Get a grip girl, this shouldn't really be that difficult."
Then, after taking a deep breath, she turned the key.

As she slowly pushed the door open, she was surprised to breathe in the familiar smell of 'home'. She was fully expecting the place to have been neglected for the last five years, but no, it smelled clean and actually quite inviting, even though it was cold. She put the hall light on and saw that mail had been neatly stacked on the table under the mirror. She presumed Patricia was responsible for keeping the place in order, and realised she would have to thank her at some point. Frankie dropped her bag and keys on the hall table and proceeded to do a walkthrough of the house. She had to admit, despite the place looking worn and tired, it was clean and tidy.

She left her own childhood bedroom until last. It didn't really look like the bedroom she'd grown up in. There were no Duran Duran or Wham posters on the wall. No clothes hanging over the end of the bed. No books all over the desk, and the closet door was actually shut properly, not just pushed to because of all the 'stuff' she just couldn't part with over the years. *'What happened to all that 'stuff'?'* she thought; she was pretty sure she didn't have any of it. She wasn't even sure what 'it' all was - hockey stick? Stuffed animals? Her first doll that she never actually played with but kept for years… maybe?

She sat on the bed, put her elbows on her knees and rubbed her forehead with her hands. She felt the beginnings of a headache; she never got headaches unless she was really stressed. Suddenly, she sat up and looked into the mirror on the wall opposite.

"You've taken the first step in this and it really wasn't that bad. Baby steps, okay." She took a deep breath and blew out slowly, "Baby steps."

After about an hour at the house she'd had enough. There was a small picture of her mother on one of the bookshelves in her father's study. It was taken the Christmas before Emily was diagnosed, eighteen months before she died. This was the only picture of her mother that appeared to be on display in the house, tucked away on a bookshelf. Frankie put it in her bag before locking up and leaving.

A day like this required something comforting. A steamy shower with six foot plus of rippling muscle, followed by slow, mind-blowing sex sprang to mind but, as that wasn't an option, Frankie had to settle for M&S carbonara and a glass of chenin blanc. She was proud of herself for going to the house so soon after arriving. She could easily have put it off until the following week, but she knew the sooner it was on the market, the sooner it would be sold, and the sooner she could get back to normal life in Canada. She sent emails to both Andrew and Kayla to update them, ran a bath, poured more wine and of course, she needed Andrea to soothe and calm her with his beautiful interpretation of a coq au vin recipe.

It was 10.05 when she climbed into bed, wondering how she had become so sad and boring, going to bed so early.

"I guess I have no life here really, do I, big guy?"

Hercules was already lying on the bed when she joined him. He stretched out, then curled into her, purring.

"Suppose I'm not here to enjoy myself, am I?" she continued, despite Hercules shutting his eyes. "Oh well, let's see what tomorrow brings. Sleep well."

She put the light out and, before she knew it, her alarm was letting her know it was 6.30.

Friday felt like a very long day for Jack. Not surprisingly, he was quiet and distant at work, but it was probably for the best that he had it to distract him. He wasn't working with Frankie, but again, he thought this was probably for the best; he was a little embarrassed about having left her, mid-conversation, without any explanation. He didn't really want to explain himself yet, but he knew he would have to at some point. He saw her in the distance, twice. She was doing a general surgery list - that Friday list was always chaotic. Mr. Patrick O'Reilly was a very good surgeon, but he was also an Irishman, who therefore loved to talk; and talking leads to teaching, and teaching leads to surgery taking three times longer than planned, which then leads to a list running so far behind you might as well plan to stay the weekend! Jack had earned so much overtime because of Mr. O'Reilly.

At 5.25 Jack was out the door. He was picking up his older brother, Anthony, at Newcastle Central station at 6.15 - plenty of time to get across town. As he walked out through the theatre suite doors into the main hospital corridor, he bumped into Denise, who was on her way back in.

"Hey Jack." She was facing the theatre doors, Jack had his back to them. "I know today wasn't easy, I'll be thinking of you tomorrow." She smiled sadly and touched his arm lightly.

As they talked, the theatre doors opened behind Jack and a small figure walked past them. The person was all in black, including a black hat with all her hair tucked up inside. He knew it was Frankie; he found it difficult not to watch her and to concentrate on what Denise was saying. When he next looked up, she was gone. '*She must have taken the stairs,*' he thought. Jack thanked Denise, explained he had to run and why. Denise was glad he wasn't going to be alone over the weekend.

At the station, Jack parked in the short-stay car park. He walked through the main entrance of the historic Grade 1 listed building at 6.05. The arrivals board declared the TransPennine Express from Manchester Piccadilly delayed until 6.40, so he decided to go for coffee. Sat alone in Starbucks, he started to think about what he'd been doing this time two years ago. He remembered being quite late home from work that evening, after the last patient of the day had arrested on the table. Thankfully, the patient had survived but it had taken a long time to stabilise her enough to move to the intensive care unit. When Jack had finally arrived home, Emma had been taking a bath, because her back was aching. She'd worked as a Community Physiotherapist with the elderly. They'd had an ordinary weekday evening; Emma had been tired around 10, not unusually, so she had gone to bed. Jack remembered her saying the following morning that she had a slight headache but she'd declared she hadn't slept that well and had put it down to tiredness. She'd left for work before he did. He remembered her giving him a quick peck on the cheek and telling him she loved him before she disappeared out the door. That was the last time he saw her alive.

Jack was sat at a corner table, with a tall dark roast coffee in front of him that he'd barely touched, when his phone beeped next to him on the table. It was Anthony.

Where are you mate?

Jack replied.

Starbucks, sorry, just saw the time. Be right with you.

Jack took his coffee and made his way to platform 4. Anthony saw Jack approaching and slowly walked towards him.

"Jacko, mate." Anthony put his right arm around Jack and patted him firmly on the shoulder. Jack did the same in return.

"Good to see you too." Jack was genuinely pleased to see his brother; his family was right, he shouldn't be alone this weekend and Anthony had drawn the short straw. Jack was much closer to his younger sister, Anna, but she was unable to get out of a work commitment. However, there was never a dull moment with Anthony around, so he knew that his brother would be good distraction.

"You came straight from work?" asked Anthony

"Yeah, thought we could pick up a curry on the way home."

"Excellent choice for a Friday night, my friend, we can always hit the town tomorrow evening."

"Oh I don't know about that - it wouldn't feel right - maybe just a drink in the local." Jack was a shy, natural loner, he hated the whole going out, getting drunk, chatting up girls scene in Newcastle; and it was the last thing he wanted to do on Emma's second anniversary. He envisioned a quiet weekend just hanging out, talking, and maybe seeing a movie, though he knew Anthony would have other ideas.

"Hey look, mate, whatever works for you, you know? I don't want to push you into doing something you don't want to do. I just want you to get through tomorrow, okay?"

"Yeah, I know, thanks. Can we just get to tomorrow and see how it goes?"

"Absolutely, you call the shots." Anthony patted Jack's back again as the two brothers arrived at Jack's car.

The rest of the evening was a fairly sedate affair. After a very large Indian takeaway and a couple of bottles of beer, Jack relaxed a little. They caught up on each other's lives and news; as always, Anthony's life, especially his love life, was far more interesting than Jack's. At the age of 33, Anthony ran his own sandwich company, delivering to the offices and businesses of central Manchester. He had gone to university there to study business, and never left; instead he'd started his own. Like Jack, he was tall, dark, good looking, and worked out so he was in great shape. He had women swooning over him everywhere he went and, over time, he'd had his share of them. He had only once really settled down, briefly, with a stunningly attractive make-up artist at a local television station. The whole family thought she would be the one to break his playboy ways, but she got offered the chance of a lifetime, to work for a television network in Los Angeles. It took Anthony three days and a one-night stand to get over her!

The interesting thing about the two brothers was that, whilst neither knew how the other one could live his life the way he did, both respected each other's choices. Anthony still found it hard to believe that, since losing his wife, Jack had not so much as looked at another woman, let alone dated one. Jack didn't understand how Anthony could use women the way he did and not feel any sort of guilt. Despite these differences, they were siblings who actually got on pretty well, and would always be there for each other, no matter what. Right now, Anthony knew that his brother needed him to just be there.

To Jack's surprise, Saturday was a pretty ordinary day. He hadn't known what to expect, but he noticed that he wasn't quite the emotional wreck that he had been this time the year before. Maybe this was the beginning of moving on, of accepting that Emma was gone. Anthony had suggested fish and chips somewhere on the sea front at Tynemouth, followed by a cultural walk taking in the Priory and Tynemouth Castle, which dated back to the 7th century. It wasn't raining for a change, so Jack agreed that this would be a good way of blowing some cobwebs away. By the evening, they were both glowing and knackered from the sea air, but as Anthony had to be on the 11am train the next day, they felt they should make the most of time they rarely spent together.

They decided to have dinner at a small, local, Italian restaurant that Jack had never been to. That it was walking distance from Jack's Kingston Park flat also made it an attractive choice. They enjoyed pasta and red wine before moving on to whisky; Jack didn't normally drink very much, so he was pretty relaxed when Anthony fired his opening question.

"So little brother... when are you going to move on and start to do some serious tomming about?"

It took Jack a minute to process exactly what his brother had said.

"What do you mean?"

"Come on Jack, it's been two years. If the shoe were on the other foot, would you have expected Emma to sit around and grieve for you for that long?"

Jack hadn't really thought about it like that.

"I suppose not, but I'm so out of it now, I just don't know where to begin; you know I thought she was my soul mate. I know you don't get that; I hope one day you will. I genuinely have no idea where to begin. Emma and I were together for so long, the thought of being with anyone else, or even just kissing someone else freaks me out; not to mention the guilt I would feel."

"But why should you feel guilty? You're a widower, Jack, free to kiss whomever you want. You shouldn't feel guilty. You've spent two years respecting her memory. It's time to go out there and find yourself a hot blonde, with big tits and legs up to her armpits, and shag her into next week!"

"Ahh, so that's what you mean by 'tomming about'. You think I should just have meaningless sex with random women before I start to look for the second Mrs. Right?"

"Basically, yes!"

Jack sat back in his chair. The restaurant was starting to empty now, as it was nearly 11. He played with a dessert spoon, thinking about what Anthony was advising him to do. It was no good; he had to be honest, he just wasn't Anthony.

"Ant, I don't think I can use women like that, not the way you do. I know that sounds crazy, coming from a bloke, but it's the truth."

The truth was, Anthony didn't know the half of it. Jack was scared of ever loving someone again, after having Emma torn away from him. As for sex, well despite his good looks and excellent physique, he wasn't sure he had much to offer a woman. He considered himself relatively inexperienced and now very rusty.

"Okay, I know, you think very differently to me. I respect that. But if you change your mind, I know some very hot totty who would be very willing to rehydrate your dry spell!"

"Thank you big brother, I'll bear that in mind."

After another shot of whisky and a disagreement over who should pay the bill, they staggered back to Jack's one-bedroom flat. Jack was pretty drunk by the time they got home. Anthony made sure his troubled little brother was safely tucked up in bed before he himself retired to the sofa. He wished he could do more to help him move on, but hoped that their conversation had sown a seed. He knew that Jack had a completely different set of morals and values from his own, and he respected that, but his brother needed to lighten up and have some fun. The most positive thing that had come out of the weekend was that Jack had not shed a single tear. Anthony hoped that this meant his brother was finally going to put the past behind him.

Frankie spent the weekend with her family. After a frustrating day dealing with estate agents, she spent Saturday evening with her cousin Thomas, his wife Jen, and their two children, Isabel who was 11, and Joshua who was 9. The children treated her like an aunt, so as any good aunt would, she had brought them gifts - from Vancouver. Joshua got a Canucks hockey shirt, of course, and Isabel a Scuba Hoodie from Frankie's favourite yoga store, Lululemon. Isabel always laughed hysterically at the name of the store, but she had made Frankie promise to bring her a hoodie just like hers when they'd last Face Timed. Frankie never needed an excuse to shop at Lululemon; Kayla was worried they would go bankrupt during the six months that Frankie was away, so before Frankie left she'd paid homage to the great god of yoga wear and splashed out on a few things, including a hoodie in Isabel's favourite colour – pink. Thomas and Jen told Frankie off for spoiling the children, but she just waved it off, commenting that she had to spoil someone's kids, as neither she nor Andrew were ever likely to have any!

A traditional British Sunday lunch of roast beef, Yorkshire pudding, and all the trimmings followed the next day at her aunt's and uncle's, again with Thomas and Co.. She had to be honest, she did miss that sort of thing, but her lifestyle beat any Sunday lunch hands down. She didn't get back to the flat until gone 7pm and was glad she wasn't at work in the morning. Instead, she had appointments with four different estate agents to value the house. She wasn't looking forward to the day but knew it had to be done, and the sooner the better.

In the end, only two of the appointments were worth the effort. Frankie cursed the British housing market and it's unsatisfactory system of buying and selling. She only had the experience of buying her Vancouver apartment to compare it to, but she was sure that hiring a realtor to do the job for you was much more effective than doing it all yourself. Still, she had to decide which company she was going to go with. The valuations and the marketing were similar for both. The only difference between them had been that one agent was female and one was male. After a quick Face Time with her brother, she decided that girl power was to win, and the woman with the killer heels would be hired.

Frankie spent the rest of the evening making a list of all the things she now had to do, regarding the house and her father's affairs. She still hadn't heard from Patricia, but then that wasn't really surprising as they had agreed to talk only when necessary. After a soak in the bath, she decided to curl up in bed and read. It would be orthopaedics again tomorrow; she started to think about Jack and wondered what his weekend had been like. Poor guy. She couldn't imagine what it must be like to be made a widower at such a young age. She wondered what had happened to his wife; it was sudden, so something traumatic most likely, car accident maybe?

When Frankie arrived in Theatre 4 on Tuesday morning, she was disappointed to find a female ODP setting up the room.

"Morning, Frankie," the young, quite pretty girl greeted her, "I'm Chloë... You don't mind if I call you Frankie do you, only that's what I was told to call you?" Chloë saw the look on Frankie's face and thought she'd stepped out of line.

"No... I mean yes, yes that's fine, I much prefer that," Frankie leaned towards Chloë, "I hate the 'Dr.' title!"

"Oh, okay, well I'll let you check over everything. I'm just going to get some supplies that we are about to run out of, back in a jiffy." And she disappeared out the door.

Frankie fished her glasses out of her bag, so she could look over the list for the day. She was standing with her back to the door when she heard it open. Not looking around, she spoke.

"Well it looks like we're in for a treat today, Chloë, two crumblies for hips; then the removal of a external fixator in a 26 year old, to make up for the old guys... Let's hope he's ho........t!" She paused half way through the last word, as she turned around and found herself looking at Jack's chest.

Suddenly it was warm, very warm. Frankie wasn't sure what was going to happen when she opened her mouth, but she knew she had to say something.

"I'm sorry," she looked up into his eyes and thought she was going to melt, "I thought you were Chloë."

"Obviously," he replied, smirking slightly. "You don't happen to know where I can find, her do you?"

"Sure, she went to get supplies... um ... g-gloves and things, I think." She was stuttering slightly; he wasn't standing that close, but whatever that scent was that he wore was wafting her way like the Bisto gravy adverts she remembered from childhood. She was sure that if he stood there for long enough, she would be lifted off her feet and float behind him wherever he went. Frankie suddenly realised she could hear Jack talking, but she wasn't actually listening.

"I'm sorry, what did you say?"

"I said I would... are you okay?" He was looking at her, very concerned.

"Yes, sorry... Yes I'm fine, not enough caffeine yet!" She let out a nervous laugh.

"Okay... Oh, here comes Chloë now... Excuse me."

As the door shut, the draught gave her another blast of his scent, to torture her even more. She stamped her foot on the floor. *'Stop it... He must be at least ten years younger than you,'* she thought.

Frankie found the day passed by quickly. Chloë was lovely to work with. Despite being very newly qualified, she was very efficient and seemed to know her job well. They were both slightly disappointed that their last patient was not in the slightest bit 'hot', which prompted a conversation between them about personal relationships.

"May I ask if you're married?" Chloë asked Frankie, as they were clearing away at the end of the day.

"Sure... no, I'm not... and yes, I'm probably too old now and past it!" Frankie replied.

"Nonsense, you must only be in your mid thirties?"

"Late actually, but thanks for the compliment, you can work with me any day!"

"You're welcome, you honestly don't look it. So, no boyfriend either, I take it?"

"No significant other and no, I'm not gay... Very, very straight. I leave all that sort of thing to my big brother. How about you?"

"Yes, I just moved in with my boyfriend a couple of months ago, we've been together for a year now. He's a policeman."

Frankie could tell, by the way Chloë talked, that she was obviously very proud and very much in love with her guy.

"Lucky you, a man in uniform... who comes with toys too!" Frankie smirked and winked at Chloë, who turned a vibrant shade of red.

"Sorry, didn't mean to embarrass you, it's my inside voice; you know when you have a thought you don't really mean to say out loud, but you do anyway, unable to stop yourself because it's already happening!"

Luckily Chloë laughed and looked less embarrassed. Frankie was done, so she thanked her for a pleasant day and left her to finish her work.

The following day, of course, was 'Train' day with Mike Anderson. Frankie was starting to see some of the same faces around the theatres. Once again Heather was scrubbed, and Frankie also recognised one of the other nurses in the theatre. However, there was still no Jack; one of the other male ODPs, Alex, was to be her assistant for the day. Alex actually turned out to be quite the joker, so there was a lot of banter between him and Mike. They were both dedicated football fans, but Alex supported his home team, Newcastle United, while Mike was a Liverpool fan. Frankie had never liked football, ever, and living in Canada she had no clue as to what went on in the English Premiership. She was now learning very quickly that you never get involved in a discussion between two men who support different teams! The most interesting bit about watching both these men was the fact that Mike was quite tall and good looking, whereas Alex was not much taller than Frankie and had not exactly been near the front of the queue when looks were handed out. Over the course of the day, however, Frankie warmed to him, even though he was not as good as any of the others she'd worked with so far, and of course... he wasn't Jack.

Before she left that day, she popped into the anaesthetic office to check her mailbox.

"Frankie, glad I caught you, your ticket for Friday." Helen handed her a small rectangle of white card with gold printing on it.

"Friday... oh, the charity thing... Yes, thank you, you got the cash I left?"

"Yes I did, thank you." Helen hesitated before saying, "You do know it's... um... a dress-up, kind of glamorous affair, don't you?"

Helen was looking Frankie up and down, prompting Frankie to look down at herself in her black yoga pants, a black and white striped Scuba hoodie underneath a fitted black waterproof jacket and heavy, clumsy shoes.

"I can do glamorous!" she replied, as she looked up at Helen and shrugged her shoulders.

"Okay, just wanted to make sure that you knew," Helen muttered, turning back towards her desk.

Frankie glanced in her mailbox: nothing, so she left. As she shut the door behind her she said quietly to herself, "Glamorous. I'll give her glamorous... cheeky cow!"

Chapter 5

AFTER SIGNING SOME paperwork and handing over a set of keys to the estate agent, Frankie decided to treat herself to a little shopping spree. She already had a dress for Friday night but she needed new shoes, bag, and stockings. Stockings were easy, M&S all the way, but she trawled around several shoe shops before she found what she was looking for. She just made it back to the flat before it started to rain. It was late afternoon by then and she was cold, and a little achy from shopping, so she hopped in the bath where Hercules promptly joined her.

"Oh, that's nice," she said, as she sank into the steaming water. "I hope this charity thing is not going to be boring, after I've just forked out £200. Still, a girl can't have too many shoes, can she?"

As Hercules made his way along the side of the bath towards her, he slipped and almost fell in. There was quite the meow when his front leg hit the hot water, but he then landed firmly on the bathroom floor, perfectly upright, as cats always do. Even though Frankie was the only witness to this event, he immediately sat elegantly on the bath mat and proceeded to wash his soggy paw as if nothing had happened. Frankie peered over the side of the bath.

"You okay, big guy?" she asked, knowing that it was only his pride that was hurt.

Hercules glanced up at her as if it was her fault he'd fallen in, then slunk off into the living room to dry off on his radiator.

Friday afternoon came around very quickly. It was Frankie's lucky day. The Leprechaun, as Mr. O'Reilly had so aptly been nicknamed, had to cancel his last case because the patient was too sick for surgery. Result: She could go home and enjoy getting ready, instead of throwing make up and clothes at herself while waiting for a taxi.

"Are you going tonight, Frankie?" asked a voice from behind the lockers. Heather stuck her head around the corner.

"I sure am!" she replied. "You?"

"Absolutely! Between three kids, two dogs, and a husband who also works shifts, I don't get out much these days. It's usually a lot of fun; I'm glad you can make it. Of course, there'll be some scandal to gossip about on Monday morning, there always is!" Heather slung her bag over her shoulder. "See you in your glad rags later!"

"See ya."

Frankie was just about to close her locker when she heard voices entering the changing room. One was Marie's, the other she didn't recognise.

"Well, it will be interesting to see what she turns up in. If what she wears for work is anything to go by, she'll not get past the front door, ticket or no ticket!" said Marie.

Frankie instinctively knew she was the topic of conversation; should she declare herself or sit it out?

"I like her," said the other person. "She's very good and funny, not like the other consultants. I actually quite like her style, she has an amazing figure; if I looked like that, I would wear what she wears."

"Hasn't got her very far has it? I mean she must be, what, 35, 36, and still single?"

Frankie looked up and mimed, "Yes!" Once again, her age had been guessed incorrectly.

"Maybe she has a boyfriend back in Canada."

Frankie was intrigued by this conversation now.

"You don't spend six months away from home without your man. She's a dyke! It's so obvious - I mean she doesn't even wear underwear, what kind of woman doesn't wear underwear?"

"A very confident one. She's not gay, Marie. You must have seen the way she looks at Jack!"

Uh-oh! Had it really been that obvious? She had no idea she'd given anything away, she thought. It seemed that Marie hadn't thought so either.

"Don't be ridiculous. Jack would never be interested in her. Jack's not interested in anyone... alive anyway!"

"Ah Marie, that's cruel, just because he won't jump into your knickers."

Now Marie was really hacked off.

"Don't be so sure, you'll all be laughing on the other side of your faces when he sees the sexy little number I have planned for tonight. He'll be begging me to take him home!"

Frankie couldn't help herself. She had no idea how long this verbal diarrhoea was going to go on for, and she had some serious getting ready to do. She took a deep breath and revealed herself.

"Catch you later, ladies."

She caught a glimpse of their stunned faces before she casually opened the door and left.

At 7.30pm the taxi pulled up outside the Gosforth Park Hotel, a contemporary building set in substantial parkland near the vibrant City Centre. Frankie was aware she was a little late, but always hated arriving at these things on time when there were only a handful of people, especially when she didn't really know many of them. This way, there should hopefully be enough of a gathering that she could just slip in and hang out near the bar with a drink, until someone she knew passed by. The hotel had provided a novelty red carpet welcome and tickets were compulsory. After dropping her coat in the cloakroom, she confidently entered the Classics Room, which was a lot more crowded than she'd expected; she didn't think she was *that* late. In front of her, the ceilidh was in full swing, with many of the participants clearly having no idea what they were doing, despite having a caller to guide them. She completed a quick scan of the room and, noticing the bar to her right, decided that propping it up was definitely the way to go.

Jack was standing with his back to the door talking to Dr. Peter Watkins, a retired member of the department who, nevertheless, attended and supported the event every year. The room was buzzing and crowded, but whilst in mid-conversation with Peter, Jack became aware of a red dress standing off to his right hand side. When he got the chance to look, the red dress was gliding towards the bar. It was very fitted, and the occupant small, but curvy in all the right places. She was wearing simple, black-heeled pumps and was carrying a black clutch bag. If this wasn't enough, the dress was crowned by an almost shoulder-length, poker-straight, pale copper-coloured bob that was elegantly swinging as she moved.

"... So we have this agreement that I'll play golf on a Tuesday and she... Jack... Jack... Jack are you okay?" said Peter, aware that Jack appeared to be miles away.

"What? Sorry... um yes, yes... Carry on, I just thought... anyway, no carry on, sorry!" Jack had taken complete leave of Peter's droning conversation. He had no idea who the red dress was; since he turned back to answer Peter, he'd completely missed Frankie turning sideways when she reached the bar.

"Well, I never," said Peter, "I'm sure that's Nick's girl... will you excuse me son, I've just spotted the daughter of an old friend."

"Not at all," Jack replied. "Always a pleasure to catch up with you, Dr. Watkins."

Moving to one side to allow Peter to make his way to the bar, Jack looked in the direction Peter was walking and noticed the red dress was standing at the bar with her back to him. Curiously, Jack watched as Peter headed directly towards her.

Jack was aware he was staring. He was right; the person Peter had recognised was the red dress. Who was she? He was pretty sure that, if it had been someone from work, he would have noticed her before now. He started to think about the conversation he and his brother had had the weekend before; it had preyed on his mind all week. Maybe he hadn't noticed the owner of the red dress because he simply hadn't been looking. Now, suddenly, he was looking and noticing. *'So I'm interested in the red dress... what do I do now?'* He considered approaching the bar, because he knew Peter, and Peter obviously knew her. He even considered waiting until Peter moved on and then approaching her... but before he knew it, Denise was whisking him onto the dance floor and he was 'Stripping the Willow'!

It had been a long time since Jack had danced and had fun. Sweating thoroughly, he needed a drink. At the bar he ordered low-alcohol beer and scanned the room for the red dress. He was disappointed to find her missing. He took his beer over to the silent auction tables, to assess the progress; even though he himself hadn't bid on anything, it was always interesting to keep an eye on who was bidding on what. As he moved along the table, a couple of nurses moved from in front of him, leaving a gap between him and the next person. The first things to catch his eye were the simple, elegant, black-heeled pumps. His eyes travelled up nude stockings clinging to shapely, toned legs. The hem of the red dress was far enough above her knee to be sexy but not slutty. The dress was hugging a small, curvy silhouette in all the right places... It was slightly gathered at the left hand side, which drew attention to her tiny waist. There was no plunging neckline, but the shift style was classic and outlined a perfect chest.

Jack inhaled sharply as his gaze travelled up to take in Frankie's heavily made-up, emerald green eyes, her simple diamond stud earrings caught by the light, her scarlet lips parted slightly, full and very kissable.

"D...D...Dr... R... Robertson!" His mouth had gone so dry that when he opened it, he could barely speak.

Frankie couldn't help noticing Jack's reaction to her, but she was also busy taking in what stood before her. The delicious sight of Jack Lee, all six feet whatever inches of him, in a black tuxedo; tidy, trimmed stubble outlined his strong jawline, and curls, a whole head of soft, sexy curls... *'Holy Mother of Medicine!'* she thought, *'This guy is gorgeous!'*

She was determined to remain in complete control of the situation, but she knew that she was about to break all her dating rules... and probably that night.

"Jack, will you please quit with the doctor title. I only ever went to medical school to piss my father off. Please, I know you think it's weird, but will you call me Frankie?" She smiled at him, probably a little too seductively; she knew what she was doing to him. He was heart-stoppingly handsome, but looked shy and vulnerable.

Jack let out his breath slowly; he genuinely had had no idea that she was the occupant of the red dress.

"Yes, sorry... Frankie. You look so different,"... *'Very hot'* was what he really wanted to say. He was sweating again; it was warm in the function room anyway, without having an incredibly stunning woman stood in front of him. He couldn't take his eyes off her. She had beautiful hair; he'd had no idea she was a redhead.

"Don't look so surprised, Jack. I am actually still a woman under those hideous scrubs, and occasionally this woman dresses up and goes out to play!"

Jack gave a nervous little laugh and looked down for a second to gather his thoughts before going for it.

"Well, she can't play with an empty glass can she? May I have that refilled for you?"

"Sure, that would be lovely," Frankie replied, looking at her almost-empty wine glass.

"After you then." Jack gestured with his hand for her to walk first towards the bar, leaving a gap between the two of them. Frankie knew exactly what he was up to, and had it confirmed when she caught a glimpse of them in a wall mirror. He was totally checking her out! She had to concentrate quite hard to stop a victorious smile escaping as she worked it, sashaying all the way to the one and only vacant barstool.

When they arrived at the bar, Frankie placed her wine glass and clutch down and turned towards Jack. She hitched herself up onto the stool in one slick move, before slowly crossing her legs. Her dress took a slow ride a couple of inches up her thigh. Jack couldn't help but admire the shiny, nude leg that was now begging to be touched. Thankfully, the bartender rescued him from his thoughts.

"What can I get you, sir?"

"Oh... I'll get a Bud Light please, and the lady will have a glass of..." He pointed to Frankie's wine glass.

"The merlot, please," Frankie informed the bartender, whose name was Sean, according to his badge.

"The merlot, thank you, that's all." Jack pushed Frankie's glass towards Sean.

Turning to face her, Jack leant against the bar on his elbow, holding a £20 note in his hand, which was shaking slightly. He looked nervous. Frankie couldn't take her eyes off him. He wasn't just gorgeous; in that tux he was 'drop dead' gorgeous. She couldn't get over that head of dark, loosely curled locks that had a slight untidiness about them. Hair you could fondle; run your fingers through and... grab!!

"What did you bid on?" Jack asked nodding towards the auction tables and bringing Frankie back from her explicit thoughts.

"Oh... the romantic weekend for two at Lumley Castle," she answered. "Not for me of course, I thought I would give it to my aunt and uncle, as a sort of thank you for looking after me."

"You're living with them?" Jack asked, looking a little puzzled.

"Oh, no, no... hell NO! I love them to bits and I'm very close to them, but I couldn't live with them, they are just very good to me." As she smiled at him, their drinks arrived and Jack paid.

"There you go," Jack passed Frankie her wine. "An apology for my slightly distant and odd behaviour last week. I... um...," Jack fiddled with the top of his beer bottle, "I just had a few things on my mind."

Seeing how he was really struggling, Frankie stopped his explanation. He had slid his hand down the bottle now and was holding it. She moved her hand from her glass of wine and put it over the top of his.

"It's okay, Jack, I know why. Heather told me when she took over from you the other day. I hope that's okay?"

"Yes, of course." He sighed with relief.

"She didn't say much, just that it was the second anniversary on Saturday and that you were still coming to terms with it all."

Jack just stared at Frankie's small, soft hand over his and nodded slightly. They were silent in the noisy room. Eventually he looked up at her, and she could see he had been fighting his emotions; his beautiful eyes were glistening slightly.

'I'm sorry,' Frankie mouthed to him and took her hand away so she could take a drink.

"So!" Jack suddenly exclaimed, "'What's your explanation, 'cause everybody got one?'"

Frankie almost spat wine in his face; she quickly put her hand over her mouth while she swallowed. Jack noticed her short, manicured nails matched her scarlet red lips. Frankie finally composed herself enough to speak. "You're a fan?"

"From the beginning, every album, three times in concert. I would have to argue that I'm Train's number one fan!"

"I'm impressed, but I think I win the number one fan status; five times in concert, including one of them twice - in Vancouver and then two weeks later in Seattle!"

"That's just sad," Jack said with a mock sympathetic look.

"Quite possibly, but proud of it!" She returned a playful smile, wrinkling her nose.

Jack was sure his heart skipped a beat when she did that, but what he was feeling scared the life out of him. Sat before him was the most attractive woman he'd noticed in a very long time; but there was more to it than that. She was confident, funny, smart; of course she was smart, she's a doctor... *'Oh, hell yeah... She's a doctor for goodness' sake!'* he thought. *'She's way out of my league... and she has to be older than me!'* He was convinced she would eat him alive, even though she was almost half his size; but he was smitten, completely and utterly smitten.

"So?" he said, taking a mouthful of beer. At that moment Frankie totally wanted to be that beer!

"So...what?" She looked at him puzzled; she really wasn't concentrating on anything he was saying.

"Your story, is it as tragic as mine, or are you just on the run from a crazy boyfriend?"

"Neither actually," she said, matter-of-factly. "My father has finally had to move out of the family home and go into full time care, so I'm being the dutiful daughter and sorting out all his affairs; selling and clearing the house to pay for however long he has left. I took a sabbatical that I couldn't really afford and didn't really want, but it was an agreement I made with my brother; long story... We can save that one for dinner if you like...oops!... Did I just say that out loud?"

Jack glanced down for a second before looking up. Frankie watched him smile; it was like it was happening in slow motion. She felt aroused by the deep creases that appeared at the side of his nose... Then dimples formed in his cheeks... Little lines at the sides of his eyes... Then there were teeth, a full set of pearly white pegs began to reveal themselves... Outlined by kissable pink lips... It was the most amazing sight, and she was sure that if she hadn't been sitting, her panties would have hit the floor; then she remembered she wasn't wearing any!

"Sorry," Frankie continued, as she wrinkled her nose again. Jack thought he was going to melt into a big, embarrassing puddle. What was happening here? No one had ever done this to him, not even his wife; he was ashamed at the thought.

"Anyway, here I am. Putting my own life on hold so I can work in the NHS for peanuts, all for a man I haven't seen or spoken to for five years." Frankie was aware that her tone had changed, that she had begun to sound angry. Jack sensed it too.

"So, if you're so angry about the situation, why are you doing it?"

"Blood is thicker than water I guess. I suppose, deep down, I feel I have to do it because he's my father and, for some crazy, messed-up reason, my mother loved him. And I owe it to her to see that he's taken care of."

Jack suddenly felt admiration and respect for what Frankie was doing. He was very close to his parents and couldn't imagine a relationship that would require him to do something like this out of duty rather than love.

"That's all very sad, I hope it works out for you. How long is your sabbatical?" Jack had to ask; what was the point in having romantic thoughts about someone, if they were only going to leave you?

"Six months, and not a minute longer!" replied Frankie; if this ended up going somewhere, she needed to be clear from the beginning that it would be a short-term thing. She drained the last drop of wine from her glass as the band started up a new dance.

"It's the Gay Gordons! Come on, I need a partner." She grabbed her clutch with one hand and Jack's hand with the other.

Oh My God! Frankie was holding his hand; he started to feel his heart pounding in his ears. One minute they'd been having a serious conversation and the next, Jack felt Frankie's tiny hand in his. His fingers seemed to close around it automatically. He remembered something about her needing a partner; he saw her place her clutch on a table next to the dance floor and say something to the person sat there. Next he was standing in a line, among his colleagues, the caller describing the dance and explaining how they should stand. It was a good job Frankie was wearing heels, as Jack had to slip his right arm around the top of her shoulders and she took hold of his hand.

"Now give me your left hand... Come on Jack, I won't bite, I promise."

'Oh God,' he thought, *'don't do that wrinkled nose thing again.'*

She took hold of his left hand as he held it out. His heart was racing; he couldn't take his eyes off her and he felt as if ten million other pairs of eyes were on them.

Frankie took a couple of deep breaths as the caller was explaining the dance sequence. She was so close to him that his scent was intoxicating. She was sure that if she just 'scratched & sniffed' it on a bottle, it wouldn't have the same effect. It was the whole package... the tux, the curls, the eyes, the stubble, the broad shoulders and the tragic past.

"Are you ready?" she asked, looking up at him. He was very flushed.

Jack nodded, not sure if his legs would actually move if he continued to touch her. "As I'll ever be!" he replied.

"I know this well, just follow me, okay?"

The band began and the caller talked them through it; they started to move four steps forward and didn't take their eyes off each other until they had to change partners. The dance would keep going until they were all back with their original partners, and throughout, Jack and Frankie exchanged glances and smiles across the dance floor. Half way through, Jack partnered with Marie, who was *almost* wearing a black halter neck tube of fabric. Frankie wasn't sure whether he did it on purpose, but he made a point of looking across the dance floor at her and smiling, not once taking notice of the two watermelons bouncing around in front of him. Frankie caught sight of Marie looking at her, with a face like a slapped arse! She raised her eyebrows at her and smirked, triumphantly.

Finally they were back together and the dance came to an end. Everybody clapped, both for themselves and the band, who were now finished for the night.
"Thank you," said Frankie.
"My pleasure," he replied, "I don't think I've danced this much since my own wedding!"
"Well maybe it's time you started," she said, smiling at him.
"Yeah... maybe." He flashed her another groin-throbbing smile.

Frankie went to pick her clutch up from the table she'd abandoned it on and thanked Gloria for looking after it.
"If you don't mind me saying, pet, you've got a secret admirer there." Gloria nodded to someone behind Frankie; of course she knew without turning around who Gloria was referring to.
"Do you think?" Frankie asked Gloria curiously.
"I saw the two of you at the bar," Gloria gave a cheeky little wink. "I have to say, pet, you look smashin' tonight; he couldn't keep his eyes off you. You know, he's a little fragile still, after everything." Gloria said quietly as if it was top secret, "but I wouldn't be sayin' no, pet, if I was 20 years younger!" Gloria looked admiringly over at Jack, who was now deep in conversation with someone Frankie didn't recognise.

It was time to leave. She'd made an obvious impact on Jack, that had not been her original intention when she decided to attend the event. It would not be good for her professionally, or for their working relationship, if she were seen with him any more that night. She headed towards the door and took one last look over her shoulder at him. He happened to glance up at the same time, so she gave him a slow, sexy smile, before she swayed her hips out of the door.

Jack stood staring at the doorway to the function room. She had left. He couldn't go after her, people would notice. What had been one of the most enjoyable evenings he'd had in a long time was over. He'd had no idea where it was going next but he hadn't expected it to just end there. Maybe it was for the best; he still had to work with her at the end of the day. He had lost interest in his conversation with Denise's husband, who was an events planner at the hotel, and was thus always able to get the room hire at a knockdown price. Jack wasn't really concentrating on anything now, so he decided to call it a night.

After saying his goodbyes, he reclaimed his coat and made his way outside. To his complete surprise, Frankie was still standing out there in the cold, windy weather, her hair flapping around her shoulders. He stood for a moment, not really knowing what he should do, or even if he should do anything. On impulse, he decided: This was his chance; he had no idea what he was going to say, but he couldn't let her get away a second time. He approached her from behind and heard her swearing at her iPhone, stomping her heel on the ground.

"Hey... Is everything okay?"

"Oh hi," she said, surprised. "Bloody cab firm... Three times they've said my cab is on it's way and as you can see I'm still here!"

She looked cold.

"You know, I have my car. I can drop you somewhere, I really don't mind," he said, hopefully.

"Are you sure? I'm in Jesmond." She began to feel all twinkly again.

"I can detour through Jesmond." He shrugged his shoulders. "Come on, you look frozen. You could wait hours for a taxi on a Friday night." *'Please come with me, you're going to chew me up and spit me out, but I want you badly,'* he thought.

"Okay, if you insist, you're sure it's no trouble?"

"No... But I think you might be, in that dress!" *'Did I really just say that?'* His brain wasn't connected to his mouth anymore.

"Jack!" She gave him a sexy little smirk. *'Oh, Mother of all Sexy Dresses... I am going to be forever in your debt!'* Mrs. Clit-tor-rus was starting to throb at the thought of this Adonis fondling her.

"Oops! Sorry... my inside voice... that's your fault!" They both laughed as they walked towards his car.

"Here you go," Jack said, as he pressed the button on the key to unlock the doors.

Frankie stopped, staring at the car. She was smiling, one hand on her hip.

"A Mini... You drive a Mini?" she said, completely surprised.

"Yeees... is that a problem? They're really quite cool, you know!"

"It's not that." *'Oh, if only you knew!'* "I just didn't expect it, that's all. You're so... tall." She gave an approving smile, before sliding into the passenger seat.

After Frankie gave Jack the address, they spoke very little on the journey. Every time Jack had to change gear, he was aware that those smooth, nude legs were almost within reach. Frankie was becoming intoxicated again with the seductive scent that filled the car. The radio played quietly in the background, breaking the silence. It didn't seem that long before they were pulling up outside the flat.

"There you go, how's that for door-to-door service?" Jack said, as he pulled up the handbrake and put the gear stick into neutral.

"Thanks Jack, I really appreciate the lift."

"Well, I couldn't have you stand out there much longer and let someone else pick you up." Jack covered his eyes with his hand. "Sorry, that came out all wrong, didn't it!"

"Don't worry, it's fine."

Frankie was still sat in the passenger seat. They both started to speak, both stopped mid-sentence, both said, "Sorry" at the same time, laughing nervously. After a short pause, Frankie decided to bite the bullet.

"Jack... would you like to come in?"

He turned to look at her; he couldn't believe she had just asked him that. He desperately wanted to, but was terrified at the thought. Something instinctively told him that she wasn't really going to eat him alive, if anything quite the opposite. He could feel himself start to shake a little.

"I mean, just for a coffee or a nightcap or something?"

Another pause. They looked at each other again. Jack swallowed hard, the engine still humming. Frankie was about to tell him it was no big deal if he felt uncomfortable; it would probably be for the best, but he spoke first.

"Okay," he said, his voice quiet and shaky. He switched the engine off.

Jack followed Frankie up the sweeping staircase to the first floor. He had no choice but to watch her pert little bottom sway from side to side as she led the way. He had never felt so nervous; he had no idea what to expect. They arrived at the front door, where she had a little bit of trouble putting the key in the lock. She couldn't believe this was really happening.

"May I first of all apologise for my roommate, he's a bit of a hairy lay-about and he thinks that I'm his servant!"

"We're not going to be alone?" Jack asked, completely shocked and now extremely uncomfortable.

She saw the look on his face, but was enjoying winding him up.

"Oh yes, we'll be alone, he'll just curl up and go to sleep!"

She pushed the door open and a loud meow greeted them. Jack started to laugh.

"You really had me going there... not funny!" he said, bending down to stroke the cat.

"Jack, meet Hercules; and Hercules, meet Jack."

Frankie slipped her coat off and hung it on one of the hooks to the right of the door.

"May I take your coat, Jack?"

"Thanks," he said, as he slipped out of his 3/4-length wool jacket. He handed it to her and she hung it next to hers. When she turned back to face him, he was stood looking quite lost. She noticed his strong jawline looked strained.

"Can I get you anything Jack? Or would you just like to just settle for me?" He swallowed hard, clenching his teeth. He couldn't speak.

Slowly, she walked over to him. He looked too good to be true. She gently took hold of his jacket lapels and ran her fingers down the front. She could feel how firm his body was under the jacket. She flattened her hands and ran them up and over his chest, sliding her hands underneath his jacket, so she could push it off his shoulders. She then moved her hands down the outside of his arms, so she could feel those thick muscles underneath his shirt. She was so twinkly inside, she was surprised she wasn't glowing; she was amazed she was so in control. She hadn't looked him straight in the eye until now; as she ran her hands across his chest once more, she noticed his heart was almost leaping out of his chest. When she looked up, he was staring at her, almost panting.

"Hey Jack, relax... You okay?" she said quietly.

He pulled away from her and sat back on a barstool.

"I'm sorry... I... I haven't done this in a long time and I was with Emma for so long before she... I just can't do this, I'm sorry... you must be wondering why the hell I agreed to come up here now?"

He was sitting with his head in his hands, his fingers pushed through the front of his hair. She noticed he was shaking.

"I spent last weekend with my brother. He doesn't think twice about jumping into bed with women, no strings attached." Jack sat up, clasped his hands tightly together. He looked up at the ceiling and then at Frankie, who was still standing in the same spot.

"Emma and I lost our virginity to each other. I know that sounds too perfect and romantic, but we never slept with anyone else, even when we broke up for six months. Anthony suggested I hook up with someone and just have casual sex, but I'm not like him. I can't use women like that and, to be honest... I'm 31 years old and feel like a virgin again. I'm scared I'm going to disappoint, be inadequate, fail to provide pleasure." Again, Jack looked down at his hands; Frankie could see he was really shaking now. He took a deep breath and looked at her again.

"I am insanely attracted to you. I know this is going to sound crazy but I have never felt the way I feel when I'm around you. When I saw you tonight, you were walking away from me towards the bar. I think you had just arrived. At the time, I had no idea it was you. You look stunning," he smiled at her, and she smiled coyly back, feeling a little bashful at his kind words.

"I don't want to use you Frankie, you're a beautiful person. I'm guessing now you know this, I'd be the last guy you would want to spend the night with." He dropped his head into his hands once more, and then ran them through his hair again. "I'm sorry." He sat, still shaking, with his head in his hands.

Frankie paused for a second before approaching him; all this had only made her want him more. She stood beside him, placing one hand over both of his, and slid her other hand gently around his neck. She slowly pulled him into her chest. As she held him close he automatically put his arms around her waist. She began to stroke his hair gently; it was so soft. The top of his head was just millimetres away from her nose, she could breathe in the masculine scent of him.

"If it helps, I'm insanely attracted to you too. I'm a consenting adult; you wouldn't be using me. I could be a kind of therapy for you... Help out for a while; get you back in the game."

Jack pulled away from her and sat back, moving around to face her properly,

"You would do that? What would be in it for you?" He was surprised at her proposition; he had assumed they could be no more than friends now.

"Isn't that obvious?" she said.

She took his hands in hers again and put them back around her waist. They were almost the same height with him sitting and her standing in her heels. She touched his stubbly cheeks softly, with both hands, and ran her fingers through his sexy curls.

"Jack, I'm thirty eight years old and still single. Women like me can only fantasise about this situation, so when it's handed to us on a plate, even just for one night, we're going to make the most of it."

She carried on playing with his hair.

"I also get to see this firm, fit body of yours; I can touch it, lick it, kiss it and play with it, but the best part... I get to feel it throbbing next to mine. You would be a great distraction, Jack. I'm going to need some fun while I'm here." The whole time she was speaking, her eyes remained fixed on his; she could see she was seducing him. He didn't really need to speak; she already knew what he was thinking.

Jack was hooked. He was scared and excited; he was putty in her hands. The way she was playing with his hair was so arousing. Her touch was so gentle, but electrifying. With the movement of her fingers and the sexy sound of her voice, he was becoming more and more turned on; something that hadn't happened in a very long time.

"Okay, Doctor... When does my therapy start?"

"No time like the present, Mr. Lee, but we are going to take this one step at a time. I want you to feel comfortable and relaxed for us both to enjoy this."

Chapter 6

FRANKIE PULLED JACK'S bow tie and slowly slid it from around his neck. Their eyes were locked together.

"I'm going to use this as a blindfold, because I want you to explore my body without seeing it. I want you to remove my clothes by touch and feel. However, there are rules... You can only use your hands, no kissing... yet! And you can't touch my breasts, or between my legs. I can guide you if you want me to, but I'd rather you explore my body instinctively. How do you feel about that?"

Jack kept his eyes firmly fixed on Frankie's and took a deep breath; he'd never done anything like that before. He slowly exhaled.

"Okay, I'll give it try. Are you going to undress me?"

"Oh yes, but your blindfold will stay on. Only I get to see." She winked at him.

"I just want to be clear here... I'm not getting myself into one of those Dom/Sub kind of situations, am I?"

Frankie laughed and gently put her hand up to his face.

"Jack, I want to play with you, but that doesn't mean I want to tie you up and use you as a toy. I want us to play together. I want to teach you how to enjoy a woman's body again, and touch is a very important part of that. I want you to find my sweet spots.

Then, I want to find yours. I'm not going to whip you or hurt you... far from it!"

She smiled at him, and then bent forward and placed her forehead on his and whispered, "You're far too attractive to damage!"

Jack instinctively went to kiss her, but she was quick to place two fingers over his lips.

"Oh no you don't... No breaking the rules before we've even started... Patience!"

"Sorry, I'm nervous... I've not been very adventurous in the past... I'm not comfortable with kinky stuff."

"No kinky stuff, okay, just stop me if you're not comfortable."

As she placed the bow tie over his eyes, she knew it was too short to tie together, so she picked up a hairclip that happened to be lying on the breakfast bar and gripped the two ends together at the back. Jack sat there, wondering what was going to happen next. After a couple of minutes he heard music; it was Bocelli, of course. Jack heard Hercules meowing across the room.

"Does he get to watch?".

"Is that a problem for you?" She was right in front of him again. "I don't have a problem with it, he's sees me naked all the time."

"Lucky guy!"

"You don't know that yet, you might not like what you see." She placed his hands on her hips as she slid her hands slowly up his arms towards his shoulders.

"From what I've felt so far, Doctor, I don't think I'm going to be disappointed."

Frankie smiled but, of course, he couldn't see her.

"Whenever you're ready... and Jack, remember, if ever you're not comfortable with something, you have to say, okay?"

"Okay... what do you want me to do?"

"I want you to get me naked."

He smirked. He had such a strong jaw line; she was desperate to kiss him but knew she too had to be patient.

Jack moved his hands around her waist towards her back. He hesitated for a second, before letting them slide down over her small, but perfectly formed bottom. Sliding them back up the dress, he followed the zip all the way to the top. He was unaware that Frankie's eyes were studying his perfect face. He hesitated again, before taking hold of the zip and slowly, steadily, unzipping her. Frankie glanced down and noticed that he was already very hard. Jack stopped at the base of her spine. She saw he wasn't sure what to do next, so she ran her fingertips up the side of his neck and began to gently fondle his ear. Jack swallowed hard. She whispered to him, "Take it off Jack. I can see you're getting uncomfortable down there... I don't want you to stop."

Encouraged by her prompting, he ran his fingers up her bare spine. He hesitated, finding no bra strap stopping him from going all the way to the top.

"Looking for something?" she asked him.

Jack smiled before slowly easing the dress off each shoulder and sliding it down over her arms. The dress was quite fitted so he gave it a little push when he reached her hips and it fell to the floor. He started moving his hands around her hips, as if he were looking for something else; he was trembling a little.

"You're already naked, you're not wearing any underwear?" he asked, surprised.

"Is that a problem? I can put some on, if you want to string this out for longer?"

"So you haven't been wearing any all evening?" This sudden realisation completely shocked him.

"Correct!" she said, as she stepped out of her dress and flicked it to one side.

"I didn't think women really did that!"

"Oh Mr. Lee... you'll be amazed at the things us women really do. You've stopped exploring. Why don't you examine that naked rear of mine, since you were checking it out so closely when you followed me to the bar?"

"You don't miss a thing, do you, Doctor? And you're really standing completely naked in front of me?"

"I really am... if you don't count the lace-topped hold-ups and my heels."

"Oh God, don't... I'm close to exploding!" Jack slid his hands over her soft, firm bottom. When he spread his hands out, they almost covered each cheek. He instinctively squeezed a little.

She was absolutely bursting for him to touch her, take her, right there and then, but she was determined to prove to herself that she could have some self control. She needed him to relax, feel more comfortable.

"I like that Jack... Do it again."

As he did, she moved forward to stand between his parted legs. She couldn't help letting out a moan when he squeezed for a third time. Allowing his hands to travel down her legs, he lingered over the lace at the top of her hold-ups.

"I think I'm going to like these when I finally get to admire them."

As he explored this area he found the crease just below her bum cheeks. He rubbed his forefingers along this crease a couple of times.

"OH GOD!" It took Frankie by surprise. She couldn't believe he had instinctively found this spot.

He stopped.

"I'm sorry... are you okay?"

"I'm fine, I love that Jack, you found a sweet spot... Don't stop." She was speaking in a low voice, then leaned forward and whispered in his ear, "It turns me on, I want you to keep doing it, because it makes me very wet."

Jack let out a short, sharp breath. Her words were so seductive, he tried to continue, but she sensed he was struggling. She gently took hold of his wrists and moved them away from her naked body.

"Why don't I take over now, Jack, and undress you. I want to see you naked." As she placed his hands on his thighs she whispered in his ear again, "I want to see what I've done to you." She gave his ear a playful lick, before moving away.

"I thought no kissing," he was quick to say.

"True... however I didn't kiss you, I licked you. Did you like it?"

"I did, very much."

"Good, because I like to use my tongue to explore. I like to use it a lot!"

Before he knew it, his shirt was being eased off his shoulders. He had completely missed her unbuttoning it; he was thinking about her tongue. Frankie let the shirt fall to the floor behind him.

"WOW! You seriously work out!" She had admired those muscles under his scrubs for the last couple of weeks, but now they were naked in front of her, they were even more amazing.

Jack smiled and looked down, even though he was still blindfolded. He seemed embarrassed by the fact that his body was so perfect.

However, for Frankie, the hottest thing was his chest hair. Frankie loved chest hair. She had to touch it; she wanted to feel it on the side of her face while she drifted off to sleep.

"You know Jack, this is one of my favourite things. I could play with it for hours. It's incredibly sexy."

She was running her fingertips over the soft hair on his pecs. With her forefinger she traced an imaginary line down the middle of his abs, circling his belly button as she passed, before hooking her finger over the top of his dress pants. Then, with the help of her other hand, she expertly undid them. She could see he was still shaking, so she slid her hands around his waist, stopping at his lower back, gently caressing the small of his back with her fingertips.

"Try to relax Jack, and just enjoy my touch."

She noticed him swallow hard again. Slipping her hands between his pants and his underwear, she pulled him towards her so he stood up; slowly she pushed his pants down. She didn't want to expose him in one move; he was clearly quite shy. The pants fell to the floor, pooling around his feet. He was wearing slip on shoes that he stepped out of while she was still holding his hips. Another pile of clothes littered the floor.

To Frankie's surprise, he raised his hands and clumsily found her face, gently touching it for a moment, before running his fingers through her hair.

"I think this is going to drive me insane when I feel it tickling my skin. You have beautiful hair."

"I will do my utmost to ensure that happens, but first I want to remove these very sexy boxers from your incredibly impressive erection, so I can admire it properly... how do you feel about that?"

"Nervous... excited... almost ready to come, to be honest."

She started to walk around him, her left hand trailing behind her, skimming the firm, taught skin around his leg, across his amazing backside and around his other leg, stopping at his thigh. As she did this, she spoke to him in a slow, sexy voice.

"I can see that. I can't even begin to tell you how much I want to ride you right now, but you know we are not going to have sex tonight, right?"

She had come full circle and was now facing him again. She pulled him close so she could feel him hard against her; her bare breasts were now touching him. He let out a gasp as she reached both hands around him and slid them over his firm buttocks.

"We're not?" he managed to say.

"We're not, but don't worry, I'm not going to leave you like this... tell me, how do I feel against you?"

Jack blew out slowly; hooking her thumbs over the top of his fitted boxers, Frankie slowly ran them around his waistband.

"You feel... soft... but your nipples are hard."

"Yeah... You like that?" She started to move a little, so her nipples were tickling his skin.

"Oh yeah, that... that's good, you're very good at this," he gasped.

"I'm very good at what?" She stopped moving, and pulled away from him. Leaving her thumbs hooked over the waistband, she slid her hands inside his boxers.

"Getting me to almost fall apart without really doing anything."

"That's the idea, Mr. Lee."

In one move she slid the boxers over his hips, stretching them slightly forward to allow him to spring free.

'Holy Anatomy!' she thought, *'He's huge!'*

She was glad he was blindfolded; her jaw nearly hit the floor. She wasn't sure she'd be able to accommodate him, but she was sure as hell going to try. Looking back up at him she slowly smiled to herself; of course, he remained oblivious to her silent outburst of glee.

"Oh Jack," she said smirking, as she moved towards him again so she could feel him, skin on skin. She ran her hands up his abs and through his chest hair, "That's a mighty fine piece of equipment you have there!"

Jack smiled, "Thank you."

He put his hands on her shoulders and slid them around her neck, then down her back.

"We are going to have a lot of fun with it."

"It's quite rusty, I'm afraid."

"Oh, it won't be for long, I promise."

"When are you going to let me see you?"

"All in good time, patience, remember. I'm not done with you yet. Follow me."

She took hold of his hands as she slowly walked backwards towards the bedroom, guiding him as he stepped out of his boxers. Her heels started clicking on the floor.

"You're still wearing your heels, with those stockings... and you're otherwise naked?" His breathing quickened, "Frankie, I'm sorry, I'm going t..." As he was trying to get his words out, they had just entered the darkness of the bedroom; she could see him falling apart, so quickly pulled him close. She slid her arms around his middle and lifted her leg, rubbing it against his so he could feel the stockings, then she ran her heel gently up his calf. Jack grabbed the back of her head so her forehead was against him. He let out a loud gasp as they both felt a warm wetness between them. Automatically he put his arms around her and held her tight.

"I'm sorry," he said, when he had stopped panting long enough to be able to speak. "God, how embarrassing."

"Why?"

"For coming... I've always come quickly, I don't know how to control it, I'm sorry."

She lifted her hands to his face, then took hold of the hairclip, and let the bow tie fall to the floor.

Jack squinted a little until his eyes readjusted and he was able to see again. The room was in semi-darkness, but he could clearly see Frankie gazing up at him with a slight smile. He also noticed her full breasts; pressed against him, they felt so good. He lifted his hand to her face, and pushed her hair to the side, so he could look at her properly.

She was beautiful, even in the semi darkness.

He desperately wanted to kiss those plump red lips. He ran his hand down her back, across the soft cheek of her bottom and made his way down her leg. She smiled up at him; he lifted her slightly and moved forwards so he could lay her on the bed. Their bodies were still pressed together, their eyes firmly fixed. Jack took hold of the leg Frankie had hooked around him and ran his hand slowly up and down.

"I want to look at you, take you all in, but it's been a long time since I looked at another woman naked."

"I took the blindfold off because I want you to look at me."

She ran her forefinger down his nose and across his lips, before rolling away from under him, so that she was positioned more in the middle of the bed. She lay flat, with one knee bent, stretching her arms above her head, forcing Jack to look; he ran his eyes along the length of her. Then she flipped onto her stomach, raised herself up onto her elbows and slowly kicked her heels back and forth. Jack propped himself up on his elbow. Reaching his hand out he tucked her hair behind her ear so he could see her face better.

"What can I say, Doctor... You are very, very hot... May I relieve you of those incredibly sexy stockings and heels?"

"Mmm, only if you do it very slowly with your teeth!"

Jack laughed. He looked down at her legs; she kicked the heels off onto the floor.

"Are you serious?"

She raised her eyebrows, giving him a very playful smile.

"You are serious!"

"And I'm not turning over again until you're done; I think it would be very distracting for you. I can already see my request has brought you to attention again!"

"Okay. I'll see what I can do, but I don't think you'll ever be wearing them again."

"Do I look like I care?" Frankie tilted her head to one side, "But remember the rules, you can lick, nibble, and touch but no kissing allowed."

Jack took a deep breath; he was so turned on, he thought he might explode again, right there and then. This was something else he had never done before. Although he was starting to relax a little, he still felt shy and self-conscious lying there, naked, with an enormous hard on, beside a woman he hardly knew and would be working with for the next six months. Whilst all these thoughts ran through his mind, he began lightly running his hand over her back. He worked his way down, along her soft, smooth skin, to the base of her spine.

"I assume you're staying?" Frankie asked, casually.

Jack slid off the end of the bed and, as he knelt down on the floor, began to use both hands to fondle her pert cheeks again.

"Do you think I'm going to be in any fit state to leave, after what you're doing to me? I feel more intoxicated now than if I'd had a skin full!"

"Excellent! Oh, ooh..." She was taken by surprise when he began licking the sweet spot under her left cheek. He did the same to her other side. Moving down her leg, he caught the top of her stocking with his stubble, causing it to roll back slightly, allowing him to grab it with his teeth. He continued to move down her leg, slowly peeling the stocking away, his hands following behind the stocking, skimming her smooth, waxed skin. Her short legs meant this process didn't take too long; he then repeated it on the right leg.

"There you go, Doctor." He dropped the second stocking on the floor and crawled onto the bed, straddling her.

"Jack, you know I hate being called that."

Placing his tongue at the base of her spine, he licked the length of her back, slowly crawling his way up. He stopped at her neck and lay on top of her, pressing his throbbing erection into her back. She groaned. He tried not to place his full weight on her; he was very aware that he was easily twice as heavy. With her hair still tucked behind her ear, he placed his ear next to hers and hugged her gently.

"I know you hate it, but I'm in therapy, so it's only right I address you correctly, and I also find it quite sexy!"

"You sure you haven't done that before? You were very slick, and yes, only while we're playing can you call me that, okay?" She rubbed the side of her head against his. "Your therapy is obviously already helping. You seem very relaxed up there?"

"I'm getting there, thank you. You're amazing."

She took hold of his thumb and started to circle her tongue around it. She sucked it, and played with it in her mouth, while Jack buried his face in her hair. She could feel his breathing quicken, she knew he was close....

"Just let go, Jack," she whispered, as she kept going until he came again. "Now I'm amazing!"

Jack rolled off onto the bed and lay on his back. He covered his eyes with his hands; he was panting slightly.

"I am so sorry; I just can't control it when you do something like that. It just felt so good, I..."

"Shh." She reached over, placing her forefinger to his lips, and moved over so she could lie on his chest and push a hand away from his eyes.

"Jack, it's fine... look at me," she gently touched his face, "look at me, Jack... please?"

He moved his other hand so that they were both above his head, then turned to look at her.

"I wanted to show you pleasure through touch. You couldn't see my body and yet it excited you just by touching it. When you told me you felt like a virgin again, I wanted to tip you over the edge, so that you experienced that pleasure without us actually having sex. Getting to know each other's bodies will make it much more enjoyable for both of us. Then, when we do have sex, it will be much more intense. And I wanted to make you come, you just need more practice!"

Jack looked up at the ceiling and exhaled slowly, then looked back at Frankie.

"I loved Emma more than anything in the world. I enjoyed making love to her, but it was always the same; I suppose I've never had anything to compare it to, until now." He reached over and began to stroke her hair.

"Don't compare us, Jack, otherwise you're never going to move on." She took the hand that was stroking her and eased herself from under him, climbing off the bed. Once she'd stood up she tugged his arm a little.

"Come on Mr. Lee, this session is over, we need a quick shower to freshen up and then some skin on skin sleep."

"Yes Doctor, whatever you say." He climbed off the bed and allowed her to lead the way.

"And that means, JACK, I am no longer DOCTOR... OKAY!"

"OKAY, FRANKIE!" he playfully shouted, as she guided him to the bathroom.

They showered separately; once the light was on, Jack became quite shy again, so Frankie took her make up off while he went first.

"I can feel your eyes all over me, Jack, hurry up in there."

He couldn't help but watch her through the glass door of the shower cubicle. She seemed completely comfortable standing naked in front of the mirror, while he showered and discreetly tried to step out without her seeing him.

"Okay, it's all yours, and you can't blame me for looking, now that I can see you with the light on."

Wrapping a towel around himself, he walked over to her. She turned around to face him as he came up behind her. She had swept the sides of her hair up into a clip; a few wisps had been left behind and hung randomly around her face. Seeing her now, without any make-up on, he noticed very faint freckles on her nose, and her otherwise flawless skin. He brushed a couple of wisps out of her eyes.

"I haven't looked at a naked woman in a long time and I'm very much enjoying what I see."

"Good, I'm glad. Now go and warm the bed up, I'll be two minutes." She playfully turned him around to face the door and pushed him towards it.

The following morning, Frankie woke to the warm feeling of a naked man next to her. Spooned into Jack, her face lay against his firm back; her right arm under his, nestled in his soft chest hair. She could tell by his breathing that he was still deeply asleep. She lay there, just breathing him in, absorbing his heat and enjoying a closeness she had not felt for a long time. She didn't really want to move, but she needed to go to the bathroom and she could hear Hercules meowing outside the bedroom door. Easing her arm out slowly and carefully, she rolled out of bed. Jack stirred and moved onto his back with his arms above his head, the sheet now just covering his hips. She stood for a moment and admired the gorgeous creature lying in her bed and wondered how she'd managed to restrain herself the night before. He was too good to be true.

After feeding Hercules and clearing the floor of abandoned clothes, she made tea, wearing Jack's shirt. It was 9.15 on a Saturday morning. She had planned to go to the house today, but it was possible she might now be spending the day in bed. She heard the bed creaking slightly, so she went back to the bedroom. Jack was stretching out, causing his morning glory to poke up from under the sheet; it was a very inviting sight. Morning sex with a natural erection was the best; she felt instantly turned on and quite damp just from watching this display. She leaned against the doorframe with her arms folded, her bucket of tea in one hand. He hadn't yet noticed she was there.

"Good morning gorgeous," she said, smiling seductively.

Jack rubbed his face with his hands as he sat up. Frankie couldn't help notice how those impressive abs became so taught as he did this.

"Good morning to you too. Have you been awake long? You should have woken me."

Jack hung his elbows over his bent knees. Frankie started to walk slowly towards him and sat on the edge of the bed next to him.

"Why? You were so deeply asleep, and you're going to need all the rest you can get if we're going to take this any further."

She casually turned sideways, bent her knee, lifting it up on the bed so her foot dangled over the side. Of course, she was only wearing Jack's shirt … and nothing else. She hadn't done many of the buttons up so the right shoulder slipped down; the shirt, being white, was a little see-through and her normally poker-straight, neat bob was now flicked out in all directions after being slept on.

"You're sitting in front of me, looking incredibly sexy in my shirt, with your legs spread and you're suggesting that I might not want to see you again? Frankie, right now I don't want to leave, you have me under some sort of spell and all I want to do is kiss you and get you naked again. I have no idea what to do with you then, but I'm sure I'll figure something out."

As he spoke their faces were moving closer and closer together, but Frankie was determined she was going to make him wait just a little longer. She pulled away from him.

"Good, well I'm glad you're not having any second thoughts. Tea?"

She went to stand up but he grabbed her wrist and pulled her down again. She just managed to put her mug on the bedside table before he wrestled her onto the bed.

Before she knew it she was on her back; he was propped up on his elbow with his arm around her, looking down. She could feel him pressing hard against her… This wasn't really happening, it couldn't be; he wasn't real. She lifted her head and looked down into the large mirror at the end of the bed.

"Is there a problem?'" he asked her, looking puzzled.

"No, not now."

"You've lost me, what do you mean, 'not now?'"

"I was just checking that you're really here, and that I wasn't dreaming this, because last night I brought home a nervous, shy but very hot younger man, and this morning I have woken up next to a more confident, even hotter, not-so-shy younger man. What happened?"

Jack started to laugh,

"Oh Frankie." Then his voice became quiet, "I think you left him out on that bar stool when you blindfolded him and stripped him naked. You'll still have to be patient with him; he's still quite shy but he wants to learn to play your games, if you'll teach him?"

One minute he was speaking, looking at her with those amazing eyes, rubbing his nose against hers and the next he was kissing her and she was kissing him back. It was slow and passionate; they were both completely absorbed in each other. She pushed the sheet away from him, and he found the edge of his shirt and pulled it up. They broke apart for a second, while he lifted it up and over her head. Their eyes stayed fixed on each other. When they came back together, they pressed noses, smiling, and then resumed their kiss. Still lying under him, Frankie gently moved her hands up and down his back, she was going insane, she needed release and she could feel how wet she was. She broke their kiss but kept her forehead and nose pressed against him.

"My turn to have no self control. Would you like to watch?" She could see he was unsure what she meant. "I'm going to play with myself," she whispered, "I need to come Jack, you're driving me crazy."

She could see the nervous, shy guy had reappeared; he had no idea what to expect. She put her finger on his lips, "Relax and enjoy, Jack, most men would give their right arm to watch this."

She parted his lips and slowly inserted her finger into his mouth; he took the hint and sucked gently. Once it was sufficiently moist she put it between her legs. Looking down, he couldn't see exactly what she was doing, but she appeared to be using her finger to circle one area, occasionally moving further down and pushing it inside herself. She had parted her legs quite wide now and was groaning and panting; he looked her in the eye and she gave him a little smile before they began to kiss again. Instinct told him she was on the verge of climaxing, so he broke their kiss to watch again and lifted his hand up to her breast, massaging it gently. He couldn't believe how full it felt; then she shuddered and let out a long moan.

"Wow!" She let out a little laugh before kissing Jack, long and hard.

"Thank you," she said, as they rubbed noses.

"I didn't do anything, but yes, it was pretty mind blowing to see. Now I need to make love to you very badly."

Frankie took a couple of deep breaths.

"Jack, I never in my wildest dreams thought that I would be in this situation, so I don't have anything, and I'm pretty confident you haven't either."

"You mean protection."

"Yes," she started playing with his chest hair, "that's why I didn't want us to do anything last night, until we'd discussed this. As far as previous partners go, I have had two serious, if that's what you want to call them, relationships without protection. Otherwise I've always been careful. The most important thing you should know is that I can't have children, so whatever we decide to do, I kind of have that covered. I trust you when you say you've only had one partner, so if you're willing to trust me, we can not use anything which will make it a lot more fun and much less admin; or if you want to think about it, we can carry on as we are until we get something, and still have a lot of fun... "

Before she could finish he was on top of her, and she could feel the tip of his throbbing erection, almost kissing Mrs. Clit-tor-rus, who was still singing at the top of her voice.

"... Or, Doctor, we could just get on with it and take my therapy to the next level." He brushed her hair away from her face. He loved touching it; it was so soft and silky.

"Okay... but I would like to prescribe a better position."

She pushed him onto the bed. Despite his size she found this easy; he was letting her take control again.

Climbing aboard, she straddled him; leaning forward she supported herself on straight arms and began to rub herself up and down the length of him.

"Can you feel that, how wet you've made me?" She then moved in such a way that she lifted him slightly and he slid inside her.

Jack let out a gasp, as Frankie slowly massaged him inside her. She looked down to see a look of surprise and pleasure, then leant forward so she could kiss him, slowly, gently.

"Relax Jack, that must feel good... it does from up here."

She sat up and right back onto him, so he filled her as much as possible; she began to ride and didn't stop until she was sure she had squeezed him dry. His length hit a nice sweet spot high inside her when she sat back, enabling her to climax again too. They were both out of breath as she climbed off him and snuggled into his side, her face against his chest and her leg hooked around his, arms tight around each other.

"Dr. Robertson, you are an amazing therapist... but I am officially worn out!"

"You younger men have got no stamina!"

Jack let out a laugh and pulled her closer. They fell asleep, tangled and naked.

Chapter 7

"Frankie... Frankie..." Jack was trying to wake her.

"Mmmmm...." She stretched.

"Frankie, the phone is ringing... shall I get it?"

"What?" She looked around, quite dazed, and then realised what he was saying. "No, no I'll get it."

She stretched across Jack to reach the phone from the bedside table, allowing her left breast to dangle dangerously close to his face.

"Hello," she said sleepily, "Oh okay, do I need to be there? ...I trust you to show them around for me, like we discussed... Yeah, that's fine, just call me if you need to discuss anything... Okay, thanks.... Bye." She replaced the handset.

"You need to be somewhere?" Jack asked as she slid back down the bed to lie next to him.

"No, it was just the estate agent dealing with the house. She has a viewing at one. I have no intention of being a part of the sale, to be honest; as long as it sells before I have to leave." She lay there playing with his chest hair.

"You're really rather fond of that, aren't you?" he said, as he pushed her hair away from her face.

Frankie just gazed up at him. She was thinking how incredibly sexy he looked when he first woke up; *oh* those curls!

"I told you, it's one of my most favourite things in a guy."

"What are the other favourite things?"

"Ahh, that's for me to know and you to find out!" She knew where this was headed, but she was hungry and needed to eat, so she flipped herself on top of him, rubbed noses and kissed him gently.

"I'm starving, have breakfast with me?"

"Only if you wear my shirt again... and only my shirt!" He touched her nose with his finger, causing her to wrinkle it. "That playful little nose of yours is going to cause me a lot of trouble if it keeps doing that!"

"Ooh, I've discovered a weak spot... and yes, I will gladly wear your shirt. It was a little fantasy of mine that I had not yet fulfilled until this morning... and you will wear those tight little boxers I peeled off you!"

"Okay... deal!"

Breakfast was more of a brunch when they realised the time was 11.15. Hercules had made himself very comfortable on Jack's tuxedo jacket, so it now had a nice, white, furry patch on the back. They sat at the breakfast bar, ate toast and drank tea. Frankie made sure that Jack was educated in how she liked her tea, in the hope that he was going to stick around for a while.

"So, I have to ask..." Jack put down his mug, "You're not really Frankie, are you?"

She laughed, "You don't like it, do you?"

"It's... growing on me!" He nodded his head a little, "And if I'm honest, it suits you."

"I was never a girlie girl. In fact my brother was always more of a girl than me. We were the wrong way round, I guess. Anyway, I'm Frances, Frances Ann to be precise; I mean, do I look that saintly?" Jack laughed and shook his head.

"I was quite the tomboy and when I was about seven my mum caught me and my two friends, male of course, climbing the scaffolding of a new housing development that was being built a couple of blocks... sorry, streets... behind us. She didn't know that it wasn't the first time, but I didn't enlighten her. After a serious talking to, I was forbidden to go again."

"But you did?"

"Oh absolutely, it was even more exciting once I wasn't allowed to go; just made sure we didn't get caught again. Anyway, after she read me the riot act, she made some comment about my tomboyish ways and said she was going to start calling me Frankie instead of Frances. It's stuck since then, and I much prefer it. I've never liked my name. I was named after both my grandmothers, neither of whom I ever met."

Jack was leaning on his hand, his elbow on the bar top. He was listening to Frankie and thinking how he liked her odd mixture of accents, British and Canadian, that seemed to get all jumbled up in the same sentence. She was wearing his shirt, as promised; her hair was quite the opposite of the neat swinging bob that had caught his eye the night before.

She looked up at him; he seemed to be in a trance.

"What?" she asked, curiously.

"I just can't get enough of looking at you... your hair is a beautiful colour." He leaned forward and pulled the bar stool, with her on it, towards him. He took the mug from her hand and placed it down. They took a moment to just look at each other closely.

"Thank you," she replied, "the red is the only natural bit, I'm afraid. I have the blonde highlights added to tone it down, and apparently blondes have more fun!"

"I have to get that suit back to the hire shop today, and as I wasn't exactly planning on scoring last night, I said it would be back to them by 2pm. Which means I have to go home and change first, then get back into town."

"So, where is home?" Frankie was a little confused, because she thought that last night's lift home was on his way.

"Er... Kingston Park." Jack looked a little sheepish at the fact he only lived a short distance from the previous night's venue.

"JACK! So, I wasn't on your way home last night."

He had started to run his hands up her bare thighs, creeping a little further under his shirt, knowing she was naked.

"No, you're right. But I promise you, I had no intention of any of this happening; I just expected it to be a lift home. To be honest, I was absolutely terrified when you invited me in."

"That's at least true... you were shaking, yet look at you now, boldly going wherever you want to go."

He took hold of her bare cheeks and lifted her onto his lap so that she was straddling him; she wrapped her legs around his waist.

"If you do that, you are never going to get that suit back on time."

"I know, now that I've got a taste for you, I want you all the time."

"That's going to make work a little tricky," she raised her eyebrows at him, "which is something we need to talk about, but later."

"Can I see you again later?"

"Jack, you have me sitting on your throbbing manhood while you're looking at me, with your sexy curls and rippling muscles... what do you think?"

He gave her the most enormous grin, and then they kissed, slowly, running their hands through each other's hair.

When they finally managed to part, Jack retrieved all of his clothes, except for the shirt.

"The shirt is actually mine, if you'd like to continue living your fantasy for now." He was buttoning up his coat, so that no one would see he didn't have a shirt on. Frankie was standing in front of him, arms folded, still wearing only the shirt.

"Thank you, I would like that. Are you happy to come over here later?"

"Of course. I have a really small place, with no cat and the tiniest mirror you've ever seen." He gave her a cheeky little wink.

Frankie went to put her arms around him, which was difficult now that he had put his coat on over his suit and all that... body!

"I have plans for that mirror..."

"Oh I bet you do. How about I see you around six? We could order takeaway?"

"Sure, sounds good."

"Okay, I'll be back later then. Take care of her for me, okay?" he said, looking across at Hercules, who was sphinx-like on the back of the sofa.

They enjoyed a lingering kiss as he reversed out of the door, before Frankie closed it. She stood with her back against it for a minute, trying to compose herself, but it was no good. She suddenly jumped into the air, punching it and shouting, "YES!" As she landed on the floor, she put both hands over her mouth to stop herself from screaming out again, but couldn't help her feet when they began to move in a fast running action; she was grinning from ear to ear.

"OH MY GOD! Hercules, I have never, never ever in my whole life even kissed anyone so gorgeous, so perfect and sooooooo hot, let alone spent the night with him! And he's younger than me; he's into me and he's mine, all mine!"

She was pacing up and down as she talked. Hercules had now sat up and was looking at her as if she'd completely lost her mind.

"Can you believe I came here expecting this to be the longest, most boring six months of my life and I'm hopefully going to end up spending most of it in bed with him! Did you see him? He's an absolute GOD! Of course you didn't, you're a cat! How lucky am I?!" She was now dancing around the living room. "Look at me, for Pete's sake, I'm acting like a teenager who just got asked out on her first date." She stopped herself and straightened the shirt, pushing her hair back before turning around to the iPod to select some music: Train, of course.

"Okay, I need to take a shower. It's okay, I've got that outta my system now, I'm going to try and remain calm about this."

As she made her way towards the bedroom, the song 'This'll Be My Year' started to play. Frankie couldn't help but start to dance, giving Hercules an affectionate tickle under his chin as she passed.

"Kayla, I have to tell Kayla... oh no, I can't, it's the middle of the night... I'll text her and see if she can Face Time before he gets here at six..." As she passed the large mirror, she caught sight of herself, stopping to look at her reflection. A slow smile appeared on her face.

"You bad girl!" she said pointing to herself; then carried on dancing.

After showering, Frankie decided to take a walk. It was at least dry outside, even though it was cold, so she wrapped up warm, plugged herself into Train and set off, not really going anywhere in particular. She needed to just clear her head a bit; think about what she was about to get herself into. She wondered if it was possible to have a relationship that you both know is only going to be a short-term fling. Of course, it was all about distraction for her and therapy for him; it wasn't a relationship, it never could be. That didn't explain the way he had made her feel the first time they met; every time they met. She had never experienced those feelings before. She tried to convince herself that it was because he was young, good-looking and very fit; lots of girls must feel like that when they were around him.

As she walked she couldn't help but smile about the previous night. He may have made lots of girls swoon, but he'd chosen to spend the night with her and he was hopefully going to spend many more over the next few months. She decided just to enjoy it for the moment; so what if it was only for six months? It would be a huge boost to her confidence knowing that she could pull a younger guy like that.

It was nearly 2.30. She picked up a latte from a coffee shop she passed by chance and started for home. As she walked, she began contemplating the evening ahead and tried to decide where Mr. Lee's therapy session should be held next... the cast iron bath, in front of the mirror, or both.

It was nearly 4pm by the time she got back to the flat. She texted Kayla now that it would be nearly 8am for her. It turned out she was at work all weekend, but she could do 8am/4pm Sunday, or she would be off on Monday.

No problem, I know I will definitely be alone on Monday, so it will be easier to talk. Let's plan for then;-) Fx

Hang on a sec hun... alone? Kx

Yes. Alone. Fx

OMG!!! Are you serious? Your hunky helper?? WTF... I only spoke to you on Thursday! Kx

I know & yes... him! Charity event last night. We ended up back here... & yes OMG!!!! Fx

Good for you... can't wait to talk! Kx

Me too! Don't work too hard :-) Fx

Frankie was a little lost now; 6pm was still nearly two hours away, this was ridiculous. She did some laundry, checked out Facebook, made a bucket of tea, paid Hercules some attention and fed him... 5.40pm. Thinking she should probably tidy herself up, after getting a little windswept on her walk earlier, she decided that he was going to have to accept her casual style. However, she decided to take off the Power Y tank she was wearing under today's sloppy sweater, ensuring she was completely free of any underwear. This started to cause some dampness, at the thought of this teasing Jack. As she came out of the bedroom, the buzzer for the front door started to make a really annoying sound. She looked at the kitchen clock - it was 5.58. With a cheeky little grin on her face, she pressed the 'talk' button.

"Helloo?" she said, trying not to sound too excited.

"Hi."

"Hey Jack, just push the door and it should open." She pressed the 'enter' button, holding her finger on it for a couple of seconds. After a deep breath, she flicked the lock on the door and opened it.

Walking towards her was a blinding smile dressed in leather and jeans, with curls and stubble, carrying a holdall and... roses!

'Oh My God', she thought, *'he's brought me flowers'*. She couldn't remember the last time someone had given her flowers.

"Good evening," he said, as she opened the door fully for him to come in. "For you!"

Frankie was leaning on the door as she opened it, still holding the handle, feeling quite weak at the knees. Unconsciously, she put out her hand to take the flowers, while smiling dreamily up at him.

"Ahh Jack, thank you, it's nice to see that romance is still alive and kicking in younger men!" She wrinkled her nose just for him.

"Can you at least shut the door, and put the poor flowers in some water before you do that." He gently touched the end of her nose, "The last five hours have already been the longest of my life!"

"I take it you're planning on staying?" Frankie nodded at the holdall slung over his shoulder.

"Is that okay? I know it's a bit presumptuous... I don't have to if you do... "

Frankie stopped him by putting her fingers over his lips, looking up at him through her lashes. Pushing the holdall off his shoulder, so it dropped to the floor, she then took hold of his jacket and slowly pulled him down to her lips. Instinctively he picked her up and sat her on the end of the breakfast bar; she lay the flowers down before peeling his jacket off his shoulders and wrapping her legs around him. Their lips met again as she found his hair, running her fingers through it, and massaging his head. Jack felt his way around her waist, where bare flesh was just begging to be touched. He wanted to feel every inch of her beautiful, pale skin. When they were finally able to tear themselves apart, Frankie ran her tongue around her lips.

"You taste soooo good, Mr. Lee, I could kiss those lips all day." She touched his lips, then fondled his stubble. Something suddenly dawned on Jack.

"A fan of facial hair also... Doctor?" His hands travelled lower, feeling his way across the top of her yoga pants.

"I might be," she said, as she carried on stroking.

Jack smiled; he knew he'd just ticked another box on her list of 'likes'.

Frankie knew that if she didn't take control of this again, they would be naked in no time. She was determined, no matter how much she wanted it, that this was not going to be just about sex.

"I think we should open some wine and order some food," she said, continuing to stroke his cheek.

"Sounds good, what do you fancy... apart from me?" He was giving her his best cheeky grin.

She couldn't help but think how cute he looked when he was being playful; he was so young. She smiled at him.

"Sushi, but I guess I'm going to have to settle for pizza. If you'd be so kind as to lift me down, I'll get the menu."

Still with her legs wrapped around him, Jack lifted her down. Letting them slide down, she placed her feet on the floor. He gave her a quick peck on the nose as he set her down, and realised how far he had to bend to do so. She really was quite petite, but he was beginning to like it; this was new to him, his wife had been quite tall.

"Why don't you make yourself at home... can I get you a glass of red?" She looked back at him as she walked into the kitchen. He had his back to her and was hanging his leather jacket up. She took a moment to admire the view from the back; his jeans were just the perfect fit. He turned around.

"Okay, I'm not big on wine, but I'll join you."

"It's a shiraz, so has quite a lot of body..." She winked at him. "Here's the menu."

Frankie opened the wine and let it breathe for a few minutes, while she put the roses in a vase that she found under the sink. As Jack scanned the menu, she poured two glasses of wine and pushed one towards him.

"There you go...cheers!" She raised her glass to him, and he picked his own up.

"To therapy!" he said.

"To distraction!" She lowered the glass to her nose to breathe in the fruity aroma, before taking a sip. Jack just launched into taking a drink.

"Mmm, you like it?" she asked.

"Yes, actually I do... I'm not a big drinker, to be honest, never have been, and drinking on your own really isn't much fun."

Frankie put her wine down and went to hug him. She slid her arms around his waist and snuggled her head into his chest. He was wearing a thin black sweater; it felt soft against her face and so good to be that close to him. She breathed in the scent that only belonged to him. With his arms wrapped around her, he bent down and kissed the top of her head. It was so affectionate, it gave her a warm, fuzzy feeling inside.

Time seemed to stand still, until they heard the loud purring of Hercules, who had started to weave himself in and out of their legs. They moved apart slightly, looking down at him, then looked back at each other.

"Group hug!" said Frankie, smiling at him. He smiled back.

"Let's order," said Jack, "Hawaiian okay?"

"My favourite, actually, good choice."

Jack ordered the pizza, which was going to take forty-five minutes to be delivered. Frankie selected Bocelli on the iPod to play quietly in the background. Sitting down with their wine, at opposite ends of the sofa, they both put their feet up so that they were facing each other. Jack was taking in the room; it was the first chance he'd had to actually look around.

"This is a nice place. What's the deal with your roommate?" He nodded towards Hercules who was now making himself comfortable on his radiator.

Frankie took a sip of wine before answering.

"It's my cousin's flat, he's her roommate. I'm very close to my Aunty Carol, my mum's younger sister. You've probably guessed that my mum's not around." Frankie swallowed hard. "She died five years ago of breast cancer."

"I'm sorry." Jack rubbed her leg sympathetically.

"Thanks. So, apart from my brother, my Aunty Carol's family is all I have. Carol and Eric live in West Jesmond. My cousin, Thomas, lives in Gosforth, with his wife and two kids. This place is Lucy's, my other cousin. She's an intensive care nurse; used to work at the Freeman, but last year she split from her boyfriend. They had been together for about four years, I think. It was a complete shock to her, and everyone to be honest. We all thought he was about to pop the question. She decided to go to Australia for a year; fresh start kinda thing. A friend of hers lived here for the first six months and by pure luck it became available for me to use; I leave the week before she gets back. It means that the big guy here gets to live in his own home, and Carol comes in every week and looks after the place for me, so everyone is happy!"

"Dare I ask about your dad?"

"You've probably heard of him, Mr. Robertson, the arrogant cardiac surgeon from the Freeman who went gaga!"

"He's your dad?" Jack had heard of him.

"Unfortunately, yes. He was diagnosed with Alzheimer's shortly after mum died. Initially everyone thought he was just not dealing very well with the loss of his wife, but Andrew, my older brother, and I knew different. He had very old-fashioned ideas about marriage and family. My mum was a medical secretary when they met. She became pregnant shortly after they were married. He made her give up work, so she could keep house. We don't think he ever really wanted kids; he had a kind of children-should-be-seen-and-not-heard attitude towards us. We're convinced it was Mum who really wanted a family. Having said that, I think he had high hopes for Andrew, and expected him to go to medical school, follow in his footsteps, but Mum and I knew quite early on that medical school was the last place he was going. Andrew and I were always close as siblings. Being younger, and a girl, I was completely invisible to my dad. When Andrew came out at eighteen and told him he was gay, Dad kicked him out and completely disowned him. Enter sixteen-year-old Frankie, who decided to get her head down at school and aim for medical school herself. Like I told you, I wanted to really piss him off. I knew he would hate to have to admit to anyone that his daughter was a surgeon."

"A surgeon? But you're..."

"I know, at the other end of the patient now. Kathy Barnes, who was at the end of her anaesthesia training when I was a Senior Houseplant in General Surgery..." Jack laughed at Frankie's name for a Senior House Officer, "talked me into reconsidering my career and switching to anaesthesia; I realised that my impatient personality required a career that provides instant gratification. I liked the fact it was very hands-on, I would get to make my own decisions and use a lot of the knowledge I'd spent five years acquiring at medical school. I prefer the short, brief interaction you have with patients, who are often more worried about the anaesthetic than the surgery. There's also a good buzz that comes from being the one that everyone calls when panic sets in. It's an art, as well a science, and of course nobody fucks with a hundred of Sux!!" she casually concluded.

Jack let out a loud gasp in complete disbelief at what she'd just said, but was quick to respond once he'd caught his breath, as Frankie took a sip of wine.

"You're right, there's no way I would argue with you if you were holding a loaded syringe of muscle relaxant. Did you just make that up?"

"No, I stole it from some guy on Twitter. Anyway, I also found out it would be a better career move for my ticket out of here."

"All I Ever Wanted; Track 1; For Me, It's You; 2006!" Jack said, pointing to her with his fingers like a gun.

Frankie was taking another sip of her wine and started choking when he said that. Jack was quick to get up and pat her on the back. He squeezed in behind her, rubbing her back with his hand in a circular motion.

"Sorry," he said, "I couldn't help myself. I shouldn't have interrupted, you okay?"

"Yes, I'm fine thanks. You took me by surprise; I'm impressed, maybe you are Train's number one fan!" She laid her head back against his shoulder.

"They write very good lyrics. Could be fun to slip some of them in here and there, then the other person has to name the song, album, track number, and year!" said Jack, tucking her hair behind her ear, as he slipped his arms around her waist, his hands finding bare flesh.

"I like that idea, but what happens if you can't name something?" She rested her hands on top of his.

"Mmm, I'm sure we'll think of something." He bent down to kiss her at the same time as the annoying door buzzer went off.

After enjoying their pizza, Frankie topped up their wine, placed a bowl of strawberries on the coffee table, and they retired once more to the sofa. Making himself comfortable, Jack sat down and put his feet on the coffee table, while Frankie sat with her back against the sofa arm, her legs resting over Jack's thighs; she rested her head against the back of the sofa. Jack noticed her sweater had slipped off her shoulder. There was no tank or bra strap visible; why hadn't he noticed this before? Or had she just taken it off while in the bathroom? He had to say something.

"I see that finding clothes to fit outside of work is also a problem for you!" He glanced at her bare shoulder.

Frankie gave him a sexy little smirk.

"Is that a problem for you?"

His sweater sleeve was pushed up to just below his elbow; she started to stroke his bare arm. *'Struth! Even his forearms were solid muscle!'* she thought.

"It will only be a problem, Doctor, if you turn up for work wearing only half your clothing." His own hands were now creeping up the leg of her yoga pants, in search of bare flesh.

Frankie relaxed, examining his biceps, thinking that he was going to have to lose his sweater soon...

"I do!" she replied.

He looked at her, wide-eyed.

"What do you mean, you do?"

"Exactly what I said, I do turn up for work wearing only half my clothes. I don't wear underwear normally." Her hands travelled down his arm back to his hand; she started playing with his fingers.

"You... you don't?" Jack struggled to get his words out. He turned his upper body to face her; he looked completely stunned by what she'd just revealed.

She was used to this kind of reaction. She continued to look down at his hand, massaging it gently, she could feel his eyes burning into her. She slowly looked up at him with that sexy little smirk she had perfected over the years.

"I haven't worn underwear in years. I do if I wear jeans, or if it's really inappropriate for me not to, but I mostly wear these yoga pants, so I don't really need to wear panties. Last night I guess I should have worn something, but my dress was very fitted and I hate it when you can see lines so... lucky you!"

"So, you're telling me that every day I saw you at work, you were completely..." He was still quite shocked and couldn't quite think straight; Frankie finished the sentence for him.

"Commando! Yes! And I will be every time you see me at work from now on too!" She could feel him beginning to harden under her leg.

"It looks like you could do with some therapy, Mr. Lee, and perhaps some dessert?"

She moved to straddle him, his expression had changed; he suddenly looked nervous and worried.

"Relax, Jack, I'm only going to feed you strawberries, but I want you to close your eyes, okay?"

Jack took a deep breath; just when he was starting to feel comfortable, she wanted him to play games.

"Okay," he said, a little reluctantly. Not knowing where she was going to take this excited him even more than the underwear discussion.

Frankie took a strawberry from the bowl behind her and held it by the stalk. Jack shut his eyes. She played with his hair while she gently ran the fruit along his lips. Every time he thought she was going to let him take a bite, she moved the fruit away so he would bite at the air. Taking hold of the stalk in her mouth, she put it to his lips, still weaving her finger in and out of his curls.

This time she let him take a bite; as he did he opened his eyes and saw two emeralds staring back at him. He bit into the fruit, leaving her with the stalk in her mouth. As he ate the strawberry, he slowly smiled.

Frankie sat up and took the stalk out of her mouth, returning it back to the bowl. She picked up another, but this time she took the stalk off, placing half the fruit in her mouth, gripping it with her teeth. Slowly running her fingers through Jack's hair, she put the strawberry to his lips; his eyes were fixed on hers again. As he opened his mouth, she gently inserted the fruit, this time allowing their noses to touch; their lips were almost kissing. Instinctively and simultaneously they both bit down causing juice to drip down their chins. Neither moved; their noses remained kissing as Frankie continued to massage his curls. Finishing her half first, she licked the juice from Jack's chin and then licked his lips. When she stopped, he needed no prompting to return the favour.

As Jack finished, Frankie slowly slid her hands down his chest and over his abs to find the bottom of his sweater. Once again their eyes were locked together, foreheads and noses touching; Bocelli murmuring in the background, reciting his grocery list. Finding the edge of his sweater she took both sides and gently slid it up his firm, rippling body. Jack lifted his arms above his head, enabling her to remove it, to land on the floor, behind the sofa. Sitting back, crossing her arms, she took hold of the edges of her own sweater and lifted it up and over her head. Jack let out a gasp; he wasn't looking at her breasts, he was still gazing into her eyes.

"Don't go all shy on me again, Jack, they're yours for the taking. I want to feel your eyes on me, your touch, I want you to play with them and make me wet." Once again she was touching his face while she spoke.

Jack looked down; Frankie could see he was shaking slightly. She had taken him out of his comfort zone again and he was worried about being embarrassed.

"Hey, Jack, look at me. What is it?"

"Frankie if I touch you, or so much as look at you, I'm afraid I'm going to come."

Frankie sighed and placed her forehead on his, rubbing noses.

"Oh Jack, does it really matter if you do? I wouldn't think any less of you if you did. It actually means that when we make love we can take our time, you can take your time. I have an idea." She sat back and took his hands as she slid back off the sofa to stand up.

"Come with me; I want to try something with you, something I've never done either."

Chapter 8

FRANKIE TOOK HIS hand and led him to the bedroom. Jack followed behind her, feeling apprehensive about whatever she had planned. Now that she wasn't looking at him, he couldn't help but admire her. She had a beautifully petite, sculptured back, which tapered to a waistline that accentuated her hips, giving her a slight pear shape that swayed as she walked. Arriving at the bedroom, Frankie left Jack at the foot of the bed, in front of the mirror, so she could turn on a bedside light. She wanted them to be able to see each other without it being as bright as the living room. Jack was stood looking down at the rug when she returned to him. She slid her arms around his waist and rested her forehead against him, feeling his heart race as she too looked down, noticing through his jeans that he was still very erect. He lifted his hands to her hair and began to stroke it; she could feel him relaxing again. Stroking her hair obviously helped him, so she let him do this for a few minutes.

When she felt he had calmed enough she moved her hands around to his belt buckle and undid it. Jack carried on stroking her hair, as she pushed his jeans and then his boxers to the floor, and he stepped out of them. In one easy move, she dropped her yoga pants and pushed all the clothes to one side with her foot. Looking up at him, she could see he had his eyes closed.

"Jack," she whispered. He looked into her eyes and swallowed hard.

"Sit in front of the mirror with your back against the bed. I'm going to sit in front of you, between your legs, okay?"

Jack just nodded and did as she asked. As he parted his legs she sat with her back up against him and crossed her legs; he wrapped his legs around her, placing the soles of his feet together. He still didn't look. She took his hands and put them on her flat stomach.

"You don't have to watch if you don't feel comfortable, but I think it will be quite sexy to watch you touch me. Remember, I'm watching you in the mirror, I'm not looking right at you. I think that might help ...but just touching, okay?"

It took Jack a moment before he looked up into their reflection and nodded. He could see how hot they looked sat together, naked, her hands resting on top of his. She smiled at him and tilted her head so that his chin could rest on her shoulder.

"And Jack," she whispered, "I like feeling you come against me, so don't worry, okay?"

That was enough encouragement for him; she moved her hands so they rested on his knees and he started to explore. Before long he was massaging her breasts. She could feel him harden more against her lower back; she loved that feeling, it really turned her on. She didn't stop watching him; their eyes kept colliding in the reflection. It was no good; Mrs Cli-tor-rus was throbbing so much, she just had to put her out of her misery. While Jack became more confident, tugging on her nipples, she reached down between her legs and began to massage herself. Jack looked up into the mirror and watched. It took very little time for her to climax; almost at the same time she felt a warm, wet sensation on her back. They were both breathless, looking into the eyes of each other's reflections.

Jack moved his arms so that he was hugging her, and she placed her arms on top of his to hug him back. They were cheek-to-cheek, skin-to-skin.

"I want you to show me how to do that for you. I want to be the one to make you come... I like that," he whispered into her ear.

"You did for the most part. I didn't do very much, believe me. I love the way you touch me, you're so slow and gentle. It's making me wet again just thinking about it. I would love you to do that for me, but all in good time."

Frankie moved away from him, turning around. She pushed his legs together and straddled him.

"The mirror was fun but there's nothing quite like looking at the real thing," she said, before kissing him, stroking herself against him.

"Do you like that Jack?"

"God, you're dripping! Ride me, will you ride me like you did this morning?"

"Oh, I intend to, and you can watch in the mirror, if you like."

She ran her fingers through his hair and kissed him passionately while her hips moved, continuing to stroke his incredible length. She let the tip kiss her very wet entrance for a few seconds before she slowly let him glide into her. This was one of her favourite positions, both sat upright. She could keep a good, steady rhythm going while they explored each other's mouths. At some point Jack moved his hands to her breasts and began to play with her nipples again. She started to groan. God this felt good; he was blowing her mind, she didn't want this to stop. He was going to make her come again; she practically never came with just penetration alone. Jack laid his head back on the edge of the bed and she looked down at him, still continuing to keep a steady rhythm going. She felt so tight around him; he was completely at her mercy. He lifted his head up once more so he could look in the mirror. It was so erotic, watching himself penetrate her. Feeling him full and hard inside her, she came just before he did. Frankie instantly collapsed onto him, her face buried into his neck and shoulder. She was so out breath, feeling almost dizzy, after two mind blowing orgasms so close together. Jack held her tight; never in his life had he experienced anything like that. How was he ever going to give this up? How was he ever going to give her up?

Having both finally caught their breath, Frankie sat back and stroked the side of Jack's face. Still resting his head back on the edge of the bed, he looked down at her and smiled. She leant forward and kissed him, very tenderly, then rubbed noses together. He was still inside her, so she squeezed him a little, taking him by surprise. He let out a little gasp and lifted his head.

"Just checking you're still with me, Mr. Lee," she said, as her hands moved down to his chest.

"Only just, Doctor." He laid his head back again.

"Will you take a bath with me?"

"Only if I can just lie in it and rest. In fact, you may have to carry me there; I don't think my legs will work!"

Frankie laughed.

"And you're the young, super fit one between us. You'd better start getting used to this, Jack." She climbed off him and headed toward the bathroom. "Your therapy is giving me a very healthy appetite." She made her way out of the bedroom, without looking back.

Jack had turned his head to watch her leave; her small but perfect bottom was wiggling a little as she walked. He let out a very satisfied sigh.

They lay in the bath. Frankie sat behind Jack, her short legs wrapped around him as far as they would go, massaging bubbles into his chest hair, his head resting on her shoulder. They were bathing in a comfortable silence, no music or words, just the movement of water. After a while, Frankie broke into it.

"You have an incredible body, Jack. You must work out often."

Jack took hold of the hand Frankie was using to wash him and locked his fingers into hers.

"Yes, Doctor, I would like you to work me out often!" Frankie laughed and hugged his cheek against hers. He continued, "I've always played sports and kept fit. When Emma died, I used exercise as a way of coping. I started doing a lot of weight training. It made me feel good about myself; the beefy exterior covered a fragile, suffering interior. It never really occurred to me that women would find it attractive, or maybe I chose to ignore it. I'd lost my soul mate; at least I thought she was. I couldn't imagine ever being with anyone else."

"I'm not going to ask about her. It's not that I'm not interested, I just think it's up to you whether or not you want to talk about her, and in your own time."

With their fingers still locked together, they played with each other's thumbs. Frankie lifted her hand and pushed Jack's hair back from his face. She pressed her cheek against his again; then he spoke.

"She died of a subarachnoid haemorrhage, an aneurysm she'd had all her life, but never knew about."

Frankie didn't speak; she just carried on stroking his hair, her thumb playing with his. She wasn't prepared for what he said next.

"She was almost twenty weeks pregnant with our daughter... obviously I lost her, too."

Frankie took a sharp intake of breath; she had been a doctor for fifteen years and this was one of the most tragic things she had ever heard.

"God Jack, no wonder you're so bruised."

"We all got bruises." Jack turned his head and gave her a sad smile.

"Bruises; California 37; Track 4; 2012." Frankie said quietly.

Jack didn't need to say anything; they both knew she was right. They returned to their comfortable silence, until the water was cool and they had to get out.

After bathing they decided to turn in for the night. Together they spooned, Frankie in front of Jack, warm and naked. It felt comfortable and familiar, even though this was only their second night together. Frankie woke at some point in the night to find they were both still in the same position. She needed to move, but was desperate not to wake Jack. The more she tried to move, the more he held on tight to her, despite being deeply asleep. She gave up trying; she loved the feeling of his warm, firm body against her, his chest hairs softly brushing her back. She didn't know how long she lay awake; she just wanted to absorb every bit of this moment, feeling his breathing, slow and shallow, his breath warm and steady. His strong arms enveloping her; she felt safe. At some point in her thoughts, she drifted back off to sleep again.

It was light when Frankie next opened her eyes, and found Jack now spooned into her, her face pressing against his back, her hand nestled in his chest hair. He was still deeply asleep. Like the previous morning, she managed to escape without waking him. As she made her way to the bathroom, she noticed that Hercules had made himself comfortable on Jack's abandoned sweater, behind the sofa.

"Morning, big guy," she spoke quietly to him as she stroked his head, "Shh, we have to be quiet, my bed slave is still asleep." She was just about to walk into the bathroom when she remembered... "And by the way," she continued, "You know I mentioned that I would be happy to trade places for a while, well, can I take a raincheck on that?"

Frankie had no idea that Jack had woken as she left the bedroom and could actually hear her. He smiled to himself when he heard her talking to the cat.

After using the bathroom, she popped her head around the bedroom door and discovered Jack lying on his back, his forearm across his eyes. He knew instantly that Frankie was standing there, so he moved his arm to look at her.

"Good morning," he said, with a sleepy smile and messy bed curls.

Frankie stood leaning against the doorway with her arms folded, admiring the view for a moment. She noticed the sheet was pushed down as far as his hips; Mrs Clit-tor-rus started doing a belly dance as her eyes wandered a little further down. *I can't go another morning without doing something with that,* she thought.

"Good morning... Glory!" she said, with her sexiest voice.

She started to move towards the bed, still confidently naked. His eyes followed her. Standing at the foot of the bed she lifted the sheet, crawled under, and slowly made her way up, climbing on top of Jack. She stopped when she was nose to nose with him, and gently kissed him. Purposely she sat straddling him, his great length pressing against her now very moist entrance.

"I hope you don't mind, but I have always thought it a terrible waste to ignore something so natural. I also think it is the best time to have sex!"

"Why would any man ever refuse such a request from an incredibly beautiful woman first thing in the morning?"

Frankie wrinkled her nose for him and smiled as she slid her hips back slightly and allowed him to slide into her slowly.

"Ohh, God!" Even though he was expecting it, her wetness created such an amazing sensation. He couldn't remember the last time he'd had sex first thing in the morning. It felt different to the other times they'd made love; much more sensitive. As Frankie glided up and down him slowly, he knew he was about to come.

"Come for me Jack, I want to feel you burst inside me," she whispered, looking into his eyes.

He noticed she was only resting on one arm; her other arm had disappeared between her legs. This was enough to tip him over the edge, into the most intense orgasm he'd had with her so far. She didn't stop riding him until she came herself a few moments later. He watched her as she enjoyed the ecstasy, her expression pure pleasure; thinking again to himself how gratifying it would be to be able to pleasure her, the way she did so for herself. Lying on top of him, she buried her head in his neck. Suddenly he rolled her over, so he was on top.

"Ahh!" she shouted out, surprised, and then laughed as he pretended to playfully bite her neck.

She wrapped her arms around him, spreading her hands wide on his broad back. Jack stopped and rubbed his nose with hers.

"I think I would like to wake up this way every morning, Doctor," he said pressing his forehead against hers.

"Oh, you would, would you? Well, that would mean us spending every night together." Playing with his sexy bed curls, she wasn't really taking him seriously. She thought he was just caught in the moment, although she couldn't agree more. What a way to start your day!

"Yes, it would, but as I only have you for a short time, I want to make sure I don't waste any of it." He kissed her softly.

"Jack, this all started only two days ago, not even, yet you're talking about practically moving in. Aren't you forgetting that we also have to work together during this time too?"

He moved to lie by her side, propping his head up on his arm so he could look at her. Her arm was still around him, stroking his back, looking up into those gorgeous, steel blue eyes of his.

"I was wondering when we were going to discuss work," he said with a sigh, gently running his hand across her stomach.

"Well, it's kinda important. I've been back in this country for two weeks and worked there for a total of only six days, and in that time we've worked together, what... twice I think. When we both left on Friday we barely knew each other and now look at us, we've spent two nights together since. I think we need to keep this to ourselves for as long as we can. It doesn't look good for either of us if it becomes apparent we hooked up so soon. I'm aware that we're on a time schedule here, but we could just as easily get bored with each other and it could be all over next week. This way, no one at work need ever know. I guess what I'm saying is that I think we should enjoy it for the moment. No expectations, no one interfering or having an opinion, no strings... what do you think?"

They lay there looking at each other, Frankie waiting for Jack to speak. She could see he was thinking, processing what she'd said.

"I think you are very sexy when you are being serious, especially when your beautiful, full breasts are staring up at me just begging to be kissed. I am going to agree with everything you've said, but on one condition." Now he was trying to be serious.

"What's that?" She looked at him curiously.

"You allow me to make love to you again before breakfast."

"Now there's an offer I can't refuse, but only if you take charge. A little test to see how well your therapy is going."

"Okay, I'll see what I can do." He bent to kiss her lips before moving down to her breasts, letting his hands drift across her stomach, down her hip and her leg. He wanted to touch her between her legs; Frankie sensed this and spread them slightly for him, but it was out of his comfort zone; he just couldn't. Again she saw his hesitation and took his hand, brought it to her lips and kissed each of his fingers. He stopped and looked at her; she had seen that nervous look enough times now, but she was determined she was going to let him take the lead. She placed her hand on his chest; his heart was thumping.

"Play with my hair, Jack," she said in a quiet, calming voice. Still leaning on his elbow, he began to stroke and fondle her hair. He loved her hair. He loved the colours, the style, the feel of it, the way the ends all flicked out in different directions after she'd slept on it; but right now he loved the way it melted over the pillow like caramel sauce on vanilla ice cream. He could feel his heart rate slow down.

"That's better. Now that you've relaxed a little, would you like to continue?" she said, stroking his back again.

How did she know that playing with her hair would calm him? He didn't even know that. Smiling very slowly, he moved himself on top and positioned himself between her legs. She gave him a slow, reassuring smile, and he slowly slid inside. He was very quick to come; Frankie just held him tight and let him let go.

"I'm sorry," he said, as he buried his face into the pillow next to her.

"Will you stop saying sorry, what for this time?"

"That wasn't very good for you was it?"

Frankie rolled him off her, pushing him on his back; he covered his face with his hands. She eased herself up so she could lean on her elbow and peeled his hands away from his face.

"Look at me," she said a little more sharply than she had intended to.

He turned his head so that he faced away from her.

"Jack," she said softly, "please, look at me." Placing her hand flat on the side of his face, she encouraged him to turn and face her.

"We're going to straighten a few things out before we go any further. So you didn't make me come, big deal! Doesn't mean I didn't enjoy it; I love the feeling of you against me, touching me, kissing me, inside me -- Christ, I'm turned on just looking at you, but I'm not going to make you feel good by faking it. I don't fake it. I also, like most women, don't really climax through penetration alone. If it helps, last night, when I rode you in front of the mirror, I came again. That almost never happens to me, but it did with you. It was mind blowing, if you must know." She started to play with his curls admiring how his hands behind his head defined his shoulder and arm muscles. She was trying desperately not to let them distract her, as she continued her speech.

"And as for you coming, too soon or not in the right place... the only person who seems bothered by this is you, get over it!" This finally made Jack smile.

"For me this is not about banging each other's brains out to see who can have or give the most orgasms. I want to share an intimate connection with you. It should be comfortable, pleasurable, and fun. We don't always have to have sex, we don't always have to climax, but we do have to respect that and enjoy it. Maybe I'm expecting too much, but if you work with me Jack, you might just find you'll relax and stop cutting yourself up so much. Do you honestly think I would be lying here now, looking up your nose if I wasn't enjoying what we have?"

Frankie rested the side of her head on Jack's chest, his chest hair soft against her cheek, his firm pecs cushioning her head. They lay there in silence; Jack staring at the ceiling.

"Talk to me Jack, what are you thinking?"

There was a heavy pause.

"I'm thinking..." he swallowed hard, "How am I ever going to let you leave."

Frankie felt a sudden sinking feeling in her stomach; she couldn't say anything, her mouth had gone dry.

After showers and breakfast, they spent the rest of Sunday lounging around, getting to know each other better. Jack talked about his family in Oxford, where he'd grown up. He was the middle child of three siblings. His brother Anthony was the oldest, Anna, his sister, was a couple of years younger. His dad was a retired headmaster of the local secondary school. His mum still taught; she was a year 1 teacher at a school a few miles away from their home. Jack had always thought he might be a paramedic or an emergency nurse, but he'd ended up following Emma to Newcastle, where she'd studied physiotherapy. They had been on a break from each other, after dating for the last year of high school, However, absence made their hearts grow fonder, so he moved to be with her and failed to get a training position as a nurse or a paramedic. That's how he'd ended up training to become an operating department practitioner. Not his ideal job, but he enjoyed it and was good at it. He'd married Emma when they were both only 24; they waited a couple of years and then decided to try for a baby. It had taken her three years to get pregnant.

Jack listened to Frankie talk about the father who never once hugged or kissed her, not even goodnight. How he never really displayed any sort of emotion, or obvious love towards her mum. How he appeared to have an old-fashioned view of women and their role as a wife. She only remembered spending time with her mum and older brother Andrew when she was a child. Even family holidays were not really spent together; her father would always be writing a scientific paper, analysing some research, or reading work journals. It had been her mum who'd held it all together; she'd never understood what her mum saw in him or why she'd even stayed with him. Frankie missed her mum desperately; she thought of her every day and she wasn't ashamed to wish it had been him who had suffered and died, and not her.

She talked of her brother, who lived in New York, and designed ergonomic office furniture for a big US company. She also talked of her fondness of Andrew's long-time partner, Angus, an eccentric Scotsman and home magazine editor, who was nearly ten years older than Andrew. They had been together for eight years now and were very much in love. Frankie briefly outlined the two significant relationships she'd previously had and why they hadn't worked out; on both occasions it had been her decision to end it. She now believed she was too old to find true love and was just going to enjoy whatever came her way, hence her opinion on her relationship with Jack. As for children, she had been told at about 18, after being investigated for very irregular periods, that her ovaries didn't appear to ovulate and therefore her chances of ever having children naturally were very slim. She explained to Jack that she now very rarely had a period, which she considered a bonus, and that she had come to terms with probably never being a mother herself. She felt it was irrelevant anyway, as she was now probably never likely to find a partner; let alone someone who didn't want children!

By late afternoon it had started to rain and began to get dark outside. Mid-February was still cold, so Frankie put the fire on; Hercules was quick to claim his spot on the rug. While Jack was in the bathroom, Frankie decided to put on some Train and make tea. When he came out he walked towards her; she had her back to him, stood at the sink. She was singing along to 'Calling All Angels'; it was loud enough that she wasn't aware of Jack approaching her from behind.

"Gotcha!" He grabbed her waist to pull her away from the sink, then spun her around so he could capture her in his big arms. He completely ignored her protests.

"Ahh! Jack, you gave me a fright... what are you doing... Put me down you big bully... This is not fair!"

There was nothing she could do; he was just too strong for her, but she was secretly enjoying every minute of being manhandled by him. He picked her up and sat her on the kitchen bench, spreading her legs so he could stand between them and locked his arms around her waist.

"Oh, it's not is it, why is it not fair?" He was moving his face closer and closer to her so that eventually their noses touched.

"Because..." she couldn't think of anything; he was distracting her by rubbing noses, and giving her a dazzling smile.

"I'm waiting, Doctor, you're the one with all the answers, why is it not fair for me to playfully attack you?"

"Because, you're the one who's supposed to be having 'issues'," Frankie made little comma signs with her fingers, "If you continue to display that kind of behaviour, I might have to declare you cured and discharge you."

She leaned back on her hands and tilted her head to the side while giving a little smirk; of course she couldn't resist wrinkling her nose for him.

Jack let his hands slip from around her; she had the cutest little nose that made him melt when she did that. Every time he took a moment like this to look at her, he saw something new. This time it was the way the sides of her hair were swept up and clipped in a messy knot on top of her head; random bits of copper and blonde hung around her beautiful face. He noticed her fair eyebrows were perfectly shaped. She looked adorable. He was looking at a professional woman who was seven years his senior and had completely rocked his world in the last forty eight hours, and right then, at that moment she was just... adorable.

As Jack let his hands rest on her thighs, the song changed to 'Drops of Jupiter', a favourite of both of theirs, though neither knew this yet. Spontaneously, they both began to mouth the words, gazing longingly into each other's eyes. Jack found the edge of her sweater and lifted it over her head; she wore a bra that gave her an impressive cleavage but he didn't look, he kept miming with her, dropping the sweater to the floor. Frankie lifted his T-shirt - his impressive upper body meant it was quite fitted - and dropped it onto the floor too. She loved his chest, his shoulders, his abs, his arms, but her eyes didn't leave his to look. Continuing to mime the words, Jack took hold of each of her fleecy socks and pulled; they dropped to the floor. She undid his jeans, then with her bare feet she hooked her big toes over the top at his hips and pushed them down; still miming, she didn't look. Unhooking her bra he slid it forwards, dropping it to the floor. He took hold of the top of her yoga pants as she straightened her legs and rested them on his hips so she could ease her bottom up slightly; he pulled them down and added them to the pile on the floor. She was naked, he still didn't look. Removing his boxers the same way she'd removed his jeans, she then wrapped her legs around him. He pulled her close, still miming, eyes still fixed. It came to the part of the song where the words quicken; they both pressed their noses together to mime these words. As the words finished, they both laughed. The song continued but there was no more miming; they were now passionate, tangled skin in the middle of the kitchen.

Frankie never got her tea.

Jack planned on going home on Sunday night, as he was at work on Monday morning. However, after christening the kitchen bench, raiding the freezer for M&S ready meals and feeding each other ice cream in front of the fire (much to Hercules' disgust), he stayed. Over breakfast, they agreed that they wouldn't see each other that night, especially as they would both be at work together on Tuesday.

"Do you have plans for the day?" Jack asked.

He was freshly showered, all damp curls and sexy stubble, with that intoxicating scent he wore; sitting at the breakfast bar in the sweater he'd arrived in on Saturday, eating granola and drinking tea.

"Yeah, I do," Frankie replied with a sigh, "I have to go to my father's solicitor and sign papers, straighten a few things out so I can officially sell the house. Then I thought I would go to the house and make a start. I don't really know where to start, but I'll have to figure it out, I guess."

She was leaning across the kitchen bench in front of where Jack was sitting, with her bucket of tea in her hands. All she was wearing was the T-shirt he had worn the day before and her fleecy socks; she hadn't showered yet so she was all bedhead and no make up.

"We should exchange mobile numbers, just in case you can't live without me tonight. I'm going to the gym after work, but other than that I'll just be sitting at home, thinking of you." Jack picked up his phone.

"Sure, I guess I had forgotten we'd skipped that part." Frankie reached for her phone too, trying to ignore the other things he'd said.

They exchanged numbers and finished their tea. It was 7.15; Jack was due at work at 8.

"Well sweetheart, I guess I better go and show my face," he said, standing up.

"Are you okay?" She went to him and put her arms around his waist.

Jack put his arms around her neck and stroked her hair.

"I think so, I mean it's not like it's written all over my face, is it?" he said, looking down at her.

"Oh, I think it is, Mr. Lee," she said, grinning up at him. "Seriously Jack, it's been a huge step for you, are you okay?"

Jack bent to kiss the top of her head. "I can't remember the last time I felt as good as this, thank you."

They looked up at each other before kissing goodbye.

Frankie closed the door and stood with her back against it for a moment, before sliding down to the floor, her head in her hands. Hercules strolled across to her, stopping to stretch half way. He rubbed himself against her legs, purring. Frankie pushed her fingers back through her untidy hair before reaching down to stroke him. Letting her legs go from under her she sat with her back against the door. Hercules came and sat in her lap and she continued to stroke him.

"Oh, big guy, what the hell am I getting into here? Should I be ending this now, do you think? You know, before it gets any more serious. Grrrr! This is not supposed to happen, but he's so lovely, and very hot!" She looked down at Hercules, who was very much enjoying having his chin rubbed and appeared to be looking at Frankie with his eyes shut! She didn't care, and continued talking.

"I mean that body, I still can't believe I've had the pleasure of it all weekend. He's just so affectionate, the way he strokes my hair, the way he rubs my nose... Oh God, listen to me, I've regressed back to my teenage years again. Come on."

She stopped stroking the cat and lifted him off her knee so she could stand up. "Time to face the world, I guess, and whatever delights it has in store for me today. I bet by the time he gets to work he's been in touch." Hercules just sat with his tail curled around his feet, looking up at her. She looked down at him. "Okay, yes, right, I know I'm rambling... go shower, I get it!" She turned towards the bathroom, waving a hand at the cat as she walked.

Chapter 9

JACK ARRIVED AT work at five to eight. He felt really weird, a feeling he couldn't describe to anyone. It was a mixture of *'I've just had an amazing weekend'*, *'What the hell is happening?'*, *'Did all that really happen?'* and *'If I don't tell someone soon I'm just going to burst!'* He texted Frankie, testing her number and letting her know that he was missing her already. She promptly replied, informing him she had just stepped out of the shower, naked and dripping! Enthralled with what he was reading, Jack proceeded to walk into a laundry cart; luckily no one saw him. He texted her back, telling her to behave as he was about to get changed and the changing room was quite busy. She fired back,

Oh, Mr. Lee. Do I have you standing to attention... again?

As he walked back out of the men's changing room, Denise took him by surprise.

"Morning Jack, have a good weekend?"

'Oh God, what should I say to that, I'm sure to give something away.' He swallowed hard before speaking.

"Morning Dee, yeah, not bad thanks, you?" He surprised himself at how calm his voice was.

"Yes, thank you... a little fuzzy on Saturday morning, you know," she said as she nudged his arm, "but nothing that a couple of Co-Codamol and a fry up didn't fix!"

Saturday morning! Was it only Friday night they had all been out? It seemed like such a long time ago. So much had happened since then.

"Anyway Jack, I have a meeting at eight, which - oh hell - I'm late for... Catch you later." She disappeared off down the corridor.

Jack went to check the schedule; he was in Theatre 1, doing a plastic surgery list with Dr. Richardson -- a female anaesthetist who worked part time, juggled four kids under six, and occasionally saw her high-powered lawyer husband. Jack was actually pleased to be working with her because she hadn't been at the event on Friday evening, so hopefully he wouldn't need to talk about it. However, he couldn't help noticing that the following day, and Wednesday, he was going to be with Frankie. He looked up and let out a big breath. That was going to be interesting. He made his way to the anaesthetic room to set up.

It was lunchtime before he heard anyone mention Friday night. A group of nurses were doing a post-mortem of the evening in the staff room; who had looked good and who hadn't, which dresses they liked, which ones they didn't. Then he heard her name as he stood in the kitchen, and almost allowed his glass of water to overflow.

"Honestly, she looked amazing, I mean you know how you just see her in those black jogger things, well honest to God she walked in this slinky red dress, killer heels, nails, hair, make up and everything. I swear she turned heads."

"I'm not surprised, she's really quite pretty you know, and I don't think she's married. She must have a boyfriend though."

Jack was glad to have his back to this conversation. He knew the nurses who were talking, and if they were to see the huge grin on his face it would have been game over. He took a drink and composed himself for a moment before turning round to face them and heading towards the door. As he left the room, he caught one last comment from the first nurse that he'd heard speaking,

"And I swear he didn't take his eyes off her all night..."

Oops! He wasn't aware he had been that obvious. It was no good now; he had to text Frankie again.

Well, Dr., it would appear you turned more than just my head on Friday night! Jx

It was 12.45; he wasn't sure what she would be doing, but it only took a minute for her to reply.

Really? Yours was the only one I noticed ;-) About to go into my appt, catch you later. Fx

While he was reading her text, Heather walked into the theatre in which he was about to check over the anaesthetic machine.

"Well good afternoon, Jack, and how are we this fine Monday? I'm afraid you have the pleasure of my company now. Vicky's back is killing her, after scrubbing this morning. Poor girl; I didn't scrub at her stage, I mean she's so big now she could hardly reach the patient over that bump." They both set to work while Heather talked. "So I've told her she needs to talk to Dee, she hasn't got long before her mat leave starts anyway."

Jack didn't respond to Heather, he just listened.

"Oh Jack, I'm sorry, how insensitive of me, I shouldn't talk about... I didn't think." She went to Jack, who was crouched down, fitting new ventilator tubing. She put her hand on his shoulder as he stood up.

"I should know better Jack, I'm sorry."

He turned to look at her,

"It's okay, really. I'm moving on; I'm fine, honestly." He smiled at her before disappearing around the back of the machine again.

"So!" Heather said, "You had a good time on Friday evening?"

"I did, yes, thank you. You?" He could tell she knew something.

"Oh yes, it's always a good night." Heather had her back to him, laying out the trays for the first case of the afternoon.

"I thought Dr. Robertson looked fantastic. It's amazing how we all look the same every day at work, then we put our glad rags on and WOW! Someone always steals the show, don't you think?"

Jack was no longer concentrating on what he was doing. *'She knows...'* he thought.

"I suppose, she looked very nice, yeah!" He was glad she wasn't looking at him.

"Yesss, but not the kind of dress you want to be wearing when you have to climb into a Mini?" Heather turned around and winked at Jack who was peering over the top of the machine, frozen.

"Don't worry, Romeo, your secret is safe with me. Can't say I'm surprised; there's been a couple of occasions since she arrived when I've almost told the two of you to get a room!"

"Was it that obvious?"

Heather moved back over towards Jack.

"Jack, when you're both in a room together, there is so much chemistry, I'm surprised the anaesthetic gases don't spontaneously combust! Look, I know how hard this last couple of years has been for you. It's about time you got a proper workout and had some fun."

"Heather!"

"Just be careful, Jack. She's not here to stay and I don't want to see you go through any more grief."

"Yes Mother, thank you," he said with a smile; she was smiling back at him. Jack was very fond of Heather; she was like a mother or a big sister to everyone. She wasn't afraid to give an opinion, but she was very genuine and would do anything for anyone.

"And watch where you do your canoodling when you're both here. The walls have eyes and ears, you know." She winked at him again, before returning to her trays. Jack just smirked.

Frankie spent nearly two hours at the solicitor's office. It hadn't all been as straightforward as she'd expected it to be. She was brain dead by the time she came out, and it was raining again. *'Great!'* she thought, stood there in heels and a short skirt. She had decided she needed to make some sort of effort; after all, she needed the solicitor on her side to stop Patricia trying to gain control of her father's finances. Pulling up her hood, she made her way down the street, in search of 'that wretched box on wheels', as she now called it. Once inside it, she headed straight for home, desperate for a bucket of tea.

Arriving back at the flat, she changed into comfy, dry clothes and curled up on the sofa with Hercules. She opened her iPad to update Andrew on the meeting that afternoon. She replied to emails from Kayla, arranging a FaceTime with her at 5pm, and finally, one from Lucy, who had been camping in the outback for a couple of weeks. She wanted to catch up on how things were going with the flat and cat etc.. She replied to Kayla, confirming that five was fine, and then sent quite a long reply to Lucy, updating her, but leaving out the obvious. Frankie figured that Lucy didn't need to know what was going on in front of her mirror or on her kitchen bench; it was bad enough that her cat had been watching! Before she knew it, her iPad was ringing, asking her to accept a call from Kayla. She pressed 'Send' and Lucy's email went whooshing into cyberspace, then she switched to Face Time and accepted.

"Hey!" they both said at the same time.

"How you doing, hun? Did you manage to get any sleep this weekend?" Kayla was dying to hear all about it and couldn't help launching right into it.

"Kay, it's not like that..."

"The hell it's not, if he's as hot as you made out. I bet the two of you didn't leave the apartment all weekend!"

"Well, yes, we were getting to know each other. You know, it's all happening a little fast..."

"You're telling me; you didn't even like the guy the last time we spoke."

"Well, I found out some things about him after that. He's a little fragile..."

Frankie explained everything to Kayla, who used half a box of tissues while listening. She made it clear to her that this was a short term 'arrangement', although she didn't like calling it that, so it was known as 'therapy and distraction'. It was all still early days and might not even work out, but she was enjoying it for now.

"Well, hun, I hope - for your sake - you're going to be okay about walking away from this at the end. Sounds to me like this is more than just distraction for you. But, please!!... Tell me one thing, just one teeny, tiny, hot little detail... "

"What?" Frankie knew what she wanted to know.

"Was he good, you know, even though he was a little rusty?"

Smirking, Frankie bit her smiling lip, while coyly looking down at her hands. Kayla had her answer.

"Oh yeah! Good for you, hun."

And on that note they signed off, with plans to speak the following week.

Frankie looked at the clock: 6.05. She wondered if Jack had finished work, or was he already at the gym? Suddenly, she felt a sharp stab in the left side of her neck.

"Hey! There's no need for that, are you jealous?" She lay back on the sofa, where Hercules was stretched out; the paw containing the claw that had just attacked her was now dangling beside her.

"I promise you can keep me warm tonight," she tickled under his chin and he began to purr, "although, I'm sure it's not quite going to be the same, even if you are rather handsome."

Unable to refrain any longer, she texted Jack.

Hey! How was your day? Fx

She waited. She made tea and waited. She made dinner and waited. At 7.33 she got a reply.

Sorry! Ran out of battery at work. Day was ok & interesting, Heather knows, she saw us leaving together.

Frankie wasn't surprised someone had seen them; she was just glad it was Heather.

Oh! She seems like a pretty discreet person... yeah? Fx

Yeah, she's ok. I know her well and it won't go any further - she's not surprised :-) Jx

Really? Anyway, how was your workout... better than me? Fx

My workout will never be better than you!

Oh, is that right... why?

There was a pause before Frankie received a reply.

Well... I now know what a full marathon feels like... Dr.! Jx

This made Frankie smile. She was dying to say, "Get that fit ass over here now, so I can lick you all over," but she was determined that they should have a night off.

No more half marathons for you, Mr. Lee. Will I have the pleasure of working you hard tomorrow? Fx

Frankie meant after work, so his answer took her by surprise.

Oh yes, we're together tomorrow AND Wednesday! Jx

You gotta be kidding me!

Nope! I'm all yours for two whole days... & nights I hope ;-) Jx

You bet! Sleep well before our rendezvous in Theatre 4 tomorrow am ;-) Fx

You too. Jx

Although disappointed that she wasn't spending another night with Jack, Frankie was proud of herself for not giving in and inviting him over. The weekend had been intense and she thought that they both needed some space to digest what they were getting into. Facing work together the next day would be challenging; there would definitely be some fallout from Friday night. After a soak in the bath, and remembering to take the red nail varnish off before bed, she had the worst night's sleep she'd had in a long time.

Jack sat in his small, lonely flat, watching TV and eating pasta. He had never really settled in there; probably because it was bought on the rebound, after he'd sold the house he'd bought with Emma just before they got married. Apart from sentimental keepsakes and a few personal items, the only thing he had held onto was her Mini. He'd purchased it for her when she found out she was pregnant; a red Mini One, not quite what she wanted, but all he could afford. She had loved it. He had known that once they had a baby, she wouldn't ever get one. He couldn't give it up. He had sold his own car so he could keep it, and if the truth were known, he loved it. It was like a fun, happy reminder of Emma. However, seeing another woman in the passenger seat just a few nights ago had changed all that. He felt as though he was betraying Emma, almost committing adultery. This was another thing he had to get over. Deep down, he knew she would want him to be happy and get on with his life. Uninterested in watching the TV, with tiredness creeping in, and knowing that working with Frankie for the next couple of days would be challenging especially if they spent their nights together, he headed to bed. He, too, had the worst night's sleep he'd had in a long time.

In separate flats, the following morning they both woke feeling awful. Having completed their normal morning routines, they each set out on their commute to work. Jack had no choice but to drive, while Frankie jumped on the Metro, one stop, from Jesmond to Haymarket. As she walked the few streets towards the Infirmary she started to feel quite nervous, despite Jack saying that apart from Heather, no one else seemed to have noticed anything. Jack turned the corner into the hospital car park, and was able to park in his usual spot. He took the stairs to the third floor. Walking down the main corridor, he saw the back of her disappear through the theatre suite doors. She was unmistakable now, her black yoga pants, her long black waterproof jacket, her colourful back pack; all her things had a funny little symbol on them – a curly sign in a circle - that he had never seen before. And, of course, her hair was trussed up in her black hat with the little peak at the front. His insides leapt when he saw her.

Frankie walked into the theatres changing room, calming her nerves; there weren't many people inside. She was successful in finding some smaller scrubs, so at least she would spend the day decent in Jack's presence, even if the rest of her time with him had been anything but. If the truth were known, she was actually quite excited about seeing him, especially in a situation where they were going to have to be controlled just to look at each other. After pushing up her washed-but-unstyled hair into a theatre hat, she calmly left the changing room. Walking towards Gloria at the front desk to pick up her list, she happened to glance up at the monitor on the wall. Normally this screen, which was slaved from the front desk computer, had messages, emergencies, and list changes on it; it was basically the centre of the universe for the theatre suite. Anything anyone needed to know could be answered by the monitor or, of course, Gloria, who controlled it. Frankie froze on the spot, staring at the photos currently streaming across the screen. They were from Friday night; the one that she happened to see was a picture of her and Jack looking right at each other while dancing The Gay Gordons with other partners.

Even she could see how hot that look was! She had that 'Oh My God' kind of sinking feeling in her stomach, until she was brought back to reality by Gloria's voice.

"Mornin' Frankie... Frankie?" Gloria was about to stand up and touch Frankie when she snapped out of it.
"Oh... sorry Gloria, good morning. Sorry, I didn't sleep well last night, I need more caffeine!"
Just as Gloria was about to hand Frankie her list, an all-too-familiar voice behind her spoke, causing Frankie to breathe in sharply and forget to breathe out.
"Oh dear, Doctor, did you not sleep well? Funny that, me neither... You should have called me - we could have counted sheep together, or something."
Jack walked past the front desk without making eye contact with anyone; he just carried on down the corridor until he arrived at the door of Theatre 4. Turning to push the door open he took the chance to glance back. Frankie blindly managed to take the list from Gloria, whilst looking in Jack's direction. As he disappeared through the door she saw him wink at her. Her stomach did the biggest summersault, at which point she suddenly remembered to breathe.
"See pet..., he's sweet on you," Gloria commented, winking at Frankie, who let out a nervous little laugh. Thinking, *'Oh Gloria, if only you knew!'* she made her way down the corridor for a quiet word with her ODP.

Entering the anaesthetic room, Frankie had intended to be mad at Jack, but all he had to do was flash his gorgeous smile and she just couldn't be angry with him anymore.
"Good morning. Looks like you missed me as much as I missed you; and there is only one way to cure this problem, you know! "

Jack was stood at the bench, preparing to draw up drugs; he was still smiling. Frankie was starting to feel all twinkly inside, seeing his beautiful, white, straight teeth beneath those perfect pink lips; he looked incredibly hot in his scrubs.

'To whoever designed these hideous sacks,' she thought, *'I take it all back, it should be against the law to look that good in scrubs!'*

"Jack, don't you dare do that again! Especially in front of Gloria; she had already noticed the way you've been looking at me, and then there's the picture up on the desk screen! We need to at least try to be discreet about this, otherwise we might as well..."

As her mouth was racing through everything she needed to say, Jack put down his syringe and walked towards her. She didn't quite finish what she was saying before he bent down and kissed her, long and tenderly. She couldn't help but kiss him back, she had missed him so much, and right there and then she didn't care if they were seen. He slowly pulled just millimetres away from her, rubbing noses. Their eyes locked.

"Is that better, Doctor? I think we'll both get through this day much happier, now that we've got that out of the way, don't you?"

Frankie couldn't say anything; she just smiled and looked down as he moved back to the bench to continue what he'd been doing. When she eventually looked up, he was about to draw up some saline from a vial; he glanced sideways at her and gave a cheeky little smirk. After placing her backpack down, she pushed her glasses further up her nose and picked up her patient notes. She gave him her sexiest smile and spoke in a slow, low voice. "I'll go and see the first patient then," she pointed to the door.

"Okay," he said with another sideways glance.

As Frankie walked to the day suite, her phone vibrated in her pocket.

Dr., those glasses are very sexy... l would like to see you in them & only them ;-) Jx

Frankie let out a loud laugh as she entered the day suite, causing everyone to look at her.
"Sorry," she said quietly, feeling a little embarrassed at her outburst.
She replied to him as she walked towards the main desk.

Mr. Lee, you really are coming out of your shell now, aren't you, and becoming so demanding?

Instant reply:

Well, you're very good at what you do, Dr.. Now, about those glasses?

I am very good at doing you, Mr. Lee, but only if you promise to be a very good boy for the rest of the day ;-)

Jack was in the theatre when he got her reply, the room was now busy with nurses setting up. He, too, let out a very loud, spontaneous laugh and smacked his hip on the edge of the operating table.
"Something you would like to share with us, Jack?" asked Marie, who was assisting in that theatre for the day.

"Oh, no... Nothing," he replied, grinning a little, rubbing his side. He texted her back, aware he was being watched.

I'll do my best ;-)

They managed to make it through the rest of the day without giving anything away, until the very last case. Frankie had been given a message late morning; could she check in with Helen and arrange to pay for the weekend away at Lumley Castle, for which she had successfully bid in the silent auction? So, immediately before the last case of the day, she popped over to the anaesthetic office. Helen complimented her on her stunning appearance at the event; this had not been the only time someone had complimented her that day. Frankie wrote her a cheque and Helen informed her that she would forward her the details of the weekend, which was booked for the first long weekend in May.

Frankie returned to Theatre 4 as Jack was setting up for the next patient.

"Paid your debts?" he said.

The room was busy again, with nurses setting up trays and cleaning. Olivia, the nurse currently scrubbed, was stood waiting for Marie to open the first set of drapes containing her sterile equipment, so that she could set up her table. Looking across at Frankie, she remarked, "In debt already, you've only been here about two weeks!"

"Oh, it's just my bid from the silent auction," Frankie replied, opening her patient notes to read them.

"What did you bid on?" asked Marie.

Frankie looked up at her, and as she spoke, she couldn't help glancing towards Jack, and then back at Marie.

"Errr... The romantic weekend for two at Lumley Castle!" she replied, smiling at Marie.

Jack spoke up.

"Nice. Taking anyone special?"

Frankie shot him a look, knowing that Marie and others in the room were looking at them; he did a quick raise of the eyebrows with that cheeky grin of his. It was almost the end of the day and he looked hotter than ever. A couple of curls had escaped from under his hat and were clinging to his forehead. His mask was tied around his head but pushed under his chin revealing rough stubble, and his eyes were sparkling blue. Frankie's mouth went dry.

"I-if you must know; it's a gift for my aunt and uncle," she stuttered, trying to be matter-of-fact about it and not daring to look at Jack, but deep down she knew that, if all went well with this 'arrangement', Carol and Eric wouldn't be going anywhere near Lumley Castle. She had to break the awkward silence that was now present.

"Right, Jack, we should check those drugs!"

Knowing all eyes were on them, Frankie turned and walked back into the anaesthetic room.

Jack left work before Frankie; it turned out he had predicted that he wouldn't be going home that night, and had brought an overnight bag with him. While clearing away at the end of the day, he had suggested he cook for them; there were only so many freezer meals he could tolerate, even if they were from M&S. He would pick some things up at the supermarket on his way to her place and meet her there. Frankie also had some shopping to do. It was quite likely he would arrive before her, so she gave him her keys.

'What on earth am I doing?' She had done it without any hesitation, but it somehow felt right.

Sure enough, there was his bright red Mini, parked a couple of doors down from the front door of the flats. Luckily for her, Penny, Mrs. Whitfield's daughter, was coming out of the front door as Frankie reached it. They said 'hello' to each other and Penny let Frankie in. Arriving at the front door of the flat, she noticed that Jack had left the door on the latch, so she was able to just push it open. When she entered, she was not only greeted by Hercules, but she was swept up into the arms of a very excited Jack. She just had time to drop her backpack by the door before he picked her up and sat her on the end of the bench.

"Jaaaack! At least let me get my coat off!"

"I have wanted to scoop you up like that all day; I think I have shown admirable self control for the last nine hours!"

They enjoyed a lingering kiss before Frankie pulled away.

"I need a shower!" she said.

"Wouldn't you like dinner first and then we can bathe together?" he asked, removing her hat so he could run his fingers through her now very messy, flat hat hair.

Frankie looked behind her at the display of chopped veggies and various other ingredients around the kitchen.

"WOW! You really are cooking a meal."

"Yep, why is that so surprising?"

"I don't know; I just didn't expect it, that's all. You're so macho and manly, I guess I just didn't consider cooking to be one of your fortés." Frankie looked back at him; they just smiled at each other.

"How about you take your coat off, sit down with a glass of wine and tell me all about your day, while I make you dinner... dear!"

"Oh, I could get used to this," she said, as he lifted her down from the bench. "All the men I've dated and not one of them ever made me dinner." Sliding her arms around his waist, she squeezed him into a tight hug while he stroked her hair. She looked up at him tenderly, as he brushed hair away from her face.

"So we're dating now are we?" He bent to kiss her.

She felt all twinkly inside; she hadn't really thought about what she'd said. They stopped kissing and looked at each other; she could feel Jack's heart racing.

"I'm sorry, my inside voice, I didn't mean it like that." Frankie was worried her stupid mouth had pushed him too far.

Jack bent down, resting his forehead on hers.

"It's fine, I think I'm okay with dating, as long as I still get my therapy!"

Relief washed over Frankie as they smiled at each other, rubbing noses before they parted.

After dinner - one of the most delicious risottos Frankie had ever tasted - they cuddled on the sofa and talked. It was beginning to feel rather like any other relationship in its early stages; they were truly getting to know each other. No matter how much they pretended this was some kind of 'arrangement', they were headed toward much more together. They agreed that the subject of this being a short-term thing was not going to be discussed any further; what would be would be. They made love on the sofa, then bathed together. In the midst of their love making, she found the back of his neck, underneath those sexy curls, to be quite a sweet spot for him, whilst he discovered that she was extra sensitive behind her ears. Frankie really wanted to try some different things with Jack, but seeing him now more relaxed and comfortable, she didn't want to push it. They eventually fell asleep spooned together.

Chapter 10

As usual, Frankie woke before Jack, but this time she just lay there, enjoying the warmth of his body, his hand cupping her breast; his slow, steady breath across the top of her ear and, of course, that firm part of him that she loved to feel pressing into her back. All too soon, the alarm went off and real life had to begin again. As Jack started to move and stretch, Frankie reached across to switch it off. She turned back to Jack, who had his arms above his head, his eyes still closed. She leisurely kissed him. His stubble needed a tidy up, so he was a bit prickly, but she didn't care; she loved it!

"Good morning. I trust you slept better?" she said. Jack opened his eyes and looked down at her.

"Umm, not surprising, since you made me run two marathons before bed."

"I didn't notice you protesting," she retorted, fondling those crazy morning curls. She thought he was still quite sleepy, but all of a sudden she was on her back and he was on top of her.

"Oh no you don't, I'm making it a rule; there will no therapy before work!" she said, very seriously.

"But I thought this was your favourite time, and it's a shame to waste this," he said, as he rubbed himself against her.

"Tempting; very, very tempting, but if I give in we will both be late. Save it for the weekend, when we're not clock watching." She gave him a quick peck on the nose and pushed him off her, so that she could get up and take a shower.

"I'll break you, Doctor; I will have therapy before work... You'll see." He lay sprawled out on the bed as she left the bedroom, throwing a random piece of clothing at him.

"In your dreams, Mr. Lee, in your dreams."

"Oh you are, you're Breakfast in Bed." He waited for her answer; it only took a moment before she popped her head around the corner again.

"Save Me, San Francisco, Track 10, 2009," she said, smugly, and disappeared again.

"That was an easy one," he said quietly to himself, but he had to confess he wouldn't have known the track number; he just trusted that she was right.

They decided that it wouldn't look good for either of them if they arrived at work together. Jack dropped Frankie off before the hospital, making it look as if she'd walked from the Metro. They were in theatre together again for the day; at least it was Mike's list, so good music and banter were the order of the day, which would be good distraction. The nursing crew was Heather, Alex, and Megan; there was also a surgical registrar and a medical student assisting Mr. Anderson. Frankie had just finished getting the first patient ready on the table when Mike made his entrance.

"Ah! Good morning Dr. Robertson. Might I compliment you on your stunning appearance last Friday? It's about time we had someone show this lot how to dress at these events - no offence, ladies," he said as he nodded towards the female nurses in the room.

"Thank you Mike, I'm flattered... So... which of your patients has a problem that you haven't told me about?" Frankie replied.

She wasn't stupid; he might have meant what he'd said, but there was a definite ulterior motive here.

"Oh! You're pretty and smart!" Mike was laying sterile drapes over the patient with Heather, while talking. "The last case - may possibly have underestimated how complicated it might be after just reviewing his latest scan. Now, where's our music, Doctor? I think we'll start with Save Me, San Francisco."

Frankie and Jack couldn't help exchanging looks, after Jack's comment that morning. In fact, throughout the album, as they listened to the lyrics they discovered just how suggestive eyes could be when the rest of your face is masked.

Heather caught Frankie alone that afternoon, when they were between patients. She told Frankie how delighted she was that Jack had finally moved on and that she was pleased for them both, but she was concerned that Frankie was only around for six months, and then what? Frankie explained to Heather how she understood her concerns and how both she and Jack had decided to not go there yet; it was still early days and they were just planning on enjoying the moment. Heather reassured Frankie that their secret was safe with her; she was quite excited that she was in on it, usually being the last person to know anything. However, she wanted to know one more thing.

"I trust you're making good use of, and enjoying, every inch of that heavenly body?" Frankie grinned.

"I'm working on it, Heather. There's a lot of it, so it will me take some time... And yes, so far it's been very enjoyable, thank you."

Frankie left Heather fanning herself with a packet of sterile gloves.

It was Thursday morning, Frankie wasn't at work that day and Jack didn't need to be in until eleven, so Frankie bent the rules slightly and made sure that his morning glory didn't go to waste. Afterwards, they enjoyed a long, hot shower together, something they hadn't yet done. Needless to say, Jack went to work a very happy man.

Frankie spent the rest of the day at the house. Having decided to take one room at a time, she tackled the living room first, by taking pictures down off the walls and making four piles in the centre of the room: charity, keep, garbage, and sell. Both she and Andrew had decided that they would only take small keepsakes, mainly from their mum; neither wanted furniture, pictures or ornaments. Once she got going, it was fairly easy to sift through everything. She exchanged the odd text with Jack throughout the day; he was acquiring some boxes for her, courtesy of Gary, one of the hospital porters whom he knew quite well. Gary usually took away all the flattened theatre supplies boxes; he made sure several were put to one side so Jack could pick them up on his way out.

She stayed at the house until 7.45 that evening. Jack was working until 8.30 so there was no point in rushing back to the flat. She had given him a spare set of keys anyway, so that she could have her own back. He walked through the door of the flat at 8.55, tired and hungry. All he wanted to do was eat, shower then cuddle up in bed with her. In the morning, they had to make sure all evidence of him staying in the flat was out of sight. It was Carol's cleaning day and Frankie wasn't ready to explain herself yet, though she knew that if he carried on practically living with her she was going to have to come clean soon.

They didn't work together the following day, which made things a lot easier; it meant they didn't feed the gossip queens any new information. Of course it was Friday and Mr. O'Reilly, the

Leprechaun, was in teaching mode. Frankie could tell once the first case got underway that it was going to be a long day; she texted Jack to let him know. He replied suggesting that he go to the gym, check on his flat and pick up some clean clothes for the weekend, before heading back to her flat and letting himself in if she wasn't there.

It was 7.30 before Frankie walked through the door that evening. The smell of Chinese food was the first thing that hit her. Unusually, Hercules didn't greet her; then she noticed the bathroom light on. She peeked around the door to find him sitting in his usual spot on the side of the bath, pawing at bubbles. However it wasn't Hercules that really caught her eye; cascading over the end the bath was the best thing she'd seen all day - curls... thick, dark, damp Jack curls. She got that warm, fuzzy feeling; at the same time Mrs Clit-tor-rus started playing the bongos.
"Good evening. I thought you might want a soak before we eat, after your long day."
Jack didn't move or look around when he spoke.
Without replying Frankie took off her coat, followed by her hat, her messy bob sticking out in all directions, just hovering over her shoulders. She kicked her boots and socks off, then removed her hoodie and threw it on the back of the sofa. *'Time to take your therapy up a notch, Mr. Lee'*, she thought, and he'd handed her the perfect situation on a plate.

Walking slowly and silently into the bathroom she knelt behind him and, with both hands, began to massage his head. She was already very turned on, but touching that beautiful head of hair and breathing in its manly scent made her ache even more. Jack let out a groan, "Oh God, that's good, but shouldn't I be doing that for you?"

"Shhh," she said quietly in his ear, "I swear, I could come just touching you like this."

Frankie glanced down at the bath water and noticed Jack's erection rising out of the bubbles. Her nipples stood to attention, joining in. Slowly she moved around to the side of the bath, gently skimming her hand over his shoulder and down his arm as she went. She stopped with her back to him, crossed her arms in front of her and took hold of either side of her tank top. In one sleek move, she lifted the tank up and over her head, allowing it to fall to the floor. Hercules was quick to jump down and claim it for a nap. While she had her arms up, she gathered up as much of her hair as possible and twirled it into a knot, reaching onto the shelf above the sink next to her for a clip to grip it together. She then began to slide her hands down her body, touching her breasts, still with her back to him. Hearing Jack's breathing quicken behind her, she slid her hands down to her hips, letting them slide into her yoga pants and eased them down. Naturally, being naked underneath, she purposely bent over to remove them. Jack let out a gasp as she stood, running her hands up her smooth legs as she straightened, letting her hands settle on her hips before she slowly turned around.

Jack sat up in the bath to make room for her. It was a large, wide tub so she was able to climb in and straddle him. Facing him, she could see he was nervous and excited at the same time, his hands gripping the curved sides of the cast iron. Frankie ran her hands up his legs before gathering bubbles in her hands.

"Watch and learn, Mr. Lee…," she said, seductively.

Slowly she started rubbing the bubbles over herself, touching her breasts. Jack sat there mesmerized, as if the striptease wasn't enough. This was a woman who knew her body well, knew what she liked, and wasn't afraid to show him. Clearly she was very comfortable and confident touching herself for him, something he had never experienced before. He could feel himself getting harder and knew that at some point he would probably spontaneously come. He was more comfortable with that now and wondered if that was her intention. His eyes continued to follow her hands, her nipples becoming very hard as she started to play with them. Reaching one hand down between her legs, she moved some bubbles to one side, so Jack could see what she was doing, before she took two fingers and slid them inside herself. She continued to pull and tug at her left nipple with her other hand; her eyes were fixed on him, even though he was watching her hands. She slid her fingers out and began to massage herself a little further up between her fair-haired lips. Frankie knew it wouldn't take much; as soon as she started, she saw Jack let out a gasp as he came. It was enough for her to climax too. Once her orgasm began to fade, she gently lay down on top of Jack, who wrapped his arms around her and kissed the top of her head.

"Good evening to you too, now I'm relaxed, thank you," she said, snuggling into his chest hair and he slid a little further down the bath, so that the water covered her.

"I like your idea of relaxing. That was... quite a show," he said, holding her close.

"I take it you enjoyed it then? Were you comfortable watching me do it?"

"Oh yes, I very much enjoyed it; I'm getting much more comfortable with watching. Nothing surprises me with you now and I'm learning that, even though I'm not satisfying you directly, you are clearly satisfied by being with me. That makes me feel good."

"Do you think you're ready to do that for me?"

Frankie looked up at him, she had both hands flat on his chest, with her chin resting on top of them. Jack was using his hands to cup water onto her back.

He looked down at her messy, copper hair clipped up on her head, with damp strands hanging around her face and her neck. Her mascara had smudged a little and her make up was washing off her face to reveal pretty freckles across her nose.

"Say something Jack, have I scared you?"

There was another pause while he continued to study her, still cupping water.

"I just love to look at you. I want to make sure I remember every tiny little detail of your beautiful face."

"You still have plenty of time to do that, and you're avoiding the question."

"I think I'm getting there, okay, but I'm getting very hungry. Let's get out and eat!"

They sat on the sofa, eating a Sainsbury's Chinese meal for two. Frankie wore one of Jack's T-shirts, and only the T-shirt, at his request, while he wore some old sweatpants, no underwear or shirt, at Frankie's. They drank red wine and caught up on each other's day.

"What's the funny little sign in the circle that appears to be on almost all your clothing?' Jack asked, pointing to the hoodie that Frankie had thrown over the back of the sofa. The sign was visible on the back of the hood.

"Lululemon," she replied, matter-of-factly.

"Bless you!" he said, as if she'd sneezed.

"Haha! Lululemon was born in Vancouver; it's very well known across Canada and is now trying to take over the closets of all North American women. It's essentially yoga wear, but a lot of people, like me, just... wear it."

"And wear it well, I must say." He winked at her as he placed his plate on the coffee table. "You do yoga?"

"Oh good God no! I hike, bike, swim, ski, paddle, roller blade, snowshoe, and I have tried to rock climb. I will not tie myself in knots or hum round a candle. 'Strewth!" she exclaimed, imitating her friend's thick Aussie accent. "I would also have to give up meat and eat herbs four times a day!"

Jack was now rolling around on the sofa, laughing so hard that he was holding his abs. Frankie started to laugh at him laughing. She noticed that his gorgeous face, full of laughter lines, lit up the room better than a 220-watt bulb. He had such an infectious laugh.

"Oh sweetheart, that's the funniest thing I've heard in a long time," he finally said, when he was able to compose himself.

"I'm glad I amuse you," she said, smiling, as she bent to put her plate on the coffee table.

Jack took a sip of his wine then, suddenly remembering, he put it down as he swallowed.

"I forgot; Carol left you a note." He got up from the sofa to look for the Post-It that Carol had left on the bench. He walked over to the breakfast bar.

"Here you go, um… She did all the usual stuff and folded the laundry that was in the dryer. Can you let her know if you're going over on Sunday?" Jack read from the note, then put it back on the bench before sitting back down.

"Right, Sunday lunch; I should go, I would like to go, I didn't see them last weekend. It will be two or three hours, is that okay?"

Jack let out a big sigh and tried to give her his saddest face, before reaching forward and pulling her into his lap.

"I don't think we're quite at the stage where I can take you with me yet," she said, looking up into his dreamy eyes and fondling his hair.

"No, not yet, so I'll just have to keep you prisoner in the bedroom that morning and I will expect you to strip for me again on your return." He rubbed noses.

"Oh! That sounds terrible," she replied, "but if that's what I have to do to see my family, I guess I can manage!" She wrinkled her nose for him as Hercules jumped down from the back of the sofa; he knew what would happen next, he'd seen it all before.

The rest of the weekend consisted of a lazy Saturday, most of which was spent in bed, followed by sofa canoodling in front of a movie in the evening. On Sunday, they didn't spend the entire morning in bed, but by the time they finally did manage to leave the bedroom, it was 11.45. Jack went to the gym and checked on his flat, while Frankie went for Sunday lunch. It was the usual family gathering: Thomas, Jen and the kids at Carol and Eric's place; roast beef and all the trimmings. Afterwards, the men vegetated with beer in front of an English Premiership game, and the kids played in the garden with the dog, while the three women cleared up and put the world to rights. Carol and Jen quizzed Frankie about work, the house, and how she was settling back into British life.

"So, have you been out much since you arrived? I can't remember if you still have friends here," asked Carol, as they sat back down at the table with cups of tea.

"None really. Most people have either moved on or we've lost touch, especially since I moved abroad. I attended a charity event from work, but that's it, I'm afraid."

Frankie was sure she hadn't given away even the tiniest hint that she'd spent most of her spare time naked in the arms of her hot new toy boy!

"So…" Carol got up from the table and walked towards the kitchen; she pulled something out of a drawer and turned around, dangling the item. "I was wondering if you knew who was missing this?" she said.

Having just taken a mouthful of tea, Frankie nearly choked. Carol was walking towards her, holding Jack's bow tie. She had a sudden flashback of the moment she'd removed it from Jack's eyes and let it fall. *'Shit!'* she thought, *'we must have left it on the bedroom floor.'* She took a deep breath and swallowed hard before answering.

"Not a clue, but if you find him and he's really hot, can you send him my way? Where did you find it?"

Jen was sat next to Frankie, smirking slightly, trying not to laugh. It was very obvious to her that Frankie knew exactly where the tie was found and to whom it belonged.

"On your bedroom floor, under the bed!" Carol said matter-of-factly; she too was trying to keep a straight face. She could tell that Frankie was hoping the ground would open up and swallow her at any moment.

"Really!" Frankie said, desperate to keep this to herself for a little bit longer. She tried to look surprised and frowned a little.

Carol nodded her head, "Hmmm, really!! I'll pop it back in the drawer; let me know if he asks for it back." She winked at Frankie as she turned back into the kitchen.

The Frankie that everyone knew and loved was never shy, embarrassed, or lost for words. For once, however, she sat there speechless, her cheeks growing hotter by the minute.

Chapter 11

THE WEEK STARTED with a day off for Jack; he was working Saturday instead. He took Frankie over to the house with all the boxes he'd acquired, as they were still piled up in the back of his Mini and there was no way she would get them in the Smart car. She showed him around the house she'd grown up in, talking about her life as the daughter of loving mother and a cold, selfish father. She explained that on the days her father was in the operating room, he would often return quite late at night, well after she and Andrew had gone to bed; they had rarely seen their father during the week. She described how he'd never taken any interest in their schooling, even though he'd paid for them both to attend very good private schools. He'd had no idea who her friends were or what she was interested in; he'd never asked or made any attempt to make conversation with her, or Andrew, about anything. She admitted she'd never understood why he behaved the way he did, and this had led to her having a very low opinion of him.

Frankie had arranged for an antique dealer to come and take a look at the furniture and some other items she thought might be of value, so Jack left her to it for a while to run some errands of his own and go for a workout. Frankie loved the fact that he looked after his body; it was to her advantage so she didn't mind missing him for a couple of hours, and it meant she could focus on what needed doing. He picked her up on his way back that afternoon, by which time it was almost 4.30 and she was tired, hungry, and in desperate need of feeling Jack's firm, naked body against hers.

The rest of their week was fairly straightforward. They didn't actually work together, but often saw each other around. They texted regularly throughout their days, even while eating lunch at opposite ends of the staff room, or in adjacent anaesthetic rooms. The gossip from the charity event seemed to have died down and they appeared to be old news now. They spent their days pretending and their nights close together. Again, on Friday, they made sure that there was no trace of Jack around the flat, so that Carol wouldn't suspect, but they agreed that, if he was going to live there now, Frankie needed to talk to her, and soon.

Frankie was late home again on Friday evening; the Leprechaun had been on a high because he'd just found out he'd been successful with a large grant application that would allow him to do some fairly significant research. Jack had finished early, so he'd decided to cook for them. Once they'd finished dinner, Frankie wanted a soak in the bath, so Jack cleared the dishes while she relaxed, and then he joined her.
"No note from my Aunty Carol today? I presume she's been. I must call her; she'll want to know if I'm going over on Sunday again." Jack was lying between her legs, his back against her front.
"I didn't see a note, but maybe just check I haven't missed it. I dumped all the groceries on the bench when I came in and didn't think to look. She's definitely been today, everything's clean."

'"Okay, well I'll call her tomorrow... Speaking of clean, I think we both are, but I would like to take this into the bedroom, Mr. Lee, and get very dirty again," she said licking his ear.

"Oh, Doctor, you have such a way with words, look, you've made me all hard!"

Jack pulled the plug, stood up out of the bath, and then turned to lift Frankie out. He removed the clip from her hair, enjoying watching it fall down to almost touch her shoulders; he loved the way it stuck out in all different directions. It seemed impossible for them to keep their hands off each other when they were all slippery. They both loved the feel of warm, wet, naked skin. Skipping getting dry, they just enjoyed that feeling together.

On this occasion a long, lingering kiss led to Jack picking Frankie up in his arms and carrying her to the bedroom. He gently laid her down on her back, before lying next to her on his side. Propping his head up on his hand he began to run his hands over her wet breasts, while she ran her hand down his back, then traced across his perfect pecs before playing with his chest hair. Jack's hand was creeping lower and lower, across her ribs, over her stomach, towards her hip and down her leg. For the first time, Frankie noticed, he didn't keep eye contact. He actually watched his own hand glide over her neat little curves. As he moved his hand back over her hip she bent her knees and parted her legs, stopping his hand from travelling back up her body. Immediately he made eye contact with her, knowing what she wanted him to do. She kissed him tenderly and whispered in his ear, "Play with me Jack, I want you to touch me."

His breathing quickened as she licked his ear then whispered again, "It's warm and wet... I know you like warm and wet... Just let your fingers explore."

She moved her hand away from his so she could touch his face, leaving him free to make his choice. He hesitated; she could feel him shaking slightly. Slowly he started to move, his eyes fixed on her. He allowed his hand to slide down until he reached her soft pubic hair, stroking her gently. As he moved his hand further, she let her legs fall a little wider and his fingers found her warm, wet entrance. He stopped for a moment before letting his fingers explore, moving in a circular motion, as he'd watched her do.

"Why don't you slide them inside," she said to him quietly.

He could feel just how wet she was, turning him on, making him throb even more, then slowly and as gently as he could he slid his long, thick, middle finger inside her. Frankie let out a satisfied groan as he felt himself starting to come; he too let out a surprised groan. Placing his forehead to hers, he mouthed the word, 'Sorry'. She kissed him and put her finger on his lips, then slowly began to move her hips so that his finger would glide in and out of her. Understanding her need, he began to do this himself.

"I like that," she said, still touching his face.

He carried on for a little longer. Frankie could tell he wasn't really sure what to do next, so she took the hand that was supporting his head and placed it on her hair. He smiled at her and started to stroke it.

"Slide your finger out and move a little higher up. I'm very turned on, so you'll feel where you need to be."

He did as she said until he touched a spot that made her jump a little. He could feel it was quite prominent, so he instinctively began to rub. He could see she very much enjoyed this, but something told him that it just wasn't the same as her doing it for herself. He stopped.

"I'm sorry," he said as he buried his head into her shoulder.

"Hey! Why? Don't stop!" She turned on her side, so that they were face to face.

"I could tell it wasn't the same as when you do it."

"So what? It felt amazing to have you touch me. I was really enjoying it. I don't want it to feel the same as when I do it, otherwise what's the point?" She was now stroking his hair.

He smiled; she had a point.

"You, Mr. Lee, just need a lot of practice!" She wrinkled her nose for him. "Now, may I have the pleasure of this ride?"

"How can I refuse, Doctor?" He had now relaxed again, and was back in his comfort zone.

Frankie climbed aboard and enjoyed him slowly, before bringing herself to climax as he came again. Afterwards, she lay on top of him, and they drifted off to sleep.

It was becoming the norm that Frankie woke first; even on her days off she was always awake before Jack. He wasn't due into work until twelve that Saturday, so they could enjoy a lazy morning together. It was about 9.30 before she finally decided to get up and make tea. She was stood at the sink, filling the kettle, when she felt warm hands sliding around her bare body and soft, sweet kisses behind her ear. He had quickly learned that this was enough to make her melt. She placed the kettle down in the sink. He began massaging her breasts, which were always more sensitive first thing in the morning. She could feel his huge erection throbbing against her back.

"Come back to bed, I need you right now or I'm going to explode," he whispered into her ear.

"Well, we can't have that, can we?" she replied, "I don't think you'll make it to the bedroom, I think you need to take me right here."

Tilting her head back, he was kissing her neck and playing with her nipples.

He turned her around and lifted her up onto the edge of the sink; she wrapped her legs around his waist and her arms around his neck so she could caress the sweet spot beneath his curls. She was so turned on; she knew that as soon as he entered her, she would explode. Sure enough, as he slid her onto every inch of his glorious, thick manhood, she felt a warm, sweet feeling in her stomach that was building very quickly. She had never enjoyed this position before, but Jack was strong enough to hold her, sliding so deep that he could hit a part that no one else had ever found. Moving slow, but deep, it only took a few moves before they both let go. Jack felt his legs weaken despite their strength, so he perched Frankie on the edge of the sink again. They caught their breath for a moment, foreheads pressed together, looking into each other's eyes.

"Oh... My... God!" Jack panted.
"Oh My Giddy Aunt!" exclaimed a very surprised voice from behind.
They both froze, shocked and wide eyed, foreheads still pressed together before Frankie, who knew exactly to whom the voice belonged, quickly darted her head to the side of Jack's.
"Aunty Carol!" she squeaked, grabbing a tea towel from the bench so she could cover Jack's behind.
Surprised but smiling, Carol stood in the doorway of the flat, holding a large bag of cat food.
"Ahhh don't do that, I've had my blood pressure tablet this morning, I think you could at least let me have a moment to enjoy the view!" Her eyes were scanning the fine figure of a naked man stood just a few feet away from her.
"Aunty!" Frankie knew her aunt well. Carol wouldn't be shocked by what she had witnessed; she would see the funny side of it and want to know... everything!

"Could you just give us a few minutes... maybe?" Frankie asked.

"Absolutely, no problem pet. I'll just pop this down here," she left the cat food next to the door, "and I'll pop back up in a bit with the litter." She gave Frankie a little nod and a wink before shutting the door.

Frankie and Jack looked at each other and burst out laughing.

While Jack was in the shower, there was a knock at the door. Carol made sure this time that she didn't cause any further embarrassment. Frankie had made herself decent by throwing on her yoga pants and Jack's T-shirt from the day before. Frankie opened the door for Carol, and stood holding the latch and leaning against the edge, the sound of the shower faint in the background. Unable to look at her aunt at first, she watched Carol's feet enter the flat, before she looked up. The two women looked straight at each other for a second, then both let out a short laugh.

"He's in the shower," Carol said quietly, pointing towards the closed bathroom door.

"Yeeess, he is."

"Ooooh," Carol said, as she fanned herself with her hand.

"I'll introduce you properly when he has some clothes on!"

"Spoil sport!"

"Where's the cat litter, I thought you were bringing that too?" Frankie asked, looking at Carol's empty hands.

"Oh! Silly me, forgot it, it's in the car. Maybe your 'friend'," Carol made commas with her fingers, "could help me get it, when he's dressed, of course."

Frankie gave her aunt a cheeky little smirk.

Frankie heard the shower stop; she suddenly felt a little nervous for Jack having to walk out of the bathroom with just a towel around him. Carol had made herself comfortable on a barstool.

"Pop the kettle on, love, I might as well have a brew while I'm here. You obviously didn't get the note I left you yesterday?"

"No, I'll be honest I got in from work late, we had dinner and got a little distracted," Frankie became coy as she spoke. "I forgot to check if you'd left one."

As Frankie spoke, the bathroom door opened. Jack couldn't have looked any hotter if he'd tried. His towel wrapped around his hips, a few inches below his belly button, revealing a very sexy line of hair that went all the way down to there... he was all muscle, damp skin, wet curls, chest hair, and... oh, if it weren't for Carol, Jack would have been late for work.

"I'll just go and get dressed," he said as he paused for a second, pointing to the bedroom.

"Can I get you some tea and toast before you go?" Frankie asked.

"That would be great. I'll just be a minute." And he disappeared into the bedroom.

Frankie looked sideways at her aunt, hoping that she wasn't looking, but Carol was looking right at her, wide-eyed, with an *'Oh, do you have some explaining to do, young lady!'* kind of look.

"The kettle...." Frankie said, having completely forgotten what she was doing.

A couple of minutes later the bedroom door opened, revealing a clothed Jack, in jeans and a white, long-sleeved T-shirt that had buttons at the top. He had left them open, revealing some of his chest hair escaping out of the 'V' at the bottom. His hair was still damp and he smelled delicious. Frankie walked towards him and took hold of his hand, walking a few steps into the kitchen.

Carol was still sat on the other side of the breakfast bar, making no effort to take her eyes off him.

"Aunty Carol, I would like you to properly meet Jack," she looked back and forth between them both as she made her introductions, "and Jack, this is my Aunty Carol." She looked back at Carol, still holding Jack's hand.

Frankie knew that this wouldn't be easy for Jack; he was gripping her hand quite tightly. Carol stood slightly and leaned across the breakfast bar, offering her hand.

"Pleased to meet you, Jack. Might I say you look as good in clothes as you do out of them?" Jack took her hand as Carol winked at him.

"Aunty! Please!' exclaimed Frankie, with a little smirk.

"It's nice to meet you too, Carol, with my clothes on, and thank you for the compliment." Jack smiled back at her, squeezing Frankie's hand a little more.

"I'll make tea," said Frankie, letting go of him and turning towards the kettle that was just boiling.

Carol proceeded to do most of the talking, while Jack and Frankie both ate breakfast. It was all small talk; she'd spoken to Lucy, who was well and having a great time in 35 degree temperatures; Isabel had been picked to play field hockey for her school; and Joshua was costing her a fortune because she'd agreed to give him a pound for every goal he scored for his school football team, and so far he'd earned £8!

"So, now that this is all out in the open, I'll expect the two of you for a roast tomorrow." Carol surprised them both by putting them on the spot.

"Um... I hadn't really... thought about it." Frankie genuinely had no idea how Jack would feel about that. "We'll talk about it and I'll let you know, okay?" She was looking at Jack for a sign.

Looking back and forth between the two women, Jack said, "I'm okay with it." He shrugged his shoulders, "It's been ages since I've had a proper home-cooked Sunday spread!"

"Are you sure? You'll be under the spotlight," Frankie warned him.

"Sweetheart," Jack reached around to the end of the bench where Frankie was standing and pulled her towards him. Frankie instinctively put her arms around his waist. He looked down at her and pushed a strand of hair out of her eyes, "After this morning, how could I be any more exposed?" He kissed the top of her head.

Carol sat there, watching this beautiful display of affection towards her niece, from a man she could have only known for a couple of weeks.

"Anyway!" Jack said, lifting Frankie's chin, "As adorable as you are, wearing my T-shirt, with your messy hair, I have to go to work." He started to move off the bar stool and Frankie let go of him.

He grabbed his jacket from the rack, and picked up his keys, wallet, and phone from the coffee table.

"I'll see you tomorrow, Carol." He took Frankie's hand, to get her to follow him.

"Yes, looking forward to it. Have a good day at work, wherever that is!" Carol watched them go out of the door; Frankie looked back at her Aunt who was grinning like a Cheshire cat.

Frankie thought she'd shut the door behind her but it sprung open a little; Carol was able to see them at the top of the stairs. She didn't want to spy on them but she couldn't help it. She was intrigued by the intense chemistry between them. She could see Jack standing a couple of stairs lower than Frankie, so that their heads were at the same height. Frankie's arms wound around his neck; he had his hands all over her, running them up the back of her T-shirt; his T-shirt, apparently. Carol witnessed a very tender kiss that made her feel all soft and gooey inside. She loved Frankie like she was her own, and would have given anything to see her find a decent man to settle down with. She noticed them rub noses when they stopped kissing, and press their foreheads together for a moment before parting. Frankie stayed at the top of the stairs, watching Jack disappear out of the main door. Carol quickly got up and legged it over to the kettle. She was refilling it when Frankie came back in and stood with her back to the door, pressing her lips together in a hard line, waiting for her aunt to speak. Carol looked at her niece very seriously.

"Put your bum on that sofa, I'll make us more tea and you are going to talk. I want to know every little Fifty Shades of detail because you two didn't just hook up last night!"

Frankie didn't say a word; she just did as she was told.

Chapter 12

"HE'S AN ODP, we met on my first day, worked together a couple of times and then got talking at the charity event. We didn't really get along very well at first. I guess you should probably know that he was married. His wife died suddenly two years ago from a subarachnoid haemorrhage. She was twenty weeks pregnant," Frankie explained.

"Poor guy, that's..."

"Pretty tragic, I know."

They both took a drink.

"Aunty, I don't know what it is about him. I felt it the first time we met. I know that sounds ridiculous but there was this..."

"Chemistry?" Carol chipped in to help Frankie out.

"Yeah, chemistry, it's crazy, he makes me feel like I'm sixteen again for God's sake!" Frankie laughed a little, before becoming serious again.

"When I left the charity event that Friday night, I had no intention of pursuing it any further. I called a cab three times and it didn't arrive. He offered me a ride home; said it was on his way, which it wasn't of course, and I asked him in."

"Hell, yeah!" said Carol, interrupting her, "Sorry love, carry on." Frankie laughed.

"He was hesitant, but accepted. When we got up here he wasn't the guy you would imagine. He was so nervous, so scared. He had been together with his wife since he was 18, no one since. He had no idea how to move on and start again. So I'm kinda helping him. 'Therapy' we call it, and 'Distraction' for me. The last two weeks have been the weirdest but the most amazing; I just can't describe it. He's amazing, not just physically – although yes, I'm aware he's gorgeous," Frankie said shyly.

"Can we not go there again, or I'll start having another flush!" Carol was wafting herself again with a cushion. Frankie smiled.

"I feel like I've known him forever. He treats me like no one ever has before."

"What's going to happen in July if this becomes serious?" Carol asked.

Frankie hesitated and looked down at her empty mug, starting to circle the top with her forefinger.

"I have no idea. We started out agreeing that this is an 'arrangement', but I'm falling fast. We're just enjoying ourselves for now, and I guess we'll see where things lead." She didn't look up.

Carol slid across the sofa to sit next to Frankie. Taking the mug from her, she placed it on the coffee table and took Frankie's hands in hers. Frankie looked up at her.

"Pet, you're sat here in his T-shirt and you haven't stopped smiling since I arrived. What I witnessed this morning has gone far beyond any sort of 'arrangement' as you put it. The way he looks at you, he's hooked; and it's about time you had a bit of luck with that part of your life." Carol squeezed Frankie's hands affectionately, pulled her close for a hug, then eased away.

"Am I right in thinking he's younger than you?" she asked cautiously.

Frankie pressed her lips together before answering.

"Yes... he's only 31," she said smugly.

"Frances Ann Robertson!" Carol was wide-eyed, "No wonder you look so tired!"

"Aunty!"

Frankie had known that her aunt would be great about the whole situation. Despite having been very close to her mum, she knew that if it had been her mum walking in on her and Jack, it would have been a whole different conversation. Emily had been a bit of a prude; Frankie assumed that that had stemmed from years of living with her father. Carol was a very open minded person for someone of her generation. She had been a nurse in Accident & Emergency for thirty-five years so there wasn't much that she hadn't seen; it took a lot to shock her.

Jack's shift was one of the busiest Saturdays he'd had in a long time. Despite being really tired when he got home, however, just the fact he wasn't walking into an empty house was enough to give him a second wind. When he walked through the door, the flat was warm and cosy, with the fire on. Frankie was curled up on the sofa, with a glass of red wine and her iPad. Hercules was stretched out on the rug in front of the fire and the glorious smell of cottage pie was wafting from the kitchen. It was like he'd been doing this all his life. After a shower, and dinner, they talked for a while, but Jack was falling asleep.

The following morning Frankie got up and let Jack sleep in; years of crazy hours meant her body clock no longer understood the concept of sleeping in. It gave her a warm, fuzzy feeling to have him sleeping in her bed, while she quietly padded around the flat in his T-shirt with her bucket of tea. Occasionally, she peeked around the door to watch him; the first time he was still lying on his side facing away from her, the way she'd left him. The second time he had turned onto his back, his left leg uncovered; it was long and thick with firm, toned muscle and covered in soft, dark hairs. The sheet was teasing her, not completely covering his hip, a cheeky strip of flesh screaming out to be kissed. She moved away from the doorway, smiling to herself. Hercules was sat on the back of the sofa, systematically washing himself after enjoying a breakfast of salmon paté. Frankie went to join him.

"It doesn't get any better than this, does it, big guy?" she said to him quietly. "How is it possible for someone like me to get so lucky?" Hercules stopped washing and jumped down onto her lap, purring as she began to stroke him.

"I just want to be with him every minute, every day; he makes me feel so... special. And it isn't just the sex, even though it's pretty mind blowing; it goes so much deeper than that, like there's something more, you know? I've never felt like this before... never."

Jack had woken just after Frankie had moved away from the doorway. He sat up in bed with his knees bent, elbows resting over the top, listening intently to Frankie talking to the cat. He wasn't surprised by what he heard - he felt exactly the same way - but it scared him a little to realise that he, too, had never felt like this before. He'd loved Emma with all his heart, but this was different, he too recognised it as something deeper, and so much more intense. How could he ever tell Frankie this; she wasn't staying and she'd made that clear from the start. After rubbing his face with his hands he looked at the clock. It was 10.15 - wow! He must have been really tired. He got up and made his way to the door.

As he entered the living room, stretching, he saw Frankie sat sideways on the sofa with the cat. Hercules jumped down and went over to his radiator. Frankie looked up at Jack, all sleepy, naked, and glorious. Kneeling up on the sofa she rested her arms across the back, her head on her hands.

"Well good morning handsome," she said, admiring the view.

Jack walked towards her, amazed at how comfortable he now felt having her watch him so exposed. Because of her position on the sofa, when he stopped in front of her, she got a full frontal, inches away from her face. Not ashamed to stare, she was admiring him closely when, suddenly, she was looking straight into Jack's eyes. He had dropped down to a crouch and put his hands on the sofa so he, too, could rest his head on his hands.

"Good morning beautiful, thank you for letting me sleep," he rubbed noses with her.

"Well, it was worth it just to watch you rise in front of me."

"Cute... very cute, as are you in my T-shirt, again. With your copper bedhead and your small but perfect cheeky behind teasing me."

"Oh, I think if anyone can be accused of teasing it should be you, giving me an eyeful of candy and then taking it away."

Frankie couldn't help it, she loved those messy morning curls; she just had to fondle them.

"Oh, it's still there, and getting very uncomfortable!"

She wrinkled her nose for him, knowing he would come undone. Leaning in, he kissed her gently, before climbing over the back of the sofa and pulling her towards him. They paused, looking at each other for a moment, while Jack slowly lifted his T-shirt up and over her head, throwing it towards the rug in front of the fire, not taking his eyes off her.

"That's better," he said, " no more teasing, we are now equals."

Jack slid down the sofa pulling Frankie on top of him as they kissed. She had wanted to explore him with her tongue for a while, and decided now would be a good time to see how Jack would respond. As he opened his mouth, she slowly entered, searching for his tongue. To her surprise, he returned the greeting. After a while Jack broke away.

"Ooh, I like," he said, pressing his forehead against hers, "You have a very adventurous tongue, Doctor."

"Oh, Mr. Lee, just you wait and see what this tongue can really do!" Frankie rubbed herself against his hard, throbbing length.

Jack was on the edge, the feel of her full, firm breasts and hard nipples rubbing against his chest; his hands on her firm, little behind, while she glided, rubbing, stimulating herself. This was almost as mind blowing as being inside her; he loved it. He could feel how wet it was making her, and the best part; the anticipation, never knowing when she was going to allow him to slide inside; she had complete control.

After making love, they enjoyed a late breakfast before showering. Time was ticking by and lunch was at one. Jack dressed casually in jeans and a blue and red checked shirt, pulling off a *'smart enough to meet your mother'* look. After drying her hair and applying some makeup, Frankie got dressed while Jack tidied up the kitchen. Even though it was the beginning of March, it was still quite cold, so she decided to wear her dark, skinny jeans with one of her favourite sweaters, a dark wine-coloured, fine, fitted cashmere with a scooped neck; her favourite knee high black boots with an ornate heel; an animal print scarf; and her mother's diamond stud earrings which finished the outfit off perfectly. She walked out of the bedroom.

"Okay, ready when you are," she said, looking around for her phone.

She had her back to Jack when she felt his hands touch her bottom.

"Ohh! Wait a minute... come here and let me look at you." He turned her around in his arms and, holding her hand, pulled back so he could admire her properly.

"Sweetheart, you are smokin'." He couldn't believe how different she could look: red dress, yoga pants, scrubs, and now hot jeans with boots. "Give me a twirl, I have to examine that rear again."

"Jack!" she said, swatting his hand away. "Behave, or I'll have to go change so you can keep your hands off me."

"Baby, you could wear a bin bag and it wouldn't stop me... Come here, I need to smudge those perfect red lips of yours." Pulling her back into his arms, Jack gripped her bottom and kissed her passionately.

"Now then, jeans equals underwear, if I remember correctly!" he said, with raised eyebrows and a hopeful smile.

"That's for me to know and you to find out... later! Now let's go." Frankie handed him his leather jacket, prompting her to decide that her own would be the perfect finish to her ensemble.

"Oh God, you are sooo going to get it when we get back, you bad girl!" he exclaimed, when he saw the jacket on; a plain, short, fitted, smooth leather, with a hidden zip at the front.

Frankie just wrinkled her nose.

Jack insisted on picking up some flowers at Sainsbury's on their way to Carol's. He didn't like arriving at anyone's place for dinner without something to offer the host and Frankie thought that this was incredibly sweet. While they drove the short distance to Carol and Eric's house, Frankie reminded Jack who would be present and what he could expect from the afternoon. She warned him that Carol and Jen would dissect him; Eric and Thomas would talk and watch sport; Joshua would be glued to his DS;

and Isabel, who was nearly 12 and already hormonal, could quite possibly try to elope with him.

As they got out of the car outside the large, semi-detached house, Frankie saw Jack take a big breath in and slowly let it out again. He was nervous, not surprisingly; he not only had to face Carol again, but he was meeting Frankie's family, which was a huge step in any relationship. Frankie waited on the pavement until he joined her. She took his hand and pulled him close.

"Try to relax, they won't bite, I promise!" she said, and he bent down to kiss her before they walked up the driveway.

Unbeknown to them, Jen and Carol were watching out of the living room window, catching the look that passed between them, followed by their gentle, meaningful kiss.

"They're here everyone, now please can we give them some space, okay, he's not on trial!" said Carol, as she walked towards the front door.

"Oh my God, Carol! I see what you mean, he's..." Jen started to comment, but was quickly interrupted by her husband.

"Not nearly as handsome as me, is that what you were about to say, dear?" said Thomas, flashing his wife his best Clark Kent smile.

"No, I'm afraid that's not what I was going to say but, if it makes you feel better, I'll let you think that." Jen rubbed Thomas's shoulder as she passed.

"Hi, come in both of you, let me take your jackets and then we'll introduce everyone in a sec; Eric will get us some drinks started..." Carol's mouth was working overtime; she was so excited that Frankie was with someone.

"Hi, thanks Aunty." Frankie handed over her jacket, as did Jack, who was trying not to look at everyone.

"Oh, for you, Carol," Jack said, nervously handing her the flowers.

"Ahh pet, that's very thoughtful, thanks," Carol went to hug Jack, taking him by surprise, "Oh come here, I'm not letting her have all the pleasure, I think I can have proper hug!"

"Sorry," he said, putting his arms out and hugging her properly, "I'm a little nervous," he whispered as they embraced.

Carol gave his bottom a little tap as she pulled away. "No need, pet," and she winked at him.

He should have been embarrassed then, but there was something about Carol that made him relax.

"Okay, Jack," said Frankie, as she worked her way around the room, introducing everyone, "this is my Uncle Eric, my cousin Thomas and his wife Jen, Isabel, and Joshua," They all smiled and nodded.

"Everyone... this is Jack!" She looked up at Jack, smiling and pulled him close; he returned the gesture, putting his arm around her.

"Is he your boyfriend?" asked Joshua.

They both let out a simultaneous nervous laugh and avoided looking at each other, aiming their gaze at the floor until their heads turned and their eyes met. Jack answered the question without taking his eyes off Frankie.

"Yes... yes, I am." They both smiled slowly at each other before Jack bent to kiss the top of her head.

"Well, who'd like a drink?" asked Eric, to break the ice. Everyone in the room seemed aware that Jack and Frankie had just shared a special moment.

Sunday lunch was an important weekly event that this family shared. Carol was an excellent cook, so it was always a magnificent spread, cooked to perfection, followed by a traditional English pudding of some description. This week it was rhubarb crumble and custard. Eric had grown the fruit on his allotment, and it was to die for. Jack had seconds of everything and Carol was in her element, feeding another healthy appetite. Jack had slotted right into place, like he'd been part of the family for as long as Frankie. She was really proud of him; it couldn't have been easy. When Eric and Thomas invited him to watch the football with them while the ladies cleared up, he wasn't sure that that was the right thing to do; Carol had clearly spent all day in the kitchen. He approached Frankie from behind and slid his arms around her waist, pulling her towards him. He'd done pretty well to keep his hands to himself up until then, but he couldn't help holding her as she was bending over the table collecting dishes. He held her so that they were cheek to cheek, facing the open plan kitchen.

"Would it be okay if I watched the match while you're chained to the kitchen sink?" he asked, swaying her slightly while he hugged her.

Frankie turned her head to face him, fully aware that Carol, Jen, and Isabel, who hadn't taken her eyes off Jack since he'd arrived, or said more than a 'hello' to him, were pretending to get on with what they were doing but were watching intently out the corners of their eyes.

"When you put it like that, how can I say no?" she replied, giving him a quick kiss.

"Let me know if you need me for anything, okay?" He let go of her, and lovingly squeezed her bottom as he moved away, thinking that no one had seen, but they all had. Frankie just smirked at him.

"Oh, Jack, wait a second, pet," Carol called after him, "I think I have something of yours, let me get it." Carol walked towards the kitchen drawer.

"Oh no! I forgot about that." Frankie mumbled quietly to herself, head in her hands, knowing exactly what Carol was getting from the drawer.

"I believe this might be yours?" Carol turned around with Jack's bow tie once again dangling from her hand. She was desperately trying not to laugh, and knew she was embarrassing both of them.

Jack, surprisingly calm, and trying not to smile at the memories it brought back, glanced over at Frankie, who had one arm wrapped around herself supporting the other arm, her other hand covering her eyes.

"Er... yes, I believe it might be mine, thank you." Jack started to reach towards the tie but then Carol spoke again,

"What I don't understand is, why is there a hairclip attached to the end?" Carol opened her hand to reveal the hair clip that Frankie had used to hold the tie in place around Jack's eyes. Frankie couldn't have been any more mortified; she had nothing to lose. She looked up at Carol.

"Use your imagination Aunty, you've read Fifty Shades of Grey!" Frankie said, rolling her eyes.

Jen took a sharp intake of breath. Jack sucked his lips in and bit them hard, to stop an embarrassed laugh from escaping. Carol could only manage two words.

"Oh my!"

Reaching across, Jack took the bow tie, winked at Carol and mouthed 'thank you,' before turning and leaving the room. He didn't dare look at Frankie.

"He's quite the catch! I'm surprised you've managed to leave the flat," Jen said to Frankie, raising her eyebrows.

"Don't you start, it's bad enough that this one," she gestured towards Carol, "found his tie on my bedroom floor and walked in on us yesterday." Frankie was trying to be serious, but it was difficult when Jen and Carol were smirking at each other.

"Oh no!" said Jen, putting her hand over her mouth. "You walked in on them? Do tell."

Carol and Jen proceeded to talk as if Frankie weren't there.

"In the kitchen, I got quite the eyeful, and very nice it was too!" said Carol.

"I bet it was," replied Jen.

"Excuse me, I'm still here, and that's my..." Frankie paused for a second; she found what she was about to say strange but nice, "...boyfriend you two are ogling." Now she was serious.

"Oh pet, come on, we're just having a bit of fun, we're just really happy for you..." Carol put her arm around her niece and gave a little squeeze, "...and only a teeny bit jealous!" Carol smiled up at Jen and then Frankie, who returned the smile as they carried on clearing the dishes.

Jack got on really well with Eric and Thomas; they spent the entire football match giving their own commentary. After the ladies had cleared up and put the world to rights over a cup of tea, Frankie joined Jack in his armchair, cuddling into him. He was so comfortable to lie on; she felt it would be ever so easy to fall asleep, as Jack stroked her hair rhythmically. When they finally left at around 6pm, it had all gone far better than she could have ever hoped for; almost too well.

As soon as they entered the flat, before they even got their jackets off, their lips were locked. Jack lifted Frankie up, sitting her on a bar stool, before breaking their kiss. He wriggled out of his jacket and put it on the back of the sofa. Hercules was trying to get some attention but gave up and headed back to his radiator. Jack took hold of either side of her jacket and pulled her close, whilst she slid her arms around his waist. They looked at each other for a moment before Frankie spoke.

"I have an idea, if you can wait just a little longer?" she asked quietly.

"Okay," Jack replied reluctantly; he had wanted her so badly all afternoon, in those tight jeans and leather.

"Wait here, I won't be long." Standing up off the stool, she let her hand slide around his stomach as she slowly walked away towards the bedroom without looking back.

Jack took his shoes off and hung up his jacket. He was becoming a little nervous about whatever she had in mind but, knowing that so far everything she'd done had eventually led to blowing his mind, he was also quite excited. After about five minutes the bedroom door slowly began to open and his heart started to race again as he sat on the bar stool, anxiously waiting. From the angle he was sat at, he could only see the left hand frame of the door. He saw one hand appear on that frame, and the edge of a leather sleeve.

"Close your eyes, Jack," she said.

"Okay, they're closed," he replied.

Frankie moved to lean her body against the doorframe, where she'd previously rested her hand. Placing her hands behind her back, against her bottom, she seductively angled herself, bending her knee.

"Okay, you can open them and enjoy the view!"

Jack thought his heart was going to thump right out of his chest; he had no idea what to expect. He slowly opened his eyes, looked straight at her, and let out a gasp.

"Problem?" she asked him, running her tongue along her top teeth.

It took him a moment to speak.

"Only in that my jeans are now too tight!"

"Ooh, good! I can do something about that." Frankie pushed herself away from the doorframe and slowly walked over to him, working every step.

Jack was trying to take in her black leather boots; now no jeans, just smooth, pale legs. Her leather jacket zipped half way up to her impressive cleavage, no sweater and possibly no bra. If that wasn't enough for him, she was wearing the sexiest, tightest, smoothest black boy shorts. He had never seen anything so hot in all his life and she was standing right in front of him; she was his for the taking.

Frankie placed her fingers on his abs, just above his jeans. She could see how she was affecting him; he was right, his jeans did look too tight! She considered relieving him of them, so she could watch his impressive erection spring towards her, but instead she decided to play with him a little bit longer, letting her fingers walk up his abs towards his chest, where there was a little tuft of chest hair sticking out of his open-necked shirt. Jack had been watching, following her fingers as they climbed, but was now looking into her eyes as she curled her fingers around his hair. Slowly, she started to unbutton his shirt with one hand. Before he knew it, she was tugging it out of his jeans and the last button was free. Jack was now panting a little. Their eyes remained fixed.

"I was only going to strip down to my underwear for you, then I decided to keep on some of the things you like. I can see that you approve of my choice." Frankie walked her fingers back up his firm abs, all the way to his mouth. When he opened it, she slid her fingers inside, encouraging him to suck them; then she slid them back down his body to the top of his jeans. She pulled him towards her so that he stood up. Before Jack knew it, his jeans hit the floor, her black boot stepping on them, allowing him to step out. She walked behind him, sliding his shirt down his arms, tossing it onto the barstool.

"I think I would like to play in front of the mirror, what do you think?" she asked him, as she slid her hands over his impressive back.

Jack found himself concentrating so hard, willing himself not to come yet; but she was in charge, he had no control.

"I think I'd like that very much. What did you have in mind?" he struggled to ask.

"Oh, you'll see!" However, she knew, before they even got to the mirror, that one touch would undo him. This was exactly what she wanted, ensuring he could then concentrate solely on her.

Stepping in front of him, she slid her hands into his boxers and started to slide them down, bending her knees so she was at eye level with them as they went. He sprung free, almost touching her nose as she passed; she just carried on, even though all she could think of at that moment was how much she'd like to take him in her mouth. When she reached the floor, he stepped out and she tossed them to one side. She placed her hands on the outside of his legs and gently ran her fingers gently up them as her own legs straightened. Once his impressive erection was back at eye level, she stuck her tongue out and slowly licked its length.

"STOP!" Jack shouted, pulling away from her, putting his hands on her shoulders to keep her at arms length. He was gasping, looking down at the floor.

Frankie, a little confused about what had just happened, lifted her arms to his and rubbed them gently.

"Jack I…I'm sorry, I don't understand."

Looking down at her, Jack relaxed his arms and pulled her close.

"No I'm sorry, you took me by surprise...I...I've never had... erm...Emma never..." He struggled even to say it.

"Went down on you?" she looked up at him.

He looked at her, taking in a deep breath, "No, never...and I'm not sure I want you to... yet... Sorry, I'm sorry for shouting at you." He hugged her tight. She hugged him back.

"Listen, I told you to stop me if you were uncomfortable and I'm glad you did. We won't go there until your ready, okay, but you should know, it's something I like to do and it's something I would like to do for you. I think that, when you're ready, you'll really enjoy it. What are you worried about?"

"I'm not sure really, I guess, because I'm quite... big, I don't know how it will feel in your small mouth and I expect it can't be comfortable for you. And what would you do when I come?" Jack sat down on the barstool, so his face was almost at Frankie's level.

"First of all, I already told you I like doing it; it's certainly not uncomfortable. Second, I have a good gag reflex and third, it's a good source of protein!" Frankie explained, running her hands through his hair.

"So you... swallow... it?"

Frankie gave him a sexy smirk and shrugged her shoulders.

"Just think about it, but right now, we have some unfinished business to attend to." She took his hand and led him to the bedroom.

Stopping in front of the mirror, she left him there for a second while she turned a light on. Jack watched her move around the bedroom. She looked so good, he became very turned on again. Once she was stood in front of him, he reached out to the zip of her jacket and slowly pulled it down. He had been right, no bra.

Her breasts fell out in front of him, full and beautiful. As he threw the jacket onto the bed, Frankie turned to face the mirror.

"Stand behind me Jack."

He did as she asked; they looked at each other's reflection. She pressed her back against him as he started to massage her breasts, pulling and tugging on her nipples, making them hard, making her wet and wanting. She pushed her shorts down, letting them fall to the floor, flicking them to one side. She stood there naked, except for her black boots, and Jack couldn't hold on any longer.

"Oh God, Frankie, that looks so hot!" He grabbed her breasts and leaned into her as he came.

"Sit on the floor," she said, as he caught his breath. "I want you to make me come."

They sat the same way as the last time they'd used the mirror, only this time Frankie spread her legs as wide as she could; boots still in situ.

"Look at how wet you've made me Jack; it won't take much, you just have to find my sweet spot." She took hold of his right hand and placed his middle finger in her mouth, making it very moist, and then guided him down between her legs.

"I'm going to watch you in the mirror; I like to see what you're doing to me," she told him, leaning her head into his neck. "Go ahead Jack, make me come."

Somehow his left hand found a breast and slowly, with his other hand he touched her; she was so moist. She moaned as he moved his finger up a little, finding that little bump; this time it was very prominent.

"Jack, meet Mrs. Clit-tor-rus, she likes to be massaged; just circle the tip of your finger over her and she will explode for you... Oh God, Jack, right there, don't stop..."

Jack didn't stop; it was amazing to finally be able to give her as much pleasure as she gave him. The look on her face was of pure ecstasy, and he had done that. He moved his finger down while she was still coming and pushed inside her; she instinctively contracted around it as he moved in and out slowly. He kept doing this until she relaxed.

"I think I might have got it right this time, Doctor," he said, as he removed his fingers and wrapped his arms around her.

"You more than got it right. Believe it or not, you are the first man to have ever gotten that right for me," she replied to his reflection.

"You're just saying that to make me feel good."

"I promise you, I'm not a very good liar; did it make you feel good?"

"It did, very much, can't you tell?" Jack replied, rubbing himself against her back.

"I know exactly what I need to do about that. Straighten your legs, I'm going to straddle you and show you reverse cowgirl!"

"Oooook."

"Don't sound so unsure, I love this position."

'You're a sex addict, Doctor; you love everything!"

"Just do it and trust me...I am a doctor!"

Jack did as she said; she straddled him, kneeling, still facing the mirror, with him behind her as she hovered over him.

"You might have to help me out a little; this position is more difficult for me to ease you inside, just push yourself forward so you're straight."

Jack followed her instructions until he almost entered her. Frankie watched him put himself in position; watching like this always turned her on more.

"You okay?" she asked.

"So far."

He moved his hands so they rested on her hips.

"Okay, I'm going to ride hard and fast."

As she let him enter, he let out a gasp. She moved slowly at first so as not to take him by surprise before she really started moving. Jack slid his right hand round between her legs; he wasn't sure he would be able to concentrate on both giving and receiving, but he wanted to try.

"Oh yeah, Jack," she said, smiling at him.

As she rode him faster and harder, he found he didn't have to move his finger too much; Mrs. Clit-tor-rus was rubbing herself. The feeling was exquisite; the new angle meant she felt different inside. This was the roughest sex they'd had so far; it felt exceptionally raw. Frankie was close to screaming; Jack was panting fast; becoming harder he started to come, almost forgetting about her. Remembering, he started to rub her a little harder, feeling her tighten around him, squeezing him, milking him. She climaxed violently, the orgasm ripping through her.

He leant forward to rest his forehead on her back as she too leant forward, with her hands on her knees. They were both out of breath and sweating.

"You...are...one...hell of... a...cowgirl!"

He was so out of breath he could hardly speak. Sliding his hands down her arms he took hold of her hands, wrapping them around her in a joint embrace. They stayed like that until they'd both calmed down.

"My legs have gone to sleep," giggled Frankie, suddenly needing to move; she had pins and needles in her feet. "Lie next to me on the bed, Jack."

Hauling themselves up, Frankie removed her boots and they lay close together, skin on skin. After a few minutes she spoke.

"Thank you, that was amazing," she started to stroke his chest hair, "What did you think, did you like that?"

"I sure did, but it didn't feel intimate; I like looking at you, kissing you, touching you. It felt a bit raw, like it was just sex... is that okay?"

"Sure, of course it's okay. I just wanted to open your mind. I didn't really appreciate that your experience had been so... basic and mechanical, but I guess if neither of you had anything else to compare it to and you were happy..."

Jack let the conversation die, not wanting to talk about the past now; he was more concerned about the future and whether there could even be one.

Chapter 13

JACK WORKED A regular day shift on Monday; afterwards, he planned to go to the gym and check on his flat. Frankie was determined to make some noticeable progress with the house. She sent a couple of emails, touching base with Andrew and Kayla, and browsed Facebook for a while, over a tea. She walked through the front door of the house at 9.35am. It was a grey day again, leaving her feeling cold and miserable. She fired up the heating, knowing that she planned to be there for most of the day. With the living and dining rooms completed, there were now boxes everywhere; she needed to start moving some of them on. Realising that between the Mini and the Smart car, they were never going to move much themselves, she exclaimed to herself, "Oh bugger it! A skip and a house clearance company are what I need. Who cares, the crazy old fool can afford it."

She walked around the house, talking to herself, looking for a Yellow Pages directory. She found one in the cupboard under the stairs, four years out of date, but better than nothing. After making a bucket of tea she sat down at the kitchen table and waded through the directory, thinking she should look for a gardener while she was at it. Flicking through, she noticed a couple of pages had been marked with Post-It notes. Curious, she turned to them. The first one was a page of plumbers, no big deal, but the second one was for headstones. She sat staring at the adverts - small pictures of graves with ornate, engraved, marble stones at their heads. Quickly, she shut the book and gazed, unseeing, at the cover. Visiting her mum's grave had been at the back of her mind; she hadn't been since the day of the funeral. Frankie started to feel bad that her relationship with Jack had gotten in the way of something so important, something that she should have done long before now. But, did she want to go? Would it be wrong not to go? It wouldn't change the fact that her mum was gone; it would just drag up old emotions. Who knew if that would be a good thing? Her mind raced on and on, posing many reasons to not go. She went outside for some fresh air.

Once she had cleared her head, she was able to carry on. She hired a skip and spoke to three house clearance companies, but failed to find a gardener.
"Oh well, two out of three ain't bad…huh, I think that was a Meat Loaf song," she said to herself, scanning the downstairs, trying to decide what to do next. She looked in her father's study, but there was no way she was in the right frame of mind to tackle that yet, and she needed some of this other stuff out of the way first. She decided to go upstairs.

Her parents' bedroom had, like most of the house, always been a very plain, uninteresting room, lacking in character. There was no colour, or texture, or warmth; it was just the room in which they had slept and dressed. There really wasn't much in the room; a couple of pictures on the wall and a few knick-knacks. She presumed that Patricia had taken whatever her father needed to the home already. So, unless there was anything obvious that should be kept, it could all go. She started by opening all the wardrobes, finding them mostly empty of clothes; obviously nothing of her mum's was left. There were some of her father's suits, shirts, and ties; she decided that he was unlikely to need them again.

While on her hands and knees, emptying the base of one wardrobe, she came across her mum's jewellery box, which had been pushed to the back by an old suitcase. It was a beautifully carved wooden box; she remembered her mum receiving it from her father one Christmas, when Frankie was six, maybe seven. It was heavy but she thought that that must have been the weight of the wood, as jewellery just wasn't something her mother had been into. Pushing it across the carpet, Frankie then sat leaning against the bed with her legs out in front of her. She lifted the box into her lap and slowly opened it.

She was right, it wasn't full of any hidden treasures, some costume jewellery and old coins, no longer in circulation; a string of pearls that Frankie knew was authentic, so she'd need to get them valued; and a small, navy, velvet box. Opening it, Frankie hoped it would contain what she was looking for, and sure enough, it did. She sat looking at the contents, moving them around so that the stones would catch the light. Carefully, she removed her mum's diamond engagement ring and a full eternity ring, putting the velvet box back in the jewellery box. She remembered that, despite the unhappy marriage her mum must have had, she had never once seen her without her rings on. At Emily's request, she had been buried wearing her wedding ring; her father had refused to let Frankie or Andrew keep these other two rings, stating matter-of-factly that, as he had bought them, they were his, end of story! Emily's diamond stud earrings, which Frankie now possessed, had been taken by Carol shortly before Emily died. They had previously belonged to their mother, Frankie's maternal grandmother; Carol had wanted to be sure they stayed in the family.

Frankie just sat there, staring at the rings. They needed cleaning, but they were still beautiful, simple and elegant. Having previously discussed with Andrew the possibility of finding them, they had come to the arrangement that she would keep the engagement ring and Andrew would keep the eternity ring. Either way, neither of these rings would fit Frankie, as her mother's hands had been very petite. She returned them to the velvet box, lay her head back on the end of the bed, placed the box over her heart and closed her eyes, letting out a big sigh.

"Oh Mum, why?" she whispered, "Why you first?"

Neither she nor Andrew had thought it fair that their mother was taken from them when she'd been the one to hold the family together, and put up with their father. They had independently wished it had been him first, something neither was ashamed to admit.

After a few minutes, she moved to put the rings back in the jewellery box. Only then did she notice that the box had a second layer, if she lifted out the tray at the top. Underneath, Frankie found some letters addressed to her mum, and some old photographs. The letters were very yellowed, and on closer inspection she saw that the postmarks were dated between 1968-1970, and that the writing was not her father's. She knew that her parents had met in 1969, so these letters, whatever they were, were written during that time. Although curious, Frankie wasn't emotionally ready at that moment to delve into her mum's past and discover things she'd never known. Putting the letters and pictures back, she replaced the tray and closed the box. She would be taking it back to the flat with her anyway.

That afternoon, the skip was delivered. All the house clearance company representatives with whom she'd made appointments came and gave estimates, and she received a call from the antique dealer who had previously been to value some of the furniture and pictures. Frankie felt it had been a really productive day. She'd now completely cleared the living and dining rooms of junk and had started on her parents' bedroom. By 5.45 that evening she was beat; she needed a shower, some food, and Jack.

Jack too was tired when he arrived at the flat at 7pm. He'd texted Frankie a couple of times during the day, so he already knew how busy she'd been. They chatted about their day over dinner. Whilst clearing away the dishes, Jack nervously started to speak.

"Sweetheart... I... I've had an email from my mum asking... um... asking if I'm still going home for the Easter long weekend," he paused for a second; Frankie carried on washing dishes and didn't look at him. "I'm off all weekend and I... I said some time ago that, because the whole family would be there, I would go too; it's also my sister's birthday."

He stopped drying the plate that was in his hand, put the tea towel on the bench and wrapped his arms around Frankie's waist, resting his chin on her shoulder.

"I haven't seen them since Christmas. I really want to go, but..."

Frankie stopped washing, her gloved hands hung in the water, as she brushed her cheek against his hair, breathing in his freshly showered scent.

"So you should go. It's important you spend time with them. Don't worry about me, it will probably do us good..."

He interrupted her, "No, no, no... You don't understand," he hugged her tighter, "I want you to come with me. I want you to meet them."

Oh no! She hadn't seen that coming; this was getting way too serious, meeting the parents, meeting the siblings, and spending a weekend with them. No, she wasn't ready for that; it was only three weeks away, too soon! She stood at the sink with all these thoughts racing through her mind; she didn't know what to say. Did he not realise that once you start meeting parents and spending weekends with them, you're declaring this relationship serious? She had no idea what to do; she needed to think this through.

Slipping the gloves off her hands, Frankie hugged Jack's arms around her. She was waiting too long to answer him, she could feel his heart beating fast against her back.

"Well?" He kissed her neck.

"Oh Jack, this is all moving way too fast, meeting parents is huge in any relationship; I didn't really expect us to be introducing each other to any family while I'm here. We kinda had no choice with mine. I don't understand why they have to know, or what you'll say to them?" Her voice was quiet and calm but she wasn't sure she was choosing the right words. She really needed more time to think about this.

They stood hugging each other for a moment, before Jack let go of her and turned away. When Frankie turned around to look at him, he had his back to her, running one hand through his hair, his other one resting on his hip. Even in that moment of tension, Frankie admired his physique; she loved the way his shoulders looked when he lifted his arms; even through his T-shirt she could see his bulging muscles. She rested her forehead in her hand. It felt like a long time before Jack spoke.

"I thought that when we'd agreed we were now dating, and you'd seemed happy introducing me as your boyfriend in front of your family, that we were taking this more seriously, you know?"

"Jack, we met barely three weeks ago and, in that time, we have seen each other every day and been apart for only one night; you've just about moved in with me..." Frankie paused; she had no idea why she was getting so emotional about this, but she felt like she was going to cry. Turning to face the sink again, she placed her hands on the bench, shrugging her shoulders. She was really tense, scared about what she might admit to him. Jack went over to her; he wasn't sure what was really going on here, but he knew this wasn't just about meeting his parents. Taking her in his arms, he hugged her close, kissing the top of her head. She would talk when she was ready.

For the next couple of days there was an obvious tension between them. They tried to carry on as normal, and the conversation about Easter remained unresolved. Jack was working a late shift on Thursday but he didn't spend the morning with Frankie, having decided instead to go to the gym before work. Before going to the house that day, Frankie decided that she too needed some exercise and fresh air; some time to think. It was a beautiful day and the weather was definitely improving, so she went for a walk. She had no idea where she was going; she just plugged herself in, hit shuffle, and took off. It wasn't until she was thinking about heading home that she noticed where she was. Walking a little further along Jesmond Road, she saw the entrance up ahead. She felt a strange, nervous pain in her chest; she wasn't sure she would be able to walk past without going in. Suddenly, she found herself standing at the gates. Just the words 'All Saints Cemetery' made her feel sick to her stomach. Five years had passed but she could still vividly remember watching the coffin being slid out of the back of the hearse. She took a deep breath and walked in.

She could only vaguely remember where the plot was; she knew it was at the end of a row next to a very elaborate, marble headstone that marked the resting place of a young girl, maybe about eight years old, she recalled. She meandered along the rows, nervous and sad, noticing the wide age range of people buried there. A ninety year old next to a two year old. Her glance fell across a very worn headstone, which stated that the person had died in 1905, and she thought to herself that there must come a time when you get forgotten about; no longer does anyone visit your resting place, especially when you've been there for over a hundred years. She walked as she read, her music quietly humming in her ears. Beginning to wonder if she had misremembered completely, she finally saw the elaborate headstone of the child ahead. Trying to swallow, she found she couldn't; her mouth was dry and she felt choked. As she walked closer and closer, she became aware that she was trembling. She could feel her eyes welling up but no tears fell. Then she saw the words, the dates, flowers... and her name.

As she stood at the end of the grave, her hand flew up to her mouth and the sobbing began; the tears, the despair and the reality of it, all hit her at once. Putting both hands over her mouth, she shook her head saying, 'no, no, no,' over and over again. She had no idea how long she stood there. Eventually she calmed a little, tears still falling, enough to walk up the side of the grave; it didn't feel right to walk over it. She dropped to her knees when she got to the headstone, and knelt there, looking at the engraved words.

In Loving Memory of a Dear Wife, Mother, Sister, and Aunty
    Emily Jane Robertson
    21st January 1947 - 7th January 2008
    May You Rest In Peace

Tracing the word 'Mother' with her finger, Frankie suddenly started hitting the headstone violently with her side of her fist. Crying loudly, her face flooded with tears, streaking her mascara. She collapsed forwards, her forehead resting on the marble, her hands above her head gripping the edge. She was sobbing uncontrollably, thumping once again with her fist.

"Why did you leave me? WHY? WHY did you leave me? I need you Mum, I need you to help me... Please, tell me what to do... I don't know what to do...."

All the anger, the frustration, the pain, the confusion and the tears that had built up, not just in the previous four weeks, or the last five years, but in her entire lifetime, were finally spilling out of her. It had been a lifetime of needing to feel loved and wanted; a feeling she was now realising was possible, but feared she just couldn't have.

As she knelt, sobbing her heart out, the words of a Train song popped into her head; she searched her phone for the track, 'When I Look To The Sky'. As the song played, she started to calm down, the sobbing subsided and the shaking eased.

'Cause when I look to the sky,
　Something tells me you're here with me,
　And makes everything all right.
　And when I feel like I'm lost,
　Something tells me you're here with me,
　And I can always find my way.'

She looked up, just as the lyrics suggested, feeling slightly stupid that she found this comforting, even though she was alone.

'*And when I feel like there's no one*
  That will ever know me,
  There you are to show me....'

As the song came to an end, she stopped the music and looked back at the headstone, touching the name on it.
 "I miss you so much, Mum," she said quietly.

Having now pulled herself together, she noticed the built-in vase at the base of the headstone was currently empty. Next time, she thought, if there was a next time, she would remember to bring some flowers. She was suddenly overwhelmed by tiredness and hunger. Sitting back on her heels, she glanced one last time at the words, then kissed the tips of her fingers before pressing them against the word 'Mother' and mouthing the words 'I love you'.
 She got up and slowly walked home.

Once back in the flat, she ate some lunch. Time really had run away with her; it was 2.30 in the afternoon. She didn't really feel like going to the house anymore; she wasn't in the mood and she felt emotionally drained. There was something else that she thought she should do, seeing as she was already an emotional heap. She made herself a bucket of tea and placed it on the coffee table. Hercules had been by her side since she had gotten back; it was as if he knew she needed looking after. He jumped up and snuggled next to her on the sofa, as she lifted her mum's jewellery box onto her lap.

"Well, big guy, let's have a look at these letters." She stroked his head and he began to purr.

Opening the box, she lifted the tray out, took hold of the stack of letters and pictures and sat back on the sofa. Firstly, she quickly scanned each envelope; they were all addressed to her mum at her old address in Fenham, the part of Newcastle where she'd grown up. Frankie knew the house; it was where her maternal grandparents had lived.

Behind the letters were some very old photographs of a man, and one of a couple. On closer inspection, even though it was a poor quality picture, she could clearly see that the lady in that picture was her mum when she was young. The man she didn't recognise, but there were half a dozen pictures of him, at least three of which had him dressed in what looked like a military uniform. It was very obvious from the photo of him and her mum that they were a couple. She realised that the letters she was holding must be love letters. Immediately she put the letters back in the box, feeling that it wouldn't be right to read them; they were private and personal. But she was intrigued to know who this man was and why her mum had kept pictures of him for all these years. She slowly turned over one of the pictures of him in his uniform.

Frankie got the shock of her life; the name on the back was Donald Robertson, her father's brother, the uncle she had never known but had heard about. He had been a pilot in the Royal Air Force when his plane went down and he was killed. Frankie didn't remember how or why, but that didn't matter; she was more interested in why her mum had pictures of him, and presumably letters from him, hidden in her jewellery box. She came to the realisation that the only person who would probably be able to answer that for her would be her aunt.

"Oh Hercules, why does everything have to be so complicated? Why does everything in MY life have to be so complicated?" She put the box back together and left it on the coffee table, and then sat back, Hercules curled up on her lap. Her head was starting to throb.

Jack finished work early. It hadn't been a particularly busy day, but he was a little worried about the tension between him and Frankie, so he felt tired. As he entered the flat, he thought it was odd that it was dark; she had said she would be home. About to put the light on, he glanced across the room and saw her sleeping silhouette on the sofa; Hercules curled into the crook of her knees. She had obviously been asleep for some time because it was 7.25 and it had been dark for well over an hour. He decided to switch on the lights underneath the kitchen cabinets, so he could see her better and the main ceiling light wouldn't startle her. Carefully, he hung his jacket and slipped his shoes off, dropping his bag next to them. Hercules was beginning to stir; he got up and stretched in that way only cats can, where they squeeze their front and back legs together, arching their back so they look half their size. He let out a loud meow when he saw Jack and jumped down to greet him. Frankie was still sound asleep.

Walking over to the sofa, Jack knelt on the floor in front of her. The light was just enough that he could see her face. Although sound asleep, lying on her side, Jack could see she looked terrible, make up all smudged and her eyes looked puffy. He was worried she was unwell so decided to wake her. Gently he stroked her hair and kissed her forehead. He didn't usually get much opportunity to study her this closely while she slept. He noticed some faint freckles on her forehead that he'd not seen before. She had small, perfectly shaped ears; he tucked her hair behind one so he could see it better. Her skin was so smooth; she looked like she'd never suffered a pimple in her life. Her soft pink lips were parted slightly; he loved the shape of them, full but not big. He kissed them, oh so gently.

Frankie became aware of being kissed. She instantly knew it was Jack; his kiss was unique. Smiling with her eyes still closed, she started to move and stretch. As she opened them, there he was, right in front of her, their noses almost touching.

"Hey," he said, stroking her hair again, "are you okay?"

"What time is it?" Now that she had come to properly, she was a bit disorientated.

"7.45. We finished early, so I was let out for good behaviour. Are you okay, you don't look good?"

"I'm fine, can't believe I slept so long... what do you mean I don't look good?"

"Frankie, you have puffy eyes and look like a panda! I was worried you were unwell."

She sat up and touched her face, but by now it was too late, it was dried on from all her tears.

"Um, yeah, maybe I'll just go and wash my face, wake up a bit."

She eased herself up off the sofa and disappeared into the bathroom.

When she came out Jack was pouring two glasses of red wine.

"I've no idea if I'm allowed to open this, but I have, because you look like you need it." He set the bottle down and handed her a glass.

"Thanks," she said, as she took a sip and stood looking at the floor.

Suddenly, she couldn't stop them; the tears just came in floods and floods. Jack quickly put his glass down, taking hers from her hand and placing it on the bench before scooping her into his arms and just holding her. He didn't need an explanation; he just needed to be there for her.

It was a few minutes before she calmed down enough to look at him and speak.

"I'm sorry, you don't need this."

"Don't be stupid. Whatever it is, I'm here for you, okay. Now, take this," he handed her the glass of wine, "and come with me." He took her free hand and led her over to the sofa.

They both put their wine down and before Frankie could sit, she was being given a tissue, and pulled into Jack's arms, so he could sit her across him and hold her close. She laid her head on his chest. He smelt of the hospital, but there was also a faint hint of his own scent there. She started to relax a little.

"I really missed you today," he said, as he stroked her hair.

"Me too."

He was wearing his t-shirt with the buttons, none of which were currently done up, allowing tufts of comforting chest hair to soothingly stroke her face.

"Did you go to the house?"

"No." Suddenly wanting to pour her heart out to him, she sat up, turned to face him and began.

"When you decide to emigrate and start over fresh, you always know that one day you'll get a call that will change a part of you forever. My mum was sick for almost eighteen months before she died. I tried to be with her when I could, when I felt it mattered. I visited just before Christmas; she looked so frail and fragile, so sick. The way my father behaved during her illness was selfish and self-centred. It was like he was the only person suffering and losing someone. He would also bring work to the hospice, make phone calls, discuss patients' diagnoses and prognoses in front of Mum; it was very distressing for her. Mum tried to say it was just his way of coping, but I could see his behaviour upset her. The last straw for me was when he arrived one evening when she was eating dinner. She tried to maintain some independence, but she was so weak that even feeding herself was difficult. He walked in, announced the pig of a day he'd had, bent to kiss her while she had a mouth full of food, then walked over to the TV and switched it on. I sat completely speechless; he didn't look at her or me; didn't even say hello."

Frankie paused and swallowed hard, linking her fingers with Jack's.

"The following day I told Mum that if I stayed any longer I would say or do something I would later regret. She was amazing about my decision to leave; she completely understood. We both knew that it was a final goodbye. She made me promise I would continue to be me and not what people wanted me to be. She felt she had missed this opportunity herself by marrying a man she didn't love, but who loved her and wanted to take care of her. I don't think I'll ever understand why she thought he would do that because I never saw any evidence of him doing so at a time when she really needed him to. I left without saying goodbye to my father. Carol told me he asked about me. She told him he'd driven me away, but he never made any attempt to rectify that."

"She lived longer than anyone expected, but when she was finally slipping away, despite the distance, I knew; I didn't need Carol to call and tell me, I just knew. And yet I wasn't there, Jack; I left her when she needed me. A selfish part of me that, I guess, I get from my father, decided that my own life was more important."

Frankie began sobbing again as Jack pulled her towards his chest. He held her tight while she let it all out. After a few minutes she spoke again.

"The last time I was at the cemetery was the day she was buried, until today. I don't know how I ended up there, but when I was out walking, clearing my head... I did. Today was the first time I've visited the grave; I never thought seeing a name on a headstone could be so powerful, so emotional. I miss her so much, Jack; she wasn't the best mum in the world, but she did her best. I would give anything to hug her one last time and tell her I love her."

Frankie looked up at Jack, who wasn't making a sound, just listening, but as she caught his eye she suddenly realised and remembered that he knew exactly how she felt. Slow, silent tears were rolling down his handsome face as he sat staring at her; she sat up and slapped her hands over her mouth, unable to believe she'd been so insensitive.

"Oh my God Jack, I'm so sorry, forgive me please..."

He just grabbed her and pulled her close again; they sat holding each other, until his grip loosened. She pushed herself up slightly so that she could look at him for a moment before speaking.

"I've never met the parents of anyone I've dated; even the long term relationships I've had were never that serious. I've never been part of another family before. We have something very different to anything I've ever had before and it scares me because..." It didn't need saying; they both knew this was a time sensitive relationship. "Well, I don't want to waste any of that time, so if the offer still stands, I would love to spend Easter with you and your family."

Jack remained very still, but a few moments after she'd finished speaking he slowly began to show her his beautiful smile. She reached up with her tissue and wiped away his tears, as he pressed his forehead against hers.

"Thank you," he said quietly, "The offer does still stand; I want to show everybody why I'm so happy again."

Frankie let out a little nervous laugh. Jack continued speaking, "I'm sorry for being a bit of a girl, you made me realise I still have a lot of stuff to deal with."

Frankie lifted her hand to his face, her touch making him shiver.

"*I made your body shiver...*" she said, raising her eyebrows, hoping he knew what she was expecting.

Jack smiled, big and wide, pearly white teeth and everything; a classic Jack smile.

"*And when you took my breath away*," he continued, "Go on then, hit me with it!"

"Okay!" she said throwing her head back and looking at the ceiling, "Brick by Brick; Save Me, San Francisco; 2009; track..." she had to think about it, "8 or 9...maybe... 9, I'll say 9." She looked at him, waiting in anticipation, was she right?

"Pass me your phone, I'll have to check!" he said; she tried to playfully attack him but he was too quick and too strong. They ended up lying on the sofa, him on top of her, kissing with gentle passion. Jack stopped abruptly and looked at her.

"Take a bath with me; we need to wash away the day and start again tomorrow, and, I need to feel your hot, wet, naked body on mine."

"On one condition," she said.

"Name it," he said, curiously.

"I do something first about that long, hard, throbbing lump that is sticking in my hip!"

"Oh Doctor... I thought you'd never ask!"

Chapter 14

BEAUTIFUL, WARMER WEATHER was forecast for the weekend. Jack suggested, due to failed attempts to hire a gardener, that they should tackle the job themselves. Frankie informed Carol that they would miss lunch on Sunday, but that they would pop in for a cup of tea when they were done. They arrived at the house by 9.30 on Saturday morning, and stayed until almost 6. Both very dirty and sweaty, they took a long hot shower together, and then ordered a well-deserved take away. They laughed at the fact it was 9.45 on a Saturday evening and they were both curled up in bed, too tired to even make love.

They carried on with the gardening on Sunday, finishing the front and moving to the back. At around 1pm they stopped for lunch. While Frankie used the bathroom, Jack cleared everything away. When she returned, he wasn't in the kitchen or outside; she found him standing in her father's study, looking around.

"Sorry, didn't mean to be nosey; I just noticed you've tackled every room downstairs except this one," he said.

He was stood with his hands in the pockets of his jeans, wearing an old checked shirt with the sleeves rolled up to just below his elbows. Frankie stood in the doorway looking at him. He truly was gorgeous, tall, dark, and very handsome; and right now he was dirty and sweaty, a very hot and sexy combination that she rather liked. Slowly, she walked towards him, wearing her yoga pants, and a sloppy sweatshirt with a tank top underneath, feeling just as dirty and sweaty.

"It's ok, you're not being nosey. I'm just not ready to deal with what I might find in here." She stood in front of him, running her hands up his abs and onto his chest.

"I think I like this dirty look on you, Mr. Lee. It's very hot."

She started to unbutton his shirt from the top.

"You're pretty dirty yourself, Doctor... what do you say we get absolutely filthy?" Bending his knees slightly, so he could grab her bottom with both hands, he lifted her onto the desk. Continuing to unbutton his shirt, she pulled it out of his jeans and then slid her hands over his bare skin and around his back.

"Thank God for ugly net curtains!" She pulled him towards her as they began to kiss, breaking for a second so Jack could lift her sweatshirt over her head.

Deepening the kiss, he slowly lowered her down onto the desk and slid his hand into the back of her yoga pants so he could feel her bare skin. She was just about to push his jeans down when...

"FRANCES ANN ROBERTSON!" shouted a shocked voice from the doorway.

They both stopped, stunned at having been caught like this for a second time. Simultaneously, they looked sideways towards the door where a tall, thin woman stood in a long black coat, black shoes, a handbag hanging from her forearm, and her hands clasped together in front of her. She had a look of absolute disgust on her face, but didn't take her eyes off them.

"Have you no shame?" the women said sharply, directing it at Frankie.

Jack scrambled to get up, having no clue who this woman was. He buttoned his shirt up so it could hide his very large erection.

"Patricia," Frankie said sweetly, smiling at her as she swung her legs around and hopped off the desk, "How lovely to see you too." She was now pulling up her yoga pants, which had been revealing a little bit too much.

"Really!" Patricia said, averting her eyes slightly while they both sorted themselves out.

"I guess I should introduce the two of you. Jack, this is my father's sister, Patricia," she looked at Jack and then gestured to Patricia and smiled at her. "Patricia, this is my toy boy, Jack; he's making sure I don't get bored while my life is put on hold to do this thankless task." She rolled her eyes around the room as she finished. Jack nearly choked at what she'd just said and Patricia looked like she had swallowed a lemon... whole!

"Can I get you a cup of tea?' Frankie asked her.

"No, thank you, I'm not staying. I saw the car outside and just wanted to be friendly." Patricia, who was a very cold, hard-faced woman, had never been married, and Frankie was sure she was still a virgin.

"Friendly, really?" Frankie said, as she walked past her towards the kitchen, muttering under her breath as she walked, "I didn't think you did friendly!"

Jack heard what she'd said and was now smirking; he went to follow her, but Patricia had the same idea and they almost collided, heading through the French doors at the same time.

"After you," Jack gestured to her to go first.

Patricia just looked at him with her serious, 'sucking on a lemon' face. Not sure what came over him, he winked at her. It caught her completely off guard; she turned and bumped into the doorway before storming towards the kitchen. Jack followed behind her, desperately trying not to laugh as they entered the kitchen. Frankie was leaning with her back against the sink, arms folded.

"I'll head back out and carry on, okay?" Jack said as he passed her, affectionately brushing her hair away from her cheek. "Let me know if you need me." Frankie looked up and nodded as he moved towards the door to put his boots on.

"I see you've wasted no time spending your father's money," Patricia said curtly.

"Excuse me?" Frankie said, surprised; what was she getting at? "Exactly what is that supposed to mean?"

"That monstrosity on the driveway, requesting money to have a company clear the house, employing a gardener..."

Jack was just doing up his second boot when Frankie interrupted Patricia.

"Jack, would you mind hanging around for just a minute? I may need a witness to this conversation," she said, without taking her eyes off Patricia.

"Sure," he replied, standing up and putting his hands on his hips, looking from Frankie to Patricia.

"Okay, first of all, I don't know where you've got this information from; I can only presume you've got some deal going on with the solicitor. Secondly, I'm only doing what we all agreed I would do. I don't know how you expect me to clear a house using a Smart car, when there's over 40 years' worth of junk in it. And thirdly, it's none of your damn business anyway!" Frankie was calm but firm as she spoke. She was so mad that she had agreed to do this as a dutiful daughter, yet this woman, her so-called aunt, couldn't even be civil.

"How dare you speak to me like that! Who do you think you are, turning up here after all these years? Your father needed you and you just abandoned him. Now you think you can take control of his finances and spend whatever you like completing your so-called good deed, even though it's the least you could do for him. Not to mention turning his home into a brothel!" Patricia was almost purple. Frankie couldn't believe her ears; she was lost for words at the garbage that was spilling out of this woman's mouth. Luckily, Jack stepped in.

"That's enough," Jack put his hand up, signalling Patricia to stop speaking, and then pointed his finger at her. "If you haven't got anything sensible to say, lady, then I think you had better shut up. I don't know how involved with all of this you are, but Frankie hasn't mentioned once, in all the time we've been together, that she's seen you or that you've even contacted her. YOU have no idea what she has gone through or is going through! She's completely put her life on hold to make sure a man, who doesn't sound worthy of the title Father, is taken care of for the rest of his sorry life. YOU have no right to come in here, without knocking, and accuse her of using his money. Now, I suggest you leave your key on the table, because you won't be needing it again. Should there need to be any further discussion, it will be done through the solicitor." Jack was calm but assertive the entire time he spoke.

Frankie's eyes darted back and forth between Patricia and Jack as he spoke. She was in awe of Jack; she had tried to stand up to Patricia many times over the years and had never put her in her place the way he just had. This angry Jack was so hot; she thought he might spontaneously burst into flames. She wanted to go up to him and kiss him all over, but opted to wait until they were alone again. They both stood there waiting for Patricia to put her key on the table. Removing it from her key ring, she slid it across the kitchen table towards Frankie, refusing to make eye contact with either of them.

"I'll see myself out," she said, and she turned and walked towards the front door.

They both watched her leave. Once the door shut behind her, Frankie went straight to Jack and wrapped her arms around him tight, resting her head on him. With his boots on, and her only in her socks, she was even smaller against him than she normally was. He hugged her back.

"I'm sorry, sweetheart, if that was out of line, but I couldn't just stand back and watch her accuse you like that; does she have any idea what your father was like?"

"Yes, she does, but to her he was a saint. I sometimes wondered whether if she could have married him, she would have; I know that sounds weird, but she's always thought the sun shone out of his backside, her brother the great surgeon, she never had a good word to say about my mum. You weren't out of line; she needed someone to put her in her place. I'm just glad you were here... Thank you." She raised her head as he looked down at her.

"You're welcome." With intimate affection, he kissed the top of her head, "Now, let's crack on for another hour or so before we go and stuff ourselves with bad things at your Aunty Carol's!"

They turned up at Carol's in a disgusting state and weren't allowed to leave the kitchen. She had baked an amazing chocolate cake and Jack insisted it would be rude not to eat at least two slices. Although Frankie hadn't talked to Jack about the letters and photographs, she couldn't wait to ask Carol about them, and as Jack wasn't allowed to go anywhere else, she had no choice but to ask Carol in front of him.

"Aunty, may I ask you something about Mum? It's just something I found at the house, going back to when she met my father." Frankie and Jack were leaning against the kitchen bench, quite close; Jack had one arm resting on the bench behind Frankie, a cup of tea in his other hand; Frankie stood with both hands on her mug.

"Of course, pet, you know you can always ask me anything. I've always been honest with you; if I can answer your questions, I will." Carol had a feeling she knew what was coming.

"I found Mum's jewellery box at the back of the wardrobe. I was looking for her rings, which you'll be pleased to hear I found," Carol smiled at her, "but there was a tray in the box which I had either forgotten about or didn't know was there. Anyway, I lifted it out and..." Frankie paused and swallowed hard. Jack put his mug down and put his arms on her shoulders, massaging them gently. Frankie looked up at him and gave a smile of appreciation.

"I found some old letters and photographs..."

Carol interrupted her, "Good grief, she kept them after all this time." She was genuinely surprised.

"You know what they are? Who they are from? Who's the man is in the pictures? It's my father's brother, right?" Frankie's heart sank; she wasn't sure she wanted to hear what had gone on with her uncle before her parents were married.

"Come and sit down, love, this is not a conversation we should be having stood in the kitchen." Carol started to walk towards the dining room.

"But what about…?" Frankie looked down at her dirty clothes.

"Don't worry, just don't make a habit of turning up here looking like that!" she replied with a little smirk.

"Are you sure you want me around? I can..." Jack wasn't sure he should be a part of this conversation.

"Don't be silly pet, I wouldn't dare try and separate you two at the moment... anyway, if she sits on your knee it will only dirty one chair!" Carol said, winking at Jack.

He smiled at her. "Okay, I'm not going to argue with that," he said, as he raised his eyebrows to Frankie with a cheeky little grin.

They did just that; Jack parked himself on a chair and pulled Frankie down on his knee, putting his arms around her waist.

"But behave yourself," Carol said, nodding at Jack, "this is a serious conversation, I don't want parts of your anatomy distracting her."

"Aunty!" Frankie couldn't believe how blunt her aunt could be.

"I promise, Aunty Carol, I will make every effort to control myself... if I can." He gave her a wink and his million-dollar smile, without knowing it affected her too. It was clear that Jack was becoming quite fond of Carol and very comfortable.

"Ok, you have to understand that I was at nursing school when all this happened, so I only got snippets of it at the time. Anyway, your mum met Donald first. He was on leave from the Air Force; they met at a dance. Your mum was working as a doctor's receptionist at the time. She was always the quiet, pretty one between us; everybody liked her. She dated Donald during his leave and met your father at some point, as a result of meeting their parents. Of course, your father had just graduated from medical school, and he was quite taken with your mum. Donald returned to duty and they wrote to each other. I happened to take your mum along to a party, can't remember the details, but there were a lot of doctors there and your father was one of them. I think the way you put it nowadays is that he was hitting on her all night. So that's how it all started..." Carol paused for a moment; she was looking at the table, brushing some imaginary crumbs away.

Jack gave Frankie a supportive squeeze. With her hands resting over the top of his, on her stomach, she gave them a little rub in appreciation.

"She loved Donald, it was very clear from the beginning; they were a couple that were meant to be together, but you could see that your father hated it. It was only a few days after he'd returned to the Air Force base again that she got the call that all service wives and girlfriends dread. There'd been an accident, a tragic accident during a normal exercise he had completed many times. He was a good pilot; no one really knew what happened. Then suddenly, she was marrying your father and expecting your brother. She never really loved him, Frankie, but he was willing to take care of her under the circumstances. Very few men in those days would have done what he did."

As Frankie sat listening to her aunt's explanation, she began to realise the enormity of what she was trying to tell her. She suddenly took a shocked breath in.
"Uncle Donald is Andrew's father…" She breathed out quietly.
Carol closed her eyes and bowed her head shamefully at the secret she'd kept. However, when she finally looked up again at Frankie, who was fixed in a jaw-dropped stare, she looked like an enormous weight had been lifted from her shoulders. Carol spoke with relief.

"She confided in me shortly after she realised she was pregnant. We were at the hospital when your father saw us leaving the Obs and Gynae unit. He just took one look at your mum and he knew why we were there. A day or two later he came to the house and asked our father for her hand, without even asking her first. You both probably think that's odd, but that was Nick. I never really understood if he did it because he really did love your mother, or if he did it for his brother. Either way, it was an admirable thing to do, even if it had disaster written all over it."

Jack held Frankie tight, supporting her the only way he could at that moment. He, too, was completely stunned by what Carol had revealed. Eventually Frankie was able to speak. She swallowed hard before she asked Carol to confirm something she already knew.

"I guess Andy doesn't know, but somehow I don't think it will come as a great shock to him." Carol gave an indication that Frankie was right. "I guess if I really think about it, I, we, could have worked this out by the way he treated Andy once my father knew he was gay - but up until then he treated us the same. Why?"

"I think he really wanted to raise Andy as if he was his own - after all, he was his nephew - but he just became more bitter and twisted over the years, because he knew he wasn't Donald. Then Andrew gave him the perfect reason not to try any longer. Your mum tried in the early years, when you and Andrew were young. This probably explains a lot about your childhood. I'm sorry pet, we should have had this conversation long before now, but once your mum passed on and your father became sick, I didn't really think it mattered anymore; it didn't change anything, you know."

Frankie sighed, and spoke.

"Thank you for telling me now. I appreciate you being honest. It's so sad really. I can't imagine marrying someone I didn't love." As Frankie said those words, she felt Jack's heart rate quicken against her back. She continued, "I guess I'm glad she knew love once. It's quite romantic that she kept his letters and pictures, especially after everything that happened. At least she got to keep a piece of him to always love"

"You have to remember, pet, that *you* and Andrew were her world. She did everything possible to make sure you two were happy, and I know for the most part that you were. Don't dwell on it, pet, you've got enough going on at the moment. I'll let you decide when is the right time to tell your brother. Right, you've sat there for long enough now that if you don't get that boy home, I'll have to go and make up the spare room!" Good old Aunty Carol, she could always get a smile out of you no matter what the situation.

Jack rested his head against Frankie's back, sniggering.

"Never mind hiding, that just confirms I'm right! Go on, the two of you, you're starting to smell bad. Look! Even the dog's left the room!"

As they got into the Smart car, Jack leaned over to Frankie and took hold of her chin, looking at her for a long moment.

"Come here, you." He placed a gentle kiss on her lips.

When he stopped, still holding her chin, he rubbed noses and then gazed into her eyes. That was the moment she fell completely; she knew right there and then, but she also knew she couldn't tell him. Like her mum, she thought, it was going to be better to have loved and lost, than to have never loved at all.

Chapter 15

BY THE MIDDLE of March, they hadn't worked together for two weeks. When they did, it always seemed to be on a Wednesday, for Mike's list, with Heather and Alex. On this particular Wednesday the room was quite busy. A student nurse, who looked about twelve, and seemed to have noticed Jack, was working with Claire. Mike had two surgical trainees with him and there was also a medical student hanging around in the corner, looking very green. Mike chose to start the day with Train's California 37 album. There was always a great atmosphere in this room, with good banter, and the list always ran on time. Mike was peering into the cystoscope as the third track finished.

"Okay team, are we up for a little duet this morning?" Mike was obviously in a good mood.

Frankie and Jack caught each other's eye, each knowing the other was smiling behind their masks. The fourth track of the album was a catchy song called Bruises. The rhythm had feet tapping and hands drumming. At certain lyrics, Frankie and Jack exchanged looks; they knew this song well. In fact, it was like that for the rest of the day; they were connecting thoughts through the lyrics. After the album had come full circle again and the last song of the day was coming to an end, Frankie happened to look up at Jack as the words, *'Don't go... I'll show you what it's like to be loved'* played.

It was one of those moments when they felt like there was no one else in the room but them. They broke their stare when Mike spoke.

"When you two have quite finished having eyeball sex over our patient, Mr. Singh, remember him...? Perhaps you would be so kind as to wake him up."

They both looked at Mike and then around the rest of the room. "Just a suggestion, no rush!" Mike continued as he started to remove his gloves and gown.

Despite the team still having their masks on, Frankie knew they were all smiling and sniggering. She thought to herself, as she dragged her attention back to Mr. Singh, that it was getting to the point that they either had to come clean or somehow avoid working together.

Frankie loved it when Jack went into work late and she was off. Even though she woke early, she would just lie there, cocooned in his warm, naked body and thick, strong arms. She would listen to the world going to work outside and smile to herself; his slow, steady breathing in her ear, soft stubble tickling her face and a large, throbbing erection pressing against her back. It was all hers; nobody else's but hers. She pressed her back into him a little more so she could be as close as possible; he stirred, making a sleepy groaning sound, his hand cupping her breast a little tighter.

She was becoming quite moist just lying there, wanting him badly, desperate for him to wake soon. He must have sensed her need. The hand cupping her breast started to massage it, as a deliberate breeze blew over her ear. She smiled to herself. Slowly, his hand moved away from her breast and travelled over her stomach, down her hip to between her legs. Mrs. Clit-tor-rus almost grabbed him and pulled him towards her, but he knew where to go now without any help, and he was getting very good at it. He lay back slightly so he could slide his arm under the pillow they were lying on, and curled it around her, finding a pert nipple to play with. Lying on her side, Frankie opened her legs for him. She was very wet and very horny, he could tell. He was learning to not make her come quickly; he liked to play and tease her.

Jack knew he was on the edge but didn't want to deny Frankie her pleasure, knowing how much she enjoyed it. He slid his fingers out of her and up; she came very quickly, with quiet moans of ecstasy. He didn't wait for her to come down, he gently rolled her onto her front, lay on top of her and slid himself in from behind, keeping his fingers between her legs. This was a position they had just started experimenting with. Jack liked it; they still got to be close, whilst he could take control and still play with her. He didn't need to move much before he came and a second orgasm caused Frankie to tighten around him. He loved that feeling; it sometimes felt so tight that he might get stuck in there forever. This intense morning lovemaking was swiftly becoming his favourite too; they wouldn't say a word until they were finished.

He began to kiss her neck and shoulder; the hand between her legs now moved to hug her.

"Good morning, I hope the wake-up call was to your liking, Doctor," he said in a low, deep, sexy voice, while placing gentle kisses across her neck.

"Good morning to you too, that was my kind of wake-up call, Mr. Lee, but I'm not properly awake, so I think I may need another one."

"You, Doctor, are becoming very demanding." He moved her hair and kissed her behind her ear, knowing it would make her melt.

While Jack was at work, Frankie Face-Timed with Kayla, feeling the need to pour her heart out to her. Firstly, she filled her in about her mum, the letters, her visit to her grave, and of course the fact that Andrew was only her half brother. Then, she updated her on the progress she was making with the house; how Jack was a huge help and she didn't know how she would have done it all on her own. She explained how Jack had fit right into her family and that she would be meeting his at Easter.

"Whoa! Hang on a minute hun; you don't normally meet family, especially this early in a relationship! I need to get all this straight. You're telling me he's pretty much moved in, he spends time with your family, you're about to spend the weekend with his, he's helping you do all the stuff with the house, you're still blowing each other's brains out, and you're leaving in four months... am I missing something here?" Kayla sat on the iPad in front of Frankie, waiting for an answer.

Frankie took a deep breath and looked up to the ceiling.

"I know, don't remind me. I nearly told him I love him the other day, because I do."

Kayla had never heard Frankie talk like this before. She suddenly realised just how serious this was becoming and she needed to help and support her friend, because instinct was telling her that this was not going to be a fairy tale ending.

"Well hun, I guess I'm just going to have come over there and assess the situation myself, before you go and do anything crazy!" Kayla had been waiting for the right moment to tell Frankie her news.

"Oh my God! Did you book flights?" Frankie was so excited. They had talked about Kayla coming over, but she needed to do some overtime first before she could book a flight.

"I sure did, I arrive on May 17th and leave May 24th. It's only a week, I know, but that's all I could get off work."

"Kay that's fantastic! You can obviously stay here, there's a spare room. I'll see if I can take some time but, if not, I only work three days anyway." Frankie was thrilled; she couldn't wait to tell Jack.

"And lover boy, what about him? I don't want to spend a week listening to you two shagging each other senseless!"

"You know me better than that; he works full time and shifts so we'll have plenty of time together and he could always spend a night or two at his place, so we can have some girlie time."

"Yeah right, then I'll have to listen to the 'we've-been-apart-for-two-days sex'," Kayla said, making little commas with her fingers. "Look, we'll work it out. It's still a couple of months away, but I have to say, I'm pretty excited about meeting him. I've never seen you this smitten with anyone before."

Ten minutes after Frankie signed off with Kayla, her iPad was ringing for another Face Time; this time it was her brother, Andrew. She took in a very surprised breath. Unprepared and nervous about speaking to him, she reluctantly accepted the call.

"Sis! You sly old dog, you! Carol tells me you have a man!" Andrew didn't hesitate; he just came right out with it.

"I might have, and I'll kill her!" Frankie was actually relieved that the conversation would be about her and Jack.

"Oh come on, you know what she's like; can't hold her own water sometimes. Well, come on doll, spill it, I want to know everything... I believe he's pretty hot?"

"He might be..."

"Which means he is, come on tell me; you know I'm a sucker for romance and gossip."

"Okay, okay, you're like an old woman!"

"No sweet pea, Angus definitely wins the old woman award." As Andrew was speaking, there was a voice in the background, "I heard that!"

"Where are you, at home? Don't you two have jobs you should be doing?" Angus's face appeared in front of Andrew's; his broad Glaswegian accent started to boom out of the iPad.

"Helloooo darlin', are you aaaalllll right?"

"Yes Gussy, I am, and you?" Gussy was the pet name Frankie gave to Angus, when he'd started dating her brother; no one else used it.

"Oh you know, ca-nae complain, your wee bro' here has made me take some time off, said ah nee-did a wee holiday so he's taking me down to a wee island called Barbados for a week, bit of R'n'R you know?"

"Very nice, lucky you." Frankie thought how amazing it would be to spend a week with Jack on a tropical island, having him all to herself to do with what she wanted, whenever she wanted...

"Anyway darlin', I'll let you tell your wee bro' here all about the new boy...I'll be eavesdropping while I pack, take care." Angus was the female half of their relationship. Frankie loved him to bits; he was like the big sister she'd never had.

"Okay, talk!" said Andrew.

Frankie told Andrew everything. It wasn't worth being selective. They were close and he was going to find out anyway, when he and Angus came to visit her. The only part she did leave out was the fact that she'd fallen in love with him. Andrew wasn't stupid; he knew his sister well enough to read between the lines and work that out for himself.

"So, Sis, where is this going, because down the aisle is not going to be straightforward if you're five thousand miles apart?"

"I know, what will be will be, I guess."

"I don't want to see you get hurt, sweet pea. He sounds wonderful, and so do you. I don't think I've ever seen you like this about a guy."

The voice from the background spoke again, "Except me, remember, she loved old Gussy first and always will." Frankie and Andrew laughed.

"Yes, Gussy, it was always you first. I'll let you be the one to break that to Jack, okay!" She knew that if the time ever came when Jack did meet her brother and his partner, it would be a very interesting and amusing event.

The two wrapped up their conversation with a quick house update. Frankie actually felt like a weight had been lifted off her shoulders, now that the people closest to her knew about Jack. Although apprehensive about meeting Jack's family, she now felt more positive about it and was looking forward to getting to know that side of him. It was nearly 8pm, Jack would be home soon; where had the day gone? She hadn't even made dinner. Deciding to run a bath instead so he could find her naked and wet, she was just sliding down into the wonderful satsuma-scented bubbles when she heard the door open.

Chapter 16

AFTER ANOTHER WEEKEND in the garden to finally finish the job, Frankie's hard work was rewarded with an update from the estate agent. A couple, with a young family, had made a second appointment to view the house. They were very interested but over their price limit. Frankie told the estate agent that if they want to place an offer she would discuss it with her brother, but she couldn't promise anything. With the garden now presentable, Frankie carried on tackling the house; she missed Jack when he was working. He made the process a whole lot easier, way more fun and, of course, they could get up to no good whenever the mood took them.

They had fallen into a routine that would have had anyone believing that they had been living together for four years and not four weeks. Jack continued to use his gym three times a week and check on his own place; a place he wasn't that fond of anyway, so it suited him fine to just pop in and pick up his mail. At work, Heather was still the only person who knew, and even she did her best to pretend she didn't. Of course, Heather being Heather, she couldn't keep her mouth shut all the time, so whenever an opportunity arose to pass comment or ask outright how things were going, she did. All was going just fine until the Friday before Easter.

Frankie and Jack were preparing to anaesthetise the second patient on the Leprechaun's list. Mr. Collins was a 78 year-old man who didn't take particularly good care of himself. Frankie had commented that she could smell him from the elevator, when she had gone to see him pre-operatively on the ward. He was unshaven, had several missing teeth and the remainder rotten, was pretty much bald and weighed approximately 7 stone, if that! Whilst she was checking over the charts before his hernia repair, he had made a couple of suggestive comments, but nothing more than she'd heard before so she just ignored him. He was currently being wheeled into the anaesthetic room, sat up on the trolley.

"Ooh there she is, the lovely Dr. Robertson; going to put me to sleep, she is," he told the theatre porter, who just laughed and wished Frankie good luck.
"Mmm, thanks Jimmy," Frankie said, as he turned and left, smiling at her.
"Hello again, Mr. Collins, I'm relieved to see that you remember me. Let me introduce you to my colleagues and tell you why they are here." Mr. Collins sat smiling around the room at everyone, whilst they held their breath against the foul odour. Jack, who was stood behind the trolley, caught Frankie's eye and waved his hand in front of his face, acknowledging the bad smell. Frankie smirked a little.
"So, this is Jack, he'll be helping me with your anaesthetic today; this is Heather, one of our nurses, she has a student nurse with her who would like to watch, if that's okay? And Marie here is also a nurse; she'll be observing today as part of a course she's completing. Bit of a full house; it's not normally this busy, but if

you're okay with it, we can help these people with their learning." Frankie looked at the old man, who was grinning at all the women.

"Fine by me Doctor, none of them are as pretty as you, mind." He winked at Frankie. Jack had his back to them and cleared his throat; Frankie thought she was going to be sick and Marie burst out laughing.

"Ahh that's sweet, isn't it Dr. Robertson," Heather said, smiling at Frankie. She returned the gesture with one of those gritted teeth smiles, exuding the hidden meaning, *'I'll get you back for that, thanks!'*

"Right then, Mr. Collins, let's get you lying down so we can begin," said Frankie, desperate to put this dirty old man to sleep. She placed his IV without difficulty.

"Okay Mr. Collins, a little injection now, you should start to feel quite relaxed..." Frankie injected the drug into the cannula she'd just inserted into his hand. "Okay?" she asked him.

"Oh yes, Doctor, you know you are lovely, a good looking lass isn't she?" Mr. Collins turned and asked Jack, who looked over at Frankie for help. She smiled back at him without thinking, then quickly caught herself and returned to looking at the patient.

"Are you feeling relaxed yet, Sir?" Frankie asked him.

"Ohhh yes, pet." Frankie could tell the drug was working, as he slurred his speech a little, "Sssssshe's verrrrry pretty iiiiisn't she, vvveeeeery." One minute he was asking Jack the question, and the next he was asleep.

"Thank God for that, dirty old beggar!" said Heather. "He's got the hots for you, Miss Frankie; you never know, he might be worth millions." Heather was raising her eyebrows at Frankie, who was trying to get on with her job.

"I'm pretending I can't hear you so I don't throw up!" she replied to Heather, flashing her a little smirk.

Once Mr. Collins was safely on the table in the theatre, Frankie wiped her forehead with the back of her hand.

"Well Doctor," said Jack, "there's an offer you can't refuse." She knew he had a cheeky grin on his face under his mask. He raised an eyebrow to Frankie, nodding down at Mr. Collins.

She looked back at Jack as she was about to walk into the anaesthetic room. "I prefer a real man!" She winked at him as she walked away. Unfortunately Marie was looking straight at her.

Jack couldn't help but watch her disappear through the door, feeling very satisfied as his eyes met Marie's.

"That was a very suggestive comment. Something you want to share with us, Jack?" Marie was a troublemaker, but she wasn't stupid.

"Even if I did, you would be the last person I would tell," he said to her quietly.

"Now, now children, let's show a little bit of love for the sake of our students. We don't want to look like a soap opera, do we?" said Heather, as she walked between them.

The list didn't run late for a change; Jack was able to pick Frankie up outside M&S at 5.40. She was armed with wine, chocolate, and an Indian meal for two, which she planned on enjoying in that order. Once back at the flat, Frankie declared she was unable to function any further until she had washed away Mr. Collins in a hot steamy bath, with Jack's help, of course. Whilst the bath was running, she fed Hercules and paid him some attention, then they both sank down into the velvet bubbles of blackberries; Jack sat between her legs.

"I think we might have blown it with Marie... sorry," Jack said sheepishly, as he enjoyed Frankie's hands gliding over his chest.

"Don't be sorry, I really don't care, she's not the one bathing with you and washing your heavenly body," Frankie replied, as she licked his ear.

Jack turned his head so he could look at her, wisps of red and gold hair framing her face and an out-of-control palm tree sticking out of the top of her head. Her eyes were so bright against her pink cheeks, and he was sure her lips were only made for him to kiss.

As they lay there, close in the warmth of the water, Frankie noticed Jack was semi-hard.

"Jack," she whispered into his ear, "can I play with you?"

There was a pause before he answered, his breathing quickening.

"Sure," he said, swallowing hard, "I think I'd like that."

"I'm afraid, despite your impressive length, my short munchkin arms won't reach, so we'll have to get out."

Jack laughed and lifted her arm up.

"These are very beautiful munchkin arms and I wouldn't have them any other way!" He kissed her arm all the way down, "But these hands, I think, are my favourite. I love the way they touch me." He kissed the tip of each finger, before slowly standing up, still holding her hand.

He stepped out of the bath and pulled Frankie up, lifting her out. She wrapped her arms around his neck as he carried her to the bedroom, grabbing a towel as they passed the rail. As they entered the bedroom Jack was about to put her on the bed.

"Wait!" she said, "how do you feel about sitting in front of the mirror again?" She looked at him, trying to read his expression; worried she'd killed the moment.

Jack started to slowly smile.

"Okay," he said.

For the first time, Frankie felt he actually seemed relaxed with them trying something different. He placed her down in front of the mirror and she laid the towel on the floor, partly because they were still wet and partly because cleaning the rug afterwards would be very unromantic!

"Lie on your side, I'm going to be behind you; I'll get you a pillow." Frankie reached onto the bed and grabbed a pillow as Jack lay down, placing his arm under the pillow to support his head more.

"You okay? Comfortable?" she asked.

Jack nodded at her reflection, his eyes fixed on hers.

"You look very delicious, Jack, take a look at your amazing body."

He continued to look at her, so she started to let her hands slide over his skin, down over his abs and onto his hips. She gave him a taster by gently letting her fingers skim his now very large erection; he let out a little gasp.

"Watch me touching you, Jack," she whispered.

Taking the length of him in her hand, she stroked him gently, making sure he enjoyed her touch before she slid her hand up and down rhythmically. It didn't take much before he was groaning; as he came, she continued to move her hand in the same rhythm. All the time she watched him in the mirror. She then moved her hand down and cupped him, massaging gently, making him shudder and gasp; continuing her hand gently down his leg and back up over his chest, she then climbed over him so she could lie next to him.

They lay facing each other as Jack leaned forward and kissed her forehead.

"Thank you, Doctor. Is there anything those hands of yours can't do, apart from cook?"

"Toss a frisbee!" Frankie said. Jack burst out laughing; he really wasn't expecting an answer, let alone that one.

"Everybody can toss a frisbee!" he said.

"Not this girl. No idea what happens but it definitely doesn't fly! I know, really embarrassing, promise you won't tell anyone?"

"Sweetheart, you are so adorable, how could I possibly share that moment with anyone. Come here."

He pulled her close and kissed her, exploring her mouth with his tongue.

It was the day before Good Friday. Frankie had approached Helen earlier in the week, asking about a recommendation for a hairdresser and a beautician. She needed to have her hair trimmed before she met Jack's family and she wanted various bits waxed. He had informed her that they would be going out for dinner on the Saturday evening for Anna's birthday. She genuinely had nothing suitable to wear. So, with Helen's help, and unbeknown to Jack, because he was at work until five, she had appointments for her hair and full waxing. Whilst she was at the salon they were also able to squeeze her in for a mani and pedi to finish the job off. Three and a half hours later she stepped out onto Northumberland Street feeling a million dollars! After a quick lunch in the M&S cafe, she started to shop.

When she set out on her shopping spree she had no intention of purchasing more than just a dress for dinner, but she was in the mood to shop. After all, it wasn't every day she met her boyfriend's family and she wanted to make a good impression; especially as she was potentially going to whisk him away from them or break his heart. *'Break his heart'* she thought, is that what she was going to do? That was the reality if they couldn't work this out. She couldn't bear thinking like this. Everything with Jack was wonderful right now; she couldn't dwell on those kinds of thoughts.

After she had reached the point where she couldn't carry any more bags, she caught the Metro back to the flat. She didn't walk through the door until 5.15 that evening; Jack had just texted to say that he was on his way. She dumped all her bags on the bedroom floor and put the kettle on. Just as she was making her bucket of tea, Jack walked through the door with his beautiful smile, topped by hat hair. She went straight to greet him.

"Look at you," he said, holding her at arms length to admire her, "Why didn't you tell me you were going to the hairdresser's?"

"I wanted it to be a surprise." And if the truth be known, she wanted to see if he noticed, and he had, immediately, so he passed the test. "And that's not all I've had done!" she said, with a cheeky little grin, while Jack hung his coat and took off his shoes.

He walked towards her and took her in his arms.

"Oh really, Doctor." He picked her up as she wrapped her arms around his neck; sliding down his body a little, they kissed.

"I only got a mani and a pedi as well; I wanted to look good for you this weekend."

Jack stopped, staring into her eyes, still holding her off the floor. Frankie was playing with his hair.

"Say something, Jack."

"I'm blown away that this is as important for you as it is for me, and you would have looked fantastic just the way you are, but thank you, it means a lot to me."

While Jack showered, Frankie quickly packed her new things; she wanted to surprise him over the weekend, so she made sure he wouldn't see them by packing some of her regular clothes on top. They planned to leave early in the morning, so they went to bed early, and just cuddled up and crashed. It wasn't until the following morning, when Frankie felt Jack's hand travel down between her legs, that he found out what else she had done.

As usual, she had woken first; Jack woke a short time later, knowing she was awake. He loved the fact that she just lay there imprisoned in his arms. Her small frame seemed to fit perfectly into his body, like someone had taken a mould of him in that position and made her to fit. He revelled in the feel of her curvy little bottom against his hips, his throbbing manhood burrowing into her back. He knew how much she loved waking like this and he was beginning to understand why; it really did feel good. Her hair often tickled his face and nose, but he loved the feel of it and the smell; it was like caramel or fudge. He squeezed his hand a little tighter around her breast; they always felt so full in the morning, her nipples soft and warm. His hands were the perfect size for them, and they responded so well under his touch. As he massaged gently she gave a little moan of approval. He slowly let his hand travel down her warm body; she leaned into him, opening her legs for him. As his hands slid over her lips, he stopped in complete surprise; moving his fingers, he explored further. He leant up on his elbow as she gently fell onto her back with a little smirk on her face.

"Lost something, Mr. Lee?" she asked, knowing exactly what he was looking for.

"No, but you have, you're completely... shaved!" His fingers were still exploring the area to make sure there was nothing left.

"Yep, I got a Brazilian; I thought you might quite like it, especially in the mirror. What do you think?"

"I think I need to take a look... right now!"

Frankie laughed out loud. She had known that he would be a little shocked, but she was hoping that it would excite him. She grabbed the sheet he was about to pull down.

"Shut your eyes, we're going to do this properly."

Once his eyes were shut, she got out of bed and stood posing, her hands on her hips, one foot in front of the other, and her knee slightly bent.

"Okay... open!"

Jack opened his eyes wide; his mouth fell open, but then he was very quickly smiling.

"Oh, baby, come here; I really need to examine this more closely!" he said, grabbing her hand.

Frankie climbed back on the bed as Jack moved over, making more room for her. She lay there, enjoying watching him while he looked and touched.

"WOW!" he said, "I've never seen that!"

"Do you like it?" It was clear that he did, but she had to hear it.

"Absolutely! It's very, very sexy; I know you wax pretty close, but I love being able to see all of you."

"You wanted to examine me closely. Now would be the perfect time to use your tongue."

Putting her hand to his face, she turned and kissed him, allowing her tongue to wander.

"Just explore the way your fingers do. I'm pretty turned on, so I should respond well, just try it."

"But what if..." Frankie interrupted him by putting her fingers to his lips.

"No what ifs, just try it; you know me now, I won't be disappointed. I'll get enjoyment out of just watching you."

Jack moved himself down between her legs, taking a moment to enjoy the view; then he slid his hands up her thighs and under each cheek. He glanced up at her for a brief second; she was watching him, her arms above her head. Moving in closer, he could see how wet she was.

"Use your fingers as well, Jack, if you want to and send me through the roof."

Up close, with nothing to impede his view, he could see exactly where he'd been and where her sweet spot was. Releasing his hands from underneath her, he started to play; sliding two fingers inside her, he placed his tongue over *that* spot and began to massage it the way he would with his fingers. He glanced up, noticing she had started to massage her own breasts, pulling and tugging on her nipples. Aroused to new heights, he felt his own release as she climaxed too. Wanting to make it last for her, he quickly crawled on top and entered her, slowly pumping until they both came again, the second time even more violent than the first.

They lay together, breathless, Jack still on top.

"Are you sure you haven't done that before?" Frankie asked him.

"Never, but I promise you, I'll be doing it again!"

Frankie let out a little satisfied laugh and hugged him tight.

Chapter 17

THEY WERE ON the road before noon. Jack texted his mum, to let her know that they were on their way. The roads were quite busy but they didn't get delayed too much; by late afternoon they pulled into the driveway of an amazing old converted barn, in a beautiful small country village on the outskirts of Oxford.

"Looks like everyone is already here. How are you feeling?" Jack asked, concerned that this was going to be overwhelming for her.

"I think I'm okay. Do I look okay?" Frankie was wearing her dark skinny jeans and a new, pistachio-green sweater she had bought the day before.

Leaning over to her, Jack kissed her gently before saying, "You look like the sort of girl I would take home to meet my mother!" He kissed her again, "Come on, let's get this over with, so we can both relax."

Frankie swung a new pair of flat, silver-coloured pumps out of the car whilst Jack waited there to take her hand. Locking his fingers into hers, he led her to the front door. Barely registering what was happening, she realised they were both inside and standing in the hallway.

"HELLO," Jack called.

"We're in the conservatory, come through," the voice of an older woman called; Frankie assumed this was his mum.

As she walked the short distance to the back of the house, Frankie started to feel quite nervous. She hadn't asked Jack what he'd told them about her; it was pretty obvious to most people she was a little older than him, but she didn't know if he had told them how old she was. As all her thoughts raced through her mind, they arrived at a large, warm and sunny conservatory, overlooking a colourful, well-kept garden.

"Hi!" Everybody seemed to speak and move at once. Jack's fingers didn't leave Frankie's; they both held on tight while Jack hugged everyone in turn with his free arm.

Then, all eyes travelled to her. Frankie just stood there, smiling at the faces that filled the room. Jack proudly lifted the hand he was holding; he was beaming, white teeth from ear to ear, when they looked at each other. He kissed her knuckles.

"Everyone, I would like to introduce you to the woman who has completely taken over my life." As he looked at her, she looked back, grinning. "This is Frankie... sweetheart, this is my wonderful mum, Christine; my dad, Bob; my older brother, Anthony; and my younger sister, Anna."

Christine was the first to move and welcomed Frankie with outstretched arms.

"It's lovely to finally meet you, he talks about you all the time; welcome to our home."

"Thank you Christine, I'm glad to finally meet you too; and you Bob." Frankie moved over to Jack's dad to shake his hand. "Nice to meet you."

"You too," said Bob, "we're all excited to meet the woman who has finally helped him turn his life around again." Frankie smiled back at him sincerely, before moving on to Anna and Anthony, who were both equally as welcoming.

"Well, make yourselves at home and I'll put the kettle on. Tea?' Christine asked, as everyone took their seat again.

"Oh yes Mum, there's something I forgot to mention. Frankie keeps Tetley in business, so I hope you have a new box, and you might want to serve it in a bucket from the garden!"

"Hey!" Frankie playfully hit Jack on the arm that was still glued to her hand. "Don't listen to him, Christine, I'm not that bad." Frankie pulled a face at Jack, who took hold of her chin and kissed her in front of his family audience.

Sitting down on a bamboo sofa with big squashy cushions, Jack pulled her in close, unable to let her go; he wanted everyone to see how together they were. Anna went to help her mum, while Bob asked about their journey down. A few minutes later, Christine returned, carrying a large tray full of tea and goodies. Soon they all had a drink and a slice of cake in their hands, everybody sat together, chatting in the bright afternoon sun which was still pouring through the windows of the conservatory.

"So, Frankie," Christine began, "I believe you're from Vancouver?"

"Yes, I've lived there for the last seven years, but I'm originally from Newcastle."

"And you're now a Canadian, is that right?"

"Yes, I became a citizen last year. My roommate and best friend, who is from Australia, arrived in Canada at the same time, so we became citizens together."

"So, do you have both passports then?" asked Bob.

"Yes, I do. Thankfully, I didn't have to give up my British one."

"Wow, I've always thought one would look quite important walking around the airport with more than one passport!" Anna said, admiringly.

"I don't know about important, but I feel very proud and honoured," said Frankie, leaning forward to place her plate on the small bamboo table and pick up her tea.

"Why Vancouver?" asked Anthony.

"The first time I went there was to ski, the winter after I graduated. I had been skiing in Europe since I was five and wanted to go somewhere different. The guy I was with at the time suggested Canada. We went for two weeks, ten days skiing then a few days in Vancouver. I didn't want to leave. So, I just kept going back whenever I could and decided to make it my goal to live there someday. I was at a conference in London shortly before I finished my anaesthesia training, and just happened to be in the right place at the right time. I got talking to the Head of Department; nine months later I was on a plane to start my first Attending or Consultant post and a new life!" Frankie looked down at her mug, "I've never once looked back and regretted my decision, even when my mum was terminally ill."

There was a short uncomfortable pause, before Jack put his arm around her and squeezed her into his side. She smiled up at him and put her hand on his firm, thick thigh, rubbing it gently, as he kissed the top of her head. Bob broke the silence by changing the subject.

"So, what are everyone's plans for tomorrow? I've booked the table for 7.30, but we thought we would have drinks here around 6, taxis at 7." He was looking around the room at everyone for feedback.

"Well, the girls are taking me for a birthday lunch and maybe shopping, so I won't be around much during the day, hope that's okay?" Anna asked.

"I don't see why not, it's your birthday, honey, we'll fit in with whatever works," said Christine.

"I think Dad and I have some plans in the Duke of Wellington, isn't there a game on?" Anthony asked Bob.

Bob was looking a little sheepish; he hadn't discussed this with his wife.

"Well, I'm going to show Frankie around the village; where I went to school, all that stuff that girlfriends like to see," said Jack.

"Okay, sounds like we're all taken care of," said Christine standing up, loading the dishes onto the tray. "Dinner tonight at about 7 if that's all right with everyone. Jack, I've put you and Frankie in the guest room, so you've got your own bathroom and a bit more space. Hope that's okay?" After what she'd seen so far, she was pretty confident it would be.

"Great Mum, thanks," replied Jack, "we'll take our bags up and unpack." Jack shuffled to the edge of the seat and helped put some dishes on the tray, before standing up and holding out his hand. "Come on you."

"But Christine, don't you need some help?" Frankie asked, as she took Jack's hand and stood up.

"No, don't be silly. Please, just get settled in and enjoy being a guest," replied Christine, smiling warmly at her.

Frankie smiled back; Jack was already whisking her away; he wanted her to himself again, just for a little while.

They carried their bags across the upstairs landing to the far end of the house. This felt like a real family home; there were pictures and photographs of all the kids at various stages of their lives covering the walls. Frankie had never known this in the house she had grown up in; her father hadn't liked photographs on display. It was obvious that Jack was part of a very loving family.

The guest room was bright and sunny. The bed was located against the wall opposite the door. There were windows on the two adjacent walls, looking out onto the front of the house and the large back garden. There were doors on either side of the main door, one for the closet and the other entering into a good-sized en-suite shower room. It was all decorated in terracotta and beige tones, making it very welcoming.

"Well, sweetheart, what do you think?" Jack had watched Frankie check out their accommodation with a big grin on her face.

She went to him and slid her arms around his waist, looking up into his sparkling blue eyes.

"I think you have a wonderful family, and I am a very lucky girl to be part of it, thank you." As she finished speaking she began to fall backwards onto the bed, locked in a very passionate kiss. Entwining their hands in each other's hair, there were tongues exploring, teeth nibbling, and legs tangled and then....

"Can you two at least close the door!" Anthony's voice came from a nearby room; they just smiled at each other as Jack stretched his arm out and pushed the door closed.

After some very restrained canoodling on the bed, they unpacked most of their clothes. Frankie managed to keep some things out of sight so she could surprise Jack. He had inquired what she'd bought during her shopping spree and she had been selective in her answer. He had trusted her with the task of purchasing Anna's birthday gift, after discussing ideas with his mum. Frankie had taken the liberty of getting a little something extra from herself.

"Do I need to change for dinner, or am I okay like this?" Frankie asked, as she touched up her make up in the bathroom.

"Get changed? Certainly not!" His head popped around the door. "I'm hoping you're wearing those hot little shorts under there." His wicked grin made him look so young.

"Oh, you are, are you? And what exactly do you plan on doing with me, if I am?" She turned away from the mirror to face him, a large blusher brush in her hand.

"As much as possible!"

"Oh really, and under the roof of your own parents' home!" she replied, as if disgusted with him, then she playfully touched the end of his nose with the brush.

Before dinner, Jack wanted to show Frankie the main rooms of the house. He took her into the living room, where there were many pictures of him as a boy. He held her hand as he explained where they were taken, how old he had been, and recounted all the funny stories. Standing behind her, with his arms over her shoulders, his chin on the top of her head, he tried to explain to her why he had a black eye on the particular school photo they were looking at.

"I was in year 2, so I was seven. I think Ant and I had been up to no good..." His mum overheard when she came into the room.

"Do you not remember, Jack? The two of you had been caught catapulting slugs back into old Mrs. Jenkins' garden," Christine came to stand next to them. "There was this old lady, Frankie, a couple of doors down from us. She was an obsessive gardener and used to throw any slugs or snails she found on her plants over the fence. When those two saw her come out to do an inspection, they would wait on the other side of the fence and catapult them back at her. This particular day she caught them, and Bob heard them answering back and being quite rude to her; he marched them into the house and sent them to their rooms. When he went up to speak to them, Jack was behind the door as Bob opened it. His eye got the full force of the door handle... As you can see, the school photo was two days later!" Christine pointed to the photo.

"Oh yes, that's right, I forgot we used to do that - that was fun!" Jack was smiling and nodding his head as he remembered.

"Cute and naughty even then," said Frankie, tipping her head back, looking at him upside down.

"Thank you sweetheart, I don't think my mother needed to hear you say that!" Jack hugged her tight.

Christine just smirked at Frankie as she left the room.

They all sat around a large dining room table and enjoyed a beef casserole washed down with red wine. The atmosphere was relaxed and Frankie was fitting in well with the Lee family. The conversation flowed as they discussed current affairs and news. Frankie insisted on helping clear away dishes, but Jack was never far from her side. He hadn't been worried about the weekend; he knew Frankie well enough now to know that she could hold her own in most situations. He'd had no doubt his family would like her, but there were two things he had been apprehensive about: the fact that she was older than him, which, it had turned out, they were absolutely fine with; and that she was leaving in July. He wanted to show his family how great they were together and how he felt about her, before that subject was brought up. He was also enjoying the luxury of having her around him all the time, and able to be themselves outside of the flat; it made him really happy.

Once all the clearing up was complete, they retired to the living room for coffee and nightcaps. Jack led Frankie to an armchair.

"Come and sit with me, I need to hold you," he whispered in her ear.

"You're going to get to hold me all night," she replied quietly, although she had to be honest, she couldn't get enough of his affection.

"Son, leave the poor girl be for five minutes." Bob had followed them into the room.

Jack pulled Frankie a very sad face.

"Please?" he mouthed.

"Only if you behave yourself," she whispered with a smirk, knowing what usually happened whenever she sat on his knee.

"Frankie, can I get you a nightcap?" Bob asked, as he made his way over to a large cabinet at the back of the living room.

"Sure, do you have a single malt?" Frankie was making herself comfortable on Jack, with her legs across him.

"Oh Jack, you didn't tell me she was a whisky girl," Bob said, turning around to look at them.

"That's because I didn't actually know." Jack looked at Frankie, who smiled sweetly at him and shrugged her shoulders. He gave her a slow admiring nod.

Moments later Bob handed Frankie the caramel liquid. "So, my dear, let me know what you think of that. Now, a splash of water?"

"Yes, a splash would be good, thanks. What am I drinking?" She held the glass out for Bob to drop in, literally, a splash of water from the jug he was holding.

"This is Ardbeg," he replied.

"Ahh, an Islay malt, my favourite." Frankie said, smiling at Bob.

"I'm impressed," Bob replied, quite surprised. "Now, Jack, what can I get you?"

"Well, it looks like I'm going to have to join you, so as not to be outdone by my better half."

Jack, too, found himself quite impressed and surprised. He suddenly felt that there was so much he still didn't know about her.

"What are we impressed about, Dad?" Anthony walked confidently into the room, closely followed by his mum and sister.

"It turns out that our doctor here knows her whisky!" Bob waved the glass he was holding for Jack in Frankie's direction.

"Oh, well, that puts all of us further down the list, in fact we might as well all go and shoot ourselves now!" said Anna, looking at Frankie, as a roar of laughter filled the room. Anna had not inherited the whisky gene.

They all sat around the living room, classical music playing quietly in the background, small groups of chatter. Frankie and Bob talked whisky while Jack just sat and listened to them. He was enjoying the interaction between the woman he was falling deeper and deeper in love with everyday and the man he had worshipped all his life. Christine, Anthony and Anna were having a separate conversation about Anthony's business. At 10.45 Jack let out a big yawn, for which he apologised; it had been a long day and he needed to sleep. Draining their glasses, he and Frankie said their good nights before Frankie took Jack's hand and led him upstairs. She had bought some sleepwear for the occasion, thinking it only right when she was sleeping at her boyfriend's parents' house, but neither of them could bear having anything between them; it had to be skin on skin. Frankie spooned into Jack and they were asleep in no time.

Frankie woke in almost the same position; she had slept so deeply, which she put down to a couple of glasses of wine and a whisky. As usual, Jack was still sound asleep, so she slid out of the bed and headed for the bathroom. She slipped into the short, black, silky and very sexy night dress she'd bought, with matching silk robe slightly longer in length, and killed the look altogether with a pair of her slouchy, fleecy socks, before heading off in search of tea. The house seemed very quiet, no one appeared to be up and about; but then it was only 7.30 on a Saturday morning. In the kitchen, she filled the old-fashioned steam kettle and sat it back on the Aga stove. She hadn't seen an Aga in years and stood admiring its beauty. Her Aunty Carol had always wanted one; Frankie thought she might need to omit telling her that Jack's mum had one. Finding a mug was easy; they were suspended on hooks under a large crockery rack, and she only had to look in two cupboards before she found the tea. The kettle seemed to boil really quickly; it had a very loud whistle that she scrambled to stop before it woke the entire household.

She was leant over the bench, drinking tea and looking out into the peaceful garden, which seemed to be constantly busy with birds, when she got the fright of her life. Two large, familiar arms were sliding around her waist; she let out a gasp of surprise as she quickly stood up.

"I'm sorry, I didn't mean to scare you. I missed you."

Jack pulled her in close, resting the side of his head against hers. He was shirtless, but brushing over her legs was a soft fabric. *'Oh wow!'* she thought, *'Pyjama pants'*. The very thought of what he was going to look like, naked on top and sexy pj pants hanging around his hips, made her drip with desire.

"You know I don't like to disturb you, and my tea levels were dangerously low," she said, as he started to nibble her neck.

He was warm and firm against her; she was desperate to turn around and look.

"And I always appreciate that. I suppose finding you draped over the bench in this very risqué robe was worth missing you for. Come back to bed with me, sweetheart, I need some urgent therapy."

"You're wearing pj pants, aren't you?" she asked, as he moved behind her ear, making her weak.

"I'm sorry, is that going to be a huge turn off for you? They can be removed very quickly," he said quietly into her ear.

Slowly, she turned around, looking into his eyes, her hands over his chest hair.

"Oh no, Mr. Lee, far, far from it, in fact, if we were alone, you wouldn't make it back to the bedroom... may I?" she asked, as her eyes darted down and back up quickly.

"Be my guest," Jack said, as he took a step back and put his hands on his hips.

Frankie's mouth fell open and her eyes almost popped out of her head. She took him in, working from the top down. Stood before her was all that rippling muscle and flesh she already knew and loved, his messy bed curls were, well… messy. His hands rested on his hips, either side of that 'V' of muscle that men get when they are very toned. Hanging around his hips were green and navy plaid pyjama bottoms; they were loose and baggy, and very, very sexy.

"Breathe, Frankie," he said, with a big grin on his face.

Her eyes travelled back up to his handsome face; she took a big breath in, and then slowly breathed out.

"Bedroom, NOW!"

Stepping forward, she grabbed for his hand and proceeded to walk out of the kitchen, just missing Anna, who was about to walk in. "Morning Anna, Happy Birthday!" Frankie said, as she passed her.

"It would appear my pj's are hot! Happy Birthday!" he remarked, as he shrugged his shoulders at her, as if he didn't understand.

"Too much information, Jack, way too much information!" they heard her reply as they disappeared.

She pushed Jack against the closed door. He stood looking at her while she undid her robe and let it drop to reveal her nightdress.

"Oh baby, and you think I look hot!" Jack groaned, as he looked down at the sheer fabric, which left nothing to the imagination.

Frankie could see just how turned on he was becoming by what he was seeing. She took a few steps backwards towards the bed, leaving Jack paralysed against the door. Sitting down on the edge, she bent her knee giving him an eyeful; then she pushed herself back. Propped up one arm, she beckoned him with her forefinger to come to her.

Without hesitation Jack walked to the bed, let his bottoms drop to the floor, and crawled up to her. She straightened her leg so he could straddle her, and within seconds they were kissing passionately, as he slowly lay down on top of her. Her hands were desperately kneading and grabbing at whatever they could find. He lifted her nightdress; as sexy as it was, it had done its job and he wanted her naked. Once it was removed, he rolled onto his side so he could allow his hand to explore; while his mouth carried on licking and nibbling. He slid his fingers between her legs; she was gasping but trying not to let out any sound. As his tongue circled her nipple, he found Mrs. Clit-tor-rus and began bringing her to climax. Giving her a moment to enjoy, he then pulled her on top of him, knowing she wouldn't need to move much before he would explode. Sliding into place, she slowly rode him, while he used his thumb to continue pleasuring her. Just as he came, she sat right back allowing him to hit that sweet spot that only he could find, and she squeezed him dry while she exploded around him for a second time.

Sated, she lay down on top of him, while they caught their breath.

"Frankie," Jack said, as she rolled off him to lie on her side, curling her leg around his.

"Yes," she said, as she played with his chest hair.

"You still have your socks on!" He let out a little laugh and put his arm over his eyes.

"I believe I do... sorry, they're obviously not the passion killers I always thought they were."

"Sweetheart, only you could make ugly, thick, black fluffy socks look sexy and hot."

They both lay there, tangled and laughing, until the smell of bacon persuaded them to shower and dress.

Jack could have headed downstairs and left Frankie to finish getting ready, but he enjoyed watching her morning rituals. He liked the way she stood naked, and smoothed lotion over her pale, soft skin, followed by a spritz of body mist; a scent he found to be unique to her. He lay on the bed and observed the systematic drying of her gorgeous hair until it was swinging around her neck. She disappeared into the bathroom again, and he must have shut his eyes; a few minutes later her soft lips were gently brushing his as she rubbed his nose with hers.

"Worn you out already, have I?" He opened his eyes to look into hers, "Come on, we'd better show our faces before they start talking about us," she said, "and don't forget Anna's card and present."

"I should imagine they are already doing that!" he replied.

"Good morning to you both... again!" said Anna with a knowing little smirk.

"And Happy Birthday to you, again, little Sis," said Jack, as he let go of Frankie's hand so he could hug his sister and give her gifts.

"Yes, a proper Happy Birthday, Anna," said Frankie, leaning in and saying quietly to her, "Sorry about earlier."

"It's okay, I thought it was quite sweet actually, even if it was my big brother," she replied equally quietly, smiling at Frankie.

They said their good mornings to the others as they moved towards the large, old wooden kitchen table and sat down.

"What do you mean, again?" Bob asked, looking between Anna and Jack, "Did I miss something?"

"Apparently, Jack looked very hot in his pj bottoms. I just happened to be the poor unfortunate soul to witness him being dragged back upstairs," said Anna, matter-of-factly, while opening her card.

Jack had unfortunately just taken a mouthful of his coffee; he started to cough and splutter. Frankie began to pat him on the back, sucking her lips in, trying not to laugh at his obvious embarrassment.

"Well, there's not a lot we can say to that, is there!" said Bob, winking at Frankie.

Frankie shrugged her shoulders.

"What can I say, I've had a thing for men in plaid ever since Braveheart." This made everyone laugh.

Jack had re-composed himself, placed his arm around Frankie, and kissed her head affectionately.

"Adorable," he said to her, quietly.

Chapter 18

AS PLANNED, THEY spent the day together, with Jack showing Frankie around the area where he'd grown up. They passed his schools, where he'd played football, and some of the places he'd hung out throughout his childhood. Frankie was interested and excited to learn about all the things that contributed to the Jack she now loved. Most of all, they both just enjoyed spending time together as a normal couple. They talked, laughed, held hands, stole kisses, and playfully fought. By mid-afternoon it had started to rain lightly, so they decided to retreat into a local Starbucks for coffee. Frankie arrived at the counter first.

"What can I get you?" she turned and asked him.

"Oh! Just a small coffee will be fine, thanks," he replied, directing it at the young girl waiting to take their order, who smiled back at him shyly. Frankie wasn't the jealous type, and it was very obvious that she and Jack were together; she just smiled to herself, thinking *'Hands off lady!'* She also couldn't resist a bit of fun...

"And I'll get a triple grande, non-fat, no foam, extra hot, half-sweet vanilla latte, thanks." She spoke so fast, in her best Canadian accent that the girl just stood there, the paper cup in one hand and her marker pen paused in the other.

"I'm sorry," she finally said, "could you say that a little bit slower for me, please?"

Frankie then repeated her order extra slowly, leaving long pauses between each part of the order. The girl looked at her sheepishly.

They moved over to a table near the pick up area.

"That was a bit mean," Jack said, as they took their jackets off and sat down, "and what was all that sweet hot foam stuff?"

"Sorry, but she was totally checking you out, and I was just ordering the way I do at home," she replied, as she shrugged her shoulders.

"Mmm, was she now..." He leaned back to take another look at the girl.

"Hey, hot coffee over your head could have very nasty consequences!" Frankie reached for his cup, just as her latte was called ready, so Jack quickly got up to get it for her. He looked back and stuck his tongue out.

"You American girls can't have anything straightforward can you, it's got to sound fancy and expensive!" he said, as he placed the drink down in front of her.

"Oh, you'll pay for that, Mr. Lee, just you wait." She took a sip of her coffee while Jack sat grinning, rubbing his hands together.

They arrived back at the house around 4.30.

"I think I'll take a shower," Frankie said, as she started to undress.

"Come here first." Jack reached out to grab her wrist; she was stood in her bra and jeans.

"No, because I know what this will lead to, and you're in my bad books," she replied, resisting him, but as usual his strength allowed him to get his own way.

"No it won't, I promise. I have something for you," he said, taking her in his arms. "Sit on the bed and close your eyes." He let go and she sat down.

"Okay, you win... it's Easter, so it had better be chocolate or you can consider yourself discharged from therapy." As she spoke, she felt his lips on hers, placing a gentle kiss.

"Shut up and hold your hands out, and no peeking till I say," he said.

She smiled, doing as he asked, and felt a box being placed on her upturned palms.

"Okay, you can open them."

Frankie stared down at a chocolate egg in a clear plastic case, with the words *'To my sweetheart at Easter'* written in white icing on the front. She let out a little laugh and looked up at him.

"Well Mr. Lee, you got lucky!" she said.

Jack crouched down, bringing himself to her level.

"Why don't you open it," he prompted her.

The weight of the box suggested that this was not just an egg, so she went ahead and carefully lifted it out of the plastic box. She paused for a second and looked at him.

"It feels heavy, so I'm guessing there's not just a packet of chocolate buttons in there," she said.

Jack just smiled back at her, "Well, open it and find out."

The egg separated easily; inside was a box with the name of a Newcastle jeweller that she recognised; a jeweller whose shop she had passed a few times and stopped to admire all the beautiful shiny things in the window.

"Oh my God, Jack! You shouldn't have done this." She was stunned and she hadn't even opened the box yet.

"Just open it, will you. I wanted to get you something special that you could wear tonight." He was anxious for her to see his gift.

She slowly opened the box, letting out a gasp when she saw the contents: a delicate, white gold bangle with two small hearts entwined together; one was diamond encrusted.

"Do you like it?" he asked.

Frankie gazed, speechless, into the box, with her hand flat over her heart.

"It's... it's... it's beautiful Jack, thank you!" She flung her arms around him and kissed him hard. "I love it!" she said, as she pressed her forehead against his and rubbed his nose.

"You're welcome. It's a long time since I've bought anything like this. I just wanted to give you something special. I'm glad you like it."

"It's a good job I had the same thought, although my gift is not nearly as shiny I'm afraid. Okay, your turn to sit on the bed with your eyes closed."

They both stood up and swapped places. Jack closed his eyes.

"It had better be a Porsche or you'll be finding your own way back to Newcastle!" he said.

"Haha... Okay, hold your hands out."

Jack felt a gift bag being placed in his hands.

"Okay, you can open," she said.

Jack took a deep breath before he looked. Intrigued, he opened the bag and pulled out the gift wrapped in delicate tissue paper. He gave her a look that said *'You shouldn't have done this'* as he carefully unwrapped his gift. Then, after putting the tissue paper to one side, he held up a smart, navy waistcoat.

"I wasn't sure if it was something you would wear, so I can take it back if you don't like it. I thought it would suit you, something you can wear smart or just with jeans. I thought it would suit you," Frankie repeated; he hadn't given her a reaction yet.

"I love it!" he said, as his smile erupted, "I shall wear it tonight. Thank you!" He pulled her in close and kissed her. "Can I shower with you?"

"No, we'll end up in there for hours... I will be worth the wait, though, I promise." She gave him a peck on the nose and headed for the bathroom. Jack fell back on the bed, smiling, with his eyes shut.

Frankie was still in the bathroom with the door closed when Jack informed her he was ready and would see her downstairs. She was just putting on her new dress, and then she would be joining him. She walked into the living room just before six.

"Good evening, my dear," said Bob, handing her a glass of champagne, "you look lovely."

"I love your dress," said Anna, "that colour really suits you."

"Thank you. Jack assured me I needed to dress up, so I treated myself to something new."

Anthony, who was choosing music, nodded and raised his glass in her direction to acknowledge her. The unmistakable sound of Enya began to fill the room via small, wall-mounted speakers.

"Jack and Chrissy are just fixing some nibbles," said Bob to Frankie. "Now, tell me, what's the golfing like over your way?"

As Jack walked out of the kitchen, with a plate of appetisers in one hand and a glass of bubbly in the other, he looked across the hallway into the living room and stopped dead. Frankie was stood talking to his dad about something that was making him laugh; lifting her left hand to tuck her hair behind her ear, so her simple diamond stud caught the light. She was wearing an elegant, short-sleeved wrap dress in an unusual colour, somewhere between lilac and light grey. As his eyes travelled down her, he noticed nude legs with grey, animal print, low-heeled shoes.

She raised her hand to sip her drink and her bangle caught his eye. Suddenly, he felt fingers underneath his chin, pushing it up, and heard his mum's voice.

"Close your mouth honey, and breathe for me."

As Christine walked away from him, she turned and winked; this simple exchange between them told him that he wouldn't have to tell her how he felt. She was his mum; she just knew.

A starving Anthony relieved him of the plate as he entered the room. Frankie looked up at him as he approached. She was already smiling, but the sight of him made her absolutely beam... His lovely dark curls, freshly trimmed stubble, a light blue shirt, beige chinos, and his new waistcoat. She put her arm out as he walked towards her, slipping it around him when he got near.

"Well I must say, you look rather dashing, Mr. Lee," she said.

Jack hung his arm over her shoulder and bent down to whisper into her ear.

"And you, sweetheart, look positively radiant. Once again you've left me speechless." He kissed her neck as Bob interrupted them.

"Right, well, when these two lovebirds have finished, I would like us to raise our glasses and wish the birthday girl many happy returns of the day."

Lifting their glasses, they all sang out a chorus of 'Happy Birthday'.

Anna then surprised everyone by raising her glass, looking at Jack, and speaking.

"I would also like to propose a toast, to the woman who has put the smile back on my brother's face. We've missed it."

"Hear! Hear!" said Bob.

Jack looked down at Frankie, who felt a little self-conscious at being singled out.

"I'll definitely drink to that," he said as pulled her closer, bending to kiss her.

They arrived at The Purple Onion restaurant a little merry. Bob insisted on sitting between his daughter and Frankie, while Christine wanted the chance to sit between her two boys. This created a perfect boy/girl arrangement around the table, but it meant that Jack and Frankie ended up sitting opposite each other. Frankie thought this was good; she got to enjoy looking at him throughout the evening, and he would have to keep his hands to himself. Little did she know, Jack had similar thoughts about being able to look at her as much as he wanted.

The food was excellent, the wine flowed, and the conversation was easy and amusing. Relaxing over coffee, they were exchanging funny work stories. When it got to Frankie's turn, Anthony said, "Oh, this is going to be a tough one for you, Doctor. You must have so many to choose from."

"Yes, but not many I can tell in front of my boyfriend's parents, whom I've only just met!" she replied. Everyone laughed.

"Oh come on, give us one of your best ones. Mum and Dad don't shock easily," Anthony pleaded.

Frankie looked around the table at everyone waiting in anticipation.

"Oooo-kay", she sat forward, picking up a teaspoon from her cup and saucer, "when I was in my final year as a Registrar - funnily enough, at the Infirmary I'm now back at - I anaesthetised a very nervous woman in her forties; can't remember what she was having done. Everything went well, but she was slow to wake up so we wheeled her to recovery with her breathing tube still in, breathing spontaneously. Suddenly, she woke up with a look of absolute horror on her face, so my ODP quickly handed me a syringe to deflate the cuff. The woman was grabbing at the tube herself, desperate to get it out, which is quite understandable; I'm sure it feels pretty uncomfortable. Anyway, as we pulled it out she let out this big gasp and said..." Frankie composed herself for a second before doing an impression of the her patient, "Dave, Dave, take it out, you know I don't like it!"

This caused some gasps before everybody dissolved into fits of laughter. Christine was the first to compose herself enough to speak,

"Oh, the poor woman! I bet she was mortified... what did you do?"

"Nothing, she just lay back and completely crashed out after she said it. I did have a little difficulty speaking to Dave afterwards though," Frankie admitted, to further laughter.

Declining the offer of nightcaps once they were home, they headed up to bed while everyone else retired to the living room. Jack guided her though the bedroom door as their lips met. He gently touched her face, her neck... His hands were travelling everywhere, while he kissed her with hungry passion. She could feel him growing hard against her. Sliding her hands under his waistcoat, she pulled at his shirt in search of firm, bare flesh to touch; he was kicking his shoes off and trying to find the opening of her dress,

"Sorry," she said, as she broke the kiss, "it's a fake wrap, it will need to come up and over."

A slow, sexy smile appeared across Jack's face, as his hands travelled down her back and over her bottom. He stopped there and gathered up the dress, slowly lifting it; she raised her arms and it was off. As it hit the floor, Jack looked down and his mouth fell open as his eyes widened. Placing her hands on her hips, she posed seductively for him.

"WOW!" he gasped.

She was wearing a silver-grey basque that was completely see-through. As his eyes travelled down, he noted the suspenders holding up her stockings and the tiniest triangular thong barely covering her. The icing on the cake was the fact that she was still wearing her heels.

"You can either unwrap me or just lose the thong, I don't mind which," she said.

"I think I like the idea of just losing the thong, but..." he replied, looking at the item in question, puzzled.

"But you're wondering how? Let's just say, if that's the way you want me, then I won't ever be wearing it again!" She raised her eyebrows, hoping he would catch on to what she was suggesting.

"Seriously... you want me to rip it off?" He was shocked and now very turned on.

She moved towards him, allowing her hips to sway more than usual. Sliding her hands under his waistcoat, she removed it in one move.

"I think that will be your quickest option because, looking at you right now, you're not going to be able to wait until I'm naked," she said, as she undid his shirt.

He slid his hands around her bare cheeks and squeezed them slightly, before taking hold of the shoestring straps of the thong.

"Go on Jack, all that working out, you don't want a teeny little thong to get the better of you... and it will really turn me on," she urged, whispering the last comment. As soon as the words were out of her mouth, he ripped the strings.

Unbuttoning his chinos, she pushed them to the floor along with his boxers; he sat on the bed removing them, along with his socks. Pushing himself back on the bed, she climbed on top and teased him for a moment. She rode him slowly, knowing he was on the edge, but the sight of her on top of him, still in the basque, excited him too much; he couldn't hold on. As he came she stopped moving and squeezed him hard.

"Oh, God, I love it when you do that!" he said with a gasp.
"I want every last drop, Jack, because I want the next one to last a very, very long time." She bent to kiss him as he relaxed.

The following morning Frankie managed to extract herself from underneath Jack. It was 7.40 on Easter Sunday and she needed tea. Quietly, she put on Jack's shirt and boxers, along with her slouchy socks, before leaving him to sleep; she couldn't help turning to watch him for a moment. He was lying on his side, facing her, with his arm under the pillow. His messy bed curls were melting over the pillow, his mouth slightly open; for the first time she noticed his long, thick, dark lashes sweeping along his eyelids. She wanted to lean over and trace every well-defined muscle and name them, to see how many she could remember. Smiling to herself, she crept out of the room.

Christine was also up; she was stood at the kitchen sink washing whisky glasses when Frankie walked in.
"Oh! Good morning," Frankie stopped in the doorway. "I didn't expect anyone else to be up. "How are you this morning? Did you guys stay up much longer?" she asked, as she made her way to the kettle.
"It's just boiled," Christine nodded towards the kettle, "would you be a love and make me a strong black coffee?"
"Oops! I guess that answers my question. Do you need me to whisper too?" asked Frankie, speaking quietly.
"Cheeky! I only ever drink that much when all the gang are here, so I'm blaming you lot," Christine replied, moving away from the sink and drying her hands on a towel. Pulling the edges of her toweling robe together to keep herself decent, she sat down at the table.

"There you go, maybe a couple of Tylenol or sorry... um... Paracetamol will help?" Frankie asked.

"I beat you to it, had two before I came downstairs."

Frankie smiled and sat down with her tea.

"You two were awake late, your light was still on when we came to bed at whatever ridiculous time that was!" Christine looked across at Frankie with an *'I know what you were doing'* sort of look.

Frankie let out a little laugh as she played with her thumbs on the side of her mug. After a moment she spoke."Yeah! Well, you have a very demanding son and... He's pretty irresistible!" She looked up at Christine with a smirk, took a drink of her tea, then said, "Did I just say that out loud?"

Christine let out a laugh as she looked down at her mug and started to trace the pattern on the handle. "It's lovely to see him so happy. We were beginning to think that he would never move on. This - the two of you - has all happened very quickly, but somehow it all seems very comfortable. He's always been a loving boy but for him to openly show affection the way he does with you is new to us. However, as a mother, I can't help but have concerns for where this is all going, you know, once you have to go back to Canada."

Christine looked up at Frankie, who noticed she had eyes the same shape and colour as Jack's; her hair was greying but it had once been dark, like Jack's. Frankie took a sip of her tea before answering, "Christine, I was honest with him from the beginning and told him I wouldn't be staying in the UK. We came to an agreement that we would just have some fun, but I think we're both realising that this is more than just fun. I'm going to be brutally honest, in case you have any reason to think I am using Jack... I have never felt like this about anyone before. You have a wonderful son, Christine, he's kind, loving, caring, considerate, funny, I could go on and on about him."

"I appreciate your honesty, but it doesn't answer my original question," Christine spoke seriously. Frankie could feel her eyes start to fill; she was fighting not to cry, suddenly feeling quite choked. Swallowing hard, she composed herself, taking a couple of deep breaths.

"I just don't know. I can't stay. I have a job and an apartment, and a life that is 5000 miles away. A life I've worked hard to build. I can't just give that up, but I don't want to give up Jack either. We keep saying what will be will be, while trying to enjoy the time we have. Believe me, when I got off that plane in January, I was the most miserable person on the planet. I just wanted to get the job done and get back to my life. Never, in my wildest dreams, did I think I would..." Frankie hesitated, realising she needed to be honest with herself, and not just Christine, as she whispered, "find love."

Christine put her hands over Frankie's and rubbed them. Frankie looked up at her. Christine didn't say anything; she didn't need to. She just smiled sadly. Frankie did the same.

It was a beautiful, sunny Spring day, so they all decided to go for a walk along the river. The dirt path was only wide enough to fit two abreast, and they fell into pairs naturally as they got talking. Jack and Anna led, followed by Christine and Bob, with Frankie and Anthony bringing up the rear. Frankie was interested to know more about Anthony's business and life in Manchester. She knew Manchester well, having attended medical school in Liverpool; she had often gone to concerts, enjoyed nights out and shopped in the much larger, more vibrant, neighbouring city. Anna was glad to finally have her brother on his own; there was so much she wanted to ask him about his new-found happiness.

"So, tell me, who asked who out? Was it at work? How do you manage to work together? It must be strange, with her being a doctor? What are...." Anna couldn't stop herself; she linked his arm and wasn't going to let him go until she knew everything.

"Hey! Slow down," Jack replied. He was close to Anna, always had been, and he wanted to be honest with her. He took a deep breath before he began.

"I can't explain it, but I knew there was something between us the very first time I met her, which was only very briefly. I was caught up with Emma's anniversary so I wasn't very friendly, but she played on that, and even made me laugh when it was the last thing I felt like doing. You know there'd only ever been Emma right?" He looked down at Anna, who nodded.

"Well, you know the charity event we have every year." Again, Anna nodded. "She turned up looking nothing like I'd seen her at work. At first I didn't know it was her, I just kept seeing the back of this red dress and then... There she was in front of me, all slinky, in heels, with that beautiful hair. I had no idea even what colour her hair was until I saw her that night. God, Anna, she looked stunning! I honestly thought a woman like that wouldn't be interested in me." He paused and looked at Anna, who smiled up at him.

"Anyway, as nervous as I was, I bought her a drink and we danced... then, she left."

"Oh!" said Anna, disappointed.

"'Oh!' indeed, but, she was standing outside, still waiting for her taxi, when I left, so..."

"Oh, please tell me you gave her lift?" Anna was squeezing his arm tight.

Jack looked down at her and let out a short, sharp laugh.

"You did, you did... sorry, keep going."

"When we got to her place, I was practically shaking when she asked me in, I didn't expect to be that way. She was honest and told me she wouldn't be staying beyond July; it was just supposed to be a bit of fun, you know what I'm saying... But whatever was there from the beginning was just too intense to ignore." Jack stopped talking and was looking down at his feet while he walked. Anna squeezed his arm again.

"You're in this right up to your neck aren't you?"

"Yep! And falling deeper and deeper every day." He rubbed his free hand over his face.

"She's lovely, Jack. I can see by the way she looks at you that the feeling is mutual. I hope you can work something out; you look good together."

"Me too, sis... me too."

They kept on walking.

Easter Monday morning, they were packed and ready to leave by mid-morning, realising they would probably get snarled up in holiday traffic and not wanting to be too late home as they were both back to work the following morning. They said goodbyes to Anthony and Anna in the kitchen; Christine and Bob followed them out to the car.

"Thank you for a wonderful weekend, Bob, it was lovely to spend time with you," Frankie said, as she hugged him.

"Ditto, my dear. Take care of yourself and hope things continue to go well with the house, etc.," Bob replied.

"Thanks, I'll let you know."

In the meantime Jack was hugging his mum. "Thanks Mum, for everything. This was huge for me and I know I can't have been easy for you." Jack hugged his mum tight. When he pulled away from Christine she took his face in her hands and said,

"I'm just so glad to see you so happy again. You know where we are if you need to talk, okay?" Christine replied, trying to convey to Jack that she was aware that this wonderfully romantic situation could end in heartache.

"I know. I'll keep in touch."

Christine kissed her youngest son, before they all swapped over.

"Thanks Dad, look after that back of yours and lay off the golf for a bit, maybe."

"Yes, yes, I expected the lecture from the doctor, not you. Come here, and give your old man a hug." Bob pulled Jack towards him and patted him on the back, quietly saying, "It's great to see you smiling again, son."

"Christine, thank you so much for a lovely weekend and for being so welcoming." Frankie had been apprehensive about the whole thing and now, as she was leaving, she was wondering why she had thought it would be such a big deal.

Christine put her arms out to hug her. "You are so very welcome. Keep him smiling for me, will you?"

"I'll do my best." Frankie smiled at Christine before Jack took her hand and led her to the car.

There was a lot of waving as they drove away in Jack's Mini. Frankie looked over at Jack after they'd turned out of sight.

"You okay?" she asked.

He looked over at her, put his left hand on her thigh and squeezed.

"Never better... you?"

"I'm good." She put her hand over his and squeezed it a little, smiling at him and taking in his profile as he drove. She noticed the dimple in his cheek hiding under his stubble, the shape of his chin, his thick, dark eyebrows, the way his sideburns hid under his curls and faded into his stubble... He was perfect.

"What?" he asked, as he glanced sideways, noticing her staring.

"Nothing, I like to look at you, is that okay?"

He moved his hand up, rubbed the back of it against her cheek and smiled, keeping his eyes on the road.

"Look as much as you like sweetheart, I'm all yours."

She smiled, shrugging her shoulders, looking like a lovesick teenager.

Chapter 19

"Morning Gloria, did you have a good Easter?" Frankie bounced towards the theatre reception desk.

"I did, thanks pet, you?" Gloria was tapping away on the computer; she briefly glanced up over her glasses as she answered.

"Yes thank you, ate and drank too much, of course!" Frankie was looking over her list for the day.

"Isn't that what holidays are for?" Jack had snuck in behind her, and was looking over her shoulder at the schedule that was on the desk next to her. "Did you do anything nice, Doctor?"

There were a number of people around the desk now, and Frankie felt as if they were all listening.

"I did, yes." She didn't look up at him; he was almost touching her and smelled so delicious. "I spent it with family." She knew what she'd said would affect him in some way; she heard him draw breath a little. Turning her head, she looked him in the eye and smiled. "You?"

He gave her one of his signature smiles.

"I, too, spent it with family, eating and drinking too much!" he said.

"Was the Easter bunny was good to you then, Jack?" said Marie, who seemed to have appeared from nowhere.

Jack looked at her, then back at Frankie, who was gathering up some patient records.

"Oh yes, she was very good to me," he said with a straight face, looking at Frankie and then back at the schedule.

Frankie could feel Marie's eyes burning through her. She picked up the patient records, trying really hard not to smile.

"Come on Chloë, let's get started," she said, actually quite glad she wasn't with Jack that day, as he was in a playful mood after their successful weekend. She had already had to restrain him that morning, trying to stick to the 'no therapy before work' rule.

"I always thought the Easter bunny was a he," said Denise.

"Ooooh no, not in my head, that adorable little bunny is very much a she!" Jack was quick to say, as he moved away in the opposite direction. He looked back, but Frankie had already gone into her room.

Jack went around all day smiling, laughing and joking; he was so noticeably different to the quiet, serious Jack that people had gotten used to. It was near the end of his shift when Denise asked him if she could have a word with him before he left. He finished up in the anaesthetic room and went to her office. Having no idea what it was all about, he felt a little nervous when he knocked on the door.

"Come in," he heard Denise call.

He took a deep breath before entering.

"Hi Dee, you wanted a word?" He hovered at the door.

"Ahh, yes Jack, come and sit down." She gestured to the chair in front of her desk, "Just give me a sec to save this and close it."

Jack sat down and dropped his backpack beside the chair.

"Is everything okay?" he asked.

Denise was clicking away on her mouse; finally her desktop screen of her two children appeared.

"Right, sorry, yes, everything is fine. I just need to organise with you a good time to do your annual review and I, and many other people, can't help noticing that you seem to be finally getting back to your old self. You know, getting past that two year mark, you seem to have suddenly put it all behind you and moved on... It's a positive thing, Jack, don't look so worried."

Jack smiled, relaxing.

"How would next Monday work for you? You're in at 11 so we could do it at the very start of your shift, if you like?" Denise was looking at her diary and the staff scheduling.

"Sounds good." He sat on the edge of his chair, ready to get up and leave.

"Great! I'll make sure it's on the schedule for that day... So, is there anything specific, anyone specific, that's contributed to the return of the Jack we lost?" Denise was desperate to know. Jack looked at her and sighed, smiling.

"Yes Dee, there is someone. Happy now?" He leant down to pick up his backpack.

"Anyone we know? Sorry, none of my business, you don't have to answer that." She knew he wouldn't answer. "She's a lucky girl, Jack."

Jack let out a little laugh; he wanted to tell her, he wanted to tell everyone, but it was actually fun to keep quiet and play secret games with Frankie.

"Thanks Dee, I'll tell her that, and I'll see you tomorrow," he said, as he got up, and slung his backpack over his shoulder, smiling at her.

"You have a lovely smile, Jack," she said to him, "I've missed it. Take care and I'll see you tomorrow." She smiled back at him as he shut the door.

After working together on Wednesday, they enjoyed a slow Thursday morning at home. Jack wasn't in until eleven, so she let him sleep in. The phone rang while she was in the shower. Jack had just got up, he saw that it wasn't a work number, so he answered it. Frankie had just switched the water off when Jack walked into the bathroom.

"It's the estate agent. She needs to speak with you." Jack held the phone while she dried herself enough to not drip everywhere. She wrapped her hair in a towel, then took the phone from him.

"Thanks. Hi Carmen, sorry, I was in the shower... Oh it's okay, it was my boyfriend, I should have mentioned him..." Frankie looked out of the bathroom door, across at Jack, who was busy in the kitchen; they exchanged smiles. "Oh really, the family that came for a second viewing, that's fantastic!... Right, okay, that's quite a bit under the asking price... I know... yes... Okay, well I'll need to discuss it with my brother and get back to you... Sure... yeah... Thanks, bye." Frankie walked towards the breakfast bar in her towel, to replace the handset.

Jack turned around and handed her a bucket of tea. He leaned his back against the sink and folded his arms.

"An offer?" he said.

"Yeah, but it's sixty thousand below the asking price, and it's already priced to sell. The market is so bad right now, Carmen thinks it should be considered. We could barter a bit with them, but they really want it, apparently." She sounded so down.

"Come here," Jack said, as he put his arms out for her to go to him. Walking over, she put down her tea and slid her arms around him. His big arms folded around her were so comforting.

"You're doing this because you're a good person and you want to do it right, but it's not worth stressing about. Talk to Andrew first, but maybe see if they'll meet you half way. You know, sweetheart, at the end of the day, you just want the damn thing sold with the least amount of hassle." He took hold of her chin and lifted it so he could look at her, brushing his thumb across her lips, which made her smile.

"That's better, now go and put some clothes on before you make me late for work!"

"Thanks." She smiled and placed her head against him again, hugging him tight.

Andrew agreed the offer was too low, but he also agreed that they needed just to be done with it, for Frankie's sake. They decided to counter-offer, asking for thirty five thousand under the asking, expecting them to come back with an offer a little bit more than their original one. Frankie got back to Carmen just after lunchtime and then spent the rest of the day at the house. By 6pm she had heard nothing in response, and decided she had done enough for the day and needed a glass of wine and a hot bath.

As Jack was working at the weekend, he was off on Friday. Frankie had the list from hell: the Leprechaun was in a foul mood, nobody knew why; none of the patients were straightforward; her ODP was a guy called Peter, whom she'd not worked with before, and hoped never to work with again! And to top it all, she was trying to negotiate the house with Carmen, while texting back and forth with Andrew in New York. She finally walked through the door of flat at 6.40, completely exhausted.

After a big, warm, welcoming hug, followed by a long kiss, Jack poured her a large glass of red wine.

"So," he said, as he pushed the glass towards her, "what did you finally settle on?"

Frankie took a big breath in; she couldn't believe it was actually sold.

"Forty under the asking, but I agreed to take care of whatever comes up on the survey." She blew out all her breath, making her hair move. Jack raised his glass.

"Good for you, congratulations!"

They clinked their glasses together and took a drink. Frankie sat at the breakfast bar, swirling her wine around the glass, while Jack served up spaghetti bolognese.

"How would I have ever gotten through any of this without you?" she asked.

"You obviously weren't meant to, that's why I'm here!" he replied, as he placed two steaming pasta bowls down and walked around to sit next to her.

"You believe in all that fate stuff?" she asked him.

"Not really, but the way we met, the timing, the circumstances, it's all so..." Jack stopped twirling pasta around his fork to think.

"Meant to be?" Frankie said for him, before putting a loaded fork of spaghetti in her mouth.

"Maybe," he replied, with a shrug of his shoulders.

There was a short, silent pause.

"My mum always said that everything happened for a reason. I'm still looking for some of those reasons, like the reason why she died first and not him. I hate myself for thinking it, but it's the truth. The crazy thing is my brother, completely independently, said the same thing to Angus. This is really good, Jack, why can't I cook like this? I'm a woman, for God's sake!" Frankie was trying to be serious and mad, but Jack just laughed at her.

"You have other amazing talents, sweetheart, like saving lives... including mine."

"Ahh yes, the whole doctor thing. That's just my job, I was trained to do all that. Jack, does what I do bother you in any way?" Jack looked at her, a little puzzled, even though he knew what she was getting at. "Okay, I'll just come out with it."

"You normally do, I don't know why you're hesitating."

"Thanks, I'm trying to find a nicer way of asking you if it bothers you that I have the more superior job, career, whatever you want to call it. But I can't think right now, my brain is too tired." She carried on twirling spaghetti once she'd finished speaking.

Jack put his fork down and turned to face her. He took her fork and put it down, turning her around to face him.

"I feel like I've always known you, even before I really knew you at work. Think about it, we'd worked together for what, two days, then spent most of a weekend in bed. I love the fact that you're smart, intelligent, clever, as well as funny, playful, quick witted, and very beautiful. I could go on and on. I might play with the 'Doctor' title 'cause it's kind of fun and sexy, but you should be proud of it. But when you're with me, you're... Just like a mornin' sun you turn me into someone I would rather be." Jack waited. Frankie let out a little laugh.

"Very clever. How long have you waited to slip that one in?" she asked.

"Not long actually, and you're stalling to think about it."

"Your Every Colour; My Private Nation; 2003, track..." she hesitated, "it's near the end of the album so I'm going to say...10!" She knew she probably wasn't right, but as she listened to all the albums on shuffle so often now, she'd forgotten the order of them. "I can tell you the rest of the words if that makes up for the fact I'm wrong." She was clutching at straws.

"9!" said Jack, "now, finish your dinner!"

"Oh, I was so close," she said with a sigh.

"But wrong, sweetheart. Wrong!" he said, playfully.

Frankie ate her last mouthful. "Thank you dear, that was delicious." She rubbed one hand over his broad back and the other hand over his thigh. "Dessert in the bath, maybe?"

"Don't think you can turn all cute on me and I'll forget that you were wrong. You, my dear, are going to clear away these dishes while I slide into a nice hot bath!"

She sat back, pretending to sulk while taking a slow drink of her wine. Then without taking her eyes off him, she got down off her barstool, unzipped her hoodie, threw it on the back of the sofa as she passed, and walked around into the kitchen.

Wearing only her tight yoga pants and a very tight Power Y tank that showed a little bit of cleavage, she bent over the bench to retrieve the pasta bowls from the breakfast bar.

"Nice, but you'll still have to do better than that." Jack turned away and got off his stool, heading straight for the bathroom.

After a busy but productive weekend of house clearing, lengthy FaceTime sessions with Andrew and Kayla, and no Jack for the most part, Frankie was determined that their day off on Monday should be spent together. She wanted to take a walk around Newcastle, especially along the Quayside; she hadn't done that since arriving back and it had changed significantly over the last few years. They had come to the decision that if they were seen together, then so be it; they were going to just have to take the risk and accept the consequences. Hopefully, with it being a weekday, most people would be at work.

It wasn't the nicest day, a bit dull and cloudy, but at least it wasn't raining and the temperature had hit double figures. They took the Metro into the city centre and just walked and talked, before finally finding themselves under the Tyne Bridge. Frankie stood up against the wrought iron railing that ran along the riverbank, with Jack pressed against her back, his arms wrapped around her, ear to ear.

"When did the boat go?" Frankie was surprised to see that the floating nightclub, the Tuxedo Princess, had gone.

"Your standing in a historical city with its own castle behind you, and you're asking me where that tacky old nightclub went?"

Frankie just laughed at him.

"That heap has been gone for a few years now I think," he continued.

"It was always a part of this view. It doesn't look right without it, even if it was the tackiest nightclub I've ever been to!" Frankie said, as they started to walk east along the Quayside, holding hands with their fingers interlocked.

"The Sage is pretty nice," said Jack, looking over at the large music venue on the south bank of the Tyne.

"It looks like a giant metal slug!" exclaimed Frankie.

Jack laughed out loud, and tried to defend the look of the building.

"It's supposed to have excellent acoustics, I think that's why it's that shape.... and of course, it's a piece of modern architecture."

"It still doesn't get away from the fact that it looks like a slug!"

"Okay, so moving on... what else do we have..." Jack loved the way she constantly made him laugh.

As they walked on, Frankie described the Quayside market that she remembered as a child. How her mum and Aunty Carol would bring her and Andrew, Lucy, and Thomas there on a Sunday. She remembered the area being very run down, but now it was rather swish, with modern flats and converted warehouses.

"Yay!" Frankie said suddenly. "The Pitcher and Piano is still here. I'm starving Jack, come on, lunch is on me."

"Do I have a choice?" he asked.

"No, I guess not. This used to be one of my favourite places when I was training here. I don't know what it's like now, we'll just have to go in and see."

Jack bent down and kissed her.

"Okay, let's eat!" he said, rubbing noses.

She smiled and wrinkled her nose for him.

"Any more of that kind of behaviour and we'll be getting in a taxi, bound for home... I don't care how hungry I am!"

He took her hand again and they went for lunch.

It wasn't quite the same as Frankie remembered it. They sat close on a leather sofa overlooking the Baltic Flour Mill, which was now an art gallery. They ate a large lunch, while watching the Gateshead Millennium Bridge - or the Blinking Eye as it's known – rotate to allow a tall ship through. It didn't really matter where they were; they were together, like any normal couple dating, and they loved it.

They walked back to Central Station to get the Metro home. It started to rain as they walked and by the time they got off in Jesmond, it was absolutely bouncing down. They were huddled together, dripping wet, as they fell through the main door of the flats from the street, giggling.

"I can't wait to get you out of those wet clothes," said Jack, playfully nibbling at her neck; he hadn't noticed they weren't alone.

"Hi Frankie. I see it's raining quite hard now!" said Penny, as she walked down the last couple of stairs and stood on the tiled floor.

Frankie looked up and saw the slightly embarrassed look on Penny's face.

"Oh! Penny... Hi... I'm sorry, we were..." Frankie started to explain, only to be cut off by Penny.

"It's okay, I'm presuming this is your young man? I've seen him come in and out a few times but we haven't been introduced."

"Oh! Okay, Penny, this is my boyfriend, Jack... Jack, this is Penny, Mrs. Whitfield's daughter; the lady who lives next door."

Jack nodded and smiled at Penny, who returned the gesture.

"Nice to meet you," he said.

"Pleased to meet you too. Well, if you'll excuse me..." Penny moved sideways slightly to walk around them.

As Frankie opened the door to the flat, she looked around at Jack, to find him smirking at her.

"So, I'm your young man, am I?" he said, as they walked through. Hercules came to greet them, but then thought better of it when he got severely dripped on.

"It would appear so," she replied with a sexy little smirk, as they both hung their coats and kicked off their shoes.

"Well, this young man has a very big hard on, which he would like you to sit on," Jack propositioned, walking towards her as she started to retreat back towards the bedroom.

"Oh! He does, does he? Well, he'll have to catch me first!" She ran into the bedroom and leapt up onto the bed, and over the other side. She started to scream as Jack followed her, stopping at the foot of the bed in front of the mirror. "There's nowhere to run, you'll have to surrender," he said grinning.

"Okay, whoever gets undressed first... takes charge!" she said.

"Deal. Go!"

There was a mad scramble as they stripped their tops off first, followed by their jeans, but Frankie discovered that wet skinny jeans were impossible to remove quickly. Jack had just taken his socks off when she finally stomped on the last bit of soggy jeans and pushed them off, her own socks with them. Suddenly, Jack stood in front of her naked, whilst she still had her boy shorts to remove.

"I think that makes me the winner," he remarked, with his hands on his hips, his glorious erection throbbing before her and damp curls framing a very large wicked grin.

Frankie gave a little smile with a very big sigh.

"I guess it does.... I surrender!" She lifted her arms out to the side then let them drop as she spoke.

He slowly walked towards her and took her in his arms, pulling her close. She grabbed his firm, bare buttocks as he lifted her chin with one finger.

"Let's see, first I want to take you here, in front of the mirror... Then on the kitchen bench... After that, in the shower... And then on the sofa. We are going to work off every bite of that lunch," he explained, as he bent to kiss her.

They managed to tick off most of the locations. By 10pm they were both pretty knackered, but very happy.

"I don't think I've ever had this much sex in such a short time," Frankie said, as she lay on his chest playing with the hair around his belly button.

"I can confirm that, without a doubt, I have never had this much." Jack was stroking her hair.

"How would you like to spend a whole weekend doing this in a nice hotel not too far from here?" she asked him.

"Lumley?"

She looked up, giving him a slow smile.

"After I paid for it, I decided to hang on to it for a bit to see how we worked out. It turns out that Carol and Eric wouldn't be able to go anyway, sooooo... what do you think? Bank holiday weekend, bound to be raining; the perfect opportunity to spend a weekend in bed." She raised her eyebrows while giving him a cheeky little smirk.

"I think you have a serious addiction, Doctor."

"I do, Mr Lee... it's you!"

"Well then, I'd better make sure that I keep feeding your habit, so I suppose my answer is yes!"

She gave him a big smile and stretched up to kiss him, before rubbing noses.

"Time for sleep, young man... you've worn me out!" She snuggled down next to him and he reached up to switch off the bedside light.

The following week they had Sunday lunch at Carol and Eric's with the family. Finding an opportune time, whilst Frankie was in the bathroom and Jack was pouring more beer for the start of the football match, Carol cornered him in the kitchen.

"Jack, do you have any plans for Frankie's birthday?" she asked him.

"Excuse me?" he answered, surprised, "When is it?"

"She hasn't told you? It's the weekend you're going to Lumley, Saturday the 4th. I can't believe she hasn't told you," Carol told him quietly, in case Frankie reappeared.

"No, she's never mentioned it, though to be honest, I've never asked when her birthday is; it never really crossed my mind."

"Well, now you know, and you're going to be away... Make the most of it." Carol nodded and winked at him.

"I'll see what I can do... Thanks!" he replied, picking up the beers just as Frankie came through the kitchen door.

"Okay, sweetheart, you know where I'll be if you miss me!" he said as he passed her. Frankie gave his bottom a playful squeeze.

"I'm sure I'll cope!" she replied without looking.

Frankie continued into the kitchen and picked up a tea towel to start helping with the dishes.

"Things still going well then?" asked Jen.

"Mmmm, too well," Frankie replied.

"What are you going to do when you have to leave?"

"Don't go there, I have no idea. I made it clear at the beginning that I wasn't staying, so I guess that can only mean one thing. He either comes with me or..." She couldn't say the words; she didn't want to believe that it would actually come to that.

"Do you think he would? Go with you?" Jen asked.

Frankie shrugged her shoulders and took a deep breath; she and Jack hadn't even talked about this yet. She looked up at Jen, a wave of emotion hitting her at the thought of even discussing this with him, never mind him saying no, which would mean it would be over.

"I knew in the beginning that this was only going to be short and sweet. I wasn't meant to fall for him." She took another deep breath, desperately trying to hold back the tears, because she knew that once they started, they might not stop. "I'm sorry."

Carol took off her gloves and left the dishes; she went to her niece and hugged her.

"Ahh pet, come here, you'll have me in tears in a minute. Jen, be a love and pop the kettle on," she pushed Frankie away slightly and looked down at her, "or do we need brandy?" she asked, which made Frankie let out a short laugh.

For the first time, the following week they worked together every day. By the time they got to Thursday evening, they agreed that it was becoming more and more difficult to hide their relationship.

Lying in the bath that night, the subject came up yet again.

"Why don't we just come out?" Frankie asked, as she rubbed bubbles onto his chest, whilst he lay between her legs. "Is it really such a big deal? Everyone is talking about us anyway, and they're going to work it out when I leave, and you decide what to do."

Suddenly, Jack got up and stepped out of the bath. He didn't look at her, just picked up a towel and started to dry himself. Wrapping it around his waist, he left the bathroom.

Frankie sat alone in the bath, hugging her knees. Hercules jumped up onto the side and meowed. She scooped up some bubbles in her hand and spread them on the side of the bath for him to play with.

"What are we going to do, big guy? Do you have any suggestions?" She spoke to the cat quietly, even though Jack was presumably in the bedroom, "I know what I would like him to do..."

"What would that be? Although I think I know the answer." Jack was stood behind her, leaning against the doorway; she didn't look around when she heard his voice.

Hercules jumped down.

"Go on then," she said.

There was a heavy silence while she waited for his answer.

"I don't think I can, Frankie. You're asking me to leave my family, my job and everything I know."

"I haven't asked you to do anything, you have to make the decision on your own. It's going to depend on how you feel about us... about me."

"So why don't you stay?"

He walked back into the bathroom, still wearing only his towel, and sat down on the toilet seat. Bending forward, he rested his elbows on his knees and ran his fingers through his hair. Frankie couldn't help notice his legs were parted enough for her to have an unobstructed view. Looking away, she placed her forehead on her knees, took a deep breath and exhaled it slowly.

Jack sat watching her. He knew her answer; she didn't need to say it. Curled up as she was made her look fragile and vulnerable.

He hated it; he hated himself for what he'd just told her but they had to talk about this, it wasn't going to go away. Emerging from his own thoughts, he realised she was crying; her shoulders began to shake and he could hear her quiet sobs. Quickly, he reached down and lifted her out of the water; she wrapped her arms around his neck as he sat back down on the toilet seat and held her as close as he could, her face buried in his neck. He rocked her slightly as her sobs got louder; removing her hair clip, he threw it in the sink and stroked her hair gently, whilst his other hand gripped her bare waist. Kissing the top of her head, he suddenly felt overwhelming emotion. He had no idea what to do or what to say. He had no control over the tear that rolled down his face, though he didn't want her to see it. He couldn't bear the thought of ever giving her up.

Chapter 20

"SO, WHAT ARE you up to tomorrow?" Jack asked.

It was Sunday evening and they were cuddled up on the sofa after watching a movie.

"Well, I think after spending all this weekend at the house again, I might have a proper day off. I need to go into town and take Mum's pearls and her rings to the jeweller, see what he can do." Frankie replied whilst she played with Jack's hand, linking fingers.

"What would you like to do with them?"

"Well, the ring is beautiful, but it's too small for me, so I thought I might have the diamond made into a pendant. The pearls I'll have cleaned and valued. I'll probably keep them. I have very little jewellery of my own; it's not something anyone has ever bought me... In fact, you're the first person to ever buy me anything." She looked up at him and smiled.

"Really, how come?" Jack asked, surprised.

" I guess, not being a typical girlie girl, guys thought maybe I wouldn't like it. I don't know." She carried on playing with his fingers.

"Would you?"

"Definitely. I love the bangle you gave me, it's simple and elegant. I don't like fancy things, just smart and sophisticated.

The jeweller in Eldon Garden, where you bought my bangle, has lots of beautiful things in their window I would be very happy to receive." She kissed his knuckles.

"Oh, would you now," he replied, brushing her hair away from her face as he kissed the top of her head.

"I think I'm ready for bed. All this house stuff is really taking it out of me." She went to stand up.

"Sweetheart, it's only 9.30!"

"Well, come and join me and I'll string it out until 10!"

The following day, after visiting the jeweller, Frankie decided to do a little shopping. She hadn't told Jack it would be her birthday at the weekend of their stay at Lumley Castle, because she felt old. She would be turning 39, and he wouldn't be 32 until November, a fact she only knew because she had seen his date of birth on his driver's licence, on display in a clear window in his wallet. He hadn't asked her when her birthday was, so she thought she would just let it ride for this year and pretend it wasn't happening. She realised this was stupid; he had said many times that her age didn't bother him, it was just a number, and she didn't look it.

She decided to treat herself to another new dress and shoes. Knowing Jack was going to the gym and checking on his flat after work, she felt no need to rush home. She took her time to find the perfect outfit for a romantic weekend away. She checked out lots of sexy underwear, but couldn't decide on anything; she planned on spending most of the weekend naked anyway, so decided it would just be a waste of money. By 4.30, she was done; she picked up some food in M&S and took the Metro home.

Back at the flat, she put everything away and made some tea. She had only planned on sitting down for a few minutes, to catch up on her email and Facebook, when suddenly she felt Jack's lips on hers; she must have fallen asleep.

"Hey sweetheart, sorry to wake you, but it's 7.30. You okay?" Jack asked. He was crouched down next to her, stroking her hair, smelling all freshly showered.

She sat up, stretched and yawned.

"I'm sorry, I only sat down while I drank my tea." She rubbed her face to try and wake herself up.

"Would that be this one here that's now stone cold?" Jack commented, looking down at the almost full bucket of tea on the coffee table next to him.

She laughed.

"I guess so. I was just so tired after shopping."

"Oh, poor you, honestly, your life!" he said, with a mock sad face.

She hit him with a cushion as he lifted his arms to defend himself. They both laughed.

While they ate dinner, Jack talked about his day. He had worked with Dr. Annabel Richardson and she had driven him mad.

"Honestly, I don't know how the woman has managed to make it this far in life. She is the most disorganised person I have ever had the misfortune of working with. How does someone like that get through medical school?" Jack was quite animated as he spoke.

"She was probably okay until she had her kids. I think most women go soft in the head once they have a baby; it's quite normal. I guess as long as she's doing her job and she's safe, then there's really not a lot you can do but be glad she's only part time."

Frankie was peeling an orange as she spoke. Even though Jack said he didn't want any, she knew him well enough now to know that he loved it when she fed him messy fruit.

"Anyway, enough about me; how was your stressful day off?" he asked.

"Well," she started, ignoring his gentle mockery, then took a bite of a segment. Jack leaned forward with his mouth open slightly. "I know you too well, Mr. Lee, I knew you wanted some." She ran the orange over his lips and as he opened his mouth wider she pushed it in; he sucked her fingers as she slowly pulled them out.

"I always want some, sweetheart, I've never seen anyone make eating fruit look as sexy as you do."

"In that case, I'd better tell you about my day before I eat any more... So, I went to the jeweller; it's no problem to make the diamond into a pendant. They are also going to clean and value both the eternity ring and pearls for me. They should all be ready towards the end of next week just before we go away. Oh, and they had the most unusual, gorgeous, square, yellow diamonds set in platinum; earrings and a pendant. I didn't dare ask what they cost. Marcus said they just got them in at the end of last week; apparently they're quite rare. I guess there's a lucky lady somewhere out there that will have the pleasure of them... sadly."

Frankie picked up the orange again and started to separate another segment.

"After that, I treated myself to few things to take away; I haven't had a good reason to buy nice things for a long time so... I did!"

She bit into the orange, but this time Jack moved her hand away so that half the segment was poking out of her mouth. Bending down, he bit into it, their lips touching as he did. Juice ran down her chin.

"Oh... allow me," he said. She was about to catch it with her fingers, but he caught her hand and licked the juice with his tongue.

"Jack Oliver Lee, I'm not stupid. Shall I just take my clothes off now, then we can be as messy as we like?"

"Oh baby, now there's a thought," he said.

'*Oh! That smile*', she thought.

"Well, tough!" she replied, playfully shoving another segment into his mouth before getting down from the stool. "There will be no hanky panky until these dishes are done, then we can get as messy as we like!"

"You're so bossy, Doctor," he said, getting down from his stool and following her into the kitchen. "I may have to have a word with your superior and make a formal complaint about the way you treat me."

"Really? And how do I treat you, exactly?" She turned round to find him right behind her; he grabbed her and lifted her up onto the bench. She let out a surprised scream.

"Let's see... you tease me, you get me all wound up, you eat fruit in front of me, for God's sake," he stopped speaking to kiss her. "You have me completely under your seductive little spell, and then you make me do dishes!" He pulled back, leaving his hands resting on her hips; he was trying to keep a very serious, straight face.

Frankie burst out laughing, then straightened her face and tried to be as serious as he had just pretended to be.

"Okay. You talk to Kathy. I'm sure she'll be very interested to know about the terrible way I treat you before I have my wicked way with you. Now, Whipping Boy... dishes!"

"Cute, very cute," he said, now smiling. "Well Doctor, that would be Drops of Jupiter; 2001; track 9!"

It was Wednesday; they were both in with Mike Anderson. The afternoon list had been cancelled because both patients were too sick for surgery. Jack was already having lunch when Frankie entered the busy staffroom; he was sat on the far side of the room. The only seats left available were next to the door, so Frankie parked herself and proceeded to eat. After about ten minutes, the room began to empty, and soon the only people remaining were Jack, Frankie, and two nurses who were sat in the middle of the room, opposite Jack, with their backs to Frankie. She had just finished her salad and reached for a banana. Glancing up, her eyes caught Jack's, who looked up at the same time. He peeked across at the two nurses, who were engrossed in the news on the TV, before he looked back at her and smiled.

She looked at him, then looked down at the banana with a very cheeky grin. *'Oh yeah'*, she thought, *'I make fruit look sexy, do I?'*

She held up the banana and proceeded to peel it very slowly. Jack was reading a newspaper, but kept glancing up at her. Once all the skin was hanging around her hand she began. She wound her tongue around the tip of the banana, slowly letting it sink into her mouth. Working with her tongue and her mouth, she kept going until she got all the way down to the skin, then she looked up at Jack with the entire banana in her mouth. His eyes were like saucers, and she could see he was holding his breath. She smiled with her eyes, as he exhaled slowly. Closing her lips around the banana, she slowly glided them back up the fruit, and then down and up again. She didn't take her eyes off him; she knew that look - he was definitely turned on. When she reached the tip again she bit really hard and proceeded to eat, turned her head to look away from him, and pretended to watch the TV.

Within seconds her phone buzzed in her pocket. She saw out of the corner of her eye that he had started to pack up his things. Casually, she retrieved her phone.

The teaching room... 5 minutes!! Jx

Putting the phone back in her pocket, she carried on eating. Jack walked passed her; she looked up at him and gave him a cheeky little wink. He couldn't help but smile back at her before he was out the door.

A few minutes later Frankie arrived at the dark, locked room at the back of theatres and tapped gently on the door. He opened it, and as soon as she'd closed the door behind her, he pulled her to him; he was rock hard. He whipped her very large scrub top over her head, her hat and I.D. badge flying off with it. She was wearing a black bra, a favourite of his. Lifting his scrub top over his head, he lost his hat and I.D. too. She had never seen him dressed solely in scrub pants before. *'Holy Hospital Laundry'* she thought, he was hot, so hot he was a fire hazard! Pulling the tape on his pants, they loosened enough to fall. She pushed him onto a table and eased down his boxers; he sprung free. He was panting already, though neither spoke; they knew they needed to be quiet. She took him in her left hand and cupped him between his legs with her right. He let out a sharp gasp. Taking a second to glance up at him, he nodded slightly, letting her know he was ready for her to do this; she gave him a little smile before she let her tongue get to work.

He grabbed at her hair, not meaning to pull, but he needed to hold something. The sensation was exquisite; she was doing exactly what she had done to the banana. Then, she had him, all of him, in her mouth; he had no idea how, but she did. He knew that as soon as she closed her lips around him he was going to come; he couldn't help it, the sensation was amazing. He'd never experienced anything like it and she didn't stop; he was coming hard and she just kept going, until he relaxed. Regaining his composure, he looked down just as she kissed the tip, and he saw her swallow. Slowly, she kissed him all the way up his abs, between his pecs and onto his nose. She whispered quietly, "I'm sensing you enjoyed that, Mr Lee. I'll be happy to do it again later in a more appropriate location if you like."

He let out a satisfied little laugh just as they heard voices and someone trying the door handle.

"Quick... here... I presume you've got the key from the office?" said Frankie, handing him his scrub top as he pulled up his boxers and scrub pants.

"Yes, of course, but other people have keys too... Here." He handed her her hat.

Very quickly, they were dressed and decent, listening by the door to see if whoever it was had gone.

"I think we're okay," said Jack; he quickly bent down and kissed her. "Thank you!" he said, rubbing noses.

"You're welcome," she replied, smiling, giving his firm bum cheek a playful squeeze.

Jack unlocked the door and slowly opened it, popping his head outside; all clear. They both left the room and Jack locked it behind them. He gave Frankie a moment's head start so they didn't appear together, and then he followed, replacing the key on his way.

As Frankie strolled along the theatre corridor to the front desk, to find out if there was anything else needing to be done, Kathy burst through the front doors.

"Oh Frankie, the very person. You're free now, right?" asked Kathy.

"I guess so, the afternoon list was cancelled."

"Great, I know this is dumping on you a bit, but the on-call people are all busy and they need an anaesthetist up on 16. Some bloke who had a laparotomy this morning for a bowel resection is crashing. Do you mind?" Kathy seemed a little stressed about the whole thing.

"Sure, no problem," said Frankie, and headed for the door.

"I tell you what, which ODP were you with this morning?"

Jack was just walking down the corridor, about to pass them. Frankie nodded in his direction; Kathy looked behind her.

"Excellent, Jack, do me a favour and go up to 16 with Frankie will you? They're having a spot of bother with a patient from this morning."

Jack stopped and exchanged a look with Frankie. *'Absolutely! Anything! She's just given me my first blow job, how could I refuse!'* he thought.

"Sure," he said with a smile, and grabbed the transport bag from beside the desk.

"Thanks, and step on it, I think that useless SHO is up there at the moment, so God knows what sort of a state the patient will be in," Kathy said, as they pushed the door open.

They exchanged nothing else while *en route*, getting to the ward as quickly as they could. They were greeted by Alistair, the useless Senior House Officer whom Kathy had feared was involved.

"Ah, Dr. Robertson," he was looking at Jack as he spoke, "he's in the third bay, if you want to follow me."

Jack looked at Frankie and rolled his eyes, as they made their way down the ward to the bay where the patient was. The curtain was pulled around the bed, but they could see there was a lot of activity in the bed space.

"Just in here." Alistair pulled the curtain back to reveal nurses, student nurses, another House Officer, equipment and, in among the chaos, the patient.

"Okay, so can you give us a quick history?" Frankie asked him.

"Er... yes... of course." He was looking back and forth between Jack and Frankie, looking very confused, and occasionally glanced at Frankie's chest. He began to speak to Jack again; Frankie interrupted him.

"Excuse me, but do you have a problem with female physicians? Because if you are able to keep your eyes from straying to my chest for long enough, I would prefer you talk to me!" Frankie could see the patient was sick and needed her attention, so once she finished speaking, she went to the head of the bed.

"I... uh...I'm sorry, I... anyway, Mr. Len Turner here is a 58 year old man who had a bowel resection this morning for carcinoma of the colon."

While Alistair gave his speech, Frankie introduced herself to the patient and began to examine him.

"He arrived back on the ward a couple of hours ago, initially fine, but then his BP dropped, heart rate and breathing increased. Lesley here," Alistair gestured to a nurse stood next to him, "noticed his drain was full of blood. I happened to be here, so I took a look. We gave him some fluids, took some bloods, increased his O2 and here we are."

Frankie hung her stethoscope around her neck and pushed her glasses further onto her nose.

"I presume he's cross-matched, and if so can we get a unit up here, stat?" She nodded to Lesley, who nodded back and left the bed space.

"Let's get another 500 of colloid into him in the meantime, and I need to put a central line in, Jack," she looked at Jack; he nodded back at her, "can we get an O2 mask with a reservoir bag, I don't want to intubate here unless I have to. Have you been in touch with the surgeon? He's going to need to go back to the OR."

Frankie was on autopilot; some of the terms she used were not the same medical language that was used in the UK, but Jack now knew her well; he knew exactly what she was asking for.

For the next half an hour Frankie and Jack worked, together with the ward nurses, to insert lines, give blood, and stabilise the patient. At some point, the Surgical Registrar appeared and agreed the man needed to go back to theatre, which he would arrange immediately. Frankie and Jack were to bring the patient down as soon as they were ready.

Just as Frankie thought she was on top of things, Mr. Turner appeared to be having further difficulty with his breathing.

"Okay Jack, I think we'd better intubate now; I'll have a 7.5 tube please, and we're going to do a rapid sequence induction. Mr. Turner," she spoke directly to the patient, something she had done throughout, to keep him informed, "I think it's time we helped you with your breathing, so I'm going to give you an anaesthetic, just like the one you had this morning, and hopefully we will have all this sorted out when we next wake you, okay?" she explained, looking down at the frightened man.

Len slowly reached his hand up to move the oxygen mask so he could speak. It took him every effort to say to her, "Thank you, Doctor".

"You're welcome sir, you're going to start feeling sleepy now, okay."

Jack handed her a syringe and she injected it straight into the central line she'd just inserted into the right side of his neck.

She was having a little bit of difficultly, her left hand was holding the laryngoscope in the patient's mouth; the other was trying to insert the tube.

"Jack, can I have some more cricoid pressure, please," Jack pressed down harder, "Thanks, that's perfect." She was also having trouble with her glasses; they were slipping off her nose, so she was wrinkling her nose in the hope they would work their way back on.

"Allow me," said Jack, smirking a little.

Before she could answer, he gently put a finger over the bridge of her glasses and pushed them back on for her. She looked at him and smiled.

"Thank you," she said, tenderly.

"You're welcome, Doctor." he said, in the same tone, with a smile.

For a split second they forgot where they were.

"Er... Okay, so if we can tape this, I'll have a listen and then we'll start to think about moving him."

After all the drama was over, they finally transferred the patient to theatre. The surgeon, Mr. Kendal, was ready and waiting for them and thanked them both for taking such good care of his patient. They had only been in the theatre for a few minutes before Marie was very quick to make the observation.

"So what is this? When we successfully deal with an emergency, we're swapping scrub tops now, like footballers swap their shirts?" Marie looked back and forth at Frankie and Jack, who looked at each other puzzled. Then, Frankie looked down at Jack's name badge; it was hers! Looking up at Jack's face, she saw that he had also noticed their mistake. During their rush to get dressed earlier, they had put the wrong scrub tops back on in the teaching room. It suddenly dawned on Frankie: that must have been why the SHO had addressed Jack and not her.

Thinking fast on her feet, Frankie tapped Jack on his shoulder, "That's a large latte you owe me, Mr. Lee."

He looked at her, now even more confused; she looked back at Marie. "You guys have been gossiping so much about us, we thought we would have a bit of fun and see how long it would take you to notice that we'd swapped scrubs. Of course, we actually only swapped badges, you understand." She started to unpin Jack's name badge. "I told him it would be less than ten minutes, but Jack insisted it would be more... so I guess I win!"

"I guess that means you do, Doctor!" He gave her his best smile yet. He wasn't sure what he loved her more for at that moment - saving a man's life, thinking on her feet so quickly, or what she'd done for him in the teaching room that had gotten them into this sticky situation in the first place!

They both agreed to stay and see the case through. It was 7.15pm when they were finally finished; they were alone in the anaesthetic room.

"God, I am wrecked!" said Frankie, as she took her glasses off and placed them in the case.

"You know, it's pretty late. I don't like the idea of you taking the Metro now. Please, just get in the car with me?"

"Sure, why not, I'm too tired to argue."

Jack smiled back at her, wanting to take her in his arms and give her a hug, but he would enjoy it more once they got home.

"How about we pick up pizza on the way?" he asked.

"You must have read my mind," she said, as she slung her backpack over her shoulder, "I'll see you at the car."

Back at the flat they dug into a well-earned pizza.

"So, you finally trusted me?" she asked.

"I don't know what you mean!" he replied smirking.

"You know exactly what I mean, and you loved it!" She leaned sideways, nudging his arm with her shoulder.

Jack had a mouthful of pizza, but couldn't help smile. He spoke once he'd swallowed.

"Did you... love it?" He was looking at her sideways with just his eyes.

"Are you kidding me, I've wanted to do that since I lured your cute ass into my life!"

"Really!' he said, surprised, "Why?"

She wiped her mouth and hands with a paper napkin and turned on her stool to face him. Jack did the same. Placing her hands on his knees, she slowly let them glide over his thick, muscular thighs. Looking up into those hypnotic, steel blue eyes of his, she spoke quietly.

"Jack, apart from being the wonderful person I have gotten to know, you are also the most gorgeous man I will probably ever know. You look good, smell good, and taste good... you define delicious." He dropped his head and looked down smiling; she placed one finger under his chin the way he did to her, and lifted his head.

"I've wanted to explore every inch of your beautiful body with my hands, my eyes, and my tongue, but I learned I had to be patient. I am so deeply into you that you could probably ask me to do anything to you and I would... I can't get enough of you. And not just physically, emotionally too; I want to just spend time with you and share things with you." She hung her head and looked down at the floor.

Jack took a deep breath with his eyes closed.

"You were amazing today. The way you took charge of the chaos, and calmly got on with sorting out their disaster, even if you were rude to Dr. Alistair whatever his name is! I wanted to proudly stand up and tell everyone, that's my girl, isn't she amazing. I realised today that you deserve to be happy and I know that isn't here."

Lifting her head, she looked up at him; he bent to kiss her.

"Just bear with me okay, I just need some time."

She broke into a relieved smile and nodded.

Chapter 21

ANOTHER WEEK HAD passed them by, and they were getting ready for their romantic weekend at Lumley Castle. On Wednesday afternoon Frankie checked her list for Friday. It was awful! They would be arriving late and she would start the weekend even more knackered than she already was. They discussed their plans in the bath that evening.

"Look sweetheart, there's nothing you can do about it," Jack said, as she lay on her back, between his legs, linking fingers.

"I know, it just would have been nice to not have to leave straight from work; at least I have tomorrow."

"Exactly, you have all day to pack nothing!" he said, sitting up and wrapping both their arms around her.

"What do you mean, nothing?" They were now cheek to cheek.

"Well, if I remember correctly, you sold this to me as a weekend in bed. So, that would mean being naked, which means you don't need to pack anything!"

"You do know I booked us into the restaurant on Saturday evening, as we do still have to eat, especially with the amount of exercise we're planning on doing? So, I will need to pack something to wear!"

"You did mention that, fair enough. I guess it will take you all day to pack."

"Cheeky!" She couldn't move to playfully hit him as he held her tight. "If you must know, I'm going to get waxed and have my hair done tomorrow."

"Oh yeah, will you get a Brazilian again... pleeeease, for me?" He started to nibble her ear.

"I might if you're nice to me." She lifted his hands to her breasts, feeling him getting hard against her back.

"Aren't I always?" he replied, placing tender kisses on her neck.

"Always..."

As predicted, Friday was a pig of a day for Frankie. They had agreed that she would text Jack when her last patient was in recovery and he would pick her up; they'd decided they would take the chance of being seen. Carol had agreed to pop in on Hercules over the weekend. At 6.48 his phone tooted and buzzed; it was Frankie's ringtone. Having already packed the bags in the car, he gave Hercules a quick rub under the chin.

"Be good, mate. I can promise you I won't be! See you Monday."

Hercules curled up on his radiator bed as Jack locked the door behind him. Twenty minutes later he pulled up outside the main entrance of the hospital and waited for her.

After dealing with a crisis she could have done without before a bank holiday weekend, Denise was also working late. She followed Frankie at a distance down the corridor, not really thinking anything of it until she walked out of the main entrance and saw her getting into Jack's Mini. As she stood, smiling to herself, through the back window she saw Frankie lean over to Jack, and share a long, lingering kiss before she put her seatbelt on and they drove away.

Forty-five minutes later they were parking at Lumley Castle, a place they had both passed many times driving along the motorway, but neither had ever actually visited. It was absolutely stunning. Carrying the small amount of luggage they had brought with them, they entered the main entrance to check in. They were informed that it would be a busy weekend at the castle, with two weddings booked every day, but that this should not in any way affect the quality of their stay. They didn't care; they looked at each other and smiled like two lovesick teenagers.

Once checked in, they made their way through the grand hallway lined with medieval paintings and rich furnishings, to an elegant staircase that led to their room.

"Isn't it beautiful? I've never stayed in anything like this," said Frankie, looking around, trying to take it all in.

"It's certainly in a class of it's own, very... unique," said Jack, "Oh, this is us here. After you." He moved to one side so that Frankie could be the first to walk into their room.

She slid the card into the electronic slot, pushed the door open and walked inside. Suddenly, she stopped as she took in the room; her jaw dropped as she inhaled sharply. There were balloons, flowers, a large basket of fruit and champagne on ice. The balloons all had 'Happy Birthday' on them. Aware that Jack was stood behind her, she turned around slowly, as an emotional smile spread across her face. He was stood with his hands in the pockets of his jeans, looking at the floor. He knew she was looking at him, but he didn't look up.

"You did all this for me? How did you know?"

He looked up with only his eyes.

"A little bird told me. I wanted to surprise you, make it special. I hope that's okay."

She threw herself at him, flinging her arms around his neck.

"Thank you so much, no one has ever done anything so sweet. I wanted to forget it because I feel so old now! I'm going to need to have another word with that little bird." She gave him a big kiss, hugging him tight again.

"I was worried I'd gone a bit over the top," he said, looking around.

"No, I love it... You're the best!"

"Why don't you run a nice bath and crack those bubbles open? I'll organise room service for us... and just so you know, everything is on me this weekend."

"Jack, don't be ridiculous, I can't let you do that, it will cost a fortune." He put his fingers over her lips.

"And you are worth every penny. You paid for the room; it's your birthday and I want to spoil you. So shut up, get naked, and drink as much of that stuff as you want to!" He kissed her gently as she wrinkled her nose for him.

"Yes sir!" She saluted him.

She filled the bath with silky bubble bath provided by the hotel; while it was running she unpacked the few things she had brought with her. She left her dress covered up in her suit bag; she wanted it to be even more of a surprise now that Jack knew it was her birthday, and had gone to so much trouble. The room was fabulous. The centrepiece was a four-poster bed with curtains. There was a large, stone fireplace in one wall; the window opposite had a cushioned window seat; the furniture was ornate, solid wood and the furnishings were in deep rich colours of red, purple and gold.

She handed Jack a glass of champagne. "I think I am going to enjoy this birthday after all!" she said, as they clinked glasses and took a drink.

"I don't know what the problem is. So you're 39, big deal."

"I guess, because it's the last year of my thirties, and you're still only 31 and will be for months yet."

"Come here," he took her hand, put her glass down and pulled her into his arms. "I don't care, I've told you this I don't know how many times... it's just a number. You don't look your age; again, I don't know how many times I've told you that, and, I wouldn't have you any other way. You're not old, you're hot, sexy, smart, elegant, sophisticated, funny, mature, experienced," he raised his eyebrows as he said that, "and my favourite word for you is adorable; you are 39 and still adorable... And you're all mine! Now, get in that bath and relax with this," he handed her the glass back, "while I sort out some dinner."

"Okay, okay, I'm going." She walked into the bathroom, still clothed, looked back at him and blew him a kiss.

It was heaven. After a long busy day, all a girl needs is to collapse into a hot, steamy bath, scented with flowers and herbs she's never heard of, a glass of bubbly and, oh hello!... A naked Adonis to join her!

"Dinner will be half an hour, so I thought you might like some company," said Jack, as he entered the bathroom, carrying his glass.

"Oh definitely, or you could just parade that mighty fine naked body of yours around the bathroom for me to admire. It is my birthday after all." She looked up at him through her lashes as she lifted the glass to her lips.

"I think you're going to get more than enough of this body this weekend," he said, as he stepped into the bath. "Scoot up a bit, it's not as big as ours."

She slid herself up so she was sitting; the taps were in the middle of this bath so they could sit at either end.

"I can promise you that I will never get enough." She moved her foot so she could fondle his manhood with her toes.

"Ohhhh, I hope you ordered me meat?" she said, looking over the top of her glass, her toes playing with him under the water.

"A rare steak." He let out a gasp as he answered her.

"Perfect!" she smirked.

"We have about twenty minutes, and you know I have no control when you're all slippery and wet," he commented, taking a drink.

She still had her eyes fixed on his; her toes could feel him stirring. She wanted him now. A loud gurgle filled the room.

"We'd better get out then," she said, the plug dangling from her fingers.

They ate dinner in hotel bathrobes, drank champagne naked on the bed. They talked, they laughed, they kissed, and then they spooned and slept, the 'Do Not Disturb' sign hung from the door. When Frankie woke, she tilted her head up slightly, enabling her to see the clock; it was 8.58. Wow! She couldn't remember the last time she'd slept in that late. She was so comfortable, cocooned in strong, muscular arms with firm, hot, naked flesh pasted onto her. Jack was still asleep; she could always tell by his slow, steady breathing. She lay there, enjoying every inch of his skin touching her, and of course, morning glory throbbing into her back, just begging to be stroked, sucked, licked...oh! Her mind was full of naughty thoughts; well, it was her birthday after all! She decided she was going to do all her favourite things with him today, and then some. She gave a little wiggle against him. She wanted him, right now; she was absolutely dripping with need.

Jack became aware of soft, warm skin moving against him as he slowly surfaced. She was like the perfect puzzle piece; she fit into him in every way, but this was his favourite way. He could smell her hair, touch her skin and feel her breathe. This time of the day she was at her most sensitive; he knew she would be wet from him pressing against her, he knew she would be awake and wanting. Smiling to himself, he moved his arm slowly and purposefully, stroking every bit of skin he came into contact with along the way, until it rested on her hip.

She smiled to herself also; they woke like this often, never speaking until the end, making the whole experience more intense. In one swift move he rolled backwards, pulling her with him so she was lying on her back against him. Opening her legs, he was right there for her, stroking, circling, pushing; she was panting and moaning. He massaged her breasts, tugged at her nipples. Realising how close she was to coming, he rolled her onto her front and took her from behind, his fingers never stopping. He moved slowly at first so he could enjoy the moment too, knowing he came quickly in the mornings. She was gasping his name, grabbing at the sheets, still climbing. He moved quicker, she was so wet. They both reached the top together and collapsed, breathless.

After a few minutes he moved her hair away from her face so he could see her, and whispered in her ear.

"Good morning sweetheart, Happy Birthday." He hugged her close, placing soft, gentle kisses on her neck.

"Thank you, and good morning to you too. Today, will you be my birthday bed slave?"

He burst out laughing.

"You really are an addict, aren't you?" he asked, nibbling her ear. "I suppose, but only because it's your birthday," he said, with a sigh and tone that made him sound like he would be bored.

"Yes, how terrible for you, and, because it's my birthday, I want to play games and do all my favourite things."

He rolled her onto her back so he could kiss her properly, then stopped and looked at her with *those* eyes and *that* smile.

"Well, it's a good thing I enjoy playing your games, and doing your favourite things, isn't it!"

They took it to the shower and washed each other. He asked if he could wash her hair, and she was quick to point out that he was her slave for the day and that it was expected. She loved having her hair washed by someone else and wondered why she hadn't thought about letting him do it before. The way he massaged her head, teased the soapy suds out, combed the conditioner through and smoothed it gracefully sent her into a trance. She got out of the shower feeling truly relaxed and fuzzy.

They wrapped themselves in robes again. At 10.30 there was a knock at the door.

"Ahh', said Jack, "breakfast, perfect timing."

"You arranged this?" she asked, surprised.

He just smiled and winked at her as he went to the door. She flopped onto the bed and lay on her stomach, resting her chin on her hands as a large tray passed her and was placed on a wooden coffee table. Jack tipped the room service boy, before closing the door behind him.

It was quite the spread of fresh fruit, cereals, croissants, pastries, jams, tea and most importantly, birthday champagne cocktails. Jack handed Frankie her glass.

"I'm going to be pickled by the time we leave here!" she exclaimed, taking it from him.

"Excellent. I'll get to put you in a jar and keep you forever!" he said with a cheeky grin. "Now, I would like to wish you a proper Happy Birthday." He raised his glass to her; she clinked it with his, a huge grin on her face, and they both took a drink.

When they were finished eating, Jack placed the large tray outside the room door.

"Now, birthday girl, come and sit on the bed with me. You haven't opened anything yet and it's nearly lunchtime," he said, as he sat on the edge and patted the bed.

"I don't need to open anything, were here, you've done all of this," she waved her arm around the room, "and I have you." She got up anyway and walked over to the bed. Standing in front of him, she put her arms around his neck, leaned down and kissed his forehead.

"Jack, it's already quite possibly the best birthday I've ever had, which is a sad thing to say when your nearly forty!"

"So, let me make up for all the others," he said, sliding his hands around her hips so he could squeeze her bottom through the robe.

"Okay," she bent down to whisper in his ear, "but I want to take you in my mouth while you also return the pleasure when we're done."

She stood back and looked at Jack, who was sat, dumbstruck, with his mouth open. Placing a finger under his chin she pushed his jaw up, giving his stubble a gentle rub while she was there.

"Breathe, Jack," she ordered, as he swallowed hard. She wrinkled her nose for him.

"Okay," he said, and for the first time in weeks she saw a hint of the nervous, shy Jack she'd blindfolded and stripped naked in her living room, "but keep that playful little nose of yours under control until we're done with gifts, okay?"

"I'll see what I can do." She jumped up onto the bed and curled up against the pillows, tucking her legs beneath her. She felt weirdly excited; he had obviously bought her presents.

"Okay, first I have a confession to make," he walked over to his holdall and lifted out a pile of cards. "I have been stealing your mail and hoarding your cards... sorry!"

She laughed.

"I'll forgive you on this occasion, it was for a good cause."

She proceeded to open cards from Carol and Eric, Thomas, Jen and the kids, Andrew and Angus, Kayla and - the sweetest surprise - Jack's parents, Christine and Bob.

"Carol said she has something for you, but she wanted to give it to you herself... so, I suppose that just leaves this one." He handed her a white envelope that just had 'Fx' on the front.

She smiled at the reminder of how she always signed her texts.

"Thank you, I'm feeling very special," she said, as she shrugged her shoulders in excitement.

She slit the top open and pulled out the card. A little grey bear sat on the front, holding up a sign saying 'Happy Birthday'. She looked at it and smiled up at Jack, who was grinning. Opening it slowly, she read the caption inside: *To the special someone in my life*. He'd just signed it *Jx*.

"It's lovely, thank you." She leant forward to kiss him but he leaned back.

"Oh, I'm not done yet!" He presented her with a small purple gift bag. He was grinning from ear to ear and she was intrigued by what he'd bought; he had already spent so much and the weekend wasn't over yet.

"Happy Birthday, again!"

"Oh Jack, you shouldn't have." She smirked at him, in a *'But I'm glad you did'* kind of way.

She slowly reached inside the bag as she glanced up at him, but he was watching her hands in anticipation. She pulled out two items, loosely wrapped in tissue, and placed the slightly bigger one beside her on the bed. Slowly, she unwrapped the first gift, eyes widening at the name of the jeweller written on the top. It was the same jeweller where she had taken her mum's things, where he'd bought her bangle, and which displayed such beautiful things in its window, that only other women received. She looked up at him again before she opened the box; this time he looked at her and nodded for her to open it. So she did....

"OH MY GOD, JACK!!!" She was stunned, speechless, and completely blown away. Her eyes filled with tears of happiness and pure love for him, because she was staring down at the square, yellow diamond earrings that she had mentioned some lucky girl somewhere would have the pleasure of receiving. She flung her arms around him. He let out a surprised laugh, and then peeled her arms off him.

"You're still not done," he said, as he pointed to the other box.

Looking down at the slightly bigger box, it dawned on her what was probably in it. She picked it up.

"This isn't what I think it is, is it?"

"Open it and find out."

She was shaking slightly as she unwrapped it; it was another box from the jeweller's. She slowly opened the lid... She was right; it was the matching pendant.

Letting out another gasp, she held it in her left hand, placing the other over her heart that was practically leaping out of her chest. She was choked up; she could hardly speak.

"Thank you, this is all far too much, but thank you."

He could see she was overwhelmed, so he took her in his arms, kissed the top of her head and stroked her hair.

"I haven't spoilt anyone in a long time, I owe you so much; I can't even begin to explain. It made me so sad to hear that no one had ever made you feel this special."

She pulled away and looked up at him, touching his face with her hand.

"Thank you, I feel very special... and very spoilt." she said quietly.

He leant down and pressed his forehead against hers. They rubbed noses and smiled at each other.

While Jack was in the bathroom, she stood her cards up around the room wherever she could find space. She put her gifts back in the bag and placed them on the bedside table. Then she lay on the bed, naked, and waited for him. As he walked back through the door his eyes fell immediately to her. He smiled, a slow, core-tightening, Jack smile. Removing his robe, he walked towards the bed, and draped it on a chair as he passed. She was lying stretched out, with her arms above her head and her right knee bent, fallen to the side. Her hair melted over the pillow, a wanting look on her face. She took him in as he approached. He wasn't erect yet; she wasn't disappointed, she actually quite liked to see him *au natural*. He was so fit, so good looking, so hot, and so absolutely hers.

"Is there something I can do for you, Doctor?" he asked as he climbed on to the bed, lying down beside her and propping his head up on his arm.

She turned on her side and pressed against him, feeling him coming to life. It gave her a warm, fuzzy feeling to know that she had the power to do that to him, without really doing anything. She played with his chest hair for a moment then looked at him.

"69," she said quietly.

She felt his heart rate quicken under her fingers and his breathing changed. She was tracing the outline of his pecs while she spoke. He exhaled quickly.

"Play with my hair, Jack," she said quietly.

He managed a nervous smile and did as she said.

"Am I asking too much of you?"

"No, I'm just not sure how I'll concentrate on you, while you're doing that to me?" He was running his fingers through her hair and letting it fall.

"You will. As I give you pleasure, your instinct will be to want to return that feeling for me. Just play with me Jack, you do it so well now, you can always stop me if it's too much, okay?"

He smiled and kissed her forehead. Then he whispered in her ear, "Where do you want me?"

Letting out a slow smile, she looked up into those beautiful steel blue eyes.

"On your back. Our height difference might make it difficult, so I think it would be better for me to be on top."

"There's a surprise!" he said, raising his eyebrows at her.

She shuffled back on the bed so that he had enough room to lie down.

"Relax Jack, I think you'll enjoy this." She placed a soft kiss on his lips before she moved to straddle him across his wide shoulders, facing his feet. He reached up and squeezed her bum cheeks.

She felt his fingers stroking her now very wet entrance. Taking hold of his mighty erection, she kissed the tip before letting her tongue get to work. He stroked her gently before inserting two fingers inside. As she circled his tip, she pushed back for him. Allowing him to sink deeper into her mouth, her tongue didn't stop working. He pulled his fingers out, and took a moment to enjoy what she was doing, before letting his tongue stroke her; he could feel Mrs. Clit-tor-rus almost stroke him back. She tasted very sweet, but *'Oh God'*; she had all of him in her mouth... He tried to let his tongue circle and stroke her, but he was going to come, she was too good for him to concentrate on anything else. He inserted his fingers again so he could keep her aroused, but he was coming hard and fast as she allowed him to glide in and out of her mouth. It was amazing, and all he could do for her was keep stroking. When she stopped, he lay helpless, his body tingling all over. He now wanted to ensure he gave her just as much pleasure.

He pulled her back so she was almost sitting on his face and got to work. He thrust his tongue inside her as he used his fingers to stroke and massage her. She was moaning, massaging her own breasts and playing with her nipples. He loved seeing her do that, it was very erotic. He kept going like this for a few minutes before moving his tongue to caress Mrs. Clit-tor-rus. He could feel her building; she was getting wetter. Then she fell forward onto her hands, panting hard.

"I'm sorry," he said, also panting.

"What the hell for now?" She climbed off and lay next to him. He had one arm around her, the other on his forehead.

"I couldn't... You were too good... I couldn't concentrate enough on you.... "

She interrupted him.

"Enough already," she eased herself up onto his chest, face to face, and stroked his cheek. "There was nothing wrong with anything you did, you just blew my mind anyway. Stop beating yourself up every time you think you didn't do it right. There is no right or wrong, as long as you enjoy it, and did you?"

"You have to ask!" he said, with a slight laugh.

"Good, that's the right answer." She kissed him tenderly, "Now, what shall we do next?" she said, with a cheeky smirk and raised eyebrows.

Chapter 22

THEIR TABLE WAS booked for 8pm. After languishing in the bath with a very satisfied grin on her face, Frankie decided she should get out and wake Jack. It was almost 6.30; she had finally worn him out at around 4.30, when he fell asleep. Drying herself, she smoothed body lotion over her warm, pale skin, and then put on her robe. As she walked back into the bedroom, he was starting to stir. There was a knock at the door, so she threw the sheet over him as she passed the bed to answer it.

"Hi!" she said, to the room service boy at the door.

"I have an order for champagne to be delivered at 6.30, madam," he said, holding up a large ice bucket in one arm.

"Oh... er... Sure," she glanced around at the bed to make sure Jack was still decent. "Okay, if you can just pop it on the table that would be great, thanks." She opened the door wide for the guy to enter and she saw him glance over at Jack, lying very obviously naked, covered by... well not enough sheet, really.

He placed the ice bucket on the table and nodded to both of them with a hint of *'I know what you've been doing'* in his smirk.

"Sir, madam." And he left.

Jack got out of bed and stretched. Oh, how she loved to watch him stretch, it made her go weak at the knees. She walked over to him and put her arms around his waist.

"Hey, sleepyhead. I left the water in for you, and look, more bubbly!" She pointed to the ice bucket.

"I see that. It's not from me this time. You might want to check the card." He nodded towards the small, white envelope that was leaning against the glasses.

"Oh yes, I see that now." She reached for it and slid the card out. There was a pause while she read it, "Ahh! It's from Andrew and Angus, bless them. I'll text them to say thanks."

Jack had made his way into the bathroom and was sinking into the bath. She followed him so that she could put her make up on.

"Why don't we save that bottle for tomorrow and have a drink down in the bar before dinner? I thought maybe you could go down first, and then I'll follow... like a date. What do you think?" she asked, as she got out her make up and spread it out in the order she was going to apply it.

There was no answer, but she could see Jack's reflection in the mirror, smiling up at her. She turned around.

"What?" She stood, poised, with make up in one hand and a large brush in the other.

"I just love watching your little rituals when you get ready. You're the same at work, the way you spread things out in the order you'll use them and God help anyone who messes with it! And yes, I think that would be fun, waiting to see you arrive." He winked at her.

Jack made his way down to the Library Bar just after 7 to wait for her. It was quite busy and there were no tables available, so he waited at the small, ornate bar to be served. Frankie was ready;

she was just waiting for Jack to leave so that she could put on her dress with her new jewellery. She was out the door herself less than ten minutes after him.

Jack ordered two gin and tonics from the barman. He was just signing the receipt, charging it to the room, when he looked up and saw her walking towards him. Her beautiful hair was swinging just above her almost bare shoulders. Very thin spaghetti straps held up the fitted, long black dress that hung simply and elegantly on her frame. It hugged her in all the right places. His eyes travelled down to the slit that was revealing most of her right leg. She wore strappy, black, patent heels, no stockings and, he was pretty sure, no underwear. As she got closer, he could see the delicate platinum chain around her neck with the single, square, yellow diamond hanging from it, whilst on her wrist she wore the bangle he'd given her at Easter. Yet again, she had taken his breath away.

Unbeknown to them, watching from the far corner of the Library Bar was Kathy Barnes. Until the moment when a crowd of people moved away from the bar, she hadn't noticed Jack. Looking up from her menu, she saw him look towards the doorway, his jaw hitting the floor. Then Frankie entered the room and Kathy's jaw also hit the floor.

"You little minx! So it is true then. Wait till I see her on Tuesday!"

Her husband, Peter, engrossed in the wine list, glanced up, vaguely aware of her voice.

"Well, if you're thinking of having the fish, why don't we have a nice bottle of Chablis?" said Peter, initially oblivious to his wife's fascination with what she was witnessing.

Kathy wasn't paying him any attention either; she was staring as Frankie glided up to Jack, his arm immediately around her. He placed a smouldering kiss on her lips, as her clutch-free hand reached for his neck, her fingers grabbing his hair. When their kiss broke, Kathy saw him tuck her hair behind her ear, and whisper something; he seemed to be admiring something. Frankie spoke to him before he took hold of her chin and kissed her again. They moved apart slightly as he handed her the gin and tonic.

Peter looked at his wife as she sat, wide-eyed, fanning herself with the menu.

"Are you all right, dear?" he asked, concerned. There was a pause before Kathy answered.

"Of course, it's her birthday!"

"Okay, I can't have a romantic anniversary dinner with you while you're talking in riddles. Are you going to explain to me what the hell you're talking about?"

"I'm sorry darling, you remember Frankie Robertson.... Nicholas's daughter, lives in Vancouver now, but she's with me until...."

Peter cut her short.

"Oh! Yes, yes." Peter, a gastroenterologist, worked at the same hospital that Frankie's father had. "What about her?" He took a sip of his drink and returned to the wine list.

"Darling, she's stood over there with one of our ODPs, who I'm sure is significantly younger than her, and who will break the hearts of many when they find out it's true!"

"Oh! Why the fanning?"

"Female hormones dear, you wouldn't understand! I'm fine with the Chablis, by the way."

A table near the bar opened up, so Jack and Frankie sat down.

"That dress is causing me a lot of trouble, Doctor," Jack said, as she sat down next to him and crossed her right leg over her left, baring her thigh completely. He couldn't help it; he just had to touch it. Draping his arm around the back of the chair, he rested one hand on her shoulder, the other on her bare thigh.

Frankie had slid her arm around his waist, under his jacket; they were close, very close.

"I would be careful where you put your hands, Mr. Lee, or we're not going to get any dinner; and after the day we've had, I'm very hungry." She looked up at him through her eyelashes as she took a drink.

He smiled, not taking his eyes off her.

"Sweetheart, I am hot for you because of the day we've had," he said, bending to whisper in her ear.

They behaved as if there was no one else in the room. They were oblivious to Kathy and Peter walking right past them when their table was ready.

By the subtle lighting and lavish furnishings of The Black Knight restaurant, they enjoyed an intimate candlelit dinner. Frankie was quite tipsy by the time dessert arrived; the pastry chef had kindly piped 'Happy Birthday' on the plate of chocolate samplers she'd chosen. Her boss surreptitiously witnessed all this, and Frankie had no idea. Kathy was on the other side of the restaurant, among stone pillars and exposed brick, but she couldn't stop glancing across at the hottest couple in her department. She had heard the rumours circulating about the charity event, when they'd sat at the bar talking, and then danced together. Others had mentioned the way they looked at each other; the chemistry that was felt when they were in the same room. Everyone had noticed the change in Jack from the sad, grieving, shy guy that all the young nurses fancied, into the happy, confident, irresistible guy, who still didn't pay any attention to those nurses. Now she knew why.

She couldn't deny they looked amazing together, and were clearly deeply into each other. As she was enjoying coffee, she saw them get up. Jack held out his hand and linked Frankie's fingers as she slid them into his. She saw the way he looked at her; it was very intense, but loving. She couldn't help but smile to herself, happy that Frankie had finally found love, but even happier that this might mean she'd stay.

"You are, I know you too well." Jack said, as he pushed the room door closed with his foot and let his hands explore the slit of her dress further than the eye could see.

"Well, if you know, then why do you keep asking me? Remember, jeans and when it's appropriate!"

"And this wasn't appropriate?" he asked, genuinely surprised.

"Not when I'm with you it isn't. I like to tease you, it's fun."

"Oh really, fun you say?" He unzipped her dress and it landed on the floor within seconds. "Oh baby, nothing but diamonds and heels, there is a god!" he said with a huge grin, looking up at the ceiling.

He pushed her onto the bed; she looked absolutely ravishing. He undressed as quickly as he could; he was also feeling the effects of all the alcohol. As he tried to remove one of his socks, he fell onto the bed and they both dissolved into fits of giggles.

"Oh dear, Mr. Lee... too drunk to take your own socks off!" She had rolled onto her stomach with her head resting on her hands, tutting at him, trying to keep a straight face.

Finally, he stood over her, naked, as she rolled back onto her back to look at him upside down.

"Ooh, can we try this again, but with you on top this time?" She asked in an excited tone.

"Tempting, but I think I would like to feel those heels against my back while I thrust this," he stood, with his large erection hovering over her face, "deep into you and hear you beg for more."

He walked around to the other side of the bed to face her. Taking hold of her ankles, he pulled her towards him. He remained standing while she wrapped her legs around his waist, lifting her hips as he thrust deep into her. She let out a moan.

"Tell me what you want?" he asked, quietly.

"You!"

He moved in and out slowly.

"Like this?"

"Oh yes, again..."

"Play with your nipples for me, I love to watch you do that."

She did as he asked.

He moved out and didn't move back in.

"Ahh, Jack don't tease me, I want you..."

"Oh, so it's all right to tease me, but when the shoe is on the other foot..."

"Give it to me Jack, I want you so badly..."

She was tugging as he was thrusting. He reached his thumb down to stroke her, realising she was as close as he was; he knew that touching her would tip her over the edge and they would come together. He loved to watch the look of sheer ecstasy on her face as she exploded around him. Suddenly, his legs wouldn't hold him any longer; he collapsed next to her, spent.

"Well birthday girl, your bed slave is now officially off duty!"

Frankie opened her eyes and lay there for a moment, processing what she thought was about to happen. As usual, she awoke wrapped in Jack's arms; he was still deeply asleep. Suddenly, she knew she had to get to the bathroom... and quick! She took the hand that was cupping her breast and flung his arm off her as she scrambled off the bed, almost falling when she hit the floor. Hand over her mouth, she ran, bursting through the bathroom door, falling to her knees just in time to throw up in the toilet. Jack woke with a start when his arm was tossed aside. As he came to, he could hear her in the bathroom, quick to realise she was ill. Without hesitation he went to her.

As he entered the bathroom he saw her huddled over the toilet bowl, heaving into it, her messy hair flopping over to one side, trying to not get involved in the drama.

"Oh, sweetheart." Kneeling beside her, he put his arm around her, and swept her hair out of the way. She heaved again. "Okay, it's okay, I'm right here." He reached for a box of tissues and placed them on the floor beside them, taking one out of the box, and handing it to her. Then he started to rub her back. She stayed still for a few minutes; the vomiting seemed to have stopped, but she wanted to make sure. Slowly she sat back on her heels and wiped her mouth with the tissue.

"Thanks," she managed to say, as a tear rolled down her cheek. Jack wiped it away with his thumb.

"It's okay. It was so sudden, I was still asleep and it just took a moment to register what was happening. Are you okay?"

"Yeah, I think so, must have been something I ate."

He pulled her close to him and hugged her tight, rubbing her back.

He kissed the top of her head.

"How romantic is this, both sat naked on the bathroom floor while I talk to Hughie on the big white telephone!" she said. "I'm sorry."

Jack laughed.

"Don't be silly, you have nothing to be sorry for. These things happen. This is the sort of romantic thing you do when you're away for a dirty weekend with your toy boy... He looks after you!"

She looked up at him and smiled weakly.

"Thank you. I know I've joked about it, but somehow it doesn't feel right calling you that," she said, stroking his chest hair.

"I know what you mean. Obviously I never saw myself in this position, so it sounds rather strange to be described that way," he said, stroking her hair. "You feel better now?"

She nodded.

"Come on, why don't you brush your teeth; hopefully that will be it." Standing, he helped her up. He put some toothpaste on her toothbrush and gave it to her.

They made their way back to the bed; Jack fluffed up the pillows and rearranged them for her. She climbed back in and pulled the sheet over her.

"I'm just going to use the bathroom and I'll be right back, okay?"

"You'd make a good nurse, Mr. Lee," she said, as he walked away, and she heard him give a little laugh.

Jack returned and snuggled into her, sat up in bed.

"How are you doing?" he asked.

"Okay. You know, Jack, the toy boy thing... I hope you don't think that that's why I'm with you, you know, being as I'm nearly forty; here's my chance to bed a hot, younger guy before everything starts wrinkling and sagging!"

He laughed briefly and turned to her, all serious.

"Don't you think I would have realised that by now? I wouldn't have bought you diamonds, or held your hair for you whilst you were throwing up. Frankie, the way you look at me says it all, as if I'm the only one in the room and you see stars or something."

"How did you know I feel all twinkly when I look at you?" She turned in his arms to look up at him.

"Twinkly? You do? That's an interesting description, Doctor."

"Jack, you've made me feel that way since the first day I met you, when Dee stopped you leaving the anaesthetic room."

"Yeah, I remember," he paused, looking at her. "Really?" he asked quietly.

She held his gaze for a moment.

"Yes, really," she replied. "Why?"

He slid down the bed so he could kiss her tenderly, lingering for a moment. He pulled back and looked at her intensely. Then he spoke very quietly, "You did the same to me."

She touched his face, grazing her hand over his stubble and looked into his dreamy eyes. Her hand travelled up to his crazy morning curls that she loved so much. She ran her fingers along his thick, dark eyebrows, then let her thumb slide down his nose; he gave a little smile.

"For the first time in my life, Jack, I don't know what to do, because I feel that no matter what I do, it will involve huge sacrifices that I just don't think I can make, either way."

"I know, but it shouldn't necessarily have to be your decision. You were honest with me from the start. I've told you, just give me some time."

She nodded slowly.

After the morning's drama, Frankie was fine. As the sun was shining, they decided they should get some fresh air, so mid-afternoon they took a stroll around the grounds, hand in hand.

"Do you think you'll ever get married again?" she asked him.

"That depends," he said, with no hesitation in answering the question. "Yes, if I was hopelessly in love and knew that she felt the same way, then I probably would."

Frankie grinned, looking down at their feet as they walked.

"Is that the right answer?"

She wanted to say, *'Yes, Jack, I am hopelessly in love with you, and want to spend the rest of my life with you, if you'll move to*

Vancouver and don't want to have babies!' Instead, all she could manage was a slightly choked, "Yes".

He squeezed her hand, as if he knew what she had really wanted to say.

"So, would you consider any other method of having children, or even adopting?" He ventured the question; unable to look at her, he stared straight ahead.

"That depends," she raised her head, "if the person I'm hopelessly in love with doesn't mind that I can't have children naturally, and is happy to explore other options; and of course, wants children."

"It must be a difficult thing to come to terms with from a young age; most women don't usually find out until they try." He was trying to keep the conversation going, but what he really wanted to say was, *'I really don't mind and we can discuss other options'*.

"It's never weighed that heavily on me, because I've haven't actually been with anyone I've wanted to go down that road with."

She paused, before asking him, "Would you still like to have children, bearing in mind that, if things had been different, you would already be a dad?"

He stopped dead. She hadn't expected it, so she was jerked slightly as she kept walking. She turned to look at him; for the first time in this conversation their eyes met. He took a deep breath.

"It would scare me to death, to put the woman I love in that position again, for fear of it all being torn away from me, again. I know it was a rare case, a tragedy, but the last two years have been the darkest time of my life, until I met you. I don't ever want to go there again."

She hugged him close.

"I think we've had enough fresh air, I need tea!" she said, after a long moment of silence. She took his hand as they headed back inside.

Chapter 23

"Wakey, wakey sleepy head! Come on, it's nearly seven." This was the third time Frankie had told Jack to get up.

"All right, all right," he hauled himself up and sat on the edge of the bed, rubbing his face with his hands. "Can't it still be the weekend; we didn't have to get out of bed at all then."

Frankie was getting dressed in front of him.

"That, darling," she said, as she pulled her tank over her head, "is why you're so tired, and that thing," she nodded down at his large morning glory, "as impressive as it is, has no business looking at me like that; it should be as tired as you!" She kissed the top of his head before leaving the room.

"How are you so bouncy in the mornings? It's not normal," he moaned, as he passed the kitchen on the way to the bathroom.

"More years of practice, and old people don't need as much sleep!"

He closed the bathroom door with a giggle.

"Something tells me you've always been like this," she heard him say.

"I think I have actually," she said quietly to herself, as she poured granola into two bowls.

At 7.46 he dropped her off in her usual spot, so she could do her pretend walk from the Metro. She placed a lingering kiss on his happy lips, and told him she hoped he would have a good day, even though she would see him again in about twenty minutes.

Jack was stood at the front desk when Frankie appeared by his side to look at her list.

"Morning, Jack. Do I have the pleasure of your company today?" she asked, without looking at him.

"No, sadly not, Doctor, but I'll be around if you need me for anything." He looked at her and gave her a cheeky grin.

She wanted to say *'What could I possibly need that I haven't had from you all weekend?'* but she restrained herself, smiled sweetly at him, then turned to Gloria.

"Good morning Gloria, how was your bank holiday weekend?"

"Wet pet, very wet!" she replied, miserably.

"Yes, mine too." She was quite sure that they were talking about two completely different things. "Still, it wouldn't be a good old fashioned British Bank Holiday if it wasn't, would it?" Frankie picked up her pile of patient records and was about to head to Theatre 4 when Gloria stopped her.

"Sorry pet, your list is on hold; big RTA last night, no beds yet. I would go and grab a coffee if I was you, and I'll keep you posted."

"Oh! Okay, I'll duck over to the office and check my mailbox then," Frankie said, as she put the records back down.

She was standing at the mailboxes, trying to find where hers had been moved to this week, when she felt a hand on her shoulder.

"Dr. Robertson, belated happy birthday," said Kathy.

"Thanks," Frankie said, looking puzzled. "How did you know it was my birthday?" she asked her, cautiously.

"Frankie, come on, the bank holiday weekend after you passed your FRCA, it was also your birthday... remember?"

It took Frankie a moment to think back, before she suddenly looked like someone had flicked her memory switch on.

"Oh, yes... now that was a good night!" she said, smiling.

"I know, I still have a scar on my left knee after falling down the stairs at the Stage Door; how could I ever forget your birthday!" Kathy smiled too at the memory, and started to walk towards her office.

Frankie breathed a sigh of relief; for a moment she had thought Kathy knew something!

"So, how was Lumley?"

Frankie was suddenly winded. She was also aware of a couple of other people in the office, including Helen.

"Helen, can you get us a couple of cups of tea please? Come on in, Frankie, I know for a fact you've got time for a chat!"

As she started to breathe again, it took everything she had to compose herself and turn around. Kathy was stood holding the door open to her office; she gave Frankie a smile. *'Oh, God, she knows,'* Frankie thought. Declining the invitation wasn't an option and, truth be told, Frankie was glad. She made her way over to the door, slowly walked into the office, and sat down. Kathy took the tea from Helen, thanked her, and placed one in front of Frankie before sitting down herself.

"How do you know that I went to Lumley?" Frankie asked.

"I donated the weekend. Peter and I had our wedding reception there; we go back every year to celebrate our anniversary, and usually stay the weekend. I had already booked it when he had a paper accepted for a conference in Denver. So, I decided to donate the weekend for the auction."

"Oh, I see." Frankie was slightly relieved now.

"However, he didn't fly until Sunday, so we decided to have dinner there on Saturday evening anyway." Kathy was looking straight at Frankie as she said this.

All the colour drained from Frankie's face; she fell forward, her elbows hitting the desk, her head landing on her hands.
"Oh, beam me up please, this is not happening!" she said.
Kathy laughed. Frankie parted her fingers slightly and peeked through the gap at Kathy.
"I had a very interesting and entertaining dinner, although I suspect your salmon tasted far better than mine, as I didn't have six feet of rippling muscle feeding it to me!"
"Oh God, make it stop!" Kathy was a friend, and had seen her dating other guys when she was a Registrar, but she knew she hadn't ever witnessed anything like Saturday night.

Slowly Frankie removed her hands.
"So, you were in the restaurant... um, were you... also... in the bar?" Frankie was looking down over the top of her glasses at Kathy.
"Mmm, yes! Okay Frankie, I'm going to be honest with you here. I had heard the rumours about you two, but I dismissed them. You made it quite clear to me that you were here to rid yourself of a man, not gain one. But believe me, when I saw his face as you entered that bar, and the way you looked at him, I swear the temperature of the room increased by about twenty degrees!"
Frankie looked down at her hands and let out a little laugh.
"Judging by your reaction, this is no ordinary fling for you, and it's obvious that the feeling is mutual. Does this mean I get to keep you?" Kathy asked the question slowly and quietly.

Frankie continued staring at her hands; again, it was taking every ounce of effort not to burst into tears, but her eyes were welling anyway, she couldn't help that. She looked up at Kathy, choked, unable to speak. She screwed her eyes up and shook her head slowly a few times before speaking.

Kathy quickly rolled her chair over to comfort Frankie, but she put hands out to stop her.

"Don't Kathy, don't, please," Frankie sniffed, and then looked up at the ceiling. "All my life I have searched for a man who is nothing like my father. I finally find him, and I have to leave him." Kathy handed her a tissue as a lone tear escaped, and made a run for it down her left cheek.

"Frankie, I..."

"It's okay, he's still mine for another couple of months, so I'm just going to enjoy that time and take it from there." She took a deep breath and composed herself. "Has my mascara run?"

"A little, but it's fixable," Kathy said, as she laughed a little.

"Thanks, this goes no further, okay?"

"Do you really need to say that?"

Frankie just smiled weakly before getting up to leave.

Walking through the Theatre doors and straight into the female changing room, she was on a mission not to be seen by anyone, especially Jack. After a quick scan around the lockers, she was confident she was alone. Exhaling slowly, she bent over the sink. She looked up at the pale, red-eyed, mascara-smudged reflection in the mirror. Her eyes started to pool again as she shook her head, then looked down into the white basin below.

"For the love of God, woman get a grip!" she said to herself, taking a deep breath, then stood up, looking once again at her reflection.

"It's okay... I'm okay... I WILL be okay!" she said, then leant into the mirror to smooth out the smudges. "Enough already, it's not like you're getting on a plane tomorrow." Taking another deep breath, she stood up straight, with her shoulders back; she was ready to face the world again.

In Theatre 8 Jack found himself alone with Heather while they set up for the next case.

"I don't want to sound nosey Jack, but I have to ask how things..." Heather raised her eyebrows at him as she emphasised the word 'things', "are going, you know, personally?"

Jack was grinning like a teenager!

"Well," he began, "you know we went away to Lumley Castle for the weekend?"

"Oh really?! I remember her bidding on it *that night*, although she said it was for her aunt?" she remarked, setting out trays.

"Well, that was the original plan, but her aunt couldn't go, so..." Jack was checking over the anaesthetic machine.

"Soooooo!" Heather stopped what she was doing and turned around, putting her hand on her hip.

"So, we went... AND, her aunt happened to mention to me that it was her birthday, though Frankie never said a word," he continued, whilst resetting the monitor.

"And? Oh, this is going to be romantic, I just know it!" Heather excitedly tipped sterile gloves onto her tray, practically dancing on the spot.

He proceeded to give Heather a brief outline of the weekend, leaving out the obvious bits, although he knew she could read between the lines. She was suitably impressed, and told him he could arrange birthday surprises for her, with yellow diamonds and champagne, any time he liked! As other staff started to return to the theatre, Heather followed Jack into the anaesthetic room before she went to scrub for the case.

She leaned against the bench with her arms folded and looked at him seriously.

He was drawing up drugs and paused to look up at Heather.

"Where's it all going, Jack?" She looked him straight in the eye; she wanted a straight answer.

He broke eye contact and looked at the floor, exhaling quickly.

"I love her; I just can't tell her because I don't want to be responsible for taking her away from everything she's worked hard for. She said right at the beginning that she can't stay and I don't expect her to, but it will haunt me for the rest of my life if it doesn't work out." He continued to stare at the floor. Heather could see he was tormented by what he was about to say.

"But?" she urged.

He finally looked up at her.

"But, my heart followed one woman and look what happened. I'm not strong enough to go through that again, especially as this time it would mean moving half way around the world. Never mind the whole job situation and leaving my family." He let out a big sigh, and aimed the needle at a small glass vial.

"Oh Jack, I'm sorry! I didn't mean to upset you; you're just so happy these days that I thought you might have considered... well, I'm sorry. I believe Vancouver is a beautiful place though; it could be a great fresh start," she said, rubbing his arm gently. "I'm here, okay. Talk, anytime." She pressed her lips together and gave him a sad smile.

"Thanks."

By lunchtime, both Frankie and Jack had put their emotions aside and were sitting, separately, in the staff room, sending X-rated texts to each other over lunch. Frankie was determined not to put her professional reputation at further risk, following the top-swapping incident; however she was finding it very difficult not to have naughty thoughts as he sent suggestive comments into outer space and back to her. She pointed this out, and added that she wanted him, unshowered, post-workout, with damp sweaty curls and a ravenous appetite. She would be lying naked on the bed, massaging her need, until he returned in that perfect hot state!

Denise, who breezed in and proceeded to pin a large notice on the staff communication board, interrupted them.

Denise's 50th Birthday Bash!
   70's Fancy Dress - no admission otherwise!
   Saturday June 8th, 7 till late.
   Gosforth Park Hotel
   Come and let your hair down and
   celebrate my half century!

"Wow, Dee, you're really going for it. I thought you were going to have a quiet family thing?" said one of the nurses sat nearby, as Dee pinned the poster up.

"Well, you know, you have to embrace these things, and any excuse for a party! Oh, and any couples," Frankie was taken aback at the way Denise's eyes darted between her and Jack, "I expect you to be a fancy dress couple, you know... a couple of members of ABBA, Danny and Sandy from Grease, two wombles... whatever takes your fancy!"

Frankie couldn't help looking over at Jack, trying to ascertain whether or not he would even consider going to this gong show.

His look... why not!

Frankie quickly turned away from him, dismissing the whole thing altogether, but she had to admit to herself that she loved fancy dress parties.

Just when Frankie thought her day had gone to hell in a handbasket, and an early finish was a done deal, the patient on the table in Theatre 1 arrested. There was a third year registrar in there having difficulty, and as Frankie was free, she did the decent thing and offered some assistance. Unfortunately, two hours later and despite their best efforts she and the surgeon, Mr. Connelly, jointly pronounced the patient dead. At the end of what had already been a heavy day of emotion, Frankie just wanted out of there so she could enjoy a hot and sweaty piece of heaven.

One glass of Shiraz, a Cadbury's Wispa and copious amounts of affection from Hercules was enough to smooth away the day. She placed a Cumberland pie in the oven for dinner after Jack had texted her to get her kit off, as he was on his way.
"Well big guy, the things you get rewarded with for being such a good girl." Hercules was sitting on a barstool; she tickled him under the chin and poured herself another glass of wine. "My reward is on his way, so I had better do as he demands and make myself available for his pleasure." She stroked Hercules' head and turned on her heel with her wine, making her way to the bedroom.

Jack opened the door to the flat. Bocelli was quietly singing about all the ridiculous names for Ben & Jerry's ice cream, but making it sound like a romantic hymn. There was a dim lamp on in the living room, Hercules had retired to his radiator bed, and the natural glow of candles was emanating from the bedroom. Dropping his bag inside the door, he glanced at the end of the bed as he slipped his trainers and nasty socks off. All he could see were two bare feet, toes pointing to the floor, hanging over the end of the bed. He leaned against the doorway and folded his arms, grinning. She was lying on her front, her small curvy bottom like a large ripe peach just waiting to be tasted. Letting his eyes travel further, he took in the sight of the small of her back where she liked to be kissed, she was hugging a pillow, her beautiful copper hair hanging over her left shoulder, and her face resting on her left arm. She looked simply irresistible.

"I trust you are sufficiently warmed up, Mr. Lee; I wouldn't want to be responsible for you straining anything, now would I?"

"Well, as you can see, at your request I came straight home to attend to your needs."

Walking towards the bed, he removed his very damp shirt. Frankie turned over and bent her knees up before sliding her hand between her legs.

She was so turned on, just seeing him in his sweaty shorts and shirt, his hair even more curly than usual because it was damp. She couldn't help herself; Mrs. Clit-tor-rus was going to spontaneously erupt.

"You'd better hurry up, you look like a delicious naughty dessert without the calories. One bite and I will taste a burst of flavour." She was letting her fingers carefully explore, enough to keep her aroused but not enough to tip her over the edge.

Although Jack enjoyed doing this for her, now he knew how, he sometimes liked to watch her. In the candlelight, she looked like she was the star of a porn movie, for his personal viewing only. His shorts hit the floor at the foot of the bed. He didn't take his eyes off her as he crawled up next to her and began to kiss her passionately. She moaned as he rubbed his damp forehead against hers; his sweaty scent was intoxicating. As she slowly played with herself, her other hand moved over his hot, sticky back.

He could tell by her breathing that she was close, so he took her busy hand and brought it to his mouth. He slid her fingers in, so he could taste her, as she pressed her hip against his throbbing erection. When he was finished tasting, he kissed the tips of her fingers.

"You're already bursting with flavour, Doctor," he whispered. "I'm aching so much for you that this is going to be quick... sorry."

"No need to apologise, just take me, I'm on the top of Mount Everest here, I just need you to help me plant my flag!"

The words weren't quite out of her mouth when he flipped her over, pushing her left leg up so she was in a semi recovery position. Before she had time to protest, he was inside her and moving hard and fast. She loved it when he took charge like this, and was a little rough. This was a side of him she'd never thought existed, but now that he was more confident and relaxed, he occasionally surprised her. He wasn't too rough; it was passionate, deep, and just what they both needed.

He lay on top of her, taking some of his weight by leaning on one arm, so he didn't squash her. She was almost purring with pleasure. The oven timer was beeping in the background, as it had been for a few minutes. He kissed the back of her neck, which made her quiver, then he squeezed a bum cheek. She groaned and moved her hips to push into his hand.

"You really are the best therapy, Doctor, don't ever discharge me, will you?" he said, nuzzling her hair.

"I have no intention of discharging you; I would be too worried about you ending up in the wrong hands... But geography might be a problem," she said, hoping to plant a seed in his thoughts.

"Come on, before dinner is inedible, I'm famished." He always found a way to change the subject.

Chapter 24

"You haven't forgotten that Kayla arrives next Friday, have you?" Frankie asked Jack over breakfast the following morning.

"Wow! That came around quick! Do you want me to make myself scarce for the week?" he asked, tucking into a large bowl of granola and Greek yoghurt topped with two sliced bananas.

"Certainly not! I won't last a week without you," she said, winking at him. "I can't get the time off; apparently they are short that week, but Kay knew that might happen. She's pretty good at looking after herself after everything she's been through." Frankie was picking at a slice of toast, drinking her second bucket of tea.

"Ah yes, the crazy husband. You okay?" He asked, nodding at Frankie's half-eaten breakfast and rubbed her knee affectionately.

"Yeah, I just feel a little off this morning, I really should stop drinking during the week." She pulled a face and drained the last of her tea.

"You finished with this?" Jack was pointing to the half slice of toast.

"Yes, you can have it, you're like a human garburator!" she said, getting down from the breakfast bar.

"A human what?" He stood, picking up the toast and looking amused and puzzled.

"A garburator...it's a... oh, never mind, come to Canada and I'll show you mine." She smirked and gave a playful raise of the eyebrows. "Come on, let's go and see what delights await us on Mike's list." She was putting her jacket on, whilst handing Jack his.

"Thanks," he said, taking it from her, "by the way, Dee's birthday?"

"Oh yes, I meant to talk to you about that... but we got a little distracted." Frankie turned and locked the flat door as Jack headed for the stairs.

"Um, just a little." He was stood at the top of the stairs, smirking. He waited for her so he could give her a kiss. "You are very distracting, Doctor," he said, as he pressed his forehead against hers.

"I have a plan!" She pulled away from him, and looked into his sparkling steel blue eyes before they walked down the stairs.

"A plan? What sort of plan?" He knew her well enough now to know that this would either be crazy or risky.

They walked out onto the street and towards Jack's Mini.

"I think we should go dressed as if we we're a couple, but arrive separately and not really pay any attention to each other for the evening and just see what happens." She had her hand on the door handle, looking across the roof of the car at Jack, shrugging her shoulders. "What do you think?"

"I think you're wanting the world to know, without actually telling them! Which couple did you have in mind?" he asked, as they both got in the car.

"Yes, I probably have just got to the point where I want to shout it from the rooftops; however, I think it will be very difficult for us to stay away from each other. A little contest in self control! I challenge you to keep your hands off me. As for which couple..." she clicked her seat belt in and looked up at him. "Do you trust me?"

"No!"

"Oh, come on, why ever not? I don't recall doing anything that could make you feel this way, yet!" she added. Jack was driving towards a set of traffic lights.

"I don't trust you, for fear of being dressed up as Hong Kong Phooey, with you as Rosemary... or something equally humiliating!"

"Oh, get a grip, it's all good fun. You ARE going to have to trust me on this one."

"And you're not going to tell me?"

"Nope!" She gave her best smug-but-playful look, and turned away.

Jack shook his head. He was secretly quite excited at the prospect of her dressing him up, knowing it would lead to further mischief in the end.

With the second patient on the table sleeping safely, Train belting out 'She's On Fire', and Mike Anderson in a good mood as always, Frankie whispered to Jack that she needed a quick visit to the washroom. Everything was under control; he shouldn't have any problems. When Frankie returned, the conversation had shifted from the amount of money women spend on looking good, or trying to anyway, to the finer details of looking good. A good crowd of staff were joining in with the discussion. Heather was scrubbed, with Martin and Olivia circulating, a female Medical Student observing, with a registrar and Alistair, the useless SHO, assisting Mike.

"Ahh, here she is," said Mike as Frankie re-entered the room. "A Brazilian, my good doctor, we need your opinion!"

Frankie looked around the room; she knew exactly what he was asking but decided to play dumb.

"Well I wouldn't say no. I think a man with an accent is quite sexy, and they can usually move well!" Mike cut her off.

"No, no.... okay, a swab please, Heather.... You misunderstood; a wax... you know, completely off." Mike whistled and, in mid-air, circled the genital area of the patient, "You know, not the Mohawk that most women get, but gone, all of it, not a single wisp left!"

"Oh, that kind of Brazilian."

It was a good job she was wearing a mask; she didn't dare look across at Jack. "Are you asking would I, or do I?" She was very matter of fact as she injected a drug into the patient's IV line. She didn't need to look at Jack; she heard him almost choke behind her.

"Thanks Heather, I'll take another..." Mike had started to perspire in anticipation of the answer.

"Well?" said Martin, looking across at Frankie, her eyes smiling back.

Jack was still behind her; she heard him swallow hard.

"I can neither confirm nor deny!" she replied.

The poor medical student was practically hiding behind the anaesthetic machine, hoping not to be included in the conversation. Jack made his way towards the anaesthetic room.

"Oh dear, Jack, is this too much for you? You're not alone; Estelle over there is also quite red; get used to it love, this is what really goes on in theatres I'm afraid," said Olivia, nodding towards the medical student.

Jack turned around before he got to the door.

"Oh, I'm not embarrassed, I'm going to get more IV fluid. Anyway, what do the fellas think? Shall we have their opinion?

"The chap's got a point," said Mike, in his posh British accent. "I'm in favour of it personally!"

"Absolutely, I couldn't agree more!" replied Jack without thinking, looking over at Frankie as he turned to walk through the door.

All eyes were on Frankie.

She looked around, and then shrugged her shoulders. "What?" she said, trying to act surprised.

Everyone returned to concentrating on work. The case was just about done and Frankie was quietly cursing Jack. She would have to deal with him later.

The list finished on time, so they were both done by 5.30. Jack told her he would meet her back at the flat after he'd picked up some groceries. He knew he was going to be in trouble, so he decided to cook for them and see if he could soften the blow. When he walked through the door with four bags of shopping, plus his own work bag, he was met with a stern look as she leaned against the back of the sofa; one leg crossed over the other, her arms folded.

"Good evening sweetheart, don't you rush to help, I'll manage.... Um, do I detect a slight coolness in the air?" Jack knew she was trying to be serious, but if he kept up his little witticisms she might just break. He went to put the bags on the kitchen bench.

It was no good, she wasn't really mad with him; taken aback and slightly annoyed at the time, but she couldn't be mad. He had done their shopping, he was going to cook for them at the end of a day's work, and he looked amazing with his messy hat curls, tight T-shirt, and jeans. She started to feel all twinkly inside as she watched his bulging biceps lift the heavy bags, whilst still trying to look annoyed.

"I'm not happy with you," she finally said.

"Really," he said, exaggerating his surprise. He was dying to laugh at her expression, and was having trouble hiding it.

"Yes really, they all gossip about us enough as it is, without you practically putting a neon sign up that I get a full wax job!" She caved; she couldn't contain herself any longer. She burst out laughing and Jack broke into a smile.

"Ha!" he said, as he went to embrace her, "I knew you weren't really mad."

In one swift move she reached behind herself for a cushion and swatted him over the head with it.

"Hey!" he said, grabbing for the other cushion.

"Why can't I be mad with you for more than five seconds, Jack Lee... You drive me crazy," she said, as she tried to swat him again.

"Because I'm so loveable and you just can't resist me." He grinned at her, then lashed out with his cushion, knocking her slightly off balance. "You know you won't win this game, I'm too quick for you."

"Oh, is that right, well we'll see about that, won't we."

She reversed around to the other side of the sofa so she was stood in front of the fireplace. She then took him by surprise, throwing the cushion at him; bull's eye, she hit him straight in the face. However, he was right; as she tried to pass him and make a run for the bedroom, he stuck his arm out and caught her. She screamed and then collapsed, laughing. He pulled her close, with her back against his front and his strong arms enveloped around her. She was struggling playfully.

"You are a big fat meany!" she said, pouting.

He was burying his nose in her messy copper hair, breathing in her unique scent. He loved it when they played like this, especially after working together all day. They just needed to be silly for a little while, after having to be so serious and professional.

"And you're incredibly attractive, Doctor, when you're trying to be mad." He pushed his hips forward so she could feel what she'd done to him.

"Do I get make up sex then?" she asked, turning in his arms, her hands travelling everywhere.

"Once again, Doctor, you will have to educate me. What qualifies as make up sex?"

"Oh, I will be delighted to educate you, but you will have to let me go."

"Oh, no. I caught you fair and square. Why don't you run through the theory and then I can practise?"

"Okay... so, we frantically rip each others clothes off and then get down to business!"

Jack just laughed.

"Okay," he whispered into her ear.

They undressed each other, shedding each item of clothing quicker than the last. Within minutes Jack had her pinned against the fridge, naked and breathless. The stainless steel was cool against her back, but she found it refreshing. Jack was on fire, his skin was hot and he was perspiring, though that wasn't helping her; her legs were slipping down his hips, but they were both so close; one of the few positions where she came with penetration alone. His great length found a delicious spot deep inside and gave it a full Swedish massage.

Eventually his legs really gave out and they sank to the floor.

She sat on his lap, with her legs around his waist. Nestling her head into his neck, he kissed her tenderly and stroked her hair.

"Are you still mad at me?" he asked, after a few minutes.

"No," she said.

"That's a shame... I think I like make up sex!"

Frankie was washing up while Jack ran a bath for them. She was up to her eyes in rubber gloves and dish soap when the phone started to ring.

"Grrrrr," she growled at the phone, "how do people always know when it's not a good time!"

"I can get it, it's Carol."

"Okay, thanks," she replied, as she desperately tried to extricate herself from her gloves "She'll want to speak to you anyway," she said quietly, as she heard Jack say "Hi Carol" before he playfully stuck his tongue out at her.

Carol had become very fond of Jack, and he was fond of her too. Frankie had no idea what they talked about sometimes, but she didn't really care. It made her happy that he fitted into her family so easily.

"Here you go, sweetheart," he said as he handed her the phone, blowing her a kiss. She pulled a face at him, wrinkling her nose on purpose and then smirked at him, taking the phone.

"Hey, how are you? ...Yes, fine thank you ...I did, it was fabulous thanks to you..." she looked through the bathroom door at Jack who was pretending he wasn't listening. "He did ...yes, I was very spoilt ...Absolutely, the room was gorgeous, the restaurant was lovely ...Yes, of course we left the room! I can't believe ...Yeah, okay, not very much, but the weather was dreadful ...So, what about you?"

Unconsciously, she had bent herself over the end of the breakfast bar.

"No I'm off ...Okay that would be nice ...I will ...Okay, I'll pick you up at about 11 ...Bye." She hung up, but stayed draped over the bench.

"She wants to take me out for a belated birthday lunch tomorrow. I guess I can take time out of the house." Frankie felt guilty for getting distracted from the main focus of her sabbatical. Jack draped himself over her and hugged her tight.

"Stop beating yourself up every time you take a break. You've already found some skeletons in there, and I'm sure there are more surprises in that study. You need down time to stay focused. And you're allowed to have some fun you know!" He gave her a quick squeeze, and then playfully smacked her bottom.

"Oh, Mr. Lee, we're getting into that now are we? I definitely think you might be cured," she said, as she also stood up.

He smiled and winked at her, "Just keeping you on your toes, don't want you getting bored with me… come on, the bath will be getting cold, we'll finish the dishes later." He held his hand out to lead her to the bathroom.

"Oh Jack, before I forget, I was going to pick my pendant up from the jeweller tomorrow, but now I'm doing lunch, " she explained, as she followed him into the bathroom; he moved for her to get into the bath first. "Any chance you could pop in after work if you're not too late? I should have picked it up before we went away, but I didn't have time." She sank down into the hot soothing water and grimaced a little, "As it happens, I probably wouldn't have worn it anyway." She grinned up at him, as he eased himself in behind her.

"Are you okay? You seem uncomfortable?" he asked, as he gathered up her hair for her and placed a clip in it.

She lay back against him; it was one the best feelings in the world.

"I have a slightly over-used area of my anatomy that is protesting a little bit. It's fine, just stings a little when I first get in." She linked his fingers in the water.

"Ahh, poor baby, maybe we should abstain for a while?" He screwed his face up, knowing this was an impossible suggestion.

She twisted her head to look up at him.

"Wash your mouth out with soap, young man, we'll do no such thing!"

He burst out laughing at her.

"Fair enough," he hugged her tight, "and yes, I can go to the jeweller's for you, they kind of know me now."

"Oh really, what exactly did you say to them when you bought my diamonds?"

"I told them that I believed my girlfriend had brought her mother's ring in to be altered and that she had been admiring some yellow diamonds... And I wanted to buy them!"

"I bet they were all over you like a rash!"

"Mmm, they thought you were a very lucky girl!"

"Well, I am, and not just because I have yellow diamonds." She squeezed his hands in the water.

Frankie picked Carol up just before eleven. They drove out to a garden centre with a very good café, near Ponteland. Frankie knew it well; both her aunt and her mum had regularly taken her, Andrew, and her cousins there as children. It had something for everyone: playground, coffee, ice cream and, of course, all the delights a garden centre can offer the amateur horticulturist. Frankie hadn't been in such a long time; it brought back a lot of memories of her mum. Carol was sensitive to this; she saw Frankie's usual bounciness fade a little as they walked towards the café. Carol linked arms with her, giving her an affectionate squeeze.

"Come on pet, we're going to have a nice lunch and a good old natter... And I want a full, unedited update!"

Frankie gave Carol a weak smile as they approached the door.

The café had been renovated since Frankie's last visit some years ago. They had extended the seating area by building a large conservatory, which gave the illusion of being in a greenhouse. There were, inevitably, plants everywhere, and soft instrumental music, the kind you only hear in garden centres, playing annoyingly in the background. They ordered some food, then found a table by an open window.

"There you go pet, they'll be over with our lunch shortly; we just have to listen out for our number." Carol placed her tray down and decanted its contents onto the table.

"How was your long weekend?" Frankie asked, as she poured the cold, fizzy water into a glass.

"Oh, you know, that uncle of yours had me up at that golf club all day on Sunday, and it wasn't the nicest of days. Then we were back for the dinner in the evening - with the same bunch of boring old farts!" Carol rolled her eyes and took a sip of her water.

Frankie laughed.

"You really aren't into the golf scene, are you?"

"I wouldn't mind if the wives were all right, but most of them are as stuck up as their husbands. I do it for Eric's sake, but I've told him twice a year is enough, the next one is Christmas." Carol looked at Frankie intensely, trying to decide on her opening line.

Frankie was unconsciously scratching at a groove in the table when she became aware of Carol's silence, and felt her eyes on her. Looking up at her aunt, she knew what she wanted to hear.

"I love him, Aunty... It's as complicated and as simple as that, and deep down I know it's going to end when I get on that plane." She felt tears pricking in her eyes, so she nipped the bridge of her nose to stop her makeup running.

"Yes I know, look at him, what's not to love."

She looked up at Carol, who was nodding with approval and jokingly started to fan herself with her hand, making Frankie smile.

"But it isn't just that he's drop dead gorgeous, I feel like I've known him forever. It's the way he treats me, respects me, is interested in everything about me, from the fact that I don't like kiwi fruit to which shampoo I use. He's loving, caring, funny, hardworking, playful, interesting, and looks after himself; I could go on and on! God, he can even cook! I love him with every part of my being and..." Carol interrupted her.

"...And, he's nothing like your father," she said, as the waitress called their number and brought over their lunch. Placing it on the table she said, "Enjoy."

Frankie stared out of the window, desperately trying not to fall apart at the seams.

"Yes, you're right. It's the first time I've ever really felt loved by a man - properly loved - and it's amazing!"

"You don't think he might consider coming with you?" Carol asked, as she placed a napkin on her lap.

Frankie shook her head slowly. "He followed Emma to Newcastle and look what happened. I don't think he's strong enough to do it again. Besides, we don't have ODPs, so his job isn't transferable. It would be the perfect opportunity for him to re-train and do what he originally wanted to do. He's asked me to give him time, but I just know." Frankie started to nibble on her lunch.

"Well, I think you can be pretty confident that he feels the same way about you. He adores you, pet, anyone can see that, and it's lovely to see. He *is* lovely."

"You've got quite a soft spot for him, haven't you?" Frankie was smirking at Carol as she took a drink of water. Carol went a little red.

"Aunty Carol, are you blushing?"

"Well, it's not surprising after what I caught the two of you doing! Honestly, I don't know how you manage to work with him all day without dragging him into a broom cupboard every hour for a bit of nooky!" Carol said, straight-faced as she carried on eating.

Frankie nearly choked on a piece of cucumber, and took another drink.

Frankie raised her eyebrows and gave Carol a cheeky little grin, "We only let it happen once at work, and I swore it wasn't going to happen again after we ended up dealing with a sick patient on the ward, wearing each other's scrub tops!"

Carol burst out laughing.

"Fantastic!" she said, "I bet it was like something out of a 'Carry On' film."

"Yeah, something like that!" She smiled at Carol, who smiled back.

They continued talking over lunch about Frankie's relationship with Jack. Frankie talked about all the sweet things Jack had done for her birthday. She was wearing her diamonds so she could show Carol, who admired them glistening in the sunshine. She explained her plan for the fancy dress party, which Carol thought was a fabulous idea. Frankie updated Carol on the progress with the house and its sale. Then Carol treated them to coffee and cake.

It was no good; the latté that sat on the table in front of her just wasn't nice. Frankie wished she'd asked for tea. When Carol went to the washroom, Frankie got the waitress to take it away. Carol wanted to pick up a couple of things in the garden centre, so Frankie, who had not inherited a single gardening gene, sat outside in the sunshine feeling very stuffed after her 'light' lunch.

They chatted more as Frankie drove Carol home. As they pulled into the driveway, Frankie was expecting to leave and not go into the house, but Carol insisted she come in.

"I told Jack to let you know I have something for you, when he gave you your card," said Carol, as she undid her seatbelt.

"Oh yes, sorry he did mention that... Okay."

There was only the dog at home, so Carol let him out into the back garden and ordered Frankie to sit at the table while she popped upstairs. She returned a few minutes later with a box.

"I haven't wrapped it up or anything; it didn't seem right. I suppose it's not really a birthday present. Before your mum died, she gave me most of the photographs from your and Andrew's childhood - school photos, holiday snaps, and anything else she could find. As you know, your father wasn't one for family pictures. She made me promise that I would make sure that you and Andrew received them, after she died. As you can appreciate, that's not been an easy thing to do with you both living abroad, and to be honest; I haven't felt it was right until now. I took my time sorting through them and making scrapbooks for you both," Carol was filling with tears, "so, here you are, pet, look at it once you're at home. It might even be nice to sit down with Jack, so that you've got someone to share it with. He asks about you as a child, you know."

"He does?" Frankie took the box from Carol. "Thank you so much, I don't know what to say." Frankie placed the box on the table, got up, and flung her arms around Carol.

"Thank you is enough pet; you're very welcome." Carol hugged Frankie tight.

"I love you Aunty Carol, this means so much to me."

Carol eased Frankie away from their embrace so she could look at her. She took Frankie's face in her hands.

"I already know that pet, it's not me you should be telling." She kissed her forehead and hugged her again.

Jack finished work on time. He left his car parked at the hospital and walked into town. He was instantly recognised by Marcus, the owner of Elegant Touch Jewellery, as soon as he walked in. Jack handed him the receipt for Frankie's jewellery. Marcus showed Jack the pendant and the other items Frankie had left with him. Everything seemed fine; the pendant was simply set in white gold with a fine chain, and was beautiful.

"There is just one more thing," Marcus said to Jack. "The lady didn't get back to me about what she wanted to do with the ring once the diamond had been removed, so I've left it in the box. I'd be more than happy to discuss the options with her."

"Okay, I'll let her know." Jack couldn't remember what the ring looked like. "Um... may I just take a quick look at it?" he asked Marcus.

"Of course, it's a stunning ring, platinum. I was surprised she didn't want to have it enlarged, so she could wear it herself."

Jack stood gazing at the ring; it was stunning even without the diamond.

"As a matter of interest Marcus, how easy would it be to put one of those yellow diamonds in here?"

Marcus took a deep breath and shook his head slightly as he blew it out slowly.

"Difficult, but not impossible. I'd need time, and it wouldn't be cheap, that's for sure."

"Okay... thanks." Jack nodded, and handed back the ring for Marcus to place in the bag with the other items, then made his way back to his car.

Back at the flat, he gave Frankie the bag after a long 'Hello' kiss; she was thrilled with the pendant and was quick to try it on. She examined the other items; the pearls were more valuable than she'd thought, but she wasn't sure if she would ever wear them; the eternity ring had scrubbed up well and the engagement ring looked odd without its stone.

"I guess this will just get pushed to the back of a drawer and forgotten about," she sighed, closing the box and placing it back in the bag, before heading into kitchen.

Jack stared at the bag for a long moment, considering the ring and what Marcus, the jeweller had advised him about the replacing the stone.

Chapter 25

SATURDAY MORNINGS HAD become sleeping in time for Jack, with Frankie taking a short time just to enjoy the feel of him sleeping next to her before extracting herself from his safe, warm arms and padding around the flat quietly until he woke. They would then make slow, passionate love, followed by a hot shower. This Saturday while Frankie was getting dressed, she received a text from her brother, asking if they could Face Time.

"We don't have to go out yet, do we?" she asked Jack, who was clearing away the breakfast dishes shirtless, in jeans and bare feet.

"No, why?"

"Andrew wants to Face Time."

"Okay, you want me to say hi?" he asked.

"Would you like to?"

"Sure, why not," he said, apprehensive.

She kissed his back, and then hugged him tight.

"Thanks, I'll get back to him." She pulled away from him and picked up her phone.

Ten minutes later Frankie was sat in front of her iPad, accepting the call. She was sat on the sofa alone; Jack was in the bathroom. She had suggested he put on a shirt.

"Hello, my lovely," said Andrew, as his face appeared on the screen, "You're looking well. How's it going?"

"Great! How about you?" Frankie sat beaming at her brother. A familiar Glaswegian drawl in the background interrupted them.

"Halloo darlin'! I'll be wi' you in two ticks."

"Hey Gussy," she replied.

Jack came out of the bathroom and walked around the table in front of Frankie, so he was standing behind the iPad, unseen on camera.

"So, where are you up to with everything since the house sold?" Andrew asked, "and am I to presume that all is still well with your shag mate?"

"Andy, I'm not alone. He's right here, would you like to say hi?" Frankie was never surprised at anything her brother said, but she could shoot him sometimes.

"Would love to, about time we vetted him and made sure he's good enough for my little sis!"

Frankie reached her arm out to Jack, who came and sat beside her, still shirtless.

"I told you to put a shirt on," she whispered to him as he put his arm around her and cuddled up close.

"I'm too hot," he said quietly, as she rolled her eyes at him.

"Well Andrew, this is Jack." Andrew nodded and said, "Hi."

"Jack, this is my big brother, Andrew."

Suddenly the picture at their end started to wobble as Angus practically fell over Andrew to get in front of the camera.

"Oh, let me in ...I want tae see him ...Shift ya sell..." Angus fell back onto the sofa at their end. "Am here darlin'...Well introduce me, come on." Angus sat grinning from ear to ear into the camera, and spoke again before Frankie could introduce them. "Jeepers! He's like a Greek God! Hallooooo am the wife, Angus, pleased tae meet you." Angus raised his hand to Jack in a kind of wave.

Frankie looked up at Jack and mouthed, 'Sorry'. Jack just pulled her closer and kissed the top of her head.

"Give it up Gussy, you can look but not touch!" she said.

"Well, I can see he's treating you right darlin'. Okay Mr. Jack, you look after our wee lassie there or Gussy will be round tae sort you oot!"

"Don't you worry about that Angus, she's in safe hands, I promise. It's good to finally see you both; she talks about you all the time." Jack was very relaxed, despite sitting shirtless and being ogled by two horny old gays!

"Well, we'll get a chance to meet properly soon," said Andrew. "Angus here has a conference in Paris next month, starting on the 17th, for three days, so we thought we would tag on a long weekend with you lovely people before flying back on Monday. What do you think?"

"Sure." Frankie looked up at Jack for reassurance; she wanted to make sure that he was okay with that too. He shrugged his shoulders in agreement. "That should be fine. I'll be at work on the Friday, but you guys can look after yourselves, I'm sure."

"Great! Well, I'll sort out the flights and let you know about the itinerary. I can't remember, does Lucy's place have a spare room, or bed?" Andrew asked.

"Absolutely, no problem to stay with us." Again she looked up at Jack as Angus spoke.

"Ooh, it's us now, is it?" Angus said with a smirk.

"Gussy, behave." Frankie shook her head at him.

Frankie and Andrew continued the conversation without Jack or Angus. Frankie updated him on the house and her lovely birthday weekend; she didn't mention the photos from Carol because she knew he was going to receive a similar scrapbook himself. They wrapped up a short while later, everyone saying goodbye before Frankie signed off.

"I did warn you," she said to Jack, as she walked into the bedroom; he was now looking for a shirt to go out in.

"Yes you did, and they were as colourful as you made out; Angus maybe more so!" He smiled at her, and went to give her a hug. "It's fine, and important; they are your family and I want to get to know them the same way you spent time getting to know mine."

"Thanks," she said, before enjoying a lingering kiss.

"Come on, we can nail the rest of that house so that we only have the study to do after Kayla leaves. Then, I think we should go out for dinner," Jack said in a very jovial tone.

"Really? Are you sure?" She was looking at him at arms length, with her hands resting on his naked hips.

"Yes, really. Look, I'm pretty sure everyone knows already, especially after the look Dee shot us in the staff room the other day. Obviously Heather knows and now Kathy too. I think we've done well to get this far; I like our secret games, but I'm sick of not going out and just being a normal couple." He rested his arms on her shoulders as he spoke.

"Okay," she said, before burying her face in his chest hair and giving him a tight squeeze.

Jack was right, they spent the entire afternoon clearing the remaining contents of the upstairs. All that was left now was a few things they were still using in the kitchen, and her father's study. They had promised Carol that they would go to family lunch that Sunday, and as Sunday mornings often ended up the same way as Saturday mornings, there wasn't a cat in hell's chance of them doing anything more that weekend.

As predicted, the following morning was spent fooling around. They were both in a bit of a goofy mood, frolicking like teenagers and play-fighting. They had gone to a local bistro the night before, and enjoyed a romantic dinner. Frankie was sure they had put something illegal in the sticky toffee pudding they shared for dessert. They were lying on the bed, naked, and laughing at poor Hercules who had had the misfortune of joining them in the heat of the moment, and had his tail grabbed accidentally by Frankie as she came. The cat had yelped loudly then jumped off the bed and started to frantically wash himself, as if embarrassed by what had happened. It didn't end there; Jack put Frankie over his shoulder and playfully spanked her all the way to the shower for attacking such an innocent creature... And so it went on. By the time they reached Carol and Eric's they were as high as kites.

Just before they left, Eric put Frankie completely on the spot.

"So, how do you find that thing?" He was stood at the living room window, pointing to Jack's Mini. "Much different to yours?"

Frankie thought Jack was still in the bathroom; she had no idea he was standing behind her in the doorway.

"Well, I haven't actually driven it, but it feels a bit slow. It's a One, right, whereas mine is a Cooper S, so it goes like a bomb..."

"Well, well, well, Doctor... so let me get this straight," said Jack, making his presence known as he quietly slipped his arms over Frankie's shoulders, making her jump. "You have made fun of my Mini since I managed to lure you into it on a cold and windy February night, and if I just heard correctly...YOU have one!"

Frankie pressed her lips together and glanced sideways at Jack. She opened her mouth to say something, but then thought better of it and closed it again.

"Well? Did I hear correctly?" He was holding her tight, and wasn't letting her go until he had an answer.

For the first time in their short relationship, she couldn't read him. *Was he joking? Was he being serious?*

She nodded her head slowly, still looking sideways at him and biting her lip.

"Interesting," he said, as he pulled away and stood next to her with his arms folded, looking out of the window at his Mini.

Frankie looked at Eric, who was now stood with his hand over his mouth trying not to laugh. He was pretty sure Jack was winding Frankie up.

"Next, you're going to tell me it's a John Cooper Works Convertible in Eclipse metallic grey, with carbon black leather interior, light alloy wheels, sport suspension and a Harman Kardon sound system!" Jack reeled off, without taking his eyes off his own car outside.

"Almost," Frankie began, looking sheepish. "Mine also has those black and white Union Jack flag mirrors, and is wired, but the rest is pretty spot on!" She nodded, trying to look impressed.

Jack turned to look at her; his jaw had now hit the floor.

"I was actually making most of that up, after building several Minis on the w-website," he stuttered. "So, not only have you ribbed my Mini for the last three months, you OWN my fantasy Mini."

"I'm just going... to... excuse myself..." Eric made a sharp exit.

"Umm," Frankie again looked sideways at Jack, who still stood with his mouth open.

"Frankie that must be nearly thirty grand's worth of car!" Jack was now speaking to her as if she was crazy for spending that amount of money on a car.

"Fifty actually, but that's not the point; I'm sorry if I've been winding you up. You knew I had a car at home, if you'd asked me about it I would have told you, but you never did." She shrugged her shoulders, and tried an innocent smile.

"Sweetheart, a few minutes ago when I walked in and found out, I wasn't sure whether to be mad with you or kiss you. Now, I don't know whether to respect you for spending that amount on a car, or for earning that much to pay for it!"

"It probably won't help you to know that I paid cash for it then," Frankie stood with her fingers locked together in front of her, looking down at the floor.

"You...WHAT!!" Wide eyed, he stood gawping at her with his mouth open.

Frankie knew she shouldn't have said that. "God Jack, you have no idea how much I earn, do you?"

"Clearly not!!" He managed to say, placing his hands on his hips.

Frankie swallowed hard. She thought that, maybe, if he did have insight into her earnings and the fact that she could financially look after both of them, then he might just consider going back with her. There was an awkward silence between them that they had never experienced before.

"I thought this was about me owning a Mini, not how I paid for it," she said, quietly. She continued to stare at him, then turned to go and say goodbye to everyone.

They drove home in silence. Jack had intended it to be funny, but it had ended in a rift about money. He didn't earn in a year what she had paid for her car. He had had no idea she earned that much; moreover, what he didn't understand was why it was bothering him so much. *'She's a doctor for Christ's sake,'* he thought; of course she was going to earn more than him. He was mad at himself, not her. He would never be able to compete with that; he suddenly felt very inadequate. Pulling up outside the flat, the atmosphere was becoming unbearable. Part of him wanted to drive away once she'd got out, and go back to his own place to think.

"You have your keys Jack, if you decide you want to talk about this." Without looking at him, she climbed out of the car, slamming the door shut without looking back. She could tell by the way he hesitated, before switching the engine off that he was considering not following her.

She climbed the stairs, thumbing through her keys to the flat. As she shut the door behind her and leaned against it, banging her head against the wood, Hercules rubbed himself against her legs purring.

"Hey big guy," she said, after a moment of not really thinking about anything in particular. She bent down to stroke him and lifted him up for a cuddle. He was like a warm, furry power tool vibrating in her arms.

"I think I might have just blown it." She kicked her pumps off and sat on the sofa, placing the cat next to her. Her head fell back as she exhaled slowly. What the hell was that all about? One minute he was all playful; the next he was angry. All because she'd stupidly mentioned that she'd paid cash for her car. She didn't understand why it should matter; if they were going to have any sort of future together - and that was turning out to be a big if - then she would have to convince him that their salaries would just become one joint pot of money. She always saw it being that way, whomever she was with. Right now, however, she wasn't even sure if he was coming back.

Suddenly she heard the key in the door. She wanted to jump up and hug him just for not running. She didn't look around, but was aware he was stood just inside the door. Slowly, she glanced at the door; he was stood with his back to her, his hand still on the doorknob. She stopped stroking the cat and slowly got up; Jack didn't move. She approached him from behind and slipped her arms around his waist, pressing her cheek against his back. His heart was beating fast against her hands.

"I don't want something so stupid to come between us Jack, it really isn't worth fighting about."

She felt him take a deep breath and sigh before rubbing his face with his hands.

Slowly he turned around; she didn't drop her arms, instead she let him glide between them. He placed his arms over her shoulders and pressed his forehead against hers.

"Honestly, it's my problem; it shouldn't be a problem, but for some reason it is for me," he said.

"Jack I'm not sure if you realise, but I live in one of the most desirable cities in the world and that comes with a price tag; and requires a salary to match. Okay, so I have a nice car, and I own my own place, but I have a roommate for a reason. I can't afford to live on my own. I cycle to work because gas and parking is too expensive; hell, I go to a training school to have my hair cut because it only costs me 12 bucks! Jack, I earn nearly $400,000 a year, but high taxes and cost of living means I live a very normal life, a life I love and wouldn't... couldn't, give up. The only thing that's missing is someone special to share it with, and that's exactly what I would do, share it. Whatever I earn, I have, I own, would become his too." She touched his face as he kissed her forehead.

Jack sighed, then spoke.

"I know what you're trying to say, and I appreciate the offer. I've been very naïve; I only know you here, in this flat, driving that wretched box." They both laughed. "I can't picture you anywhere else but here. I've never been outside of Europe, never mind to North America; I have no idea what it's like."

"I'm still the same person, Jack, I just fit in better over there."

"Yeah, I can see you probably do." He stood straight and brushed her hair away from her face as she looked up at him. "We still haven't addressed the original issue," he said.

"Which was?"

"The fact that you own my fantasy car, and have been winding me up for months about my car." His face had softened; he now had a playful look, even a hint of a smirk. But she had to seize the moment.

"Well, the offer is there Jack, your fantasy could become a reality."

He pulled her close and held her tight for a few moments, before taking her chin and bending to place a lingering kiss on her smooth, full lips.

"It's like your lips were only made for me to kiss," he whispered.

She slowly smiled while their noses pressed together.

"We Were Made For This; California 37; 2012; track 10," she said quietly.

Chapter 26

ANOTHER BUSY WEEK flew by and, before Frankie knew it, she was receiving a text from Kayla on Friday afternoon; she'd landed safely at Heathrow Airport. She had a three-hour layover before her connection to Newcastle, which was fine, because although Frankie's list was running on time for a change, she was still not going to be done until at least 6pm. The plan was to take a chance in leaving work together, and pick Kayla up in Jack's car. Her plane was due to land at 6.25pm.

Jack finished about half an hour ahead of Frankie, so he strolled down to the coffee shop. He was stood in the line-up when someone tapped him on the shoulder; he turned to see Kathy stood behind him.

"Let me guess, you're killing time while you wait for someone?" she said with an exaggerated wink.

"Mmm, something like that," he replied, turning back to look ahead again, feeling slightly embarrassed.

"No need to go all shy on me, Jack. I'm happy for you both, and it's nice to see you happy again."

Jack reached the front of the queue and ordered.

"Thanks Kathy, we're still trying to keep it to ourselves, if that's okay." He took his change and picked up his coffee.

"I know, although I'm not too sure it's the big secret you think it is. However, I won't breathe a word… just one more thing." Kathy was well known by the barista; she was handed her usual and paid.

"Yes?" Jack said curiously, while adding milk and a lid.

"Keep an open mind; all this," she waved her hand around, "doesn't have to be it you know. It's a beautiful city, Vancouver."

Jack stared for a moment. "I'll remember that," he said, before giving her a weak smile, as his phone buzzed with a text from Frankie to say she was done.

They pulled into a parking space in the short-term parking lot just before 6.30pm.

"You want me to come with you?" Jack asked.

"Of course, why wouldn't I?" She looked at him, puzzled.

"Well, you know, you haven't seen her in a while, I just thought maybe you would like to meet her on your own, before you introduce me."

"Jack, I haven't stopped talking to her about you since we met, there is no way I'm going to get away with leaving you out here. Just remember though; she's a hard-core Aussie, her inside voice is also her outside voice, okay?"

Jack gave one of his slow, heart-melting smiles.

"I'll remember that. Come on, let's go get her!"

As they walked into the arrivals area Frankie looked up at the board and noticed Kayla's plane had just landed. They found a spot to stand, right in front of the doors.

"Feels really weird stood here; this is where Thomas met me when I arrived," Frankie said, as Jack slid his arms over her shoulders and crossed them over her chest, he bent down so they were cheek to cheek. They swayed slightly while looking at the automatic doors.

"Lucky Thomas!" he said, as he kissed her ear.

"Oh, I don't know about that; I was pretty tired and grumpy, not to mention my bad, long haul flight hair!"

Jack gave her a squeeze and purred into her ear.

"Pretty and bad hair... yummy!" he said, placing soft kisses behind her ear.

"Behave yourself, Mr. Lee. Remember, we're going to have a house guest, so you're going to have to control that bed snake of yours."

"Or what?" He asked, nibbling at her ear.

"Or, he's going to be one very lonely reptile!" she whispered.

They were so caught up in each other that they didn't notice the automatic doors open in front of them.

"FRANKIE!" Kayla shouted, as she bounded towards them, one arm open, awaiting a hug, the other pulling her suitcase.

"Kay!" Frankie was snapped out of her Jack trance by the sound of her friend's voice; at the same time Jack relaxed his arms and stood back so she could rush forward and fling her arms around Kayla.

Behind Frankie, but in Kayla's full view, Jack was lighting up the entire airport with his smile. He stood, with his hands in the pockets of his jeans, watching them both.

"Oh, I can't begin to tell you how much I've missed you! Come on, you must be shattered." Frankie broke their embrace and looked at Kayla at arms length; but Kayla was looking right at the man standing watching them.

"Me too, I'm so excited to be here hun, but don't you think you should introduce us?" Kayla nodded in Jack's direction.

Frankie turned around, absolutely beaming, and held her hand out to Jack. He took a step forwards and slipped his arm around her waist as she did the same.

"Kayla, I would like you to meet Jack," she said.

Kayla smiled and nodded, "Great to finally put a face to the name, Jack."

Frankie looked up at Jack, adoringly, "Jack, meet my best friend Kayla."

Jack nodded back at Kayla. "Likewise," he said.

Jack's first impression, he thought to himself, was that Kayla was nothing like he'd expected. She was taller than Frankie, but then most people were. She had long, crazy, thick and wavy dark blonde hair. She was very curvaceous, with a very large chest and a substantial backside. She was undeniably attractive, and seemed to ooze with energy, even after a long haul flight. He could tell he was going to get along well with her.

"Here, let me take your suitcase." He held his hand out, and Kayla wheeled it towards him.

"Thanks mate, that would be great," she replied.

As Jack turned away from them, pulling the suitcase, Kayla looked at Frankie, wide-eyed and jaw-dropped. 'WOW!' she mouthed. Frankie grinned, and mouthed back, 'Stop it!'. Kayla continued to admire the view in front of her. She was watching Jack's perfect backside being hugged tightly in a pair of dark wash jeans. She looked again at Frankie as they walked, lips pursed with an *'Oh My God, what I'd do to cop a feel of that!'* kind of look. Frankie knew her well enough to know she was just having a bit of fun with her and meant nothing by it. If the truth be known, Frankie was revelling in it. Never in her life had she dated anyone who'd had an effect on other women the way Jack did, and the best of it was for the most part, he didn't realise and didn't actually care.

After some amusement regarding Jack's car, they managed to fit all three of them and the suitcase in, with room to spare. Frankie had to confess that, as cool as her Mini was, she would never have managed that because of the design of the convertible. On the way to the flat, Kayla gave them a blow-by-blow account of her flight, which included everything from the irritating teenager sat next to her, to the stick insect stewardess, and the excellent selection of movies. She didn't draw breath from the minute she got in the car until they walked through the front door.

"Kay!" Frankie's ears were almost bleeding, even though she was used to it, "Zip it for a bit, maybe?"

"Jeez folks, I'm sorry, my mouth has got a second wind. Please just tell me to shut up!" she said, as they piled in through the front door.

Hercules was only too happy to welcome their guest. Luckily for him Kayla loved cats and had been angling for one at home, but Frankie was still thinking about it.

"Oh, he's a real beauty, aren't you, you handsome devil, you." Hercules had melted into Kayla's arms; while she stroked him rhythmically, he purred the loudest Frankie and Jack had ever heard.

Frankie had made up the study/spare room. They would all have to share the bathroom, but much to Kayla's disappointment, not at the same time. After showing her around, they all agreed a bottle of Prosecco should be cracked open, despite weariness from work and travels. Kayla curled up on a chair, while Jack and Frankie cuddled up on the sofa. They all relaxed very quickly in each other's company and chatted away until jetlag got the better of Kayla.

Kayla had never been a morning person. Especially when she combined jet lag and alcohol. Of course, Frankie was up at the crack of dawn. She was hoping for a normal Saturday morning romp with Jack, so she made tea and took it back to bed, to watch him sleep while she read. By 8.40 she could tell he was no longer deeply asleep, and there was still no other movement in the flat. She closed up her iPad, removed his T-shirt that she had been wearing, and snuggled in next to his hot, perfectly formed body. As she did so, a hand found her bare breast and her bottom pressed against his hard length. A low groan of contentment escaped from deep within him as he nuzzled her hair. His hand began to wander, and his fingers found Mrs. Clit-tor-rus almost drowning between her legs. He was so good at this now, it got better every time; he would play with her then take her from behind, so he could enjoy the feeling of her erupting around him. He always came quickly in the morning, but she didn't mind; just his touch, his hot skin against hers, his natural erection filling her while his fingers fuelled the ignition, was one of the best feelings in the world. She wished they could do this every morning, but sadly there was the minor problem of getting to work on time.

They showered together so that the bathroom would be free for Kayla. Frankie found her sitting at the breakfast bar, drinking coffee when she walked out of the bathroom.

"Good morning, I trust you slept well?" Frankie asked, cheerfully.

She had left the door open behind her to let some of the steam escape, leaving Jack in full view, stood shaving at the mirror, wearing a very small towel.

"I slept very well thanks hun, might have had something to do with the wine, mind you." Kayla couldn't help but glance beyond Frankie at the vision behind her.

"Morning!" Jack shouted over the humming of his razor, not taking his eyes off the mirror. "I'm nearly done, then it's all yours."

"Oh really?" Kayla's eyes lit up, as she raised her eyebrows at Frankie and smiled hopefully. "Can't wait!"

"I think he's referring to the bathroom, dear, but until then, I don't mind if you enjoy the view... I quite like to watch him shave, too." Frankie winked as she wandered away into the bedroom.

Kayla just smiled, then looked back at Jack and rested her chin on her hand.

When he walked out of the bathroom he nodded at Kayla, oblivious to the fact she had been watching him.

"Did you sleep okay in there?" he asked, as he stood, practically naked, by the front door.

"Yes, thank you." Kayla suddenly caught herself staring; she couldn't help it, he was absolutely gorgeous. It wasn't that she was jealous of Frankie; he wasn't actually her type, but she couldn't help admire a good-looking guy who obviously looked after himself the way Jack did.

"Good!" He gave her a signature smile and turned towards the bedroom.

She was a little embarrassed, which was totally unheard of for Kayla, so she retreated into the bathroom.

Over breakfast, the girls decided to head into Newcastle. Kayla wanted to see the city, and they thought they would do some shopping. Jack was going to go to the gym, check on his flat, and run some errands. He suggested cooking for them all that evening, and then, if the girls wanted to go out to catch up over drinks, he didn't mind hanging out with the cat.

Kayla, being the sort of person who easily made herself at home as a guest, was washing the breakfast dishes when Frankie got down from her bar stool and slid herself between Jack and the breakfast bar. His legs were saddled over his own stool, as he flicked through the paper. She wrapped her arms around his waist, lifting his T-shirt a little so she could find naked flesh on his back.

"Yes? Can I help you with something?" he asked, as she looked up into his sparkly blue eyes.

"No, just wanted to check that you're okay with our plans for the day. I feel bad that you're going to be on your own for most of it." She rested her head on his chest.

Kayla was trying to busy herself, but shot them the odd glance. She was so happy for Frankie, and she could instantly tell that Jack was crazy about her. She caught herself smiling when she saw him kiss the top of her head, and then take her face with both hands and rub noses.

"I'm totally fine, I have some things to do, and it's important you go out and have some fun. I want to make sure you're well fed before you hit the town though, and I'll be here when you get in. We can do things together tomorrow; it's supposed to be a nice day." He placed a lingering kiss on her lips, while his hands wandered.

"Behave yourself," she whispered, and playfully placed her forefinger on his nose. He tried to wrinkle it the way she did, but it didn't quite have the same effect, which made her laugh.

The temperature outside didn't quite reflect the beautiful sunny day that it was, but as long as you didn't stay in the shade too long, it was T-shirt weather. Frankie and Kayla walked along the Quayside and around the main sights of Newcastle, before grabbing a quick lunch and hitting the shops. Frankie received several texts from Jack throughout the day; he was clearly missing her. She missed him too, but was easily distracted by Kayla, who was filling her in on work gossip, various things going on at home, and a guy she had dated three times now and quite liked. Kayla made it clear it was nothing like the whirlwind romance that Frankie seemed to be having. They spoke very little about that; Kayla wanted to have that conversation over drinks that evening.

They arrived back at the flat around 5.30pm to find Jack in the kitchen. He had just started to prepare dinner when they walked through the door.

"Well, hello there ladies, I was beginning to wonder if you'd decided just to go straight to the bar!" He was grinning as he walked straight up to Frankie and scooped her up in his arms before she had a chance to take her shoes off. His hands were spread on her bottom, supporting her as he planted his lips firmly on hers, with his eyes wide open, burning into her.

"Ooh, do I get the same treatment?" Kayla asked, hopefully.

Jack swallowed hard as a very worried spread across his face.

"I was only joking, hun!" Kayla picked up her shopping bags and walked towards her room, aware she'd embarrassed him.

Frankie followed Jack into the kitchen so she could make tea.

"Chicken salad okay for dinner?" he asked her, as he returned to his chopping board.

"Lovely darling, thank you." She smiled sweetly at him and stole a small stick of celery as she gave his bottom a little squeeze. "How was your day?" she asked, as she gathered mugs and tea bags.

"Long and boring without you," he replied, trying to look sad.

"Oh, get me a sick bucket, please!" she said as she held her stomach and mimicked vomiting.

"Actually, I spent extra time at the gym, checked my place, which is fine, paid some bills, and called my mother, who says hi by the way."

"Ahh, I do like a boy who's good to his mother! Tea?"

"Sure, why not. So, how was your day?" he asked, as he continued to prepare the salad.

"We had a great day, didn't we?" Frankie looked across at Kayla as she walked towards the breakfast bar. "Tea?".

"Love one," Kayla perched on a stool. "Yeah, it's great to see a city I wouldn't normally visit if I didn't have a friend living in it. It's lovely, although I believe it's had a complete makeover in the past few years, so I can't really imagine what it was like when Frankie was a kid. I couldn't believe how the Tyne Bridge really does look like the Sydney Harbour Bridge."

Frankie handed the teas out.

"Thanks sweetheart," Jack said, smiling at her.

"You're welcome. Anything I can do?" she asked him.

"No, you ladies just sit down and put your feet up; you must be exhausted!" Jack said, trying to sound sympathetic, but failing miserably.

"Haha," replied Frankie, making her way around to the breakfast bar so she could sit opposite Jack. "What you really mean is no, because I could ruin even a salad!"

"I've tried to teach her, Jack, but I think she's a lost cause. Glad to see she hasn't starved while away from my cooking," said Kayla.

"I would never have starved, thanks to Marks and Spencer." Frankie was sat holding her tea with both hands, sipping slowly.

"So, where are you thinking of going tonight?" Jack asked, as he tossed some peppers into the salad bowl.

"There's a nice wine bar down on the Quayside that I thought we might try. Kay here is a bit jet lagged still, so it won't be a late night, just a quiet glass of vino or two."

"So, no Bigg Market for you, then?" Jack said to Kayla, smiling.

"I've heard about that place. A girl I met, when I was travelling through the States, was from somewhere called Durham, I think," said Kayla.

"Oh! That's near the castle we went to for my birthday," Frankie said, as she glanced at Jack, as he gave her a cheeky little wink back.

"Yeah? Well she described the Bigg Market as 'tacky and full of slappers' - whatever they are!" Kayla shrugged her shoulders.

Both Frankie and Jack burst out laughing.

"I think that's the best description I've ever heard," said Frankie. "We'll take a walk through it, and you can see for yourself."

Once dinner was over, Jack insisted he clear up while the girls got ready to go out. An hour later, Kayla was sat at the breakfast bar, while Jack put the last of the dishes away. He complimented her on her outfit; a new, shocking pink, strapless dress, with black heels and clutch to match. A few minutes later, as Jack was changing the music on the iPod dock, the bedroom door opened. He had his back to the room, but quickly turned around when he heard Kayla gasp and say, "WOW!" She herself then turned to look at Jack's reaction.

He was dumbstruck; once again Frankie had managed to go from plain and pretty, to jaw-droppingly stunning. She stood at the end of the kitchen in spray-on, super skinny black trousers, with a white, silky top that wasn't clingy, but just hung. It was slightly see through with thin straps, and three buttons at the top, two of which were open to reveal a sneak preview of her lacy bra, and a hint of cleavage. It was hot and very sexy. Kayla was able to see the whole outfit, and the new shoes Frankie had purchased that day. Jack was only able to see as far as her knees. Frankie stood still, glancing back and forth between the two of them, with only her eyes.

"What?" she said, with a little smirk, knowing damn fine 'what'.

"You just look, as you always do when we go out, A... MAZING!" said Kayla. "And hun, those shoes are..."

"Shoes?" Jack questioned. He put his hand over his eyes, "Oh God, do I want to even look at the shoes?"

The girls giggled. Frankie moved so he could see her feet, making a point of clicking her three-inch, patent, teal, peep-toe killer heels as she did so. Jack parted his fingers slightly so he could peek out between them. As his eyes travelled south they were out on stalks and for the second time in less than five minutes his jaw hit the floor. Frankie stood with one hand on her hip, the other holding her matching clutch, smiling slightly with perfect red lips.

"You know what, hun, I'm just gonna wait for you downstairs." Kayla winked at Frankie, as she climbed off the barstool. "Catch ya later, Jack." She raised one eyebrow at Jack, and smiled at him.

"Er... yeah... Enjoy." He was struggling to speak, his mouth was dry; all he wanted to do was turn Frankie around and take her back into the bedroom.

"I'll only be a minute," Frankie said to Kayla, as she walked out of the door.

"Take your time," Kayla whispered, smirking.

As the door closed, Frankie heard Jack swallow hard and take a deep breath. Slowly, she walked over to him, her heels clicking with every step. As he was barefoot, the extra three inches made her far less small next to him. She kept eye contact all the way, and then stopped right in front of him. Her lips were parted slightly, her copper hair sleek and neat, almost skimming her shoulders; shorter layers at the front were swept over her right eye slightly. Jack was breathing quite quickly. She put her hand on his chest and felt his heart beating double time.

"Relax, you'll get to peel it all off later; all except the heels." She began to stroke the front of his jeans with her other hand; they felt uncomfortably tight over his large erection.

"Are you deliberately trying to make me fall apart?" he gasped.

"Yes, and I'm going to succeed."

She slid her hand down from his chest, over his abs and undid his jeans.

"Put your hands behind your back, I want to make you come without you touching me."

He did as she asked. She then stroked him through his boxers until she saw that familiar look of absolute pleasure on his face. Reaching around for his hands, she took them in hers, linking their fingers.

"I hope that helped," she stretched up and gave him a quick peck on the lips. "Don't wait up." She gave him a quick wrinkle of her nose, turned on her heels and clicked her way towards the door.

"You're a bad girl, Frances Robertson!"

"I know, and you love it! We'll be at The Silk Room Champagne Bar." She closed the door behind her without looking back.

Downstairs in the hallway, Kayla was stood looking at her phone.

"Okay, ready?" Frankie asked, as she clip-clopped her way down the stairs.

"You look pleased with yourself, and not too dishevelled... AND your lippy is still in place! What did you do to him?"

"Kay really, what on earth gives you the impression I did anything?" Frankie asked very smugly.

"Hun, it's written all over your face; you look like the cat that got the cream!"

They walked out of the front door, and started down the street towards the Metro station.

"My dear, I have been getting the cream twice a day since the middle of February, this is how I look most of the time!"

Chapter 27

JACK TOOK A cold shower after the girls left. Obviously he needed to clean up and change, but Frankie had left him wanting more. She had looked so hot; he couldn't get enough of her. As the cool water ran down his face, he raised his arms and ran his hands through his wet hair, all the time thinking how much he enjoyed it when she played with his hair and how much pleasure she gained from it. He had always hated his curls, and was about to have them all cut off when he had met her. Opening his eyes, it dawned on him just how big the shower was without her in it. Squeezing shower gel into the palm of his hand, he stared at it, wishing she were there to wash him. He loved to feel her touch as she massaged his body, whilst he kissed her; water pouring down over them. Slowly, he began washing himself, thoughts of her running through his head, wishing he could feel her all slippery and wet. He loved her all slippery and wet... In fact, he realised, quite simply he loved her. Leaning forward, he placed both hands flat on the tiled wall either side of the tap, letting the water run over him once again.

He stood there for some time before he aggressively smacked the wall with his hands, and turned the water off. After drying off, he slipped into sweatpants, leaving his shirt off. Taking a beer from the fridge, he picked up Frankie's iPad, and made himself comfortable on the sofa. Hercules lay sphinx-like on the back of it, in a patch of sunlight, with his eyes closed.

"Okay my friend, let's take a look." He took a swig of his beer, placed it down on the coffee table, sat back, put his feet up, and opened the iPad. "Oh, right... password... Pretty sure it's her birthday, so let's try... 0405... No, okay... How about 0574. Ahh! Bingo, we're in!" he said, rubbing his hands.

Hercules rested his head on a paw. Jack continued talking to him.

"Right, I have no idea what to look for or where to start, so let's just google some stuff and see what comes up. I must remember to clear the history when I'm done, okay." He looked at the cat as he took another mouthful of beer.

Kayla couldn't believe her eyes as she walked through the Bigg Market. This part of Newcastle was well known for its bars and nightlife, and had been for as long as Frankie could remember. Neither Frankie nor Kayla were easily shocked. However, strolling among the loud, busy, drunken crowds that Saturday evening had truly opened their eyes. Kayla, in particular, was desperate to get away from there.

"So, you don't fancy a quick one in the Pig 'n' Whistle then?" Frankie asked her.

"I most certainly do not! Get me the hell out of here! I feel overdressed, and by that, I mean I have waaay too many clothes on!"

Frankie just laughed.

They headed down towards the Quayside, to Trinity Gardens, just behind the law courts. Frankie had heard about The Silk Room Champagne Bar and Restaurant from someone at work. The relaxed atmosphere in the candlelit bar was much more their style, with its comfy leather booths, plush silk cushions, and dark wooden floors. They settled at a small table with a bottle of Chardonnay and two glasses.

Kayla poured them each a glass, and they clinked them together.

"Cheers!" they announced in unison, as they took a drink.

"Kay, I'm so glad you came; I know it must be awkward with Jack around, but I've really missed you, despite our constant chats and messaging."

"Are you kidding me, there was no way you were gonna stop me! Man or no man, I said I would come over, so here I am. Hun, it's been clear from the beginning that what you have with Jack isn't like any of your other flings. This guy is nuts about you!"

Frankie sat, running her fingers up and down the stem of her wine glass, her head cocked to the side and a stupid grin plastered across her face. "You think?"

"Oh, I don't think; I know. Look at you turning all goofy on me. Christ, the way he looks at you, the way he holds you, and plays with your hair; not to mention the look on his face when you walked out of the bedroom earlier. Jeez, I thought he was gonna come right there and then!"

"Kay!!" Frankie exclaimed, slightly shocked, looking around the bar to ensure no one was eavesdropping on their conversation before turning back and shooting Kayla a guilty look.

"You didn't? Oh my God, you did!" Kayla's eyes were wide, as she inhaled sharply.

"Well, I couldn't leave the poor guy like that for the next four hours now, could I?" Frankie took a sip of wine with a very naughty smirk on her face.

Kayla sat back and took a long, hard look at her best friend.

"I've never seen you like this. You really are head over heels in love with this guy, aren't you?" Kayla was serious; it took Frankie a moment to notice. They sat staring at each other before Frankie spoke.

"What the hell am I going to do? For the first time in my life, I have no idea what to do, but I have to leave at the end of July, that's a done deal." Frankie was welling up fast, and she didn't want her makeup to run.

"Hun I'm sorry, I didn't mean to upset you." Kayla leaned forward again and put her hand on Frankie's, giving it a little squeeze. "Listen, I don't know what you guys have talked about, but I can't imagine he's gonna give you up that easily. I've only just met him, but I can see he adores you." Frankie was nipping the corners of her eyes to stop the floodgates from opening. Kayla continued, "He loves you too hun, it's practically written on a neon sign above his head."

"So people keep telling me, but he's never actually said it."

"Have you?" Kayla sat back and took a sip of wine.

"Oh, don't you start. I've had this conversation with Carol."

"So you haven't?" Kayla said bluntly.

"No!" Frankie sat back and took another sip of wine.

"Well, maybe that's all the reassurance he needs before he books his flight!"

"Kay, he's not going to come with me, or even follow me afterwards. He only followed Emma a few miles away from home and look where that left him. He's not going to travel half way around the world, to somewhere he can't even work, and have to rely on his professional older woman to pay his way. Not to mention the fact that, I think deep down, he still wants to have children."

"I thought you said he wasn't bothered?"

"That's what he said, but he wanted them before didn't he?"

They drank their wine, while soulful music played in the background.

"Don't give up on it hun, you seem so good together and he's just so... So perfect for you. He seems like a really honest and genuine guy. I don't believe this was all for nothing, things happen for a reason, remember?" Kayla gave Frankie a positive smile.

"Thanks, I know, and I needed this. I'm so caught up in him, I know I'm burying my head in the sand and hoping, by some miracle, it will all just work out. I can't imagine being without him now. I should talk to him, lay all the cards on the table and be honest about my feelings."

Kayla nodded and smiled, then raised her glass. Frankie did the same, and they clinked them together once more.

What was supposed to be a quiet drink out for two friends to catch up, started as a heart to heart, and finished with both feeling very tipsy after polishing off a second bottle of wine. Having put the world to rights, they fell out of the bar around eleven and hailed a cab. Laughing and giggling about anything and everything, they kept the cab driver quite amused. He dropped them right outside the front door, where Kayla paid the fare, and Frankie fumbled in her tiny clutch bag for her keys. Removing their shoes, they both stumbled up the stairs to the first floor. Frankie had trouble coordinating the key and the lock, but eventually she put the two together, and the door opened as they fell inside.

Unbeknown to them, Jack was in bed but not asleep. He had been waiting in anticipation for their safe return, knowing what Newcastle could be like on a Saturday night for two attractive women. He heard them before he heard the key making several attempts to find the lock; he lay there, smiling to himself, thinking *'This is going to be interesting'*. Finally, they were through the door, giggling like two schoolgirls.

He heard a loud 'SHHHHHH!' from one of them, and then Frankie whispered, "We don't want to wake the beast and make him grumpy."

"Oh no, then you would have to do ALL SORTS of delicious things to him," whispered Kayla.

"Ooh," Frankie was giggling again, "maybe I should wake him!" she whispered, loudly.

Jack stood in the doorway by the bedroom, in a pair of sweatpants. He wanted to look serious and annoyed, but it only took one look at them to make him smile.

"Maybe he's already awake!" he said, looking down at the pile of women on the floor. "I thought you were having a quiet drink in a classy wine bar - what happened?"

Frankie looked at Kayla; Kayla looked back at Frankie, and they both burst out laughing.

"Okay, come on, you both need a pint of water, two Co-Codamol, and bed!" He said, almost laughing with them.

"Yes Dad... Sorry Dad... It won't happen again, Dad," said Kayla.

Frankie playfully hit her, "Stop it, he's being really sweet looking after us."

Jack stood in front of them, reaching out his arms to help them up. They each took a hand, and he pulled both of them up together.

"Oh Jack, you're so strong, I don't think I can walk to my bed, you may have to carry me," slurred Kayla.

"Hands off my man, you little home wrecker!" said Frankie, trying to be serious, but bursting into giggles when she saw Kayla's face crumbling too.

Jack just shook his head, smiling; it was funny to see the two of them, intoxicated and playfully fighting over him. Walking into the kitchen, he took two large glasses and filled them with water. Bending down to the drawer, he retrieved the Co-Codamol, and popped out four capsules. Then he turned to face them; they were both leaning on the edge of the breakfast bar gazing up at him as if he were their knight in shining armour, about to rescue them from the evil Lord Hangover.

"Here," he placed two tablets down in front of each of them, "take these and drink this."

They did as they were told.

"Now, bed!"

Kayla saluted him and staggered towards the bathroom.

Frankie went to stand in front of him; she wasn't really as drunk as she appeared, but she was quite tipsy.

"Now, what are you going to do with me? I was such a bad girl before I left, and I feel like being very naughty now," she asked, in her best, seductive, chardonnay-fuelled voice.

Jack put his arms around her, and lifted her onto the bench.

"Oh you do, do you? Well, for starters, someone is going to need to help you out of those clothes. Has anyone ever told you that you're incredibly adorable when you've had too much to drink?" he replied, skimming the bare flesh under her top with his hands.

Kayla came out of the bathroom. "Night," she said, as she turned to go into her room.

"Sleep well," said Jack. "Now then, go take your face off," he ordered Frankie as he kissed her softly, "but nothing else!" He smiled a wicked sexy smile before lifting her down.

"Yes Sir!" said Frankie, saluting him, then giggled. As she turned to walk toward the bathroom, he playfully smacked her bottom.

Jack was laying on the bed, on his back, his hands behind his head, with his eyes shut when he heard the bedroom door click shut. Opening his eyes, he looked over at Frankie who was stood with her hands behind her back, leaning against the door. He moved to sit on the edge of the bed; their eyes fixed.

"Come here," he said quietly, holding out his hand for her.

Slowly, she walked towards him and took his hand, linking their fingers. Holding out his other hand, she linked fingers with that too. He broke eye contact and placed his head against her stomach and inhaled deeply. Thoughts of the things he had learnt that evening, surfing the Internet on her iPad, popped into his head; he screwed his eyes up in an attempt to push them to one side, and just enjoy this moment. He looked up at her.

"You okay? I don't want to take advantage of you when you've obviously had a little bit too much to drink," he asked.

"Don't be silly, I'm not falling down drunk. Maybe I want you to take advantage of me."

She freed her hands and ran her fingers through his hair. "I love your hair, Jack, it's very sexy."

"I know you do; funnily enough, I was going to get it cut, but I've learned to like it now. I love how you play with it...it..."

"...makes you feel all twinkly inside?" She finished the sentence for him.

He lifted her top and kissed her belly button. "Yes, yes it does." He looked up, smiling.

"It does that to me too, but you know what else it does?"

Jack continued kissing her, lifting her top higher as he slowly stood up. "Tell me, what else does it do to you?" he asked between kisses.

Lifting her arms up, he removed her top completely to reveal a white lacy bra that left nothing to the imagination.

"Running through your hair, my fingertips seem to send red hot, electric waves all the way up my arm..." Jack listened to the route, tracing it with his lips, "...across my shoulder..." He walked around her, his lips trailing across her shoulders; "...down between my breasts, so that each nipple tingles with excitement..." He sat back on the bed, bringing his eyes level with her sexy lacy bra. He buried his face in her cleavage, "...straight down my stomach, circling my belly button, waking Mrs. Clit-tor-rus... And then..." Barely breathing, she stopped speaking; he stopped licking her belly button and smiled up at her, that heart-glowing, *'I know how this affects you'* smile.

Frankie let out a gasp; she wanted him now! Sliding his hands around to her bottom, searching for something, all the time smiling up at her.

"Mmm, I'm not sure, difficult to tell, I'm just going to have to find out for myself," he said, as his fingers worked the button of her trousers loose; he slowly undid the very short zip, revealing the answer as he felt her skin behind it.

"Lie down for me." He patted the bed next to him; Frankie did as he asked, placing herself across the foot of the bed. She turned her head to look in the mirror; she raised her eyebrows and smiled at his reflection. He smiled back at her.

He took hold of either side of her trousers and peeled her like a banana, leaving them inside out in a heap on the floor.

"Do you know how incredibly attractive you are, Doctor, with and without your clothes on?"

"Back at ya, Lee!"

"Oh, you can be so American sometimes!"

"Why thank you," Frankie replied, with her hand on heart, in her high pitched mock American accent.

He let his sweatpants fall, revealing his very large erection, and climbed on top of her.

"Turn onto your side; as much as this is very pretty, I want you naked," he said, tugging at her bra. She did as he asked.

Straddling her, he slid her bra down her arms, then dropped it on the floor. "That's better."

He sat for a moment admiring her, as she raised her arms above her head.

"In fact, you are the most attractive woman I've ever known, in every way." He bent so he could take a nipple in his mouth.

She moaned. "Ever known?" she questioned.

He looked up and paused.

"Yes, ever known, and the best thing is, I don't feel guilty anymore for thinking or even saying it."

She smiled at him as he returned to work, letting his teeth nibble as his tongue circled.

"I do believe you're cured Mr. Lee, but I would like to continue your therapy for another couple of months, just to be sure." She fondled his hair, making him groan.

Locking his eyes with hers, he slowly licked up her body, from her cleavage to her mouth. Their tongues met, while she parted her legs wide and lifted them as high as she could, wrapping them around him. She felt him rub against her.

"You're drowning down there," he groaned, as he rubbed her nose.

"Well, I didn't finish explaining my happy trail... that's the effect playing with your hair has on me!"

"Really?" He looked surprised.

"Really!" she said, as she carried on wrapping soft curls around her fingers.

Turning his head to look at the mirror, he slowly entered her; she turned to look too.

"Thanks to you, I really enjoy watching us," he said, looking back at her, panting slightly as he began to move his hips in perfect time with hers.

"Oh Jack that feels sooo good." She stopped playing and just clung.

"...It does, doesn't it," he gasped.

She tightened around him, which usually took him apart, but as she came he didn't stop moving. He was watching her, his mouth open, panting hard. This was the first time he had been able to watch her without coming himself.

"Oh, Jack." She was writhing around in ecstasy; hearing her say his name, he let go, collapsing on top of her, breathless.

They lay there, his head buried in her neck, her fingers gripping his hair, locked together in their post-coital bliss. Becoming aware of his weight on top of her, he eased his body a little, lifting his head so he could look in the mirror. She turned her head sideways too; their eyes met in the reflection. He brushed his cheek against hers and they both smiled.

"I should come home drunk more often, that was amazing!" she said, as they turned back to look at each other. "I'm so glad you have a one track mind like me."

Suddenly, he rolled her on top of him; she squealed and started to giggle.

"Hey, Soul Sister; Save Me, San Francisco; 2009; track 2," he said, as he gave her a quick peck. "That was easy, and so are you!" He pressed his forefinger gently onto the end of her nose and she wrinkled it.

They folded themselves properly into bed, spooned together and slept.

Chapter 28

"Ohh... Never again," Kayla mumbled, hunched over the breakfast bar, nursing a black coffee.

"I wish I had a Loonie for every time I've heard you say that," said Frankie, leaning against the kitchen bench opposite her, holding a bucket of tea.

"A Loonie?" asked Jack from the sofa, where he sat facing them with his feet up. Hercules had started some strange obsession with washing his feet since the weather became warmer and Jack padded around barefoot.

"It's a dollar coin. Two dollar coins are known as Toonies," Frankie replied. "I have no idea why!" She shrugged her shoulders.

"So, do you have... is it dimes and what's the other one?" he asked.

"Nickels! Yes we do." She nodded and took a mouthful of tea.

A low, sorry moan came from the breakfast bar as Kayla hung her head in her hands.

"So, what are they?" asked Jack.

"A nickel is five cents, and a dime is ten cents," said Frankie, as she made her way over to Jack. Placing her tea on the coffee table, she perched next to him, on the arm of the sofa, wrapped an arm around his shoulder, and started weaving her fingers through his hair.

"So," he said, "now you two are all caught up, can I expect some decent adult conversation out of you both, without any giggling?"

"Ahh, thank you for looking after us, darling, it was very sweet," said Frankie, kissing his cheek.

"You're welcome, just don't make a habit of it. I got really tired of looking after Anthony after a skin full," he said, tipping his head back slightly, then suddenly looking back at Kayla.

"You know what you need, Kay?" said Jack.

"As long as it's something that's not too loud, you can tell me." She looked across to him, with her eyes shut.

"A full English!" he announced proudly. "Bacon, sausage, egg, beans, toast..."

"Jeez mate, I feel sick just thinking about it!" replied Kayla, as she opened one eye while the colour drained from her face.

"No, honestly, it's a well known hangover cure. Right, that settles it." He quickly jumped up off the sofa, almost making Frankie fall, turned and offered her his hand. "You and I are going to take a shower, while your friend here rehydrates. Then, we are going out in search of grease!"

Frankie put her hand in his as he led her into the bathroom; she grinned at Kayla who just shook her head.

After their substantial breakfast at a café they found in neighbouring Sandyford, they walked back through Jesmond Dene in warm sunshine, constantly chatting. Jack didn't leave Frankie's side; he held her hand, put his arms around her, and even ran after her on one occasion, picking her up and carrying her away screaming, all because she and Kayla had stopped to take pictures and some random guy passing by had offered to take one of both of them, not realising that Jack was with them. He was being very playful and attentive. Kayla found him charming and funny, convincing herself even more that he was the perfect match for Frankie. She was surprised at herself that she didn't find it as irritating as she had thought she would when they showed affection, and were all over each other. It made her smile, seeing her closest friend in love, finally... but for how long, she wondered?

The day ran away with them, which meant they didn't get back until late evening. Jack was at work early on Monday, and planned to go to the gym and pick up his mail afterwards. The girls intended to spend the day fancy dress shopping, and take in the Angel of the North and other North East sights. It was early to bed for them all.

That week went by very quickly. The girls spent quality time together, and Jack and Kayla got to know each other better in that short time. On Thursday evening they all went out for a very enjoyable dinner together, before Kayla flew back to Vancouver on Friday. It wasn't a late night; Frankie had two big cases to do the following day with the Leprechaun. Jack was working a late shift the next day, so he agreed to take Kayla to the airport in the morning. They were all up before Frankie left for work.

"You all packed?" Frankie asked Kayla, as they finished breakfast, while Jack showered.

"I am. I left the item you requested in the cupboard in the bedroom. Looking at the size, I think it should be okay, and I think the colour will suit him." Kayla winked at Frankie.

"Thanks, I'll settle up with you once I'm home, just keep the receipt."

"Sure, no worries."

"Well, I need to head off in a minute, thanks again for coming over, it's been so good to see you." They embraced for what seemed like forever.

"I've really enjoyed it, and seeing you so happy is seriously awesome; quite the change from the bear with a sore head you were those weeks before you came over here." Kayla pulled away to look at her friend, "What can I say hun, I want him to be your happy ever after, but..."

"I know, there's a 'but'." Just as Frankie finished speaking, Jack came out of the bathroom and walked across to the bedroom to get dressed. She hugged Kayla again, tears welling up in her eyes. "Safe flight, okay, text me when you land and be sure to keep in touch."

"You bet; I hope everything continues to work out with the house. Take care."

"I will," Frankie said, as she picked up her backpack and slipping on her shoes.

"I'll walk down with you," Jack said, as he opened the door for her.

Frankie looked around one last time at Kayla, who raised her hand and mouthed, "Bye"; Frankie did the same, then closed the door behind her.

When Jack returned to the flat a few minutes later, Kayla was sat at the breakfast bar with a cup of coffee, looking very serious.

"Sit!" she ordered, as she patted the stool next to her.

A little taken aback by her demand, he reluctantly went over and did as she said.

"Okay, I'm sitting," he said with a sigh.

Kayla looked at him for a moment. This breathtakingly handsome man was not going to just break her best friend's heart, but shatter it into tiny pieces, beyond repair. They needed to have a talk.

"Jack, I'm going to come straight to the point here. What do you intend to do, because I'm going to be the one picking up the pieces at the other end, and I need to know what to expect?"

Jack had had a feeling she was going to probe for information, but he didn't expect her to be quite so blunt. Rubbing his palms along his thighs, he exhaled slowly, thinking about his response. She spoke again.

"Look, she's my best friend, Jack, we look out for each other. We talk. I can see you guys are crazy about each other."

Jack glanced up at Kayla in response to her last comment.

"I've seen her go through enough heartache over the years, she doesn't deserve any more, and she's so happy right now."

"Okay, okay, I get it, but I honestly don't know the answer. I've looked into the possibility, and my job doesn't exist in Canada. I have no other skills, so working - which is something I have to do, I don't care how much she earns - would be an issue. Then there's the whole issue of moving away from my family, although I know they would be supportive, as they just want me to be happy. I still have some insecurities regarding what has happened in my past. I have a flat full of stuff from my marriage, which I would need to deal with before I could move on and make any commitments. Maybe some distance between us will give me the chance to do that and give us both some space. It's been really intense, and I have to be sure it's the right thing to do; but right now, I just don't know."

Kayla could see Jack was struggling within himself; he was clearly very torn.

"Look, it's not that I don't want to be with her, far from it. I can't see myself with anyone else, ever. But what I just don't see is, how."

"Then make it happen. You've said yourself that you would like to retrain; here's your chance. Swallow some pride, Jack, and let her help you do that; there's nothing wrong with that, not when you love someone."

She watched his reaction; the look on his face said it all. She was right; he loved her.

"I've told her she needs to be patient and give me time. I'm in a situation I never ever saw myself in and it's huge. I just need time to get my head round it all. I need her, and believe me, hurting her is the last thing I want to do."

"Just promise me you'll be honest with her; I don't want her leaving here thinking that you're going to work this out when you have no intention of doing so."

"I'm a very honest person. I'll do my best to try and work it out, but I can't promise anything right now."

"Fair enough. I want us to understand each other. You've got to appreciate I'm going to try and protect her. Can we agree to be honest with each other?" she asked.

"Yeah, of course. You're a good friend to her, Kayla. Look after her for me when she gets back?" he asked, a slightly desperate look on his face. Kayla got down from her barstool and patted him on the shoulder as she passed. She nodded, lips pressed together. She really felt for him. "Are we okay now?" he asked her, wanting to be sure he kept Kayla on his side.

"Sure. I'll finish some last minute bits of packing, then I'm good to go."

"Okay, just let me know when you're ready."

Jack sat a few minutes more, thinking over their conversation. He held his head in his hands, frustrated with the whole thing and wondered why it all had to be so complicated. The world was a much smaller place now; it shouldn't have to be this complicated. He didn't really understand what was holding him back.

Jack strolled into work a little early, after dropping Kayla safely at the airport. Their conversation still preyed on his mind; he had been so caught up in his own feelings, that he'd omitted to appreciate how leaving and returning to her normal life might affect

Frankie too. Truly, he had no idea what her real life was like; she was currently living in a temporary bubble that was going to pop at the end of July, depositing her back into her real world. He couldn't help wonder if she would just slot back into her west coast lifestyle, that had never included him, and forget he ever existed. Whereas his life would carry on as it had been before her, but now without her. He decided he needed to find out more about Canada, in particular Vancouver, as everyone seemed to give it the 'wow' factor whenever Frankie mentioned where she lived normally. With half an hour to kill before his shift, he took himself off to the teaching room to use the computer.

At 6.30pm Jack received a text from Frankie, saying she was done and would see him at the flat later; she was going to pick up some M&S goodies for the weekend on her way home, and did he have any requests? He was in the trauma theatre with Dr. Burgess; Marie and Heather were also there. He answered her text promptly.

Only that you're naked and wanting.....Jx

He smirked to himself at the thought. Frankie was still in her anaesthetic room with Chloë, clearing up. She chuckled as she replied.

I think the manager of M&S might have something to say about that! Fx

Jack felt his phone buzz as he handed Alan a syringe; fishing it out of his pocket, he let out a short loud laugh when he read it. Everyone turned to look at him. Heather smirked, presuming he was texting Frankie. He apologised to the room in general and went back into the anaesthetic room to reply.

LOL!! I feel like something naughty for dessert...surprise me! Jx

Walking past Jack's anaesthetic room, Frankie received his reply. She looked through the window, caught his eye, smiled and quickly replied.

I can be a naughty dessert...would you like me with whipped cream and a cherry on top? Fx

She hit send and slowly carried on walking. Aware of people in the corridor and at the front desk, she didn't want to draw too much attention to herself. Jack was grinning at her reply; he felt like pushing the limits and giving her a little taste of her own seductive medicine. He typed his reply, hit send then walked back into the theatre.

I think between us there'll be enough cream! Jx

As his text came in, Frankie was stood by the front desk, looking at the lists for the following week; Denise and a couple of other nurses were around. She let out a loud gasp as she read, and quickly put her hand over her mouth. "You bad boy, Mr..." she stopped herself quickly and looked up. "Sorry, my inside voice. My boyfriend," she said pointing to her phone. The nurses stared at her in silence. Frankie was already replying.

You have a dirty mouth Mr. Lee, your therapist has taught you well...... already wanting. Fx

Jack smiled, very distracted, as he replied to her text.

'Ditto' Jx

"When you have a minute Jack, after dealing with whomever is more important, I could do with another bag of fluid here!" Alan said, bringing Jack back to reality, as he looked up from his phone.
"Sorry Dr... Alan, my girlfriend, sorry, coming right up," Jack replied.
All the nurses in the room turned to look at Jack as he walked out.

At the front desk, Frankie looked up at the faces glaring at her.
"What?" she asked, just as Jack came out of his room.
"Oh, we just thought you were single?" said Megan.
Frankie caught Jack's eye as he walked past; his eyes went wide as he heard Megan's voice. He carried on walking.
"Who said I was single? Did I say I was single?" Frankie said, matter-of-factly. She knew Jack was still within earshot.
Denise almost said something, when she noticed Jack heading back towards them, carrying the requested bag of fluid. Frankie didn't dare look at him; she was already feeling a little flushed.
"Anyone we know, Doctor?" he asked as he passed, moving the bag of fluid from one hand to the other; curls escaping from his hat, chest hair peeking out from the V in his scrubs, and a smile that could power the national grid!

"Mmm, just a cute piece of ass I picked up at some charity gig! Have a good weekend, ladies, and I'll see you next week." She turned to leave as she spoke, hearing Jack laugh out loud. Megan and Olivia looked shocked at her blunt statement, and Denise spat diet coke all over her file, suddenly realising that she was referring to their theatre charity event way back in February.

"Here you go, Alan, again my apologies, I should have been paying attention," Jack said, as he walked back into the theatre.
"No problem, it's not like you, Jack, someone special?" Alan asked.
"Since when has there been a woman in your life, Jack?" asked Marie, before Jack could answer Alan.
Jack looked up at Marie, regretting he'd mentioned anything now.
"A while," he directed at Marie, "and yes, Alan, very." He looked up at Heather, who was scrubbed; he was only able to see her eyes, but he knew she was smiling as she winked at him.
"Ooh, sounds serious. Better make sure this one gets a thorough examination before you commit yourself!" said Marie.
Jack froze and glared at her. He knew she was a nasty piece of work, but a comment like that was cold and heartless.
"Just ignore her Jack," said Heather, "she's not worth it."
Heather turned around to her tray of instruments and looked straight at Marie, stood in front of her. Trying to be as discreet as possible she spoke, "One of these days, Marie Guilford, that gob of yours is going to get you into some very serious trouble, and I hope all the people you've pissed off are around to see it. You are the nastiest person I have ever known, and there is only one reason why you still have a job here, and trust me, it's nothing to be proud of."
Marie moved away from Heather, who was loading a stitch, ready to close the wound. Jack hadn't really heard what she'd

said, but he was aware that Heather had obviously put Marie in her place. Trying to put what she'd said out of his mind, he replaced it with happy thoughts of what Frankie might have in store for him after work.

"Another one?" Frankie asked him. She was lying across his front, both of them naked on the sofa.

"Where on earth did you get this crazy idea from? And yes, another one please," he said, propping his head up on an arm.

She popped her straw back into her mouth and turned towards the coffee table, where there was a large bowl of Maltesers. Placing the straw against one of the chocolate balls, she sucked hard so that it stuck to the end of the straw and carefully turned her head towards Jack; he opened his mouth and she made her deposit. They both giggled.

"I think I saw it in an advert once, and always thought it would be a fun game to play. It makes for great dessert after two orgasms and 60 calories of semen... another?"

Jack started to cough as he almost inhaled some chocolate.

"Sorry, my inside voice has been on fire today!" She moved off his chest a little bit so he could sort himself out.

"Ha! Please keep it under control when I'm eating! And yes, please do explain how all that came about? I nearly died when I walked out into the conversation." He shuffled her over, bringing her back on top of him again, as his hands reached down to fondle her naked backside.

"You know," her chin was resting on the back of her hands, laying flat on his chest hair as she looked up at him, "it just sort of came out; I really didn't plan on saying anything, but when I did, it felt really good; quite a relief actually. It's not like I told them it was you, although they're going to figure that out for sure in a couple of weeks."

He looked at her frowning, "Why?"

"Dee's party. I have found the perfect hot couple for us to be, and if that doesn't give it anyway, nothing will. Jack, I'm finally at a point where I would like us to be seen as a couple, and not just a piece of hot gossip."

"I agree; I let something slip myself." He looked up at the ceiling for a second as he owned up.

Her jaw fell open with a smile, and she breathed in sharply. "Oh?"

Looking down at her again. "Well, when I was texting you, I was inevitably a bit distracted, so I owned up to texting my girlfriend; that was just before I left the room to get that bag of fluid. Marie was pretty nasty when I returned, which took the edge off it a bit to be honest, but come Monday morning, I can guarantee it will have spread far and wide. Now then… about these costumes?"

Chapter 29

THEY STOOD SILENTLY in her father's study, with their hands on their hips, scanning the room.

"Are you ready to do this?" Jack asked her.

She looked at him, sullen-faced; she wasn't really, but it had to be done. She sighed deeply and nodded.

"Come here." He held his arms out to her, and she gratefully went to him.

This would always be one of her favourite places; wrapped in his strong, safe arms snuggled against his firm chest. It just seemed to make everything better.

"Thank you," she whispered.

"What for?" He kissed the top of her head.

"Just being here. I feel really selfish; there are so many other things you could be doing on such a nice day."

"Frances Robertson, you are probably the bravest and most unselfish person I have the privilege of knowing. You've given up six months of your life to do something that you gain absolutely nothing from."

"You're wrong there; I found you. I think I've gained quite a lot from that." She could feel his heart rate quicken as he hugged her tighter.

"That's a lovely thing to say, thank you."

She smiled up at him and wrinkled her nose.

He pressed a forefinger onto it. "Remember what happened the last time you got a little frisky in here?" he asked.

"Oh yes!! We never did pick up where we left off." She moved her hands down to his rather wonderful jeans-clad bottom and squeezed.

"Oh no you don't, you're putting this off, and I'm putting my foot down; we can pick it up once we've cleared this room."

"Okay, but I'm holding you to that," she said, breaking away from him.

"Oh, I know you will." He winked.

It was late in the afternoon. Jack was sorting through the bookshelves whilst Frankie knelt on the floor, thumbing through piles of paperwork.

"Hey, there's a box here with your name on it." Jack began to slide something off the shelf; it had been hidden among some large textbooks.

"Really?" She looked over the top of her glasses at the dusty, faded black box Jack was holding. "It's not mine, I've never used anything like that. What's inside?" she asked, as she looked back at the papers she was holding.

Jack slowly opened it. Staring back at him was a stunning photograph of Frankie in a cap and gown; she looked a little younger, but essentially she hadn't changed. He pulled back the sprung clip that was holding everything in place, so he could take the 10x8 photograph out, and see what else was underneath. Concentrating on the papers she was sifting through, Frankie didn't notice he had gone silent. Jack turned over the photograph; there was something written on the back...

'My beautiful girl graduates at the Royal College of Anaesthetists, June 2002'

He turned the photograph back over and glanced down at the box; there was another, similar graduation picture, this time in a different gown. He picked it up, staring at the photograph of a very young, longer haired Frankie. Again, she looked stunning; he turned it over....

'My girl graduates from Medical School with first class honours. I am so proud of her. June 1997

"Sweetheart, you might want to take a look at this," Jack said, as he held the pictures side-by-side.

"Why, what is it?" she asked, without looking up.

"You should come and take a look for yourself."

She could tell by the tone of his voice that he had found something intriguing.

"You're scaring me, Jack, do I really want to know?" she asked, as she looked up at him.

He turned the pictures to face her. "These were in the box," he said quietly. Frankie started to get a sinking feeling in her stomach.

"There's writing on the back that I assume is your father's. Do you want me to read it to you?" he asked. He could see that she was completely shocked, unable to move.

She swallowed hard and nodded slightly.

"Okay, this one says…" He held up the younger picture of her and read aloud; when he looked back, her jaw had hit the floor. "I didn't know you passed with a first, that's huge… WOW!" he said admiringly.

Frankie managed a little smile of appreciation at his reaction to her achievement.

"This one says..." He held up the older picture of her and read the words as Frankie hands clasped over her mouth and tears pricked at her eyes. Jack dropped the pictures and launched himself to catch her as she collapsed forward, her forehead about to hit the wooden floor. He pulled her into his arms, and held her as tight as he could while she let the floodgates open. Stroking her hair, he rocked her a little as she sobbed and sobbed. Eventually, once she seemed to calm down, he spoke.

"He loved you, sweetheart; he may have never shown it, but he clearly loved you."

He released his hold once he felt her trying to sit back. She had red, mascara-smudged eyes; it was heartbreaking to see her like this.

"I don't understand," she said.

"I know, and you probably never will, but Carol did say he did everything to treat you and Andrew equally. That doesn't mean he couldn't secretly love you, and be proud of you. You were after all his only child; if the only way he could deal with those emotions was to love you in a box, then isn't that better than not at all?" He took a hold of her chin and wiped some tears away with his thumb.

She looked deeply into his eyes. *'Say it Jack, please just say it,'* she thought. *'Now would be the perfect time to say it'*. She gave him a weak smile as he leaned in to kiss her.

"I think we should call it a day. We'll take the box back with us, and then you have it for when you're ready to find out more, okay?" He wiped the remaining tears away from her cheeks; she just nodded as he helped her up.

Frankie had been unnaturally quiet while they bathed together. They were sat on the sofa, eating pizza and drinking wine, when she finally spoke.

"You know, I haven't had the courage to go through the scrapbook that Carol gave me. I'd really like to do that this evening, with you, if you don't mind?"

Jack paused for a second, then put his slice of pizza down before wiping his hand on a napkin. He then reached over and cupped her cheek, gently stroking it with his thumb.

"Whatever you need to do, I'm here for you. I want to help."

"I really don't know how I would have gotten through all this without you. I'm starting to feel emotionally drained."

"I know. I think it did you good to have a week of distraction with Kayla. You're nearly there, and then it will all be over. Come on, I'll top up our glasses, and you get the scrapbook. I haven't seen any pictures of you as a child, but somehow, I already know you were incredibly adorable."

She looked up at him and smiled. "Thank you," she whispered.

Frankie rested the heavy scrapbook on her knee. Jack sat close to her, with his arm draped over the back of the sofa, his hand gently stroking the bare flesh that poked out from the side of her vest. Slowly, she opened the hard cover. The first page was a summary of her name, date of birth, place of birth, and her parents' names. The next double page displayed several black and white photos of her as a baby. Some of the pictures showed her being held by her mum, with her father gazing down at her.

Frankie took Jack through the album that told the story of her life; her first steps, holidays, first day of school, playing in the garden, school plays, Christmases, birthdays. She recalled stories and events; they laughed and she occasionally shed the odd tear.

She noticed that there were very few pictures of them as a family. She described how other kids would talk about what they did as a family on weekends and holidays. As she got older, she began to realise that her parents, and the family unit she grew up in, was not the same as her friends'. Now, looking back on old photographs, and knowing that Andrew was her uncle's son, she understood why. This overwhelmed Frankie with sadness. The man she remembered was not the person who had written the words on the back of her graduation photographs. She felt very confused about the feelings she now had, mixed emotions for the fact that he gave her pregnant, single mother, a woman he knew didn't love him, an honest married life. How could he do something so unselfish, and yet never show her he actually cared about her? Maybe Jack was right, he couldn't love Andrew as his own, and so he avoided showing any love or affection for her too.

"Thank you for sharing this with me," Jack said, as she closed the album. "Clearly, you have been beautiful all your life, despite what you might think."

"I was a small, smart, freckly carrot top who wanted for nothing but always felt like there was something missing." She sighed.

"Well, I like the carrot top and all her freckles; even the fact that she's a smarty pants. Besides, good things come in small packages." He took the album and placed it on the coffee table, then lifted her onto his knee. "I wouldn't change anything about you sweetheart, except maybe where you live. Come on, I think it's your turn to receive some therapy."

"More tea, or maybe coffee?" Jack asked Frankie.

They were sitting at the breakfast bar the following morning, finishing breakfast; she was still a little distant after the things she'd discovered about her father the day before.

"Mmm, tea please, I'm off coffee. I've had a couple of lattés recently that tasted bloody awful. I've decided to wait until I go home so I can enjoy decent coffee again."

"That's a bit harsh, it's not that bad here. Some of us haven't got a choice." He filled the kettle with water.

"Well, some of you could always move." She was going to seize every opportunity now to make a point.

Turning away from her, he returned the kettle to its base and switched it on. He chose not to respond and changed the subject.

"So," he said, as he took her mug from in front of her, "how are you feeling about yesterday, after sleeping on it? You seem a little distant."

Frankie was resting her chin on her hand, while gathering up a pile of crumbs. She looked up at him.

"Confused, sad, kinda angry; I'm not really sure what to do now." She sat back and scraped the crumbs into the palm of her hand before tipping them onto the plate.

"Go and see him."

Frankie just glared at him; she couldn't believe he'd just said that.

"What?" she asked, quietly seething.

"I think you should consider…" She didn't let him finish before she cut him off.

"I heard you, don't be ridiculous." She hurriedly got down from the breakfast bar and made for the bathroom.

"Oh no you don't!" He caught her arm at the end of the breakfast bar. "You're not going to pretend you can deal with this on your own, because you clearly can't." His grip was firm around her wrist.

"Let go of me Jack, you've got no room to talk about dealing with things; if it hadn't been for me, you'd still be wallowing in your own grief." Instantly, he let go of her, and she stormed off into the bathroom, slamming the door without looking back at him.

Jack decided to give her some space. He finished clearing away the breakfast dishes, before he knocked on the door to see if she was all right.

"Sweetheart," he leaned against the doorframe of the bathroom, with his forehead pressed against the door, "are you okay? Can I come in?"

He waited a moment; she didn't answer, which worried him. He was just about to turn the doorknob when the door slowly started to open. He was surprised to see that she hadn't been crying, but she looked really sad.

"I'm sorry Jack, I shouldn't have said that. I'm just..." She didn't look at him when she spoke; instead she kept her eyes on the floor.

He took her chin and lifted it so he could see her.

"It's fine, and in fact, completely true. I'm sorry for upsetting you, I shouldn't have suggested it."

"No, you're right, I'll think about it. The thought of seeing him again scares me, but maybe it will help."

"Listen, I'm off next Monday, so if you want to take a week to think about it, maybe talk to Carol. We could go together if you like. I don't have to come in with you, just be there for support. What do you think?"

"Sure, maybe I can meet up with Carol on Thursday, after I've had a chance to clear some more of the study."

"Okay, good." He took her face in both of his hands, and kissed her forehead. She flung her arms around his waist and held him tight.

"What did I do to deserve you?"

"I could say the say the same thing about you." He wrapped his arms around her neck, and stroked her hair. "Now, do you want to go to the house today, or shall we do something fun?"

"I want to say something fun, but I need to be done with that place, so we ought to crack on with it."

"Okay. I'm sure we can find something fun to do later," he said, with a wicked grin.

It was now the week leading up to Denise's party, and everyone was talking about what they would be wearing, although some people were keeping their costumes a secret. Gloria was collecting money from everyone so that they could buy Denise a gift.

"Thanks Frankie, pet, I assume you're going on Saturday?" Gloria took Frankie's contribution, and ticked her name off her list.

"Absolutely, I haven't been to a fancy dress party in years," she replied, gathering some patient records at the front desk.

"Can I ask what you're going to be?" Gloria asked quietly.

"You can ask, Gloria, but I ain't telling you," Frankie smiled at her. "You'll just have to wait and see."

"Are you... going alone, pet?" Gloria was fishing for information; there were other people around the desk and word had spread that both she and Jack had mentioned they currently had partners.

"I will be, yes," Frankie said, as she shut the records and moved away from the desk, towards her anaesthetic room. She had answered the question honestly; they had decided not to arrive together.

Mike Anderson had been called to the ward to see a very sick patient of his, so the afternoon list had been temporarily put on hold until he returned. Frankie peered through the window of

Theatre 2; she could hear Train playing 'Save Me San Francisco'. She had left Alex, Jack, and Martin setting up for the next case, although what she witnessed had nothing to do with work. Jack and Alex were playing 'Butthead' over the operating table; they both looked utterly ridiculous wearing the fitted hats, with little bows tied under their chins, trying to catch the soft balls on the Velcro strips across their heads. What made it even more amusing was the fact that Jack was almost a foot taller than Alex. The music was louder than usual, and they were all laughing at each other, Martin feebly attempting to referee. She took a moment to watch the happy, playful, devilishly handsome man she was in love with. She startled when Heather spoke behind her.

"I caught you, Doctor, watching the local talent!" She was smiling at Frankie. "Sorry, didn't mean to give you a fright." Heather put her hand affectionately on Frankie's arm.

Frankie smiled back, "Guilty as charged, Nurse, I could watch him all day," she replied, dreamily.

"Me too, love!" Heather winked at her.

Frankie gave a very bashful smile.

"What am I going to do Heather, it's all gotten quite serious." Frankie's tone had changed; it was sad and strained.

"Oh! Are you still going back?"

"Yes, I've always made that clear."

"Is he?"

"I don't know. I don't think he's decided yet. We haven't actually talked about it at any great length really; we just keep touching on the subject. The biggest problem seems to be work; we don't have ODPs so he would have to do whatever job he could find, or re-train. I think he still has some unhealed bruises which are holding him back, but I've been so caught up with my own emotional roller coaster that I haven't explored them yet."

"Do you want me to help in any way? He talks to me, and if you ask me, I think he needs to make a fresh start. I want to help,

Frankie; I had a feeling you two had fallen for each other in a big way."

"Thanks, but it has to be his decision, I don't want him to feel pressured."

"Fair enough. Are you both going on Saturday?"

"Of course. You?"

"Absolutely! Are you going as a couple?"

"Well... yes, but we're not going to arrive together, then we'll just see what happens." Frankie was smiling and raised her eyebrows.

"Great, looking forward to it." There was a loud crash as something in the theatre was knocked over. "Now then, shall we sort these naughty boys out before they wreck the room completely?"

Heather put her arm around Frankie and gave her a hug, before they pushed the doors open.

When Frankie met up with Carol in town later that week, she filled her in on what she'd found in her father's study. She expressed her mixed feelings and emotions, close to tears as she spoke. She told her how fantastic Jack had been at helping her through it; how they'd sat down together, and looked through the album. She couldn't thank her aunt enough for putting it together; it was the most amazing gift. She was grateful to have had someone to share it with, and to listen to her reminisce about her childhood, both happy and sad.

"Jack thinks I should go and see him," Frankie said, playing with a small packet of sugar.

"I think he's right, but what do you think?" Carol took a sip of her latté.

"After thinking about it for a few days now, I'm swaying towards going, but the idea scares me. Jack said he would go with me." Frankie put her elbow on the table, and leant her cheek on the palm of her hand.

"Then go. I think you'll regret it if you don't, even if what you see is traumatic. I'm not sure he's going to be around for much longer. You'll probably miss your chance if you don't go before you leave."

"I know, I've thought about that too. Okay, Jack's off with me on Monday, so maybe we'll plan go then, before I talk myself out of it again."

"Good for you." Carol put her cup down, looking like she was going to speak, but instead pressed her lips together.

"What, Aunty, spit it out?"

"He's a rare find, that fella of yours. Have you two worked anything out yet?"

Frankie sat back and ran her hands through her hair, holding it back off her face with her hands on her head. She was looking directly at Carol, who raised her eyebrows, waiting for an answer. Frankie let go of her hair; it cascaded down around her face, as she took a deep breath and exhaled slowly.

"No, we sort of skirt around the subject, but I know he's scared to make the move. It's not something he ever saw himself doing, so it's a huge step for him. I think all I can hope for right now is that he agrees to visit, and that he loves the place as much as I do when he does."

Carol gave her niece a sympathetic smile, and reached over to take Frankie's hand.

"I don't believe two people can be that crazy about each other, and not be able to work something out. Give it time."

Frankie was getting a bit fed up of being told to give him time. She wanted to know where she stood; she had waited long enough for this in her life; was it too much to ask to keep it all now?

Chapter 30

FRANKIE LED JACK into the bedroom, and told him to strip down to his underwear and socks. He had no idea what she had planned, but it was almost 6.30, and the party was starting at 7. She wasn't giving anything away. She had her make up on, and was wearing her little black robe; he could see she wasn't wearing any underwear. He did as she asked, and stood in front of her with his arms folded.

"Relax, Jack, this is supposed to be part of the fun. Now, sit on the edge of the bed; I'm going to blindfold you with this." She held up a black scarf of hers.

"Hang on a minute, you never mentioned anything about blindfolding me! What are you up to?"

"Seriously, Jack, lighten up! Just think how nervous you were the last time I blindfolded you, and look how that turned out. Now, trust me."

"Why do I instantly feel like I shouldn't trust you when you say that?"

"Give it up. I promise I'm not going to dress you up like a womble or a muppet or any other crazy children's TV character, okay? Think hot couple!"

"Yes, yes all right, just get on with it before the party's over."

Frankie took a scarf and placed it over his eyes before tying it around his head, careful not to trap any of his hair.

"Okay, can you see anything?"

"Not a thing. Happy?"

"Good! You might have to help me out a bit, okay?"

"Whatever." Jack was shaking his head at her; why couldn't she just give him the costume to put on himself, instead of playing games?

She proceeded to place a white shirt over his head; he pushed his arms through the sleeves. The front of the shirt had a V that came quite low, showing off his chest hair; already he looked very hot and he wasn't fully dressed yet. Next she slid black pants, with a red stripe down each side, over his feet, and he stood to pull them up, tucking the shirt in. She helped him into a black waistcoat, and hung a loose belt around his waist, which had plastic gun and other stuff hanging from it. As he didn't own a pair of black boots, she helped him into his shoes, then applied black, faux-leather gaiters to give the illusion he was wearing boots.

"Oh yeah, Jack, you look more delicious than the real thing!"

"Okay, I think I know who we are, can I take this off?"

"No, no, I have to put mine on first; we need to stand together in front of the mirror to get the full effect."

Quickly, she dropped her robe on the bed, opened the wardrobe and lifted out a bag on a hanger. After losing the bag, she put on the long white floaty dress over her nude bra, applied a gold belt around the gathered waist, and then tucked her hair up into the wig; finishing off the look.

"Okay," she took his hand, and led him to the foot of the bed, "are you ready?"

"As I'll ever be," he said smiling; he was actually quite excited now to see what she was wearing; visions of a gold bikini danced in his head.

"Go for it then, Captain!"

Jack pushed the blindfold off over his head. Although slightly dazzled by the light, he could clearly see, staring back at him in the mirror, Han Solo and Princess Leia.

"Bloody hell, we look fantastic!" He was genuinely amazed. "Look at you, Danish pastries and everything!"

"I know; Kayla and I found this really cool store, in Whitley Bay of all places. I bought the costumes because I couldn't bear the thought of wearing something that a million other people had worn, so it's yours to keep."

"Thank you; I suppose I should trust you more from now on. Well, if this doesn't give the game away, nothing will!"

"I know, we are pretty much resigning ourselves to coming out tonight, you do realise that, right?" She put her arms around his waist; he looked hot in this outfit, maybe he would wear it for her in the bedroom…

"Yes, I'm ready for it, but let's keep them guessing for a little while longer. We'll get a taxi and I'll hop out before the hotel." He fondled her pastries, "You go ahead, and I'll follow a little while after; then, game on!"

"Okay, sounds like a plan, let's do it!"

Frankie couldn't remember the last time she had felt this nervous as she climbed out of the taxi. Other people she didn't recognise were arriving in fancy dress; she followed a short distance behind them. As she approached the Classics function room, she could hear Wham's 'Wake Me Up Before You Go-Go'. Smiling to herself, she recalled the last time she was there, and everything that had happened since. It was obvious when she approached the door that the party was already in full swing, so she hovered at the entrance to take it in. Everyone had made an effort to dress up;

there was everything from homemade punks to a life size golliwog. Some people said 'Hi' to her as they passed, but she had no idea who they were because of their costumes or make up. Suddenly, she found herself swept off her feet by Mike Anderson, dressed as Evel Knievel.

"Your Highness," he said, bowing his tall, slim figure towards her and almost salivating over her costume. "Good evening, are you alone?" he asked, as he looked behind her.

Frankie glanced over her shoulder. "It looks like it!" she exclaimed.

"Excellent! Well, may I buy you a drink?" He held his bent elbow out for her to link it. Although she realised he probably had an ulterior motive, she didn't think one drink could do any harm, so she willingly took it.

At the bar she sipped a gin and tonic, her eyes constantly darting to the doors every time someone walked in. Mike was standing a little bit too close for comfort.

"May I say, Doctor, you make a very fine princess in your spare time. Cheers!" Mike clinked her glass with his bottle of beer, a very large grin across his face.

'Oh yes', she thought, *'he's not just being friendly... Come on Jack, where the hell are you?'*

Smiling sweetly, to be polite, she hoped he would notice that she wasn't responding by returning the compliment. The music changed to Billy Ocean's 'Get Out Of My Dreams' and, before she knew it, Mike had grabbed her hand and was whisking her off to the dance floor. Abandoning her drink on a table with ABBA as she passed, Frankie turned around and saw Heather and Claire sat with their husbands. Heather nodded at her, and Frankie gave back a *'Help me'* sort of look, but Heather just grinned and made gestures for her to just dance. Frankie rolled her eyes at her.

Jack took a deep breath before he walked through the doors of the Classics room, thinking to himself *'This is it!'* As soon as he entered the room he could feel the eyes of several people on him. He made a point of not responding, only interested in locating one person. He scanned the room until he found her; his stomach did a somersault, then took a nosedive once he realised who she was dancing with. Mike was giving an over-enthusiastic performance, but Frankie was laughing and talking to the other people around her. He smiled to himself; he could see she was desperately trying not to make eye contact with Mike, without being rude.

"Jack!" A disco diva, all clad in gold, with big hair and platform shoes was trying to run towards him.

"Hey Dee, Happy Birthday," he gave her a big hug. "You look fabulous!"

"Thanks," she stood back to look at Jack admiringly, "and may I say, Captain Solo, you too look mighty fine tonight. What, no girlfriend?" she asked, looking around him.

"There's a chance you'll meet her later," he said, as the music changed to Donna Summer's 'Hot Stuff'.

"Oh I love this song; come on, every girl should be allowed one dance with Han Solo on her birthday." She grabbed his hand, and led him to the dance floor. He had no choice but to follow.

Mike had decided to mingle, and Martin, who was masquerading as the Green Cross Code man, had now commandeered Frankie. As Jack made his way to the dance floor with Denise, Frankie looked up, and their eyes met. They couldn't help smiling at each other.

"There's a funny coincidence," Denise shouted at Jack over the music, as she nodded to someone behind him. Jack casually looked around, already knowing what she was getting at. He looked back at her, and shrugged his shoulders.

"Or did you plan it this way?" she asked.

"No idea what you mean," he said, trying to look innocent, but failing miserably.

At the end of the song Denise gave him another hug and playfully rubbed his chest, "I would love to dance with you all night, Jack, but I think Elvis would get a little bit jealous!" She gestured towards her husband, who was walking towards them in a sparkly white jumpsuit, wig, and platforms.

"People might talk about us. Enjoy your evening, Dee." She gave him a little wave as he watched her walk away to join Elvis. They were quite amusing, trying to walk in their ridiculous shoes. He needed a drink.

Frankie had left the dance floor too and went to rescue her drink from Heather's table, where she was promptly ordered to sit down.

"Well, Princess, what can I say?" Heather turned her chair so that she was facing Frankie. Jack was directly behind her, at the bar. "You couldn't have picked a more obvious couple; you two are going to be the talk of the party, you do realise that?" Heather glanced up at Jack, who caught her eye, and raised an eyebrow. Heather just shook her head at him, smirking.

"Your man is at the bar, my dear, and hasn't taken his eyes off you since he arrived. Go on, get him on that dance floor and give us some real gossip!" Heather took a drink, and nodded her head towards the crowd of people who were all dancing out of sync, doing the god-awful Macarena.

"All in good time; I need at least one more G and T first. Catch you later." Frankie got up and walked towards the bar. The Village People, who turned out to be Megan and Olivia and their partners, along with another nurse who Frankie recognised, stopped her. She saw that Jack had been surrounded by admirers, one of whom was Marie, dressed in a very tiny punk outfit. She was pleased to see that Marie looked absolutely hideous, with her blue backcombed hair and black lipstick. Jack caught Frankie's eye and winked; the crowd around him quickly turned to see whom he was winking at, but Frankie had already turned back to talk to Megan. The real ABBA began singing 'Mamma Mia' and the crowd around Jack made for the dance floor. Megan turned to respond to something her boyfriend had said, which left a magnetic gap between Frankie and Jack.

They stood for a moment, facing each other, as if they were the only people in the room. Jack was smirking lopsidedly; he looked as heart-stoppingly handsome as he had the first time she had seen him, in almost the same spot, four months earlier. Yet again she felt all twinkly inside, as he leaned one elbow against the bar, and took a drink of his beer, without taking his eyes off her. She was about to walk towards him when Gloria brought her back to reality.

"Frankie pet, why you look smashin'! A hope you didn't bring Darth Vader with you; I've seen Luke Skywalker around here somewhere!" She was chuckling.

Frankie gave Jack a little shrug of her shoulders and a 'catch you later' smile; Gloria was completely oblivious as she carried on talking. She too, had gone down the disco diva road, and was clad in a sparkly turquoise dress that made her look like one of the Supremes.

"You look great too, Gloria, and no, I didn't bring Darth Vader, but I believe Han Solo is around somewhere." She couldn't resist; it was obvious that Gloria hadn't seen Jack. "You look like you need a refill, can I get you a drink?" Frankie asked.

"That would be lovely, pet, thanks. Bacardi and coke, if you don't mind."

"Coming right up." Frankie took Gloria's empty glass from her hand, but when she looked up to the bar, Jack was gone. She scanned the area as she walked towards it, but she couldn't see him. Once she'd placed her order, she had a good look around, and found him in the far corner of the room, talking to a very small Gene Simmons from Kiss. Whoever it was had gone all out with the black and white face paint and authentic outfit. Just as her drinks arrived, she heard the DJ announce that the buffet was open.

"There you go, Gloria. Cheers! And thank you for all your help over the last few months." Frankie raised her glass to her, and Gloria did the same, looking a little embarrassed.

"Just doing me job, pet. You've been a breath of fresh air in that place. I'll be sorry to see you leave."

Frankie muttered under her breath, "You're not the only one."

She carried on talking to Gloria, and Helen and her husband, dressed as Danny and Sandy from Grease, joined them. After a while she felt hungry, and noticed that Jack had wasted no time in helping himself to a plateful of food. He was sat at a table with Zippy from Rainbow, two hippies, and a pimp! She smiled to herself and made her way over to the buffet.

Soon after, Jack was mingling with some of the other ODPs. Occasionally, he glanced around the room to keep an eye on his Princess. He saw her talking to Chloë, who was dressed as a hippy, but was unable to catch her eye. She looked fantastic; he was desperate to take hold of her and slow dance right in front of everyone, but knew he had to be patient. Several people had admired his costume and asked where he'd found it; he'd admitted his girlfriend had chosen it for him. The interesting part was that nobody seemed to quiz him about her; they didn't even ask if she was with him. He made a deal with himself that the next person to ask would be the first to find out.

During the buffet Denise made a speech, thanking everyone for coming and for making such a huge effort to come in costume. She was starting to look and sound a bit tipsy by this point, but she kept it short and ended by urging everyone to enjoy a cupcake and let their hair down. As she finished talking the DJ announced three cheers for the birthday girl, then played Tom Jones' 'Sexbomb'. Frankie looked over to Jack and caught his eye, flitted her eyes towards the dance floor and back at him, suggesting they go for it and dance, when suddenly she felt hands on her hips pushing her forwards. Gene Simmons was forcing her onto the dance floor.

"Come on Your Highness, this one's mine," said a familiar voice from behind her.

"Alex!" Frankie exclaimed, "I had no idea that was you, you look great!"

Reaching the floor, they began to dance. Frankie was quite relaxed now, after three G and Ts.

"Thank you, but I think you definitely win the prize for the hottest babe at the party."

"Are you hitting on me, Mr. Scott?"

"Just trying to get in there before Han Solo gets his hands on you," Alex said, as he raised his eyebrows hopefully.

"Alex, I hate to break this to you, but Captain Solo's hands have already been all over me!!"

She couldn't believe she'd just said that, however, it didn't quite have the effect she was expecting; Alex just laughed and carried on dancing. Sexbomb faded into Carly Rae Jepson asking to 'Call Me Maybe'. Looking up, she saw Jack talking to a guy with the biggest Afro wig Frankie had ever seen. She made her way towards the bar, in need of a soft drink.

They were at opposite ends of the room when the music volume fell and the DJ spoke.

"Okay, folks, I have a request from the birthday girl. She would like to see Han Solo and Princess Leia on the dance floor."

Frankie's stomach hit the floor with a thump. She couldn't move; she just stared at Heather, who was stood in front of her, with her mouth wide open. She had her back to Jack, who was on the other side of the room.

Jack, on the other hand, had the completely opposite reaction. His slow sexy smile spread across his face, eventually becoming all white teeth and dimples.

The crowd had started whistling and shouting out.

Looking over at Frankie, he realised that this was his moment to take charge, after everything she'd done for him. "Come on, I can see you Captain Solo; go and find your Princess," said the DJ.

Jack handed his beer to Martin and made his way across the room, to more whistling, practically electrocuting every woman he passed with his smile. Frankie realised this was it; she couldn't look around, she knew he was walking towards her, and she was already tachycardic and overheating. She put her hand over her mouth and started to laugh.

"There she is, go on, sweep her off her feet and get her up here," the DJ continued.

Frankie felt one hand slide around her waist while the other one took her drink and handed it to Heather, who was now beaming at them.

"Princess," he said, as he took hold of her hand and kissed the back of it, "shall we give these good people something to really gossip about?"

"I think you might have just done that already," she replied.

She looked him straight in the eye and smiled.

"Ooh, here they come, ladies and gentlemen."

Jack turned to face the dance floor and, holding her hands behind his back, he guided her through the tables. All she could do was follow, smiling at everyone she passed. Jack walked proudly onto the floor, looking extremely pleased with himself. As they came to a stop, he pulled her to his side and held on tight to one hand. There were a few cheers and remarks from the partygoers.

"Okay," said the DJ, "Leia, Han, I have a message from Denise. She says, you can no longer hide it from us any more, stop pretending, we all know, so give us a floor show and make this a party to remember! I presume you two know what she's on about?" said the DJ, looking down at them from his podium, while everybody started clapping and shouting, 'Kiss, kiss, kiss...' louder and louder.

They both turned to look at each other, then suddenly she was folded into his arms, the victim of the most public display of affection she'd ever been a part of. He kissed her like it was the last time he ever would, whilst all around them people cheered, whistled, shouted, and clapped. Finally, once he'd stopped and pulled her close, all she could do was wrap her arms around his waist and smile, as the huge weight lifted off both their shoulders.

"I guess that means our secret's out!" he whispered in her ear.

She just laughed at him.

"Well, that was.... erm, quite a show... Anyway, I have a tune for the two of you. Tell me, is one of you a doctor?" the DJ asked.

Jack raised Frankie's arm for her, smiling down at her as he did so.

"Oh, it's the Princess! Well this song will be just the ticket for you both... okay then, take it away Mr. Palmer..."

The volume increased as they both looked at each other, a little confused.

'*A hot summer night, fell like a net*

I've gotta find my baby yet
I need you to soothe my head
Turn my blue heart to red'

Suddenly, it dawned on both of them, and Frankie started to laugh whilst Jack began to sing along, dancing very enthusiastically, without taking his eyes of her.

'*Doctor, doctor give me the news*
I've got a bad case of lovin' you'

He pulled her in close as they danced; she had had no idea he could move so well, as he let himself go, giving them all what they'd wanted to see for months.

'*You think I'm cute, a little bit shy*
   Momma, I ain't that kind of guy'

He took hold of her chin as he sang along; she just shook her head at him, grinning. His playfulness was hypnotic; she couldn't help become a part of it. Taking her hands in his, he linked their fingers, pulling her towards him and mouthing....

'*I know you like it, you like it on top'*

There were a few whoops and cheers from their audience as Frankie raised her eyebrows, without taking her eyes off him. With a huge grin on his face, he carried on singing,

'*Tell me momma are you gonna stop'*

She shook her head at him and they moved their hips together from side to side, as he placed his hands behind his back, pulling her arms with his. Eventually, their song gave way to the Cha Cha Slide and the floor filled up again.

Now that it was game over, Jack didn't let her out of his sight for the rest of the evening. He kept her right by his side, either holding her hand or draping his arm around her. He was so happy to finally have it out in the open. The only part they were still a little vague about was how long they had been seeing each other, although it was pretty obvious to most that it had been a while. On the whole, most people were pleased for them, but Frankie could see that several female members of staff were slightly green with envy. She also felt bad that this had been Denise's birthday party, and they had stolen her thunder. She made a mental note to apologise to her when she next saw her, sober, at work.

"Well folks, we're gonna slow things down before we wrap this up for the night…" said the DJ.

Jack took her hand and led her to the dance floor. He had wanted to do this all evening and now was his chance. The DJ announced, "….with Phil Collins and Against All Odds."

'*How can I just let you walk away*
　Just let you leave without a trace?
　When I stand here taking every breath with you, ooh.
　You're the only one who really knew me at all'

They just stared at each other, holding hands at arms length as if they were the only two people on the dance floor. Frankie made the first move, and pulled him towards her. Their arms found their natural resting places; their eyes stayed fixed on each other.

'How can you just walk away from me
　When all I can do is watch you leave?
　'Cos we've shared the laughter and the pain
　And even shared the tears.
　You're the only one who really knew me at all'

Frankie swallowed hard, her heart beating so fast it was thumping in her ears. If she didn't know any better, she'd have thought Jack had requested the song on purpose, but he looked just as thrown by it as she did. They started moving... slowly.

'I wish I could just make you turn around,
　Turn around and see me cry.
　There's so much I need to say to you,
　So many reasons why.
　You're the only one who really knew me at all'

Jack knew this song well; his dad was a big Phil Collins fan. He knew the words but he couldn't bring himself to mouth a single one. All the enthusiasm he'd had before had disappeared. These lyrics were expressing the harsh reality that their blissful bubble was going to burst, all too soon.

'But to wait for you, is all I can do and that's what I've got to face
　Take a good look at me now, 'cos I'll still be standin' here
　And you coming back to me is against all odds
　It's a chance I've gotta take...'

He pulled her close to him and held on like his life depended on it. Frankie thought she was going to cry; all the emotion and the excitement of the evening were catching up with her. She managed a few deep breaths and held back the tears. She could feel Jack's heart beating, almost in time with the thumping in her ears. Eventually, he took her chin and lifted it so he could look at her.

"You ready for bed?" he said.

She just smiled lovingly at him and nodded a little. They said their goodbyes and took a cab back to the flat.

Chapter 31

BELLE VUE HOME for the Elderly Mentally ill was buried in a secluded part of Gosforth. The tree-lined driveway gave the impression of entering the grounds of a prestigious stately home. Jack parked the Mini and switched the engine off. Frankie made no attempt to unclip her seat belt. He looked across at her for a moment before speaking.

"Do you want me to wait here?"

Slowly, she turned to him; he had never seen her bearing such sadness before. It pulled at his heart, because he had been the one to suggest doing this.

"Will you come in? Maybe you could just wait outside the room or something."

Reaching over, he took her trembling hand from her lap and kissed her knuckles.

"I'll do whatever you need me to do, but don't feel you have to go through with this just because you came this far," he said, as he sandwiched her hand between his, trying to stop it from shaking.

"I know, but I ought to, I want to."

"Come on then, the longer you sit here the harder it will be, okay?"

"Yeah, okay."

He kissed her hand again before releasing it so they could get out of the car.

As they walked through the main entrance a tall, slim woman in her mid-forties greeted them with a warming smile.

"Good morning and welcome; may I help you?" she asked.

Frankie noticed she was wearing a name badge identifying her as Lorraine, the receptionist.

"I've come to see my father… Mr. Robertson, Nicholas Robertson." She struggled a little to get the words out; Jack stayed glued to her side with his arm around her.

"Of course. If you'd just like to take a seat in our sitting room, I'll let Sister know you're here." Lorraine pointed to a small room just to the right of the entrance.

"Thank you," Jack said, as he guided Frankie into the room.

They sat down on a firm green sofa. The décor and furnishings were very old fashioned, even the light fittings. Jack held her close, occasionally kissing her head, while she played nervously with her fingers.

"I'm taking you out to lunch after this," he said quietly, "and maybe some retail therapy?"

This made her smile; she had never known a man who didn't mind shopping, and up until now they had avoided going together.

"That sounds nice, thank you," she said, leaning her head into him.

As she did so, a small, round, grey-haired woman in a navy nursing uniform bounced into the room.

"Good morning, sorry to keep you. I'm Sister Eccles, but please call me Annette." She held her hand out to shake both Frankie's and Jack's hands very firmly.

They were about to stand up, but she indicated for them to stay seated as she plopped herself down in an armchair opposite them.

"Now then, I believe you are Nick's daughter from Canada?" she asked.

"Yes, although I've been over here for a few months now, sorting out my father's affairs," Frankie nervously replied.

"And you are?" Annette looked at Jack and back to Frankie.

"Jack Lee, her boyfriend." He looked at Frankie, rubbing her shoulder. She smiled and placed an affectionate hand on his knee.

"I see, okay. Well, your aunt mentioned you were over here, but that it was unlikely you would visit. I believe you and your father didn't see eye to eye, Miss Robertson?"

"Dr. Robertson," Jack corrected.

Annette looked at Jack and then at Frankie, surprised.

"Oh, I'm sorry, Dr. Robertson, my apologies... Anyway, we don't normally allow visitors in the morning, but as this is an exceptional circumstance, I'm going to make an allowance. However, in future if you would like to visit again, may I kindly ask you to respect the visiting hours?" Annette was sincere in her tone.

"Of course, I'm sorry, it never occurred to me. I wasn't going to visit at all but, well, I changed my mind." She hesitated for a second before continuing, "May I ask how he is?" Her voice was shaky.

Annette looked at Frankie and cocked her head to the side, then looked down at her hands clasped in her lap, as if she was thinking of the right words to use.

"Miss... sorry, Dr. Robertson..."

"Please, call me Frankie."

"Frankie, I'm not going to lie to you, your father has deteriorated significantly since he came into our care. To be honest, he was quite unwell when he arrived; I have no idea how he'd managed at home for so long. I know your aunt did her best, and he had some other help, but I'm amazed he didn't come to any harm. I think it's only fair to warn you that you may be quite shocked when you see him, and he will almost certainly not recognise you. When did you last see him?"

Frankie looked down at her hands.

"Five years ago, at my mother's funeral," she said quietly.

"Oh! Well, you may want to think about it for a few minutes....".

"NO!" Frankie interrupted her, in a raised voice that she didn't really mean to use, "Um…no. If you don't take me now, I'll never do it," she said, much calmer.

"Okay, come with me then, and I'll take you to him." Annette looked concerned; she wasn't sure this was the right thing to do, but she had to respect Frankie's decision.

Both Frankie and Jack stood up; Frankie took Jack's hand, holding it tighter then usual, which he took as an indication that she wanted him to go with her.

They walked down hallways, past bedrooms and through the dining room. Frankie had never been in a place like it before. Sure, she had done some elderly care in training, and anaesthetised some patients with Alzheimer's over the years. She knew what to expect medically, but she had never thought about how people with such a mentally debilitating disease were taken care of. She had selfishly shut that part out of her mind, probably not wanting to know. They approached a white door with the number 56 on it, and Annette stopped outside.

"Are you ready?" she asked, as she turned to Frankie.

Frankie just nodded slightly with a sullen face. Jack took her face in his hands and stroked her cheek with his thumb.

"Sweetheart, I should wait here. I think this is something you need to do on your own," he said.

"You think?"

"I do. I'll be right here waiting, okay?" He kissed her forehead, and let go of her.

She nodded then turned to Annette, and nodded at her too. With a sad smile, Annette turned the handle of the door.

As Frankie entered the room she felt sick to her stomach; she was terrified at what she was about to witness. The room was pleasant; tastefully decorated in cream and pale blue, with striped curtains, a blue carpet, and a chest of drawers. The TV was quietly screening a dreadful daytime show. Sat a few feet away from the TV was an armchair; Frankie noticed an arm resting on the side. Taking a couple of deep breaths, trying to calm her nerves, she unconsciously placed her right hand over her racing heart. Annette walked over to the chair, touched the resting hand, then bent down slightly.

"Mr. Robertson, your daughter is here to see you," she said, and rubbed the hand a little before straightening and moving away so that Frankie could take her place.

Frankie walked towards Annette, who gestured towards the chair; she must have looked as frightened as she felt because Annette touched her arm lightly as she passed her to stand near the door.

Slowly, Frankie took a couple of steps towards the chair, her eyes fixed on the hand that still hadn't moved. Stepping closer, she saw legs, one crossed over the other, dressed in dark brown trousers, with checked slippers on the feet. Moving in even closer, her eyes travelled further up his thin torso, noting he was wearing a beige cardigan, with a cream shirt underneath, but no tie; her father had always worn a tie. His other hand rested on the other side of the chair. She swallowed hard and realised her mouth was completely dry. Raising her gaze, she looked at the sad, gaunt face staring blankly at the TV screen. She let out a short gasp; the man sat in front of her was barely recognisable as her father. This person wasn't the tall, well respected, arrogant but brilliant surgeon she had known growing up; he was a shadow of his former self. Stripped of all his independence and dignity, he had become a sad, lonely, and pathetic creature who simply existed.

She instantly knew she'd done the right thing by visiting him. What she saw was devastating. All that she had recently learned about him flashed through her mind. She didn't see cold or heartless, arrogant or difficult, she didn't even see unloving or uncaring. Instead she saw her father, the man who'd given her life, and a roof over her mother's head, even though she didn't love him and was pregnant with his brother's child. She felt love and enormous respect.

Frankie dropped to her knees, as the man who was her father looked at her, and gave her the hint of a smile. Suddenly, from out of nowhere, she went to hug him; laying her head on his chest she could feel how thin he was underneath his clothes. She didn't know what to say, or what to do next, until she felt his arms reach over her back and tears pricked in her eyes. Slowly, gently, one of those hands started patting her, causing her to smile.

"I love you too, Dad, thank you," she said.

After a few moments, she eased herself up, taking one last look at him; she knew deep down that this would be the last time she would see him alive.

"Goodbye," she whispered, but he didn't look at her again.

She looked up at the door as she slowly walked towards it; she could see that Annette was touched by what she'd witnessed. Frankie gave her a weak smile as Annette opened the door. Outside, Jack was leaning against the wall with his hands in his pockets, gazing down at the floor. He startled a little when the door opened in front of him. Frankie walked straight into his open arms, slow, silent tears rolling down her face. He kissed the top of her head, while rubbing her back. She didn't need to say anything; he could tell she was glad she'd seen him. Annette led them back to the main entrance.

"It was nice to meet you. Please do feel free to come again and visit before you leave," Annette said.

"Thank you," Frankie replied.

"Take care." She nodded at both of them.

Jack pushed the door open and they walked out into the cool, cloudy June weather.

As they drove away Jack broke the silence.

"What would you like to do now?"

Frankie thought for a moment.

"Take a walk around Stanley Park, with your hand firmly in mine, try to spot harbour seals, gaze at the mountains…then maybe seafood at The Boathouse while watching the sun set over the Pacific Ocean…" But she knew this would always be a fantasy.

She glanced sideways at him; his head turned slightly towards her, but his eyes were still on the road; then he glanced at her and their eyes briefly met. She looked down at her hands in her lap,

"…But, I can settle for lunch at the Metro Centre; I haven't been there since I got here," she continued.

"Okay, the Metro Centre it is then," he said. *'Was it really such a wonderful place or did she just make it sound so idyllic?'* he thought.

It had just started to rain when they walked through the doors of the shopping mall. He stopped near the entrance, smiled, and pulled her into his arms.

"You okay?"

"I am, can we talk about it later?" She smiled up at him, staring into *those* eyes; she wanted to be able to look into them for the rest of her life.

Bending down he whispered, "I'm going to do this because I can, and it doesn't matter who is watching." And then he kissed her slowly and gently, in full view of all the shoppers passing by. She thought that kiss would never stop, but she didn't care; she didn't want him to stop.

"WOW!" she said, when they finally came up for air. "I think we might need to get a room, not lunch!"

He burst out laughing and took her hand, "Come on, I've seen that look on you too many times now, Doctor."

"And what look would that be?" she said, as they started walking.

He bent so he could whisper in her ear, "Your 'very horny' look, that means I will need to consume a lot of calories because you plan on wearing me out!"

She giggled, and wrinkled her nose for him. "You know me too well!"

"I do, and I..." He stopped himself, caught in the moment.

Frankie looked up at him as they walked, arms around each other.

"And what?" she asked. *'You nearly said it Jack, just say it... please,'* she thought.

"I'm a lucky guy!"

Slightly disappointed, she placed a hand on his firm and very squeezable bottom that his lucky Levis were hugging.

They sat close together in a booth in Café Rouge and took their time over lunch. While they were enjoying tea and coffee, Jack moved his arm around her waist and slipped his warm hand under her T-shirt in search of some soft, bare flesh.

"Yes," she said, leaning back into him, "may I help you with something?"

"I was hoping you would let me buy you something," he said, as he nuzzled her ear.

"Jack, you've bought me enough, I don't need anything else... just you."

His hand was creeping further up her front.

"I would like to buy you something sexy to wear, for my eyes only!" he whispered.

He gave her one of his best slow, sexy smiles.

"In that case, how can I say no? Did you have something in mind?"

"Well, it's no good buying you underwear," he said, and they both chuckled, "so maybe, just something for the bedroom...."

"So, Ann Summers then!" she said, hopefully.

"Um, actually, I was hoping for something more tasteful. You know I'm not keen on all that kinky stuff."

"Okay, let's go see if we can find sexy tasteful bedroom wear!" She took hold of his stubbly chin and pulled his lips to hers, giving him a wicked grin as she pulled away.

"You're plotting something," he said.

"Me?" she replied, pretending to look shocked. "Always!"

Boux Avenue was a lingerie store they found in the lower green mall. Wandering through the racks of bras, panties, bodysuits, and suspenders, Jack made suggestive comments as they shopped. He had never shopped for ladies' underwear before; Frankie was bringing out a side of him he never knew existed. He loved her adventurous side; it made for a very exciting, interesting, intimate relationship, and he wanted to contribute something to that. She was very experienced and seemed to be up for anything, which made him nervous and excited all at the same time. He desperately didn't want to give her up; he had never felt so alive and so in love.

"Oh yeah! What about this?" she held up a black babydoll with matching thong, and he was instantaneously brought back from his thoughts.

He gave her one of his gorgeous, all-white-teeth smiles, which should have tripped the circuit of the entire Metro Centre.

"I'll take that as a yes," she said, turning towards the changing room as she grabbed his hand.

There was a waiting area, outside the cubicles, that contained a sofa and two chairs. The sales assistant looked at the item Frankie was holding and then up at Jack, and turned scarlet. She couldn't take her eyes off him.

"Hello!" Frankie said, waving her hand in front of the assistant, "It might be for his benefit, lady, but I'm the one trying it on!"

The young girl looked at Frankie, surprised. "I'm sorry... er... Number 4 please," and she pointed to the door of the cubicle.

Frankie looked up at Jack, who was a little embarrassed, but was smirking at her.

"I'll not be long," she said.

"You take all the time you need, sweetheart." He winked and sat down.

In the changing room she stripped and put on the flimsy fabric. Looking at herself in the mirror, she admired the sixties-style, flirty babydoll. It was scandalously sheer, with flock spots and a matching thong. The ruffle scoop neck slipped easily off her shoulder for a sexier look; its length skimmed her mid-hip and swung as she moved. Smiling at the reflection, she hoped this was what he had in mind. It sounded very quiet outside the cubicle, so she opened the door slightly, peeking through the crack. Jack was looking back at her. She eased the door open further and saw that he was alone. Curling her forefinger at him, she beckoned him towards her. She watched as his eyes darted back and forth, checking there was no one around, before he got up and walked towards her.

"Quickly," she said quietly, and pulled him into the cubicle.

"I can't come in..." he stopped speaking when he saw her; his mouth fell open.

"You like?" she whispered, hands on hips and licking her lips.

He bent down to her ear.

"Baby, I'm getting hard just looking at you," he whispered.

"Good!" she said, and went to undo his jeans.

He pulled away.

"You're kidding me, not here!" he whispered, completely shocked at what she was thinking.

She cornered him, took hold of his top button and pulled so his fly popped open.

"Oh yes... here!" she held his stare as she pushed down his jeans and boxers, then took hold of his very large erection. Using her other hand, she pushed the thong down so it fell to the floor; Jack let out quite a loud gasp.

"Shh," she whispered, placing her fingers to his lips, "I'm going to face this mirror and bend over so you can take me from behind; if you lean against that mirror, we can watch each other in this one." She pointed to the middle of the three large mirrors that hung in the cubicle.

He couldn't believe they were actually going to have sex in the changing room of a lingerie store, while people shopped around them. This was the hottest thing he thought he would ever do. Moving in behind her, he bent his knees, leaned back, and took hold of her hips. She was so wet she slid onto him with ease. They both looked to the side at their reflection.
 "Play with me," she mouthed, and he reached forward to find Mrs. Clit-tor-rus, who was practically dancing with the naughtiness of it all. He began to stroke, as she began to move, and as they watched in the mirror they came simultaneously. It was quick, quiet, and very erotic.

Frankie quickly dressed while Jack sat on the bench, his legs like jelly. She hung the babydoll and the thong back on the hanger.
 "How are you doing, able to move yet?" she asked quietly, with a cheeky grin on her face.
 "I think so," he replied. As he was about to get up he stopped, stifling a laugh. "Oh no... Look!" he pointed to his own bum mark on the mirror of the cubicle.
 Frankie put her hand over her mouth to stop herself laughing out loud, then took a tissue from the box on a shelf, and wiped it off.
 "That's too funny," she whispered.

Once she had composed herself, she opened the door slowly and looked out. There was a man sat on the sofa where Jack had been sat a few minutes earlier. The sales assistant was organising a rail of underwear. Frankie, feeling thoroughly pleased with herself, boldly opened the door and strolled out of the cubicle. The sales assistant looked across at Frankie, and was about to speak when she saw Jack follow her out of the cubicle, tucking his T-shirt into his jeans. Her eyes nearly popped out of her head.

"Thank you, I'll take it!" Frankie said, as she walked passed her, smiling.

Her brazenness rubbed off on Jack, who decided he wasn't going to beat her, so he might as well join her.

"It worked!" he said, flashing the assistant his dazzling smile and a quick wink.

As they both walked towards the cash desk, they heard the assistant comment to her colleague that she thought the really hot bloke and his girlfriend had just 'had it away' in the changing room. Frankie and Jack looked at each other, then he bent down and whispered in her ear.

"You are a very naughty girl, Dr. Robertson; you are getting me into all kinds of trouble. I can't believe we just did that."

"Good. You're helping me tick them off, Mr. Lee, one fantasy at a time," she grinned.

"Well, I hope they are not all as public as that one was."

She carried on grinning, very pleased with herself.

Chapter 32

TUESDAY MORNING, THREE days after the party, there was finally no reason to pretend any longer. They arrived at work together, no longer caring who saw them. Jack switched off the engine and looked across at her. She looked really worried for a moment, and then suddenly gave him a big smile.

"That's better," he said, smiling back and squeezing her thigh, "ready to face the music?"

"Oh please, tell me they won't play anymore music! You were waaay too enthusiastic about singing that song!" she replied, as she took hold of her backpack and opened the door.

He took her chin in his hand before she climbed out.

"I thought some of the lyrics were very appropriate."

"Oh really, which ones?" *'Say it Jack, this is your chance, pleeeeease say it.'* she thought.

He leant over and gave her a quick kiss, "Well, you do like it on top!" He let go and stepped out, leaving her sitting there. She sighed before following him.

"And I like you on top," he said, as they shut their doors.

"Oh, do you now, and why is that?"

He opened the boot and took out his own backpack. She stood very close to him, looking up.

"Well?" she asked again.

He glanced around to see if anyone was in earshot. Walking towards the door he spoke quietly,

"Well, there are quite a few reasons actually. Mainly because you are in control, which I really like and..." He had one arm around her, bent over slightly so he could talk into her ear, when he was interrupted.

"Well, well, well, you two finally going to show your faces together in public, about bloody time!"

"Morning Mike," Frankie said in a dull tone without looking at him, rolling her eyes at Jack.

They all walked up the stairs together; Jack kept quiet.

"So, Princess, if I'd been ten years younger, would I have had a better chance?" Mike asked, smirking at Jack who smiled back at him with an *'In your dreams mate'* sort of smile.

Frankie just ignored Mike, and he peeled off through the doors leading to the clinics. She carried on up the stairs with Jack.

"Hell would freeze over first, Mr. Anderson!' she said, without looking at Jack, who laughed.

"I thought you liked him?" he asked.

"Yes, as a surgeon he's very good, and don't get me wrong, he's nice to work with, but really... I mean REALLY?"

"Really what? You've lost me!"

"Jack, the guy is so far up himself, he probably has a really small penis and probably the only reason he's a urologist is so he can research how to make it bigger... Oops, inside voice."

Jack was wide-mouthed, shaking his head at her. He loved the way she spoke her mind; he never knew what she would come out with next.

"You know, he bought me my first drink, and was moving in for the kill when you arrived on Saturday?"

"No way!" Jack suddenly looked furious, and started to turn back down the stairs.

"Where are you going?"

"To make his anatomy even smaller."

"JACK!" Frankie was shocked; she'd not seen him jealous and protective of her.

He burst out laughing, "Gotcha!" he said, as he dived towards her and grabbed her waist, tickling her.

"Jack, stop it! We're at work now."

"I know, that's the fun part." He stopped and gave her a lingering kiss, "I can do this whenever I want!" He grinned as he opened the door to their floor, then pinched her bottom as she walked through the door.

They both managed to change without receiving too much hassle from their colleagues in their respective changing rooms. Jack was the first one to arrive at the front desk.

"Mornin' lover boy," said Gloria, winking at him.

"Good morning Gloria, I trust you are well on this fine, sunny Tuesday?" Jack replied, checking out the schedule to see how his week was shaping up.

"Ahh pet, it's lovely to see you back to your old self. It's a wonderful thing, love."

"It certainly is, Gloria, it certainly is." He gave Gloria one of his beautiful smiles, before he strolled off to Theatre 2, without noticing that Frankie was right behind him.

She stood glaring at the screen, wide-eyed. Not only had he just admitted to Gloria that he was in love; she was now staring at a very hot picture of them both kissing, rather passionately, on the dance floor.

"It gives me a hot flush every time I see that one, too," said Denise, bringing Frankie back to reality.

"Dee, morning.... hang on a minute, there's more?"

"Absolutely, you two are like a celebrity couple now. Hottest couple since Mr. Cameron was caught with that Swedish House Officer!"

"Oh God, Dee, I'm sorry; it was your night and we completely stole your thunder." Frankie felt terrible, they should never have gone dressed as a couple.

"Don't be ridiculous, my 50th will be talked about for years because of you two," she leant into Frankie and lowered her voice, "which is good for me, because I don't remember much of it!"

Frankie laughed at her comment, and felt much better.

"Thanks, I'm glad you're okay with it, especially as it was you who outed us!"

"Listen, I was serious when I said we knew; it's been obvious for a long time, and I have a small confession to make." Denise tried to look a bit sheepish.

Frankie looked at her quizzically.

"I saw you getting into his car, Friday of the May Day weekend, after work."

"Oh! So you've known for a while then?"

Denise nodded slowly. "Now, do you want me to schedule him in other rooms, or are you still okay working together?"

"I'm okay with it, but it's probably better all round that we don't work together now. Don't ask Jack though; he'll disagree."

"Will do, look after him, okay." She gave a quick nod and a smile.

Frankie nodded, but she couldn't help feel that he was the one looking after her at the moment.

She had just put her first patient to sleep when her phone buzzed in her pocket. She quickly glanced at it.

Now then, Dr., my list...

'*Oh yes,*' she thought, '*me on top*'. So once Mr. Patel had put knife to skin, she replied.

Ah yes, me on top, in control, &...

Jack was in Theatre 2 with Dr. 'Airhead' Richardson, as he'd nicknamed her. He was in a very playful mood and he didn't want his frustrating, dysfunctional anaesthetist to spoil it, so he thought he would brighten his day with some risky texting.

It's so deep, I could get lost in there...

She was smiling to herself; yes it was deep and he could hit a very sweet spot, but...

Mmm, I think reverse cowgirl is deeper...

He still wasn't raving about that position.

Maybe, but I can't watch you come & I luv to watch you come...

She let out a long, slow breath as Chloë glanced at her with interest...

Ditto!

He gave a satisfied smile.

There is something else I like to watch...

She was intrigued.

?

'*Okay, you wanted to know,*' he thought...

...the way your beautiful, full breasts bounce up and down, it's so hot!

Frankie tripped over her stool as she walked and read, letting out a loud gasp. Looking up, she felt four pairs of eyes on her.

"Oops, sorry," she said, slightly embarrassed. Chloë smiled at her; she guessed Frankie was texting Jack.

Frankie replied a little later...

My beautiful, full breasts are tingling with excitement at the thought of your sexy eyes watching them... Later! Fx

Jack was walking back into the anaesthetic room behind another nurse, head down, reading the text; he didn't notice she'd let go of the swing door. It smacked him square on the forehead, almost knocking him over. He stood dazed for a moment, before deciding that it was best not to respond to her for fear of further personal injury.

At the end of the day he waited for her at the front desk while she took her last patient to recovery. He was chatting to Gloria, and a couple of other nurses, when she appeared at his side, sliding an arm around his waist.

"Look, we made the news!" he joked, pointing to the screen.

"Oh no, not another one! How many pictures of us do you guys have?" she asked, staring at a photo of them slow dancing, very close and looking lovingly into each other's eyes.

"I like that one, you look so in love," said one of the nurses before walking away.

Turning towards Jack, Frankie froze with a surprised, almost worried look on her face. It was the first time she'd seen Jack properly all day.

"Shit, Jack, what the hell happened?" she asked, as she reached up to his forehead, but didn't touch the large black and blue egg that had grown over the course of the day.

"Oh, yeah, that... a swing door hit me when I was a bit distracted," he replied, with a shy looking smirk.

She burst out laughing, then tried to stop herself; it looked really sore.

"Oh poor baby, I'm sorry...are you okay?" She was desperately trying to stifle her laugh.

"I will be if you keep your word," he said, raising his eyebrows.

"We'd better go home then!" She winked, and turned towards the door.

Jack looked over at Gloria and the other nurse at the desk, smiled and shrugged his shoulders. They watched as he dreamily followed her out of the doors.

Frankie pushed the flat door open, then turned around to face Jack. He wasn't even through the door when she grabbed a fist full of T-shirt and pulled him towards her. Pushing the door closed with his foot, his lips met hers. Both of their backpacks dropped to the floor; poor Hercules nearly sustained a concussion when all he was trying to do was say hello. Their kiss was needy and desperate, both already panting, still fully clothed. Frankie unzipped her hoodie and slipped it off her shoulders; another loud 'meow' was heard as it completely covered Hercules. They both smiled at the cat's reaction as they kissed. Jack was backing up into the bedroom as he undid the top button of his jeans; Frankie was tugging at the hem of his T-shirt. He helped her out by taking hold of it, breaking their kiss for a second while he hurriedly pulled it over his head. Their lips met again; her hands searching for his firm abs, travelling around to his back, over his muscular pecs and up into his crazy hat hair curls. They both kicked their shoes off and stopped in front of the mirror, all tongues and passion. Frankie slipped her arms out of her tank, and pushed it, along with her cropped yoga pants, down her body in one swift move. She was now completely naked and needed him naked too. His hands moved down from her hair, over her shoulders, down her back and around her front, coming to rest over her breasts. He tugged at her already very erect nipples, and smiled at her as they kissed. Undoing his button fly, she slid her hands inside his jeans to cup his firm behind. She pulled away to look at him in complete surprise.

"No underwear!" she said, smiling slowly.

He moved his hands back down her body and over her pert little cheeks, squeezing while he grinned, his nose pressed against hers.

"No underwear," he repeated.

"But you were wearing some this morning."

"I was, I took it off when I got changed; thought I might see what it was like and enjoy the look on your face, for once!"

"Ohh," she groaned, "it's very hot, my work here is done," she purred.

"Oh no it isn't!" he replied quickly.

He pushed his jeans down, freeing his throbbing manhood, and stepped out of them, along with his socks.

She took him in for a moment while he lay across the end of the bed. He was a beautiful sight, lying there completely naked. He placed a hand on her hip and pulled her towards him.

"Come and enjoy the ride," he said, and she climbed onto him, allowing him to slowly slide inside her.

He moaned, then took her by surprise as he sat up, and placed her right nipple in his mouth.

"Oh God, Jack, that feels so good... Make me come like this," she moaned, throwing her head back, enjoying his tongue and his touch as she sat perfectly still on his hard length. They both kept glancing across at the erotic view in the mirror.

She was so turned on that in no time at all she was shouting his name incoherently. He stopped his exquisite torture, and lay back, placing his hands on her hips. She started to move, watching his face as he too let go, and she enjoyed another mind-blowing aftershock. Collapsing on top of him, she buried her face in his chest hair and he wrapped his arms around her.

"I have needed this ever since I smacked my head on that bloody door!" he said, and they both laughed.

"Are you okay? That's quite the bump you have there." She looked up, brushing away a few stray curls, before pulling herself up to kiss the lump.

Soaking in the bath after dinner, Jack cradled her against him; letting his hands wander over her slippery body.

"I don't think I could ever getting tired of making love to this beautiful body of yours, it never disappoints," he said, as his hands slid over her stomach and back up to her chest. He nuzzled her ear and nibbled the top.

"Ditto," she replied, as she tilted her head so he could nibble his way down her neck.

"You make me feel so alive, so..." He paused, as his tongue circled the inside of her ear.

'Say it Jack, please say it, I need to hear it first,' she thought.

".... wanted." He stopped and just hugged her.

She sighed with disappointment, again.

"What?" he said, sensing her change in mood.

She took a deep breath and placed her hands on top of his, stilling them.

"All I ever wanted, my whole life, was to know that my father loved me and cared about me. Never feeling it, I've searched for that love in every relationship I've had; eventually, I'd find something about the person that reminded me of him, and I would realise I couldn't love them. When I saw him yesterday, the man who used to be my father, I felt overwhelming sadness and pity for the nobody that he's become, and I realised that he knew love; he just didn't and couldn't show it. All because he chose to spend his life with a woman who needed him but didn't love him."

"I felt so sorry for him, in the short time I stood there, looking down on him like he was a child. I went to hug him, and he folded his arms around me and patted my back. I have no idea if he knew who I was or who he was for that matter, but in that simple gesture, it felt like a lifetime of affection. It didn't make up for lost time, but since then I've thought long and hard about the man I remember. I think going to see him has helped me come to terms with why he could only secretly love me in a box of memories."

There was a long heavy silence between them while Jack digested what she had said. He knew what she needed to hear, but he was scared that if he said it, he would then break her heart because he was too weak to do anything about it.

"I'm nothing like him, am I?" he whispered. It was a rhetorical question.

She gently brushed her cheek against his arm and he knew he was right.

Chapter 33

As the cool and wet days of early summer slipped by, work had become much easier in some respects, but harder in others. They could travel together, eat together if their lunches coincided, and occasionally show affection. However, the gossip didn't end, it just moved to the next level; was she staying or was he going? Neither could have answered this, had either been asked directly. They were both burying their heads in the sand, each hoping that the other one would make the decision, or at least broach the subject. As a result, they continued to avoid sitting down and seriously talking it through. It was the same with telling each other how they really felt; each was waiting for the other to say it first, because neither wanted to have to hurt the other. There was a tension between them that just simmered in the background while they ignored the elephant in the corner of the room that was their day-to-day life.

Frankie carried on clearing her father's study. She wanted it done by the time Andrew arrived, so that they could spend some quality time together. She knew she would have to take time to tell him about his real father, in addition to going through her father's personal and financial affairs, as the sale of the house came to a close. She had made an appointment with the solicitor to ensure everything was covered, but wasn't sure how involved Andrew would want to be once he knew the truth. At the end of each day she was still feeling very tired and, more often than not, physically and emotionally drained. When she spent time on her own at the house, among her own thoughts, she tried to imagine coming back to England, and sacrificing everything else in order to spend the rest of her life looking into those amazing steel blue eyes, and fondling that beautiful head of dark curls. The reality was, she wanted the best of both worlds and she couldn't see how that could ever happen. It made her both angry and sad, and she knew that at some point it would make her cry.

For Jack, life was finally good again, but he was caught in the moment and deliberately wasn't trying to think of the future. If there was one thing losing his wife had taught him, it was to live for the moment. He could see a future with Frankie, but he couldn't see it anywhere else but Newcastle. It wasn't fair to ask her to give up everything for him; he could see she didn't belong there. Some people had suggested he take the opportunity to make a fresh start, move to this fantastic place where she lived. What people didn't understand was the reality of making a move like that; it wasn't going to be easy for him to get a job, and the distance from his family would surely be too great. Deep down, what he was really scared of was it not working out. He almost needed to put some distance between them, so he could be sure it was the right thing to do.

On the day Andrew and Angus were arriving, Jack was working a regular day shift. The boys were flying in late morning and planned to get a taxi from the airport.

"So, do you think you're ready for my brother and his 'wife'?" Frankie asked, making little commas with her fingers.

"No, I don't think anyone could be ready for those two descending for a whole weekend," he said, as he ate his last spoonful of granola.

"You're okay with the whole gay thing, aren't you?"

She was wearing one of Jack's T-shirts, nothing else, as she squeezed between his legs whilst he sat at the breakfast bar.

"It will take a bit of getting used to. For a bloke, two guys is kinda..." Jack pulled a face, "but two girls..." he said, smiling.

"Yeah, yeah, I get it. Just don't want you to feel uncomfortable, okay. It's Gussy you need to worry about, he'll be all over you."

"Um, really," he pulled another, very worried face.

"Not like that, he just likes to look out for me that's all, so expect him to give you hell until he's satisfied your not going to break my heart."

His face fell.

"Jack," she stretched up to kiss him, "I've known Gussy a long time, he's like a big sister to me, and I love him dearly. You'll be fine, now, go to work, think naughty thoughts about me, and I'll see you tonight."

He took a deep breath, took her face in his hands and kissed her long and slow.

"Mmm, already having them," he said, as he rubbed noses.

"Go!" she demanded.

Andrew texted Frankie when they landed. Her excitement mounted; it had been nearly a year since she'd last seen them. She had at least an hour before they would get to her.

"Well, big guy," she said to Hercules, who was sitting on a barstool while she made another bucket of tea, "I'm not sure how this is going to work out. He's going to get on with them, I'm sure, but you know," she leant forward and placed her chin on the heel of her hand, "I've never introduced them to anyone I've dated, and I can't help thinking I should feel nervous or something.

But I don't..." she folded her arms, still leaning on the bench. "It kinda feels right, which is really scary, because there's probably no future in it, is there?"

She reached out to stroke his head.

"By the end of this weekend, he will have met all my family, except for my father of course, and my best friend. Shouldn't we be getting married now or something? Yeah, I know; you really couldn't care less. Don't worry, it won't be long now until your Lucy will be back, and you won't have to listen to, or watch for that matter, any more of my colourful love life."

She got up, took her tea over to the sofa, and tried to wait patiently.

Just before one the door buzzed; she leapt up and pressed the intercom to speak.

"Come straight up," she said with enthusiasm, then pressed the door release.

She bounced out of the flat door and saw them pulling their suitcases across the hallway. Andrew looked up at the small, very excited figure at the top of the stairs and smiled back at her.

"Sweetpea!" he said, as he got to the top of the stairs, and wrapped an arm around her, "Great to see you." He gave her a kiss on her forehead.

"Gussy!" she exclaimed, throwing her arms around Angus next, who was just as eager to see her.

"Oh darlin', it's good to see you, it's been too long." He held her at arm's length to look at her. "You look well, my love, and you've put a wee bit a weight on, I'm sure," he commented.

"Angus, let's at least get through door before you start abusing the poor girl." Andrew looked at Frankie and mouthed, 'you haven't', while shaking his head.

Frankie just smiled at them; they really were like an old married couple.

They caught up briefly on life over some lunch, and then decided to head over to the house. That was the main reason Andrew was here, even though he was still clear that there was nothing he really wanted. He was eternally grateful to his sister for everything she'd done, and it was only right he should show some support and interest in what she'd achieved.

"So this pile over here is mainly some personal items of Mum's. I have her eternity ring for you, and this is now her engagement ring." Frankie showed Andrew the pendant.

"Nice! Why didn't you just get the ring made bigger? It was so beautiful!" he asked.

"You know I'm not big on rings, so I probably wouldn't have worn it, and this way she's closer to my heart."

Andrew gave her a hug, and rubbed her back affectionately.

"Okay, so, Mum's stuff, have a look and see if there's anything you want, I didn't want to take anything until we could do this together. That's his stuff," she waved her hand despondently at a small pile of her father's things, "and, as you know, everything else is going for clearance. All the other things we discussed have already gone."

"You're a wee star, lassie, do you know that? A wee gem!" said Angus, hugging her.

"It had to be done Gussy, and I did have some help, which made it kinda fun sometimes." She gave him a cheeky little smirk.

"Yes, well, let's not go there sis," said Andrew, holding his hand up "I would quite like Mum's jewellery box, but I understand it's a daughter thing for you to have it."

"It's beautiful, but I'm more than happy for you to have it." Frankie picked up the box and opened it. It was now empty except for the letters and the photographs that she had returned once she'd spoken to Carol. "Though there's something about it you should probably know..."

She hadn't really planned when would the best time to have this conversation, but figured that it was as good a time as any.

The three of them sat on the floor of the study while Frankie explained everything that Carol had told her. She hadn't opened the letters, she considered them private, and she knew all she needed to know. Andrew was silent throughout, taking in everything his sister was revealing. When he finally spoke, he inevitably expressed his surprise at this secretive part of their mum's history; a brief part of her life that until now, they had known nothing about, that he was the product of. Frankie and Andrew talked for what felt like hours, with Angus supplying the occasional mug of tea. They reminisced about their childhoods, bringing up memories of the past that now made so much more sense. The simple fact of the matter was, their mum had married a man who loved her and was prepared to raise her unborn child, his brother's child, as his own. She had hoped she could make a life with a man she didn't love, but it had made him the bitter, selfish, and self-centred man they remembered. And with this knowledge, they had both developed some respect for what he did for their mother, whom they loved dearly and missed desperately.

Frankie and Andrew then had a matter-of-fact discussion about what they thought they would do once their father finally passed away. Neither was emotional about this subject; however both felt that returning home to attend his funeral would be the right thing to do. On that note, they also decided to visit their mother's grave together at some point over the weekend. They hadn't realised how late it had gotten until Frankie's phone buzzed, with a text message from Jack. He'd finished a little early, and had returned home to find them all out; he was wondering if he should wait for them or grab a quick shower before meeting them somewhere.

Frankie texted him back, letting him know they were at the house, and it would be great if he could come over in the car; they'd taken a taxi because three people in the wretched box on wheels would have been illegal. Jack let her know he would be about half an hour.

For the two siblings, it had been a productive afternoon. They had covered a lot of ground and made some important decisions. It was time to move on and enjoy the short time they now had together. It was a warm, sunny evening. They were finished in the house, so went outside to wait for Jack. Frankie stood with her back to the house; Andrew and Angus faced her, admiring all the hard work she and Jack had put into tidying the garden in the Spring. Angus was the first to see him coming, though his facial expression didn't change.

"Ahh!!" Frankie screamed, as she was lifted up into the air and tossed over Jack's shoulder like a sack of potatoes. "Put me down, you scared the bloody life out of me!" She was shouting, though laughing, and smacking a pair of long combat shorts that were loosely hugging his delicious backside.

"Not in a million, sweetheart, I caught you fair and square!" He looked at the other two; Angus stood clapping his hands with glee, he loved to see this sort of playfulness. Andrew was smiling at them; it made him so happy to see that his sister had finally found someone who adored her as much as he did.

Jack slid her down his chest, and held her scooped in both arms. She wrapped her arms around his neck and he gave her a soft, loving kiss.

"Well that was very... um... lovely, darling, but maybe you should put me down so you can say a proper hello to our guests?" she said, smiling sweetly at him, stroking the back of his hair.

"Oh, don't you mind us; it's very entertaining, do carry on," said Angus, waving a hand towards them.

Jack gave Frankie another quick peck on the cheek, and slowly set her down on the ground.

"Good to finally meet you two in person," he said, as he offered them his hand, keeping tight hold of Frankie with his other arm.

"Good to meet you too, Jack." Andrew shook Jack's hand, "I see you are keeping my sister in her place," he said, nodding and smiling at Frankie.

"Doing my best; she can be quite a handful at times." He gave a Frankie a cheeky little wink.

"Oh my goodness, aren't you a big lad, pleased to meet you, my boy." Angus slipped himself in front of Andrew, and thrust a hand towards Jack.

Jack took the hand in front of him, which was poking out of a pale pink linen sleeve; its wrist adorned with a large, gold bracelet. Angus held on rather enthusiastically, and gave him a large grin through his grey goatee beard, that came to a rather neat point about an inch below his chin.

"Pleased to meet you too, Angus," said Jack.

"Right, since we're all done here, I think it's gin'o'clock!" said Andrew.

"Oh, now your talkin'; come on darlin', you and me are going to get cosy in the back of your man's wee Mini," Angus linked arms with Frankie and pulled her free from Jack, as he started walking back towards the house, "and we can giggle and pull faces at him in the mirror."

Frankie rested her head on Angus's arm as they walked. Jack and Andrew followed close behind.

They enjoyed a quiet evening in with a take away, some catching up, and male bonding over beer.

"I hope that wasn't too much of a shock to the system for you. They can be pretty full on," Frankie said, as she lay facing Jack in bed that night, close together, skin against skin. She cupped his face with one hand, while she wound the fingers of her other hand around his curls.

"It's... entertaining!" he replied.

He kissed her, their eyes open, locked together. He stroked her face, tucking her hair behind her ear.

"Oh Jack," she sighed, "I want us to be together more than I can put into words, but if you want that too, I'm afraid it has to be on my turf. I'm either out of my head or I'm out of my mind to expect you to up sticks and..." He put his finger over her lips and smiled at what she'd done.

"Very clever; you pretend to start a serious discussion just so you can slip something in there."

She tried to look like she didn't know what he was talking about. He pressed his nose against hers and whispered, "Give Myself To You; For Me, It's You; 2006; track 4."

Once again, neither chose to pursue the discussion any further; the subject was closed as they drifted off to sleep, wrapped in their own naked warmth.

The following day, while both Frankie and Jack worked, the boys had spent the day shopping in Newcastle. They had planned another quiet night in, with an M&S Chinese meal. However Frankie ended up leaving them to all to it at around 9.30. She had felt fine all day, but when she finally sat down to eat that evening, she felt nauseous and very, very tired. Deciding not to drink, she only ate one crispy duck pancake before she couldn't keep her eyes open any longer.

"I'm sorry guys, I think everything is just catching up on me; if I get a good night's sleep I'll be better company tomorrow," she said, walking out of the bathroom towards the bedroom. "Night." She lifted her hand in a weak wave.

"I'll not be a minute, I'll just see if she's okay." Jack got up and followed her.

He was able to take her in his arms before she climbed into bed.

"Hey, sweetheart, you sure you're okay?" he asked, brushing a stray hair away from her face.

"Sure, like I said, just super tired. Now that everything is wrapping up, my body just wants to chill." She snuggled into his chest, breathing in his scent, "You go and bond with my brother and his better half; if you stay much longer I won't let you leave." She looked up at him and smiled.

He took her head in his hands and kissed her tenderly.

"Sleep well," he said as he helped her into bed.

She crashed within minutes.

"Ohh, we are horny this morning, Mr. Lee, aren't we?" She turned over to face him, and he placed his hands on her naked bottom, massaging it.

"You drive me insane. I'm so obsessed, my heart is bound to beat right out my untrimmed chest..." He slid her further up his hot, naked body as she slowly smiled at him with her sparkly green eyes. They held their stare for a moment before she spoke,

"...and I'm always gonna wanna blow your mind...Soul Sister, I think you can do better than that. Now! I know I'm just here to amuse you, and I don't mean to abuse you, but if I could just use you one more time..." she said, as she pushed herself up and eased back, so she was astride him.

"You stole my line." He sat up in one easy move, his abs tight and firm. Placing his hands wide on her breasts, he kissed her, letting his tongue explore her mouth. "All American Girl from My Private Nation; 2006."

He lay back down without moving his hands and tugged on both her nipples together, and then turned them as if he was tuning a radio and said, "Track two."

She began to move slowly.

"Almost as clever as my line, but I've warned you about calling me an American," she threatened.

Jack lay sprawled out on the bed, hot and breathless.

She was lying on her side next to him looking very pleased with herself, hardly breaking a sweat.

"I told you not to call me an American, you know how it upsets me!" She lifted herself up on her elbow and rested her head on her hand.

He laughed, "Remind me not to make you angry in public, I can't believe you've worn me out already and it's only twenty to nine!"

"I know, we should get up, see what the boys want to do today."

She was about to climb over him, when he pulled her face towards his again and gave her a long lingering kiss.

"Another round maybe?" she said smirking.

"Good God, woman," he slapped his hands over his face, "are you ever satisfied?"

"Every time darling... every time." She kissed him quickly as she climbed out, grabbing her robe. "But do you know the best bit? I'm an old woman, and you, young man, can't keep up!" She turned and left the bedroom, leaving him lying there with a big goofy grin on his face.

"Good morning, gentlemen, I trust you both slept well?" she said, as she pulled the bedroom door closed behind her.

"Like a top, darlin', like a top," said Angus, looking up from his iPad.

"Very well thank you, and you, petal? Your batteries are fully recharged after your early night?" Andrew took a drink of his coffee and raised his eyebrows over the top of his mug.

"Oh, my dear brother, I don't know what you're talking about," she smiled back at him and flicked the kettle on, "but yes, I feel much better, thank you." She winked at Jack, as she passed him coming out of the bedroom, on her way to the bathroom.

"Morning." Jack looked a little embarrassed as he stood in only his sweatpants, with bed curls made even crazier by their morning romp. He walked into the kitchen to make tea.

"Mornin' my friend; you look like you've had a bit of a rough one!" said Angus, giving him a little nod of respect.

Jack laughed and coughed at the same time.

"Gus, leave the poor guy alone!" Andrew looked up from his laptop at Jack. "Just ignore him," he directed.

Jack smiled back, embarrassed as he poured boiling water into mugs.

Frankie bounced out of the bathroom, and walked into the kitchen.

"So! What would we all like to do today?" she asked.

"Well, first of all, sweet pea, I would like to arrange to take you and yours out to a very expensive restaurant tonight, and say a big fat thank you for everything you have done," said Andrew, closing his laptop.

"Oh, that's very kind of you Andy, but you don't need to do that; we agreed I would do this and," she slid an arm around Jack's waist, "look what I got out of it." She smiled up at Jack adoringly, and received the same look from him.

"No, I insist; I have been a little selfish in thinking that this was something you could do on your own, Frankie. I should have been here too, maybe not all the time, but for some of it. What you've done - taking time out of your own life, and working in a place you swore you would never work in again...." Andrew sighed; he felt very guilty.

"Andy, it wasn't that bad in the end." She rested her head on Jack's chest.

"Not the point, sis; it could have quite easily been the longest six months of your life, and there is no way I can make up for it, so, a slap up meal is what we're doing, no ifs or buts, right?"

"Okay, okay." She held her hands up, surrendering.

"Can I ask one thing, darlin'?" Angus spoke after a silent pause.

"Mmm" Frankie looked at him quizzically.

"You do have more than just yoga wear with you, don't you? Because, you know, we can always hit the shops!" Angus looked hopefully over the top of his glasses.

"Gussy, my dear, how do you think I acquired this?" She stood away from Jack, and held her arms out, as if presenting him as a prize.

Jack couldn't help but smile at the memory of the charity event, and how stunning she looked in her red dress. It seemed like so long ago.

"Just checkin' my love, just checkin'." He pushed his glasses further onto his face and returned to his iPad, slightly disappointed that he couldn't find a good excuse to go shopping again.

It was a warm, sunny day, so after breakfast they decided to take a drive to Alnwick in Northumberland. Angus was a huge Harry Potter fan, and had never been to Alnwick Castle, which features in the movies as Hogwarts. Jack was also unfamiliar with the historic town, and it had been years since Frankie and Andrew had visited. It was a cosy drive in Jack's car, and it became apparent at some point during the journey that Frankie had not been honest with Jack about also owning a Mini.

"It goes like an absolute bomb, I swear. She'd only just got it when we were last over there, and my God.... I thought, when she hit the gas, we were gonnae end up on the top of Grouse Mountain!" said Angus in admiration.

"Hey, come on, I was still getting used to it; I'd gone from a clapped out Toyota Corolla to an all-singing, all-dancing sports car. I'd never driven anything like that before. At least I appreciated the actual car itself, and not just the fact that you could open the roof with one press of a button!" she hit back at him.

"Darlin', there's nothing wrong with appreciatin' the more basic aspects of today's technology; sometimes you have to do something a few times just to get it out of your system," Angus said, trying to be very serious.

"Yes, but not every time the car stopped! Gus, you were like a kid with new toy, and it wasn't even your toy!" Andrew chipped in from the front seat.

"Laugh all you like; listen, when I was a wee boy my father was happy that his car still had its wheels every mornin', never mind its roof!" Angus said, trying to look upset, causing them all to laugh.

And so the conversation went for most of the drive to Alnwick, where they visited the castle, walked through the historic town, and ate a picnic lunch from The Olive Branch Café. Frankie was so happy that Jack seemed to be getting on really well with her brother and his eccentric partner. It was a great distraction for all of them; Frankie and Andrew enjoyed spending time together now that the reason that had brought them both back to the North East was mostly taken care of. Jack and Frankie didn't give a second thought to the future, they just enjoyed the moment; and Angus, well he was just loveable old Angus, keeping everyone highly entertained.

That evening Jack persuaded Frankie to wear the slinky black dress she'd worn at Lumley Castle. She had just finished drying her hair in front of the large mirror in the bedroom when Jack sat on the bed next to her.

"You know sweetheart, I think Angus is right, you have put a little bit of weight on," he said, as he put his socks on.

"Thanks!!" she said looking at him, clearly not pleased.

He pulled her close, looking at their reflection in the mirror.

"It's not a criticism, you still look amazing, just... fuller." He pressed his cheek against hers and squeezed her slightly, "I like it; it makes you even more huggable and very grabbable."

"I don't think either of those are words, but I think you're being very cute right now, so I'll let you use them." She took in his reflection and breathed in deeply; he smelt so very good. It reminded her of the night they had got together, the first night they had spent in that room. So much had happened since then.

"What are you thinking?" he asked.

She looked down at her hands resting on his.

"You smell the way you did when I brought you back here, that first night. I never imagined, for even a second, that we'd end up like this, in this happy place we've found together." She smiled at him, and then went to say, *"I feel something for you I've never felt for anyone else, Jack,"* but the words just wouldn't come out.

She looked up at him again; their eyes met in the reflection, and she could feel his heart pounding against her back, before realising hers was doing the same.

Jack thought she was going to finally say it, and he stared, willing her to say those three little words that would give him the security he needed to consider moving. He wasn't sure how long they stayed like that, before he became aware of how tightly he was holding her. He eased off his grip, and rested his forehead on her shoulder, closing his eyes. He needed a moment before he looked back at her reflection; she held his gaze when he looked back at her.

He hugged her close again. "Come on, the boys will be waiting."

It had been a long time since Andrew had joined the family for their traditional Sunday lunch. The weather was good, so Carol decided that a barbecue would be the best way to cater for everyone. With Eric in charge of the grill however, she was beside herself, worrying if anything would edible. Knowing Jack was a good cook, she steered him in Eric's direction as soon as he arrived and, in no time at all, Jack had it all under control while Eric made sure that everyone was supplied with a drink. The sun shone and the drink flowed, keeping everyone in a good mood. Carol was in her element, entertaining her family; she managed to elicit Andrew's help in the kitchen with a few last minute things, so they were alone.

"Well now, how's my favourite nephew?" she asked him, as she set him to work chopping peppers.

"I'm good Aunty, though I'm feeling quite guilty about having expected my poor sister to deal with all the crap over here," he admitted.

"Your sister hasn't done too badly while she's been over here." Carol nodded towards Jack, who was just outside the kitchen door, tending to some steaks.

Andrew grinned, nodding his head.

"Are you okay, pet?" Carol asked cautiously; Frankie had given her the heads up that Andrew knew about his father.

"You know, Aunty, if I'm truly honest I probably always knew he wasn't my father. But I've been given some of the best opportunities in life and I never would have had those if it weren't for him. At the very least I'm grateful for that, and owe him some respect."

Carol rubbed her nephew's shoulder. He was a very humble man and she was incredibly proud of him.

"What do you think is going to happen when she leaves next month? They seem pretty smitten with each other." Andrew decided to change the subject.

"I don't know. He's such a nice bloke, Andrew; I think if it doesn't work out, he'll be as devastated as she will. I mean, look at them."

Carol leaned against the kitchen bench and watched Jack wrap his arms around Frankie's shoulders and plant a soft kiss on her lips. As they looked lovingly into each other eyes, talking, Frankie said something that made Jack laugh and he pressed his forehead against hers and then rubbed noses. At that moment, Carol didn't care that the food might be ruined; she had never seen her niece so happy.

"Okay, is there anything else you need doing?" Andrew asked. "Hello... Aunty Carol!"

"Sorry... sorry pet, miles away," she said. "No, but listen I have something for you. It's been a long time coming I'm afraid, just give me a minute." Carol left Andrew standing in the kitchen while she disappeared for a moment.

"I did the same for your sister; she already has hers. Your mum made sure I had all your childhood photographs before she died. I've made them into scrapbooks, knowing neither of you had any pictures from when you were kids. This is yours."

Andrew was speechless, becoming slightly emotional at the gift his aunt had given him. He embraced her for a long time.

"Thank you, this is..." Andrew was unable to find the words.

"You don't need to say it Andy, I know. Take it home with you, and sit down with Angus to look at it properly. Now, go and enjoy yourself, and can you peel your sister off my chef!"

Andrew managed a laugh, before placing the scrapbook on the dining room table.

"She'll be okay, you know; she's a tough little cookie. I think it's going to be a rough ride for them, but something tells me it might work out in time." Andrew rubbed his aunt's shoulder before he headed back out into the sunshine.

Late in the afternoon, as a few clouds formed, Jack turned the car into the small parking area at the cemetery.

"I'm going to stay in the car and wait for you, if that's okay sweetheart," Jack said, looking a little nervous and uncomfortable.

"Sorry Jack, I didn't appreciate how hard it would be for you, coming here. We won't be long, okay." Frankie stroked his stubbly cheek with her fingers, and gave him a sympathetic look.

"I'll just wait here too if that's all right. A think you two need tae go alone," said Angus, patting Andrew's leg.

Frankie looked across at Jack and gave him a weak smile as he leant in to kiss her.

"I'll be right here, okay?" he said. She nodded, before opening her door.

Angus climbed into the front seat as Andrew and Frankie slowly strolled through the gates of the cemetery. He closed the door; it was still warm despite the clouds, so the car windows were wide open. He waited until they were sufficiently far enough away that they wouldn't hear him talking to Jack.

"Now then, my boy," Angus began, "you and I are going to have a wee chat."

"I thought we might."

Jack rested his arm on the window, and placed his flat hand on the edge of the roof.

"A friendly chat, Jack. Just two people who love the same person and want to make sure that person isn't going to get hurt beyond repair. Ah love that wee lassie like she was ma own sister, you know what ah'm saying?" Jack glanced across at Angus without turning his head. Angus looked very calm, but earnest, and sounded caring but matter of fact.

"You seem like a decent bloke, Jack. Ah cannae imagine what you're going through right now, trying to decide what tae do. You know, ah left Glasgow when ah was barely eighteen to go tae uni, absolutely terrified ah was. And back then, for a horny, gay bloke like mysel', the world was a very hostile place. But you know, you realise after a while that if it all goes belly up, you can always go home. Sometimes, son, you just have tae take that chance and find oot, you know what ah'm saying?"

Jack rubbed his face with his hands and then rested his arm back on the car door, his forehead in his hand. He didn't need to look at Angus.

"Ah can see you love her; she's a wonderful wee lassie, ah love the bones of her. Ah just want tae continue seeing her as happy as she is now. If you cannae commit tae that, son, you've got to tell her."

There was a long, silent pause before Jack spoke.

"I would get down on one knee right now, if I knew I could follow through. You're right, she's everything to me, and between you and me, I think I love her more than I ever loved my wife.

I realised some time ago that what Emma and I had wasn't a romantic love. It's tearing me apart to think I can't get on that plane with her, but I think we both need some distance. It's been so intense these past few months. I want to see if absence really does make the heart grow fonder, or whether we are both just so caught up in each other that, when we're apart, we realise it was just lust.

"I've tried to tell her, Angus, you know, how I feel, but something is holding me back and she's hasn't exactly declared her undying love for me either. Would it change anything if she did? I don't know, maybe." Jack was gently punching his forehead with his fist.

"Believe me, breaking her heart is the last thing I want to do, but I may have to bruise it before I can make any commitments. I trust this is all between you and me?" He glanced at Angus.

"Absolutely. Ah may be a bit of a nutter, but you can trust me, son. If you ever need a wee chat." Angus offered Jack his hand, and they shook just as Andrew and Frankie walked back through the gates.

Chapter 34

BY THE END of June the house was officially sold. Andrew had visited the solicitor with Frankie on the morning before he flew back to New York and finalised everything that pertained to him. Before the final clearance of furniture, and before Frankie finally handed over the keys, she wanted to take one last walk through the only house that she'd known growing up, and she wanted to do it with Jack.

The house was so different now. Everything echoed, and it seemed bigger... much bigger, even though there were still odd pieces of furniture left waiting to be cleared. She held on tight to Jack's hand as they walked silently through all the rooms. It was so bare, with dirty marks on the walls where pictures had hung, and deep indents on the carpets where furniture had stood for years. Frankie felt as if she wasn't just coming to the end of a chapter in this story, but the end of the book. It was all so final; she would never set foot in that house again.

As she walked slowly up the stairs, one hand sliding over the faded wooden rail, she continued to cling to Jack's hand with her other. They hadn't said a word to each other since getting out of the car. She didn't want to go into her parents' room again, but she did want to take one last look at her own bedroom. As she pushed the door open, the room felt cold, despite the warm day. It had a north-facing window with a large tree outside, so it got very little natural light, and almost no sun. Her old bed and desk were still there, waiting to be cleared; there were holes in the walls from posters, noticeboards and pictures. She touched a hole in the wall behind the door; as she spoke she made Jack jump.

"I made this when I was fourteen, with my hockey stick, trying to kill a spider; huge thing it was."

Jack let out a short laugh.

"Did you hit it?" he asked.

"No, but it fell to the floor and I think I broke a couple of its legs, so it wasn't able to run quickly enough to get away from the cookery basket I then dumped on its head!" she said, proudly. She hated spiders; it took a lot of courage for her to even look at one, let alone attack it.

"I somehow don't see you in this room as child, or a teenager." He wrapped his arms around her, and pulled her close to him. Sliding her arms around his waist, she gazed around the room.

"My father didn't allow us to put much on the walls; you know, posters of your favourite pop star or group. He just didn't understand; I think he only liked classical music; probably the reason why I hate it so much. I look back on this house now, and realise that it was just a house and not a home. I hope, if I ever get married, and if I somehow have children, I don't live in a place like this; I would want it to feel like a home."

"So...tell me, " he lifted her chin so he could look at her, "how would it be different, what do you see in that home?" He spoke softly.

"Bright, fresh colours... Practical, usable furniture... Photographs everywhere; natural ones of vacations, Christmas, birthdays, you know, fun things... Normal, everyday stuff just lying around... My kid's art work stuck to the back of the kitchen door... Wellies lined up outside in order of size... Ski passes hung on the hooks with all the keys... My husband spontaneously grabbing me in the kitchen and kissing me for no good reason other than that he loves me... and... while he's doing that... two little arms... hugging our legs." She looked down, pressing her forehead on his chest, tears prickling her eyes.

Jack sighed deeply and stroked her hair. He could see everything she'd described, with the two of them in the picture, even a small head of dark curly hair and big blue eyes looking up at them. He sniffed unconsciously, causing Frankie to look up; she saw his glistening eyes filled with emotion. She knew that her imaginary home, and family, was what he really wanted, and she would never be able to give that to him.

"Did you ever brings boys home?" he asked after a few minutes to lighten the mood.

"Hell no, my father would have flipped, strictly forbidden."

"So, you're the only person to have slept in that bed?" He sounded playful.

"I know where this is going, Mr. Lee, and yes, only me. But, if you're asking have I ever had sex in that bed, then that depends whether masturbating counts; I definitely had my first orgasm in that bed." She glanced over at it.

"Well, Doctor... I think it will be more comfortable than your father's desk." He gave her his wicked grin.

"I see, my old bed, hey? Sure, why not, but aren't we supposed to make out on it first, you know, as if we're teenagers?"

"Make out? Oh that's so American of you, Doctor... Educate me?" He tried to look puzzled.

"Well, we have to be kinda nervous, we haven't even kissed... And then, when we do, you have to try and push the limits, you know; try to touch me in all those forbidden places, but," she pulled away from him, walking backwards towards the bed, kicking her flip-flops off, "I try to stop you, because this is all new, right?" She fell back on the bed, and lay supported on her elbows. She was wearing the perfect outfit for this game; her very short denim skirt, a Power Y tank, therefore no bra, but cheeky little boy shorts.

Jack stood watching her, smirking as she spoke; he was in combat shorts and a white t-shirt. He started to walk towards her, losing his flip-flops on the way.

"What happens when you touch me in all those forbidden places?" he asked, crawling up to her; she shuffled back so he followed her up the bed.

"Well, you're a horny teenager, a walking erection, you want me to touch you, but I'm shy... I couldn't possibly touch you... there!" Her eyes darted down and back up to his.

Her head touched the end of the bed, and she couldn't move any further; he carried on crawling until they were face to face.

"And how do I kiss you, if I've never kissed a girl before?"

Their noses were almost touching.

"Oh, you've kissed lots of Taylor Swift posters, so you're very gentle."

"Like this?" His lips skimmed hers, softly.

"Just like that... Then I kiss you back." She kissed him with more force, becoming more needy and passionate.

Jack leaned on his elbow so he could let his other hand glide up her body; he was just about to touch her breast, when her hand caught his. They broke their kiss, and he moved his head back slightly to look at her.

"Slow down, I don't think I'm ready for that," she said, trying to be serious.

"Oh please, let me just have a feel; I promise I won't tell anyone." He was getting the hang of this game now.

She looked at him coyly.

"Okay, promise?"

"Promise," he said as he kissed her again, and took her in his hand, massaging her through her tank top.

She had kept her hands still on his back, but now started to let them wander until they found the hem of his T-shirt.

"Would...it...be...okay...if...you...take...this...off?" she asked, between kisses.

"I'll take mine off, if you take yours off?"

She pulled away from him, trying to act shocked.

"I couldn't possibly, I'm not wearing a bra," she said shyly.

"I know, go on, I've never seen naked breasts before. Let me see them."

She was still trying to act shy.

"Okay, but we take them off together, and no bragging to your friends."

"Scouts Honour!" He saluted as he knelt up, and straddled her.

They both crossed their arms and held onto the hem of their shirts, lifting them up and over their heads, before tossing them on the floor.

"Oh, you are very beautiful, and I'm a very lucky boy... Thank you for sharing your exquisite body with me..."

Frankie ran her hands up and over his firm chest, her fingers combing his soft chest hair.

"'The pleasure is all mine..." She didn't get a chance to finish her own compliments; he kissed her, pushing her back onto the bed. The game was over.

The month of July began the final countdown. In four weeks Frankie would get on a plane, the way she'd always planned, and return to the life she'd put on hold almost six months ago. If anyone had told her back then that she would find love during that time, she would have had him or her certified. Now that she didn't have the house to deal with, her time was her own when she wasn't at work. She missed Jack, a little jealous of her colleagues at work spending the day with him, but it was her he came home to. She began to realise that she would have to get used to that thought once she left; only then, he wouldn't be walking through the door with his panty-dropping smile at the end of the day. She had too much time on her hands now to be alone with her thoughts.

By the second week in July, Frankie was starting to think about what she needed to wrap up at work before she left. Kathy approached her at the end of her list one day.

"Ah Frankie, fancy grabbing a coffee with me?" Kathy asked, as Frankie emerged from her anaesthetic room.

"Sure, I'm gonna wait for Jack anyway; they just started their last case."

The two friends walked down to the café. It wasn't until they were sat with their drinks that Kathy got down to business.

"So, my dear, it's been quite the sabbatical for you. I bet there aren't many who can say they gained what you have."

Frankie smiled half-heartedly, and began fiddling with a teaspoon.

"And what have I gained exactly? A diamond that belonged to my mother... a box of emotion left by my father... and a handful of amazing memories with the only man I've ever loved, and probably ever will love. Yeah, I did great, didn't I!" She was on the verge of breaking down again.

"Oh Frankie, I'm sorry, I didn't mean it like that!"

"Kathy, honestly, it's fine, I just have to get through the rest of this month, and then move on. I'm not staying, and I'm pretty sure he's not coming with me. Right now, I just need to pretend that none of this is real, or I'll end up spending the next three weeks in absolute tatters."

Kathy put her hand on Frankie's arm; it was enough to make her eyes well up and she nipped the corners to stem the imminent flow of tears.

"Well, listen," Kathy changed the subject, aware Frankie was about to fall apart, "some members of the department, and the surgeons you've worked with, have approached me about giving you a bit of a send off, and I thought that was a wonderful idea. So, we would like you, and that charming young man of yours, to join us all for a private barbeque at my husband's golf club on Saturday. Bit last minute, I know, but the date works for most people, and the function room and patio are available, so I thought I would just go for it. What do you think?"

"I think that's a lovely idea. I'm quite touched that people think that much of me. I'm just a locum, for God's sake!"

"A very good one, whom I would keep in a heartbeat!" Kathy smiled at Frankie, who became slightly embarrassed; she had thought she would just slip away and leave without any fuss.

"I would love to bring my charming young man along to your little send off, thanks Kathy," she said, filling up again. "Christ, look at me, my bladder is far too close to my eyes."

"I think that's what happens when you work in that urology list with Mike too much!"

When she discussed the barbeque with Jack that evening, he seemed uncomfortable with the idea, almost suggesting she attend alone.

"I'm not going, Jack, unless it's with you. I don't understand what the problem is? Talk to me."

They were sat on the barstools, having just finished dinner. Jack was bent over the breakfast bar, while Frankie sat facing his side, in an effort to get him to talk. He took a big deep breath before he spoke,

"It's just... there wouldn't be a mixture of nurses, ODPs, people I know. This would be just consultants; people waaaay above me. I don't think I'd fit in that well."

"JACK! Look at me; I'm one of them. The woman you've been shacked up with for the last six months. We're all human beings at the end of the day. Just because we're doctors doesn't mean we're any better than you. You're the one who's always saying I should be proud of my title, when I don't like it; probably for the very reason you're talking about. People think we're something different, special, I don't know," she said, raising her arms up and smacked them down at her side while rolling her eyes, "God-like or something. Look at me... I'm really just Frankie, who happens to have chosen medicine as her career."

"Kathy, Mike, Patrick, even airhead Annabel are all just people like you; they're all paying the bills, putting food on the table and mortgaged up to their necks," this made Jack smile; she had a point. "Maybe the difference is that a lot of the doctors you work with live to work." She touched his face gently so he would look at her. "I work to live. It's a job. Yes, a job I'm good at and for the most part enjoy, but it's not the be all and end all... Come with me Jack, please! I want to share this with you, I want us to be seen together." She waited patiently before he slowly smiled, and nodded slightly.

"Okay, anything to keep Mike's hands off you!"

"Really! I mean, REALLY?" They both laughed.

Saturday came around quickly; Jack felt like someone had sped up time. Suddenly, there were only two weeks left, and every minute seemed to count. He'd tried to take some time off work on the days Frankie was off, but in the height of the summer holidays it was impossible. They were due at the golf club at 4pm. Frankie dressed in a pair of simple white linen cropped pants, a navy strappy top with white spots, and red wedge sandals. At ten to four, Jack was still deciding what he should wear.

"Jeez, Jack! I thought my brother and Angus were worse than women at getting ready, but today you're close to making that list too," she said, as she walked into the bedroom. Jack was stood in his boxers, with his hands on his hips, looking into the open wardrobe.

"Sorry, help me out," he pouted.

"Just a pair of chinos, and a short sleeved shirt will be fine." She handed him his beige trousers, then reached for a pale blue linen shirt. "There you go, easy!"

"Do you think? It's not too casual?"

"Jack, we're not going for a formal dinner, were going to a barbecue." She smoothed her hands over his firm abs as he fastened his chinos and then slid them round his waist.

"Please try to relax. I promise, this will not be as big a deal as you're making out, trust me." She looked up at him; she could tell his unease wasn't about the barbecue; it was about them. He was starting to become distant, and it scared her.

"We're going to be late," he said, as she still held him.

"Are you still with me, Jack, or is this starting to become too strained, now that the bubble is about to burst?"

He looked up at the ceiling and sighed.

"Yes, it's a little strained, but I need you; I don't want to give up on us, not yet anyway." He hugged her tight.

It was nearly 4.30 when they arrived, but thankfully they were not the last.

"Here she is, our Princess and her Captain," announced Mike, as they walked through the French doors, out onto the warm, sunny patio, and all eyes turned to them.

"Sorry we're a bit late."

Frankie held Jack's hand; she felt she needed to look after him, knowing how he felt about the whole situation.

They were each handed a glass of something pink and bubbly as they mingled with the crowd. Most of the department had been able to attend, as well as the three surgeons Frankie had worked with every week since arriving. She was surprised to find the odd person who still didn't know that she and Jack were an item.

"Frankie, my dear, I must say it has been pleasure working with you these past few months. You have made my Fridays a lot more interesting, and you'll be missed." Patrick was very sincere when he spoke.

Frankie had been stood on her own when Patrick had approached her, as Jack had gone to use the washroom; he'd reappeared at her side in the middle of their conversation.

"Oh, well hello there, Jack." Patrick looked genuinely taken aback when he saw Jack slip his arm around Frankie. "Are you two...?" he pointed back and forth between the two of them as they stood close.

"Patrick, where have you been? We've been the most talked-about couple for months, and yes, we are together," she replied, as she looked lovingly at Jack and he returned the expression.

"Oh, well that's lovely, so it is; I suppose that means we'll be losing you too then?" Patrick directed the question at Jack.

There was a moment of awkwardness that hung in the air; then his reply made Frankie's heart skip a beat. He didn't look at Frankie at all.

"Not yet, Patrick, not yet."

'*Not yet... did he really say "not yet"?*' she thought to herself.

She didn't hear Patrick's reply; she just became aware of him moving away from them, having said something. Jack lifted her chin to look at her.

"You okay?" he asked.

She just stared at him for a moment.

"Did you just say, 'not yet'?" she finally managed to whisper.

Jack took a deep breath and guided her over to a secluded bush, gesturing for her to sit on the wall.

"Frankie, I've never said I wouldn't consider it; I've actually looked into it. However, immigration and job status for someone like me wouldn't be easy. I need more time to be sure that it's the right thing to do. I haven't talked to you yet, because I don't want to give you false hope; I don't want to have false hope. You must know about all the red tape. Like I've said to you so many times, this is a huge decision for me. When you emigrated, it was part of a plan; you'd wanted to do it for a long time. I've had less than six months to consider it. Look, I think some distance between us won't be a bad thing. It's been a very intense start to a relationship, amazing, but intense."

She couldn't disagree with anything he'd said, and he was finally being honest with her.

"After what happened to Emma, I just need be sure." Jack took her hands, lifting them to his lips to kiss her knuckles, when Kathy interrupted them.

"There you are... oh sorry, I'm interrupting?" she was about to back up and leave them.

"No, no Kathy, it's fine, just stealing a moment," said Frankie.

"Well, if you wouldn't mind joining us again, we have a little something for you." Kathy pointed towards the patio.

"Oh! But Kathy, all this is more than enough."

"Be quiet for once, Frances Robertson, and follow me."

Frankie looked over at Jack and rolled her eyes. Just as she was about to get up, he took her chin in his hand.

"Don't give up on me, I'm about to come alive," he said, before kissing her softly. She smiled.

"My Private Nation; 2003; can't remember the track number I'm afraid."

"No, neither can I, come on, your fans await you."

He stood and held out his hand.

Kathy gave a little speech on behalf of everyone, thanking Frankie for all her hard work. She mentioned that initially she had thought it was going to be a bit of a chore for Frankie to slum it in the NHS for a while, but that she had found an interesting way of coping. All eyes were on Jack, who went a little red as people laughed; he saw the funny side and managed a smile. He was sat with his arm draped around the back of Frankie's chair, his hand resting on her bare shoulder. She gave it an affectionate pat when he was embarrassingly put on the spot. Kathy presented Frankie with a large bouquet of flowers and a small painting of the Tyne Bridge. Frankie was overwhelmed; she'd had no idea she had been so popular. She made a feeble attempt at thanking everyone, but was a little lost for words. After that, people started to leave; at around 7pm she & Jack said their goodbyes too and left.

Once they were back at the flat and the flowers were arranged in two vases of water, Frankie parked herself on Jack's knee, in much need of a kiss and cuddle.

"That was very nice," he said, as she finally let him come up for air.

"I just wanted to say thank you for coming with me today, and I thought you fit in very well."

"It was fun, actually. You were right, they are all just people at the end of the day, even the stuffy ones!"

"Well, you get those types of people in whatever job you do. I still can't believe they did that for me, and bought gifts; I've only been here for six months."

"I think you forget whose shoes you were filling; it was always going to be a hard gap to plug, even temporarily. You just got on with it, but you were sensitive to why you had the job too. Sweetheart, I don't think you realise just how different you are; how does Gloria put it... A breath of fresh air. I think that's maybe why I fell for you so quickly."

'Oh my God, that's the closest he's come to saying it' she thought, as she stared into his dreamy eyes.

"Tell me, exactly how quickly did you fall, Mr. Lee?"

"You wouldn't believe me if I told you."

"Try me?"

Jack lay his head back on the sofa, and looked up while he blew out a slow breath.

"Okay... I think you had me during your geography lesson."

Frankie's jaw dropped; she was wide-eyed.

"No way! That was like my first or second day at work?"

Jack shrugged his shoulders. "It's true, I just knew. What about you?"

She let out a quiet laugh and looked down at his chest. A few hairs were escaping through the open neck of his shirt; she began to fondle them. She didn't look at him while she spoke.

"When you were dancing the Gay Gordons with Marie, you didn't take your eyes off me; it was like we were the only two people in the room. I had the most amazing feeling in my stomach, more than just the twinkling, more than just a physical attraction... it was something I'd never felt before. It scared me a little, and that's why I left, not sure it was something I should have been pursuing... But then, there you were, offering me a lift and I just... knew!"

Their faces were so close, almost touching. She let her eyes find his; he almost looked like he was in a trance.

"God, you looked stunning that night," he whispered.

"You looked pretty hot yourself," she whispered back.

Jack gave her one of his full-on, panty-drenching smiles.

"I'm gonna miss that awesome smile of yours; you truly are a very handsome man, Mr. Lee, and I have been extremely fortunate to have enjoyed you and all your awesomeness... Please, don't become a stranger." She let her lips find his, as he slowly unzipped the back of her top.

With ten days left, Jack began the painful task of gathering all his things from around the flat, and moving them back to his own place. It caused friction between them, now that reality was setting in. The last Friday of July was Frankie's last day at work. The nurses had organised cake at lunchtime, and all the people who had worked with her at some point made sure they said their goodbyes before they left. She wasn't working with Jack; they had only worked together twice since the party, and it suited them better. Patrick O'Reilly was about an hour into his last case of the day; a bowel resection on a fifty eight year old woman with Crohn's disease. They were running two hours behind, which was quite good for Patrick; Frankie had become very used to always being late on a Friday. There were several people in the room, both nursing and medical staff; Heather was scrubbed and Chloë was Frankie's ODP that day.

"Oh darn it!" said Patrick, "would you look at that, torn a ruddy glove." He held his hand up.

"No problem," said Heather, as she looked over at a student nurse standing not too far away from her, "Natasha, be a love and get Mr. O'Reilly another pair of sterile size 7's would you, there are some on the bench."

Natasha disappeared, and returned momentarily with the packet. Within a couple of minutes Patrick's hands were back in Mrs. Sellars' abdomen, and Frankie was charting some observations and documenting drugs she had just given. All was well in Theatre 6 for the next five minutes. Then the background hum of the cycling blood pressure cuff was replaced by the machine's beeping alarm.

"Frankie, the blood pressure is down," said Chloë, as the numbers flashed on the screen.

"Is the cuff okay?" Frankie was looking at the other numbers for her patient. Patrick was in teaching mode with his registrar, completely unaware.

"The cuff's fine, she's paralysed, isn't she, and nothing else has moved it," said Chloë, popping her head back up from under the drapes and looking at the heart rate which was now increasing.

Frankie hit the button to take another blood pressure.

"Her sats are dropping now; they've been 100% throughout..." Instinct was telling Frankie that something wasn't right, but she couldn't think what had changed.

"Frankie, her blood pressure is still dropping..." There was a slight hint of panic in Chloë's voice.

"Okay Chloë, can you set it to take every two minutes. I'm just going to have a listen to her chest... Not sure what I'm missing here... and let's change that normal saline to... um... Haemaccel." Frankie remained calm, even though her patient was suddenly causing her great concern, and she didn't know why.

As Chloë changed over the bag of fluid, Frankie looked up at her beeping monitor again; her patient was now very tachycardic. At that moment, Jack walked in. He took one look at Frankie staring at the monitor, and knew she was concerned.

"Hey! Everything okay?" he discreetly asked her.

"Oh hi, not sure, something changed all of a sudden and..." Frankie was at a loss for a moment. "Patrick, I have a problem here." She turned up the oxygen supply to the patient, and switched from the ventilator, which was also now alarming, to the bag that allowed her to hand ventilate. "Jeez, her lungs are like a brick. I can hardly get anything into her!"

"No worries Frankie, what's the problem?" she heard Patrick ask.

"Can I help? I'm finished next door, what do you need?" Jack could tell that in parallel with her cool, calm, and collected appearance, she was deep in thought, trying to work out what was going wrong.

"Think, think, what chan..." she was about to say 'changed' when it suddenly dawned on her. " Patrick, you changed gloves. Are they latex free?" She looked at Patrick, then at Heather, who looked at Natasha the student.

"Natasha, the gloves; were they in a blue packet or a green one... where is it?" asked Heather.

Frankie turned to Jack and Chloë. "Okay, it might be latex anaphylaxis..." She took a deep breath.

"Jack, I need adrenaline, stat., we need to call a code, or whatever the hell you do here, and I'll need an adrenaline infusion setting up. Chloë, can you set up for a central line." She was calm and clear with her instructions, taking control, while Patrick packed the abdomen so he could discontinue surgery. A small voice, from the corner of the room declared that the packet was blue; not latex-free. Natasha stood holding the packet, shaking, almost in tears at what she'd done. It was known before surgery that the patient had a latex allergy.

Jack reappeared in no time with a pre-loaded syringe of adrenaline, which Frankie promptly gave.

"It's confirmed, so I'm also going to need steroids. I need to get this central line in; can you bag for me please, Jack?"

Kathy appeared beside her as she started to prep for the central line.

"Can you quickly run by me what happened?" she asked.

Frankie gave Kathy a concise summary of events, while she inserted the line into the right side of Mrs. Sellars' neck. Jack watched her as he rhythmically breathed for the patient. Here she was, the woman he loved, in an emergency situation, inserting a large needle into a right internal jugular vein, seeming as relaxed as if she was basting a turkey, while panic set in around her. Throughout, she was still able to continue to give her boss an account of what had led them to this emergency situation. Once again he was in awe, as he thought back to the night before, and what a playful pillow fight had led to; and yet, here she was, less than twenty four hours later, saving someone's life, right before his eyes.

"Okay, Jack, how does it feel?" he heard her say.

"Amazing!" he said, miles away.

"What?" said Frankie, "Let me feel?"

"What, oh, sorry!" he said, suddenly realising he had been on a little mental vacation to Hotsville.

Frankie looked at him as if he'd gone mad.

"Sorry, it feels better... yes, definitely better, here." He passed her the bag.

"Oh yes, that's much better, and her numbers are looking better. Okay, panic over, can we organise an ICU bed please?"

Frankie wiped her brow with the back of her hand and exhaled slowly, noticing how hot and sweaty she'd become.

"Well, I guess that's one way of getting your surgeon to hurry up!" she said, looking over at Patrick.

"Well done my dear, and thank you; not really what you need for your last patient, but at least you're going out in style!" Patrick replied in his thick Irish accent.

It was ten to nine before Frankie walked back into the staff room, after handing over the patient to the ICU staff, speaking to the Sellars family and filing an incident report. Jack stood as soon as she entered, and opened his arms; she couldn't get to him fast enough. Her warm, safe place; what was she going to do without him? He held her close - he wasn't sure for how long - before Heather, clearing her throat, interrupted them.

"Sorry, that is a well deserved hug, but I have someone here who would like to speak to you, Frankie." Heather ushered in Natasha, the student nurse who had been at the centre of the incident.

As soon as Natasha walked in, and saw Frankie and Jack holding each other, she turned a glowing shade of red. Frankie could see that this poor girl, who must have been at least twenty years her junior, was embarrassed. As Jack and Frankie split, Jack let his hand slowly slide away from her as she walked towards Natasha. He sat himself back down on the nearest chair.

"Hi, Natasha, isn't it? Why don't you sit down? It's been a pretty stressful evening for you, I'm sure." Frankie pointed to a chair, and Natasha nervously sat, her eyes darting across to Jack, who wasn't looking at her.

"Are you okay?" Frankie asked her.

Natasha just nodded; her eyes darted again to Jack. Frankie followed her gaze.

"Jack, could you give us a few minutes please and I'll meet you out by the front desk when I'm done?"

Natasha looked relieved that Frankie had recognised she was uncomfortable in Jack's presence, even though he had been among the crisis.

"Sure," Jack said as he looked up, "no problem." He picked up his backpack as he stood up. "Take all the time you need." He flashed a smile at both of them before them before heading out of the door.

Natasha seemed much more relaxed once it was just the two of them.

"I just wanted to apologise for all the trouble I caused, I'm really sorry, nobody told me about the patient's allergy. I feel awful." Natasha's voice was desperate.

"Hey," Frankie placed her hand on her arm and squeezed it gently, "it wasn't entirely your fault; these things are almost always caused by a chain of events; it's rarely just one person that's to blame. We all learn something from it, and it will be something different for each of us, something we hadn't thought mattered before. Try not to blame yourself, and instead put it down as an experience; I bet there aren't many students in your year that will be able to say they've seen full blown anaphylaxis." Frankie admired the student for apologising and hoped she was helping her to feel better.

"Thank you. I was worried everyone would be really mad with me." Natasha managed a relieved smile.

"Nobody is mad with you, okay. I appreciate you coming to me and talking. I hope you don't feel so bad about it now."

Natasha smiled and nodded.

"Come on, home time," Frankie went to stand up, "I need a drink... and my other half will be propping up the front desk, getting very grumpy due to lack of food."

As they reached the car, Frankie hesitated before she opened the door, looking over the roof of the car.

"Can we do something before we leave?" she asked him.

"Mmm, that depends what it is?"

"Drive up to the roof; the sun will be setting soon, and I know it won't be quite what I'm used to, but it would be close enough," she said.

"Sure," he replied, shrugging his shoulders, "why not!"

They got into the car, and Jack drove up to the roof top level of the car park. It was dusk, but as he parked his Mini in a spot that looked out over the City of Newcastle, it was still an impressive view. They were the only people up there, sitting in silence for a few moments, while they took in the view. All that could be heard were the faint sounds of the city on a busy summer Friday night, and their breathing.

"There's an outdoor equipment store back in Vancouver, that is like a candy store to anyone who is outdoorsy. It's called Mountain Equipment Co-op, or MEC for short." She stared out at the city as she spoke.

"It has a roof top parking lot that, on a clear day, has one of the best views of the city... It gives you everything: snow-capped mountains, clear blue ocean, skyscrapers, Science World, BC Place, Granville Island, Stanley Park.... It's just a breath-taking panoramic view that I will never get tired of."

She paused for a moment.

"I'm not feeling that same 'WOW' factor sat here. Sure, it's a great view, but it's not home anymore. I've seriously considered trying to make it home again, but I just can't do it. I'm sorry, Jack."

They sat in silence until the sun completely set over the buzzing city.

Chapter 35

THE WEEKEND SHOULD have been special, but Frankie had to pack. It was obvious, looking at all the extra things she'd bought, that the one suitcase was not going to get her home. So, Monday's job: a trip into Newcastle to purchase more luggage. Jack couldn't watch her do this; seeing her pack was too painful. She wanted him around, but understood that it would be better for both of them if she just got on with it. He went to the gym and worked out so hard that he almost made himself ill. Frankie packed as much as she could, which took the best part of the afternoon to do, then curled up on the sofa with a bucket of tea and waited for him to return.

Hercules joined her and made himself comfortable in her lap. She stroked him as he purred, contented. He had no idea that he was about to be deposited back at Carol's the following day, to temporarily live with that lowest form of life again, the dog! It suddenly occurred to her how much she was going to miss his company; she had never been a big fan of cats, but she had become quite attached to her furry roommate.

"Well big guy, we've had quite the time together. Promise me you'll be selective about what you tell Lucy? There are some things… well, quite a lot of things actually, that she really doesn't need to know."

Hercules tilted his head back, which Frankie took as a request for her to stroke under his chin. "You really are very lovely."

She placed her empty mug down on the coffee table and snuggled further down on the sofa. Tiredness washed over her and within a few minutes she drifted off to sleep with the cat purring next to her.

Oh, she loved the way he stroked her hair like that, he was so gentle; it made her feel all twinkly inside. The way he would tuck it behind her ear, stroking it as he did so. Oh yes, and she liked that too, combing it with his fingers and letting the hair slowly fall. *'How can he do that? Make me so aroused doing something so simple'* she thought. Slowly, she registered his kisses on her forehead, soft kisses that trailed down her eyelids, over her cheeks to her lips. *'Oh, he has the best lips; I want to feel them all over my tingling body and I swear I would come,'* she thought.

Jack rarely saw her sleeping. She was an early riser and not once in their time together had he woken first and watched her sleep. He knew she watched him often, especially at the weekend, when he would wake to find her next to him, reading, with tea, waiting and watching. He couldn't remember if there had been a weekend in the last six months when they hadn't made love in the morning. Even when he occasionally worked on a Saturday, Frankie wouldn't let him get out of bed until she'd had her fix.

When he'd walked into the flat and found her sleeping soundly on the sofa with the cat, he wanted to take in every bit of her beauty and sear it into his memory, even though he already knew it intimately. While she was sleeping, the tension that was now coming between them disappeared; he could simply pretend for a little longer. After a while he couldn't contain himself any longer, he needed to touch her, kiss her, hold her. Her hair was melting over the cushion like butterscotch. He remembered the first time he saw the back of that straight, copper bob swinging above the shoulders of her stunning red dress, with no idea that it was her. He couldn't believe he'd spent every day since that moment enjoying every strand of that hair. He knelt on the floor and began to stroke it, watching her smile and moan slightly in her sleep. It was so soft, so silky, so completely opposite to his annoying curls that he'd now learnt to love. Hers was poker straight, not a single wave; he combed it and let it fall onto the cushion as he bent down and kissed her forehead. She stirred again, as if aware of him but sleepy enough for her brain to not engage and allow her to wake. He gently pressed his lips onto her eyelids, then her cheeks, and finally found her full, pink, slightly parted lips.

Frankie slowly opened her eyes and found herself looking straight into his. They needed no words to accompany them, they just said 'I need you... now!' Her mouth started to communicate with her brain and responded, letting her tongue taste him. They kissed for a long time, letting their hands explore as they slowly removed each other's clothing, which Hercules made himself a new bed on, since he'd been unceremoniously turfed off the sofa. When they made love, there was no tension; it was slow and meaningful. Even just lying together, skin on skin, somehow felt easier.

"Can we just stay like this until its time for me to leave?" she asked, as she played with one of her most favourite parts of his body, his chest hair.

"I'm not sure that work would be very happy with me if I called in sick on Monday, having already had a request for time off turned down," he said, with one hand on her pert little bottom, while the other supported his head. He loved the way she draped herself across him like this and played. He was able to enjoy looking at her while his hand squeezed her soft cheeks. He loved every inch of her pale, flawless body.

"I guess," she said, sadly.

It rained for most of the weekend, giving them a good excuse not to go anywhere. The only commitment Frankie had was to drop Hercules off at Carol's. After a lazy Sunday morning, which extended into the early afternoon, they finally got showered and dressed, before packing up the cat and all of his things. Hercules was livid with the whole situation; he sulked in his cat box for an hour while they made small talk, drank tea and ate one of Carol's Death by Chocolate cakes. Then Carol suggested they go and enjoy their remaining time together.

As they reached the front door Carol turned to Jack.

"You know you'll always be welcome here, anytime, okay, pet." She embraced him for longer than she probably should have. She really hadn't thought that she would find this incredibly difficult. She had grown very fond of him; as she broke away from him he gave her a weak smile. She felt helpless watching him leave.

"Thank you for everything," he said quietly, as Carol patted his back.

Frankie hugged her aunt.

"See you Tuesday morning, about 8?"

Carol just nodded and gently touched her niece's face. Frankie could see the emotion welling up in her eyes, and if she looked at her any longer, she was going to fall apart herself.

Carol closed the door gently behind them, and put her hands over her face. She knew she had to keep it together. Tuesday was going to be heart wrenching.

After Jack left for work on Monday morning, Frankie took a long shower. This was her last day in England and her last night with Jack. She took the Metro into the city centre and headed straight for John Lewis, a large department store that had been in the same spot in Eldon Square Shopping Mall all her life. She knew exactly what she was looking for in the luggage department, so twenty minutes later she strolled out, towards M&S, with a large grey and shocking pink soft suitcase. It wasn't quite the colour she would have chosen, but she liked this style and needs must. She still wasn't going to have a lot of room, but she was determined to take a few comfort foods back home with her. After some shopping and tea and cake in M&S, she was back before lunch, ready to nail the rest of her packing before Jack finished work.

Jack was not in the best of moods when he arrived at work, and then having his room switched, so that he spent his day working with Dr. 'Airhead', sealed the fact that his day was just not going to go well. He was polite enough to her, he had to be, but she really did seem to be on another planet. She announced to him, half way through the morning, that she had been up most of the night with her youngest child, who currently had an ear infection. So now, not only was she going to be disorganised, she was going to be tired and disorganised. He did his best to bite his tongue, and just get on with his own job, but by the time they started their last case of the day at 3.15 he was close to losing it with her. He had given her two clearly labelled syringes, one of which was a paralysing agent. He'd even passed them to her separately, informing her what they were. All the drug labels were different colours, but recently the supplier had changed and some of the new labels were slightly different colours to what everyone had been used to. Annabel had picked the syringe up by colour code, without checking the label. As a result, she had almost paralysed the patient without first giving him an anaesthetic. Luckily, Jack happened to turn around before she administered the drug and stopped her. She tried to brush it off as no big deal, but it really didn't sit right with Jack. At the end of the day, he went to Denise to discuss the incident and seek her advice. Of course, this was the last thing he wanted to be doing, knowing an incident report would need completing. All he really wanted to do was leave, but at the same time, he was apprehensive about going to the flat to spend his last night with Frankie.

It was ten to six when he finally walked through the door of the flat. The first thing that struck him was how empty and bare it looked without all their things around it. As he stood with his back to the front door, looking to his left, he saw Frankie's new suitcase lying on the floor of the bedroom. Staring at it, his backpack slowly slid off his shoulder. He felt like the world was falling away from under him. He stood completely still, his eyes fixed on the open suitcase full of her things.

Frankie was in the bathroom when she heard Jack come into the flat. She stood at the sink and stared at her reflection in the mirror, trying to pull herself together.

Slowly, she turned the door handle and opened the door, not knowing where Jack would be. As she calmly walked out of the bathroom, she realised he was still stood at the door, staring into the bedroom. She walked over and stood close to him; he still didn't look at her.

"So this is it, you're really going?" he said quietly, turning his head so their eyes finally met.

She couldn't say anything, she suddenly felt numb; he looked so lost. She swallowed hard.

"You've just spent the last six months fucking me, and now you're just going to get on a plane and leave." His face was hard and angry.

Frankie's eyes became wide, and her mouth dropped open, as she let out a short, sharp, shocked breath. She couldn't believe what he'd just said.

A moment of heavy silence hung in the air.

"I have never once just... fucked you," she said quietly, before she walked straight into the bedroom, pushing the door closed behind her.

Jack stood frozen; he couldn't believe what he'd just said, what he'd just done. He had never seen anyone look so hurt by his words. He had no right to accuse her of something so crude; he crouched down, with his back against the front door, and hung his head in his hands. *'You idiot, you don't deserve her after that,'* he thought. After a few minutes, he realised that he had to apologise and try to take back what he'd just said. Standing up again, he tried to compose himself.

Frankie walked over to the bed and crumpled to her knees. She placed her hands flat on the bed and her forehead fell to meet them. She was too shocked to cry; that wasn't the Jack she knew and loved, or was it? Was she just seeing a side to him that had had no reason to come out, until now? She wouldn't believe it, she was sure he had just lashed out because he was angry at how this was ending. She heard the door creak behind her, but she didn't move. She couldn't look at him. He came and sat on the floor beside her with his back against the bed. He didn't say anything.

"Should we just say our goodbyes now, and not torture ourselves any longer?" she asked, sitting back on her heels, looking at him.

"God no," he said, as he met her eyes, his arms resting over his bent knees, "I don't ever want to say goodbye. Forgive me; I should never have said that. I'm angry and confused and thoroughly pissed off. It was wrong of me to take it out on you like that; if I could take it back I would... I'm sorry, Frankie."

She couldn't stop herself, before she knew what she was doing her arms were around him and she was kissing him, with her hands grabbing at his hair. He kissed her back just as passionately, straightening his legs so she could straddle him; one hand in her hair, the other holding her bottom, pushing her against him. When they finally eased back to take a breath, he pressed his forehead and nose against hers, their eyes locking together.
  "Don't leave me Frankie, please... don't leave," he said desperately, and tears began to trickle down his sad, handsome face.
  She pulled his head onto her shoulder and let him cry like a child. She tried to hold it together and stay strong, but she just couldn't do it. Shaking, she held him tight and stroked his hair. He didn't move; he just let it all out.

When he was finally all cried out, still wrapped in her arms, she slowly peeled him away from her shoulder; he sniffed as he looked down. She took his face in her hands and made him look at her.
  "I'm sorry," she said quietly, "I'm so sorry Jack, but I have to go. I can't live here, not even with you. What we've had was very special. It doesn't have to be over. But you're right, it's been intense; we could use some distance. Maybe just come and visit me, no commitment to staying, just a vacation... What do you think?" she gently wiped his flushed, wet face.

He nodded slowly and then embraced her again. He just needed to feel her close, take in her scent and hang on to her words.

Frankie had seen many grown men cry in her career; it was always a heart-breaking sight. But seeing Jack like this was different. She loved him with every part of her being, but even at that moment, when he was clearly at his lowest, she couldn't bring herself to tell him what he needed to hear. She hated herself for being so selfish, because the bottom line here was that she wanted him on her terms and not his.

"Do you want me to go?" he asked.

"Oh Jack, no, I only said that because you hurt me. I don't want to say goodbye either."

"Can I make love to you then, even though I probably look terrible?"

Frankie let out a little laugh, as she brushed some stray curls away from his face.

"You look breathtakingly handsome, even when you look terrible. I will never be able to resist you."

This made him smile; it wasn't quite up there with some of his previous arousing efforts, but it was at least a smile.

"You know, that smile of yours is one of the most beautiful things I've ever seen, Jack. At least I can leave knowing that I brought it back to life." She kissed him softly, working her way from his top lip to the bottom. Then she licked them; he tasted salty from all the tears. Before she let her tongue find his, she sat back and pulled her vest over her head so she was topless. They continued to kiss with passion whilst shedding their clothes.

Once they were fully naked, he stood and lifted her up; it wasn't comfortable on the hard floor. He pulled her back with him as he fell onto the bed.

"I'm going to run my lips across every part of your body, and I'm not going to take you until they have," he said, as she lay on top of him.

And so he did; he made sure to bring every inch of her skin alive under his kiss, leaving her breasts until last, knowing that he would probably make her come. He was very hard and throbbing almost painfully, so by the time she shattered into pieces, he couldn't help himself; the sight of her pleasure was enough to tip him over the edge. That warm, wet feeling between them was reminiscent of the first night they'd spent together, and made them stop for a second to relive it again. Jack wasn't hung up anymore when this happened, like he had been in the beginning; he knew now that he would get to enjoy the amazing feeling of being inside her for longer. He wanted to savour every moment, make it last.

Frankie surrendered herself to his lips and allowed her body to be taken over by sensation. She had successfully taught him how to enjoy and pleasure her body; something he was now incredibly good at. Just when she thought it couldn't get any better, he took her to another level. By the time his lips found her very erect, throbbing nipples she gave in and let her orgasm take over. She became aware of him stopping, with a look of sheer relief on his face, and then she felt it. That hadn't happened in a while, but she loved it when it did. Even when he took control, her body had the power to do that to him. She could see he was re-living the first time that had happened, and how he had been so embarrassed. Now, it no longer mattered to him, just as it had never mattered to her. She had no idea how long they spent just moving together; she almost didn't want him to come again so could make this moment last forever. It wasn't until he rolled her on top of him that she finally reached the top, taking him with her and placing a victory flag that caused the most enormous avalanche.

They sat in the bed, resting against the headboard, facing the mirror. Frankie sat between his legs, her back pressed against his firm chest. He wrapped his arms around her, burying his face in her hair. Frankie just watched their reflection in the mirror, as she stroked his hands, whilst they explored her body.

"I have something for you," she said.

She left the bedroom and returned moments later with a red and black bag. He noticed that a large version of the curly symbol, which appeared on most of her clothes, was on the side of the bag. Climbing back onto the bed, she sat in front of him.

"It's a hug in a bag," she said, as she placed the bag in front of him.

He looked at her, intrigued.

"Go ahead." She nodded at the bag, encouraging him to open it.

He picked up the re-useable bag that was closed with a single popper, and pulled it open. Peering inside, he pulled out an aubergine coloured hoodie, the male version of the Scuba hoodies that she wore. It had the curly symbol on the hood, in a pale yellow.

She watched the expression on his face, and then looked down at her hands nervously, worried he didn't like it.

"Kayla brought it over for me. I thought, whenever you need a hug or you're thinking of me, you could put this on... It's from my favourite clothing store, in my favourite colours." She finally glanced up at him; he was looking straight at her.

"I love it, thank you." He placed it on the bed. "Come here." He held out a hand, and pulled her into his lap. "I like the thought of it being a hug," he said, as he held her close.

At some point they decided they were hungry; there wasn't much to eat, with Frankie leaving, but toast, once again, saved the day. Frankie also needed to check in online. They bathed together for a long time, before Frankie traced every inch of his body with her lips and tongue. In the early hours of the morning they spooned together, the way they had done every night since they'd met. For Frankie, sleep wasn't important; she just needed to absorb every bit of his perfect, warm body. She lay there, completely still, after she was sure Jack was deeply asleep. This would be the last time she would be here, in this bed and wrapped in his arms. Overwhelming sadness washed over her.

"I love you, Jack," she said quietly, as a single tear fell onto the pillow.

Light poured through the window. Jack looked at the clock: 5.51. Frankie was fast asleep in his arms. He took a few minutes to pluck up the courage to move. He didn't want to do this, but it was the only way he could deal with the situation. He managed to slide his arm out from under her; she moved slightly, but didn't wake. He got up and took his clothes to the bathroom. After he dressed, he gathered the last of his things, including the hoodie, and placed them in the Lululemon bag. He picked up the T-shirt he'd worn the day before, and took a white envelope out of his backpack, standing it against a glass on the end of the breakfast bar, placing his keys next to it. Leaving his bags by the door, he slowly walked back into the bedroom for the last time. She was still fast asleep; he was shaking, his heart racing, as he placed the T-shirt on the end of the bed. He stood for a moment to take one last look and swallowed hard.

"I love you too, Frankie," he whispered.

He reversed slowly out of the room without taking his eyes off her, then picked up his bags and left.

When Frankie opened her eyes she knew. For the first time in months, she was cold. She lay there for a moment, before turning onto her back to look at the empty bed next to her. She called for him, but she knew he wasn't there. Then, she saw his T-shirt on the end of the bed; she reached out for it, bringing it up to her face and took a deep breath. Wearing it, she reluctantly went to make tea; it was 6.42. As soon as she stepped out of the bedroom she saw the envelope propped against the glass. She pretended it wasn't there, and carried on into the kitchen. She was on autopilot; she made tea, showered, dressed, dried her hair, applied some make up and packed the last of her things. Every time she passed the envelope, she ignored it.

At 7.56 Carol and Eric arrived. Before they got up to the flat, she slipped the envelope into her backpack. Carol knew better than to ask her if she was okay; she just greeted her with a solemn, "Morning, pet," and gave her niece a loving hug. Eric busied himself with taking the suitcases down to the car, while Frankie gathered her hand luggage.

"Can I just have a few minutes on my own, Aunty? I'll follow you down," said Frankie, as she placed her backpack down by the door.

Carol placed her hand on her arm and squeezed it a little. "Of course pet, take all the time you need. We'll be waiting in the car."

When Carol closed the door, Frankie stood at the end of the breakfast bar, alone. Slowly, she looked around the room, her gaze coming to rest at the barstool in front of her. The barstool, where he'd sat that first night, and he'd poured his heart out to her. She walked over to the sofa, and slowly ran her hand along the back as she moved. Looking across, into the bathroom, she stared at the large cast iron tub; was it only last night that they'd bathed in there for the last time? She turned towards the kitchen, unable to recall ever having enjoyed sitting on a kitchen bench until she'd lived here. Then there was the bedroom; slowly, she walked towards the door and leaned into the doorframe, pressing her face against the wood. Looking at the mirror made her smile; she never wanted to do anything that she had done with Jack in front of a mirror, with anyone else. It would always belong to them. Taking a deep breath, she finally turned away, picked up her backpack and closed the door behind her.

As she walked down the stairs, Penny was walking towards her.

"Oh Frankie, I can't believe you're leaving already. Listen, it's been lovely to meet you and that charming young man of yours; he's helped Mother and me on many occasions with our shopping. He's quite a catch, so hold on to him."

Frankie had no idea that Jack had been so helpful to the neighbours; and she didn't have the heart to tell Penny the truth.

"Thank you, it's been lovely having you as a neighbour."

"Well, safe journey home, okay." Penny smiled, but all Frankie could manage was a nod.

Carol and Eric were waiting in the car right outside the door. She slid into the back seat, and strapped herself in, as Eric pulled away.

After dropping her bags and collecting her boarding passes, the three of them stood at the entrance to the departure lounge.

"Oh pet! I can't leave you like this; you look so sad." Carol held Frankie in her arms, feeling helpless and, not knowing what else to do, she began to cry.

"I'll be fine, Aunty, honest... Please, don't cry, you'll set me off," she said, as her lip started to quiver; she was determined to hold it together.

Eric placed an affectionate hand on Frankie's shoulder. She looked up at him as her aunt still held on tight.

"Keep smiling my love; you know where we are, anytime," he said.

"Thank you, for everything. I love you both dearly. I'll text when I land in London, and Vancouver, okay?"

Carol began to release her, then kissed her forehead before taking her face in her hands.

"I love you too, pet. Promise me you'll be in touch if you need me, for anything."

Frankie just nodded before mouthing 'Goodbye'.

She looked back once, as she walked through the doors; Eric was holding Carol close to him. Frankie could see, by the way her shoulders were shaking, that she was sobbing into his chest. Eric simply raised his hand, but didn't wave. Frankie did the same in return, before disappearing through the doors.

She had no idea what to do with herself; as this was an internal flight to London Heathrow, the terminal was quite basic. She walked around, tried to eat, but felt nauseous; she didn't even want tea, so she bought a large bottle of water to at least stay hydrated, and just walked. Her flight was on time, so she didn't have any extra hanging around to do. When they called it, she picked up her backpack and wheeled over her roll on, offering the ground staff her passports, as she now travelled with both British and Canadian; she was like a robot. Once she found her seat, half way along the small plane, she stowed her roll on in the overhead locker and slid into her seat with her backpack. She was next to the window on a very busy flight. She rescued her headphones, music would at least help the short half hour flight pass quickly, once airborne. Before she knew it, she was up in the air, staring out of the window over fields and farms, houses and roads. She set her entire collection to shuffle, and hit play, having no idea what she would hear first.

She almost stopped breathing when the music started; of all the songs it could have randomly selected, it picked Train's 'Lincoln Avenue'. It was like they'd written these lyrics just for her, for that moment.

> *Well I guess this is where I left my life*
> *and all it's operations*
> *And I know I will never get this twice*
> *With all negotiations*
> *This feels like the place between*
> *What is and might have been*
> *So I guess this is where we both find out*
> *If this was meant to be...*

Slow, silent tears rolled uncontrollably down her face as she stared out of the window at fluffy white clouds, oblivious to everything that was going on around her.

> *And I'll tell myself, I don't need you*
> *I'll tell myself enough to get me through...*

When the song finished she turned her phone off. It would be the last Train song she would listen to for a very long time. As she put it back in her backpack, and pulled out a packet of tissues, the white envelope caught her eye. She sat for a moment, considering what to do, but in the end pushed it further in and closed the flap.

She had almost four hours to kill in Terminal 5 at Heathrow, but first of all, she needed to fix the mess that was once her makeup, and text Carol. Still unable to face food or tea, she walked and walked and walked, drinking plenty of water. After what felt like a hundred years, the departure board finally displayed a gate for flight BA85 to Vancouver. Getting to it required getting on the underground train; it took so long to get to the gate, she began to wonder if she was on her way back to Newcastle. Finally, once she arrived, she found herself a seat. Taking her passports and boarding pass out, the white envelope once again caught her eye. Reaching down for it, she noticed it felt like a card; did she really want to open it? She sat holding it, staring at the *'Fx'* on the front. Locating her glasses, she put them on. Her heart began to pound and her breathing quickened as she turned it over and slowly, carefully, slipped her finger under the flap.

She pulled the card out of the envelope to reveal a small, grey 'tatty teddy' on the front, holding a red heart, with the caption *'yours'* underneath in small print. Shaking uncontrollably, she held it, too scared to look inside. Eventually, reluctantly she did: the lyrics of another Train song jumped out at her.

'This ain't goodbye
It's not where our story ends
But I know you can't be mine
not the way you've always been
As long as we've got time
Then this ain't goodbye'
Jx

She breathed in sharply and clasped her hand over her mouth. As she closed the card she became aware of a pair of jeans stood in front of her and, above the noise of the departure gate, she heard a familiar voice say,

"Frankie?"

Acknowledgements

To everyone at FriesenPress who helped make this a reality, especially Heather, who patiently guided me through a process I knew nothing about.

To the baristas of My Cup, for making the best lattes and providing the most discreet tables.

To the great god Apple for sexy, portable and compact devices that made writing possible anywhere.

To Jim, for knowing my body better than I do and having the amazing knowledge and skill to put it all back in the right place. He never once dissuaded me from sitting in front of my computer. He is evil with needles, but my life would suck without him.

To my beta readers, Lee-Ann, Richard, Mary, Jacqueline and Eileen, I thank them for taking the time to read my crazy idea and being suitably shocked. A special thank you to Eileen, the only one who had no idea who'd written the book. Her enthusiastic hunger for more helped convince my husband that this wasn't as crazy as he might have originally thought.

To James, for saying the right thing, in the right place, at the right time. His lovely wife will now never just be a boring, part-time, female anaesthetist.

To Steph, my best friend, my partner in crime, my rock! I could never have done this without her. Thank you just isn't enough for everything she has ever done for me, and my family. When we grow up we'll be the drunk old ladies causing havoc in the nursing home!

To Tess, my girl, and the only terrier in the world who doesn't like walking! This story evolved while we walked and then she kept me company while I wrote it. I know almost all the lyrics to every Train song because of her.

To Stan and Gail, two of the most wonderful people I have the privilege of knowing, I love them both dearly. They have shown constant love and support, in everything I have done. It says a lot about my relationship with Gail that I was comfortable letting her read this. Basically I worked on the premise that if I could let my mother-in-law read it, I could let the rest of the world!

To my two amazing little monkeys; I can't imagine life with a clean house, very little laundry and no Lego. Their energy keeps me going, and their art classes and tennis lessons gave me time to write.

And finally… to my wonderful husband, the half that makes me whole, and the reason I understand the true meaning of love. He constantly encouraged and supported me throughout this journey, and showed remarkable patience during my technological meltdowns. I love him to the moon and further. Thank you, luv, for eventually believing in me. This is as much yours as it is mine.

The Author

LOUISE LINDLEY GREW up in the northeast of England. In 2004 she moved to Canada with her husband, for what was supposed to be one year. Ten years, two children, two cats and a dog later, she appears to be staying. She worked as a registered nurse until giving up her career to raise her family. When she was diagnosed with a chronic disease, she turned to writing, combining her knowledge of the medical world with personal life experiences. She lives in Vancouver with her husband and two boys. ***Bruises*** is her debut novel.